COUNTER CULT

John B Gross

One Bullet Press

Contents

Dedication   VI

1. ACT 1: SILENT PHOBIA   1
2. AS THE PRESS REFERS TO YOU   2
3. THE INCITING SERMON   12
4. BETHANY   16
5. POWER   28
6. ALL THEIR PEOPLE   34
7. VISION OF LUSTER   43
8. MURAL MURAL   48
9. THE FERRYMAN   60
10. FAULT LINES   68
11. FOR THE VAULT   77
12. ACT 2: PROOF OF CONCEPT   89
13. POKER FACE   91
14. PHOBIA   98
15. PARENT FUNCTION   107
16. THE FISHING BUSINESS   119
17. THE MAILUGIAN TIMES   131

18.	MATTERS OF INTERPRETATION	137
19.	BEHIND CLOSED DOORS	146
20.	MOTHER NATURE	152
21.	LANTERN	165
22.	FACT FROM FANTASY	169
23.	FIGUREHEADS	178
24.	ACT THREE: SPEAK OF THE DEVIL	187
25.	PROPHETIC IN WARNING	189
26.	ONE'S OWN DESIGN	197
27.	STINGING SENSATION	202
28.	GOD	211
29.	THE FERRYMAN'S TOLL	216
30.	FAME	221
31.	JEKYLL & HYDE	229
32.	DISILLUSIONMENT	235
33.	FINAL ACT: AND HE SHALL APPEAR	241
34.	THE RAGE	242
35.	THE BIG CARNIVAL	251
36.	EXODUS	257
37.	STIPULATION	263
38.	REBOOT	271
39.	REVELATION	281
40.	RAPTURE	290
41.	JUDGE, JURY, EXECUTIONER	301

Counter Cult would not exist without the love of my Grandparents. Thank you Sandy Moore, Jack Schoenfelder, and Joyce Moore for helping me become the person I am today. I am also indebted to the patience and love of my wife, Larissa Chavarria, and her family for opening their home and their hearts to me.

Thank you for choosing Counter Cult! This novel has been a pipe dream for seven years and I'm ecstatic that it's coming to life. Please enjoy!

ACT 1: SILENT PHOBIA

"Watch out for false prophets. They come to you in sheep's clothing, but inwardly, they are ferocious wolves.

By their fruit, you will recognize them. Do people pick grapes from thorn bushes or figs from thistles?

Likewise, every good tree bears good fruit, but a bad tree bears bad fruit.

Thus, by their fruit, you will recognize them."

- *Matthew 15-17:20, New International Version.*

AS THE PRESS REFERS TO YOU

"Come home, Jim. Come home."

Only one thing remained visible through the blazing, airborne sand. A woman with black hair appeared through the mist. Her white gown glimmered and swirled around her. Her gentle voice echoed. "Come home, Jim."

Sand rolled down the desert plains, nearly burying a young man. After trudging through the dunes for miles, he sank to his knees and collapsed onto his stomach. Each twitch of his excoriated hands burned, yet he kept burying his torn cuticles and pulling himself forward. Particles of dirt completely covered his black hair. Smeared blood stained his nostrils. All his emerald eyes could make out through a hurricane of sand was a violet light.

The parasitic dunes leached inside him. With each shiver, he sank deeper.

All that remained above ground was his head and arms. He reached out one last time as his bloodshot eyes flickered.

A whirlpool of sand opened in front of him, and a giant hand emerged from it.

~

Scarwood, Texas. June 21st, 2000. Midnight

Despite being abandoned for thirty years, Aceo Church lived on through Scarwood's youth. Due to the scare factor behind abandoned buildings, a circle of truth or dare would often transform into overnights at 'Old Aceo.' As teenagers became providers, Aceo became a legend.

Sometime in February, a mysterious group of outsiders moved into the decaying church and renovated it. The sign for Aceo had long been missing, but in late May, a new one took its place. Overnight, the building took on a new name: "The Sturdy." Mysterious fliers stamped with the Sturdy's address appeared across Pontifex County. They called the reader to "Watch the news on the afternoon of June 23rd," and ended with a signature from "Mr. Chessjurist."

Imaginative rumors surrounded the building and its tenants. Some passed all this off as a weird prank. Still, with no information about the occupants or their plans, most were curious.

Hearsay and personal history fueled a burglar's interest. Her approach remained as it did in high school.

An unlocked window promptly introduced itself. As the burglar opened it, her crimson, shoulder-level hair and red leather jacket fluttered through the breeze. Her soft, black eyes glimmered in the bright moonlight. She was just shy of twenty-one years old.

The first thing to become apparent upon climbing in was Queen's 'Innuendo' playing softly in the background. Keeping one hand on the window, the burglar swung a flashlight around and found nothing but the radio playing it.

The window belonged to an office area. On the other side of the room was the worship area, with a podium on a stage in front of multiple rows of chairs.

Rifling through the first few desks yielded nothing. One desk had a name tag on it that read "Susan." Searching through it presented a money clip totaling ninety dollars. Thinking she had hit the jackpot, the burglar continued digging. Instead of uncovering more treasures, she found a picture of a young woman holding a baby. She scowled and returned the cash. She placed a calling card signed "Ms. M" on the desk.

Her next step triggered a wire which turned on the light. She whirled back to the window and discovered it had been locked shut.

A mystical voice from no clear direction sang along with the music until it sputtered through a final lyric and stopped.

Her breathing intensified as she reached for a sheathed knife.

The voice proceeded toward her. Its strong, theatric tonality danced through the words. "I see it in your face, Ms. M, as the press refers to you. You've made quite a name for yourself, breaking in through forgetfully unlocked windows and doors to grab whatever your hands can procure. Then, once you're finished, you leave a calling card with 'Ms. M' written on it. The only thing I don't understand is why. It's not stylistic or clever. It doesn't convince me that you're anything more than an opportunist burglar."

Her face turned white. Her southern belle accent rang like an alarm. "How did you know I'm Ms. M?"

A man in his mid-twenties emerged from the darkness of another room. A broad smile emerged through his smooth cheeks. "I didn't."

Her heart sank like cinder blocks around the knees of a rat.

He rubbed his hands together. "I was hoping things would go this well. Tell me, are you afraid or just disappointed in yourself?" He almost fell while trying to sit, immediately shattering any whiff of intimidation.

"A mixture of both, I suppose," she muttered, snickering.

"Not funny! You'd be clumsy if you slept nine hours across three days. Doesn't help that I haven't had a cigarette in Mailugula knows–" He pressed his hand into his forehead and sighed.

Shaggy, black hair flowed neatly to his right. Thick bangs blocked his forehead and sat just above his emerald pupils. "My apologies. Now, sit down and tell me your name."

She was hesitant, "My name is Mallory. Who're you?"

A smug grin sat across his face. "You can call me Mr. Chessjurist."

"Chess... *jureest?*" She started chuckling. "That's a weird name."

Chessjurist wasn't amused. "*Chess-joor-ist.* The end is like Myst without the M."

"Can I just call you Jury?"

He tightened his lips. "No. That name is for special people. Next, give me the gun."

"Gun?"

"Gun, bat, garlic, etcetera. I'm a fan of pocket knives myself. We fixed the alarm last week, and if you don't want to hear it, I suggest you play along."

"So? Unless the police hear me admit it, you can't prove I'm Ms. M."

"You literally dropped one of your stupid calling cards on Susan's desk." He reached into his pocket and revealed a tape recorder. "Besides, between this and the cameras, they'd find you." He set down the tape recorder and extended his hand, palm up.

She handed him a switchblade and spoke with an edge of hostility, "What? You want me to sing and dance for my freedom? I'm not some puppet."

"As I, of all people, am well aware. Look, just give me a chance. Let's have a conversation. Let's be candid with one another. Then, perhaps there'll be no need for this recording."

"You're the one with the blackmail, and you're asking *me* to give you a chance?" She furrowed her eyebrows and lifted her chin. "What are you trying to do?"

Chessjurist placed his hand over his heart. "*Nothing*. I'm just the head of a small religious group preparing to make a statement."

"Ohhhhhh." She pointed at him. "You're a prophet."

He smiled and spoke in a disturbingly chipper falsetto. "No. I am not."

She managed to suppress a smirk. "But that's what they call cult leaders, right?"

Chessjurist ditched the chill demeanor. "If that's the game you wanna play, then you should know that prophets don't bluff. I am more than willing to call the police and let you *rot*." He pulled a match from his shirt pocket, "But I could never condemn a human being without understanding their circumstances," he scraped it against the desk, lighting it.

The wavering flame from the match brightened her face, but she refused to look in its direction.

"I'll spell it out for you." Chessjurist lit a candle. "Why are you doing this?"

She sighed. Her tone flipped to sincerity, "Ever since I was young, my Mama has been sick. Daddy left a while ago, and the money we got from the state was never–"

To Mallory's shock, he cut through her words with a shrieking guffaw. "Oh, please. You couldn't create a more cliche backstory if you tried," he continued to chuckle and wiped a tear from his eye. "You don't need to finish. I already know how it ends. Give me the real story, or you'll find yourself in a jail cell by the end of the hour."

Fear and confidence clashed against each other, "You don't scare me."

After shaking his sinking head, he looked back at Mallory. "I'm not trying to! Just talk to me. The chance I'm asking for isn't nearly as big as the one I'm giving you."

She released a pent-up breath, "Fine. The part about my Mama raising me alone isn't crap, but she wasn't sick."

Chessjurist folded his arms. "You never know. Maybe Dad not being around was for the best."

"*What?*" Her eye twitches. "We needed him! My Mama worked herself into the ground, for Christ's sake, all because my Daddy was a bum! Jesus! How could you say that?! You don't even know what it was like!"

Chessjurist gasped and pressed his fingers around his heart. "I am so sorry." Then, he opened up the tape deck and revealed it was empty.

Mallory shot out of the chair. "I knew it!"

"But you didn't."

"Well," she crossed her arms, "I had a feelin'."

Moonlight began tapering in from the window.

She turned away and spoke with a frown. "Does the alarm even work?"

"Oh yeah."

"And will you ring it if I run?"

Chessjurist's face stiffened. He looked angry but sounded entirely calm. "Not after what you've endured. But I still encourage you to stay and give me another chance. You have the rare opportunity to bare it all–"

"Bare WHAT?"

He winced. "That wasn't the best word choice. I mean that you have an opportunity to..." he waved his hands in a circle while jogging his mind, "Oh, how am I supposed to know? Just pretend I'm your therapist. I could tell you everything you want to hear, but it's better if *you* vocalize it. The best way to do that is to talk to me, and you can do it right now, from the heart, with nothing muddling your words."

"Is this what your religion is?"

Chessjurist smiled and extended his hands. "Mailugula has a lot to do with self-reflection and awareness. That's why you have to know where your problems come from."

"I already know where they come from."

"Not well enough to rise above them."

After deliberating, Mallory returned to her seat. Her voice became more natural and less pleading. "I've been broke my entire life. All the girls in school would constantly show off the things they had that I couldn't afford. It made me feel like dirt. I didn't even know I existed until I saw the first Ms. M report on RBLA."

"*RBLA?*" Chessjurist released a sound of genuine disgust. "I'm shocked the story made it anywhere if it came from Preston Epalit's grubby fingers."

"I didn't care. All I wanted was to be taken seriously." She turned away. "Sometimes, I feel so selfish."

"Selfish?" He looked her in the eyes and grabbed her hands. "Break yourself of that meaningless label! Nothing is selfish about wanting a better life. Still, there are other ways to reach that emerald city. If you can't think of any, my Speakers and I would love to help."

She pulled her hands back. "I appreciate what you're saying, but you're being kinda weird."

Chessjurist grinned. "We prefer the term 'eccentric.' My apologies. Just watch the news Friday afternoon. Heck, if you show me you're willing to turn a new leaf, I could help you find a new job or at least a more constructive hobby." He chuckles. "For now, no soul will know of this illegal alter-ego, but take my advice: stop while you're ahead. Another thing, notice how you livened up as soon as you started speaking the truth. The truth sets us free, Mallory! Don't you have a dream that doesn't revolve around thievery?"

"Well," she exhaled, clearing room for hope, "I've always wanted to have a loving family. I know I'm young, but I feel like that would make me chill out a little."

"Why don't you start now? Get a job. Save some money. No point in having a kid if they're going to struggle."

"There *is* no point." The baggage under her eyes shines. "It feels like God'll strike me down no matter what I do."

Chessjurist's eyes widened. "I understand how you feel, but you can trust Mailugula! With their help, you can chart your own course and search for hope! Situations like these keep Mailugula tossing and turning every night!"

"You talk about him like he's a real person."

"Who's to say that *they* are not? Mailugula can save you, but it isn't my decision." Chessjurist raised his eyebrows and glared at Mallory.

She thought for a moment but eventually sank into her seat. "Mailugula sounds nice, but aren't I beyond saving?"

His eyes widened. "No one is beyond saving, ever. I promise. That same lack of trust you fear could be the perfect anchor for Mailugula."

"I'll have to think about it," she replied, her voice lifting. "I have a question, though."

"Shoot."

Mallory pointed at a door across the room. It was adjacent to the stage but shared the same ground as the seats. It looked sunk into the wall, almost hidden. "Why is that door different from the others?"

The burgundy-colored door was taller than every other in the Sturdy. It seemed to stretch and waver in the darkness like something from another world.

"You mean the basement door?" answered Chessjurist, snapping them back to reality. "I like to call it the crypt." He caught a glimpse of the time and raised his eyebrows. "Good Mailugula, it's late. You need to get outta here."

Without a word, Mallory rose from her seat and walked toward the window. "Hey, can you wait up a second?" Chessjurist called after her.

"Didn't you just say I had to go?"

His voice was cordial. "Before that, let's make one thing clear. This *isn't* a cult."

Mallory pivoted away from the window, confused. "What do you mean?"

"The word cult has negative connotations no matter how you use it. We aren't trying to hurt anyone for our benefit. I'm using what I've learned to try and teach others to help themselves. Hence why I'm not a prophet."

She tilted her head. "But it sounds like *you're* still helping them, right? Besides, that seems like something a prophet would–"

"I'm NOT a prophet, all right?!" He seethed. His chill demeanor entirely unraveled. "I don't change lives! I drive people to do it themselves."

"If you aren't a prophet, then what are you?"

Though Chessjurist's breathing was unsteady, his voice remained grim, "They say people listen when a prophet talks. If that's true, then I'm nothing more than a fool. You're one of my firsts, Mallory. Please take my words to heart."

Mallory peered through the window before climbing out of it.

Chessjurist glanced around and, after seeing no one around, grabbed a pack of cigarettes from his pocket.

As he was pulling one out, a man appeared at the end of the hall. "Jury?"

The man was of similar age and stature. A purple bandage was wrapped around his left cheek, but other than that, his slim face was clear of blemishes. His hair was wavy and long. It was a striking shade of garnet red that seemed unnatural compared to the Latin hues flowing through him. Regardless, it complemented his hazel eyes and looked perfect.

Jury jolted out of his seat and crumpled the cigarette. He spoke lightly, "Hey, Red. Are you about to tell me you threw up? Cause that's the image you're giving me right now."

Red smiled. "You're funny." He yawned, "You put on quite a show there. Why didn't you just call the police?"

"Why didn't I call the police?" He scratched his cheek. "Uh, everyone deserves another chance. Right? It's what *I* felt was right."

Red, hand over heart, advanced toward him, "Come on. I know you better than that."

Jury sighed, "When I looked into her eyes, I saw a fragment of my youth staring back at me. It was insane. I almost got second-hand vulnerability."

"You shouldn't worry. We learned from our mistakes, and it's up to her to make sure she does too. There's only so much you can do."

Resolve filled him, "As long as we're here, I'll stop history from repeating itself."

Red put his hand on Jury's back. "She'll be okay. *We'll* be okay. Come to bed, please?"

Jury looked at Red and smiled contentedly.

THE INCITING SERMON

The Bible Belt. June 23rd, 2000

Thousands of folks watched afternoon programming on grainy CRT televisions while talking about their days. "Burglar Ms. M Strikes Again," was the lead story. Countless news anchors droned on, as did a string of sitcoms and films. Then, all at once, each channel cut to blue. The sound of interfering frequencies disrupted conversations. Fathers across the Bible Belt states rose from reclining chairs and banged on the top of their televisions. "Damn hunka junk," many muttered through bites of chalky, microwaved mashed potatoes. Before long, the screen cut again to a white male in his late twenties, sitting leg over knee in a red leather chair. He whistled and peered off to the side before transfixing his shiny emerald eyes on the viewer.

The man smiled. His eyebrows lifted and curved. "No need to fear, ladies and gentlemen," he began in a Midwestern accent, "I am Mr. Chessjurist, and I apologize for interrupting your lives." He uncrossed his legs and ascended. He was about five feet and ten inches tall. His black suit and champagne vest highlighted his toned, slim figure. "When I was fifteen... fifteen years old, I had a vision. I saw something that was taken from me, something I needed. When no one would help, a genderless, singular being I call Mailugula appeared and granted me one final view of what I sought most. Since then, I have pieced together every second of that encounter. Though it keeps returning to me, distorted through dreams." He pointed at the viewer, sincerity present in his expression, and the cheesiness of his words lost on him. "The intention and message have not been misconstrued!"

No child feared Jury, but their parents fervidly tried turning off their televisions. This proved a vain effort, as did unplugging them. Their remotes stopped working. The TVs refused to shut off. Even though it should've been impossible, Jury remained on their screen no matter what they did.

Jury's voice radiated charisma and emotion. The camera focused on him as he paced back and forth in an empty, white room. "Through this vision and other signs, I have learned that people do one of two things when faced with extreme circumstances: come apart or come alive! Some thrive, while others buckle. Why should anyone be in the latter? Why should *you* be in the latter? Many of you think that you are more than capable of helping yourselves, and you would be correct! You most definitely can, and that's what Mailugula wants. Mailugula knows you can do it yourself but is also aware of the difficulties presented by self-awareness. As such, Mailugula will help drive that internal change. They will provide the vital stepping stones needed to reach the apex of problems, the——" He extended his palm, chuckled, and smiled. "I'm getting ahead of myself. What am I saying? What even is Mailugula?"

Certain strong-willed individuals watched with their mouths agape. "This man is insane!" shouted some, reclined and cozy. Wicked grins surfaced through their curiosity.

Jury smirked. "The Mailugula I advertise to you is my interpretation, so it's only natural you have that same freedom. Religion is an idea of interpretation, and the way this world persecutes us because of it defeats the purpose. That is why we aim to offer a safe facility where people can broaden their horizons, free from overbearing familial and religious *zeal*. Mailugula is here for you to confide in while giving control instead of seizing it."

Those transfixed by Walkmans and portable game players had no idea the news had been hijacked. Jury appeared to them as another guest speaker, but he attracted their attention in a way climate experts envied. Many individuals doing chores with the television on as background noise put aside their work and lent Jury their full attention.

"Our goal is to give people hope. Grief is much more than a simple process. Mailugula and I despair over how people feel trapped in what they perceive as the cycle. We want to help. We *need* to help. Mailugula is not essential to life, and that's how it should be. You are safe and supported in our hands as long as *you* choose it. We are all people, and people need freedom. Still, those who command this world are often incapable of reassuring us that we have that right. We are ostracized for our beliefs, demonized for our thoughts. It's unnatural. It may not be a priority for those around you, but Mailugula values your decisions above all else. Even if you don't participate in what I'm offering, you are exercising the freedom Mailugula aims to emphasize. That's the beauty of it all. It's true and unpressured, as religion should be."

Jury paused. A grin overcame him. "I'm aware that the... *circumstances* you're hearing this under are strange. But you're still listening, right? You don't have to trust me, but trust yourself. The world needs another shining star, and I know one major way Mailugula will shine. The second a tradition begins to fail, it becomes irrelevant. Some people struggle because they won't accept that fact. Mailugula can comfort the people whose prayers never get answered. They can ease the burdens of those who feel trapped and restricted, those who are watching their lives pass them by, or even those seeking a change of pace. Please trust me. I urge you to experience us on June twenty-seventh in Scarwood, Texas, at three PM. It's in Pontifex County, just east of the Golgotha desert. Our address is 459 Emmaus Court, colloquially known as 'Old Aceo.' Mailugula can be an anchor, no matter the circumstance, for they are a figurehead. What does that mean? Well, if it's truly star-crossed, you'll find out, and you'll find *us*." He blinked three times, and the broadcast ended. Every signal returned to its source. Dazed and confused, reporters and producers alike tried to evaluate what had just happened.

The following day, the replay of the broadcast was everywhere. Many talk shows and news programs were dissecting the footage, analyzing everything from possible hidden meanings to its delivery. Some thought it was an elaborate hoax, but something rubbed most folk differently. Whatever Jury was planning, people were already listening.

BETHANY

March, 2000

"Bethany" was a large farm property located in Texas. Though not foreboding enough to feel cursed, a suffocating dread permeated each acre. The Zarzerous family had resided there for the past few centuries but only started tending the property when the Great Depression left them starving. The farm proved sustainable but, after a couple generations, the remaining Zarzerous family wanted out. Thus, most left Bethany, leaving the eldest brother, Grey, and his wife, Maude. Seventeen years later, the farm was coming along well. Construction of a second stable was underway, and the livestock proved profitable. Only three members of the Zarzerous family remained on the property, and one had his eyes on other avenues.

Larry Zarzerous lay in a freshly cut field while resting his poised, gunmetal eyes on clouds. The color of his pupils was so piercing that it almost overshadowed the bags under his eyes. His large nose helped distract from them further. While not handsome on its own, the beak complemented his pretty face in a way where anything else would look off by comparison. No matter how much he moved, his puffy, blonde hair remained neat, as though Mother Nature regulated each flip herself. He had a standard build and was an inch shy of being five foot six (although he knew that, he always rounded up when talking about his height).

Once he heard his father slam the barn doors, he shot upright. His peaceful expression disappeared.

His father stomped toward him, "What makes you think you can slack off? Feed the animals and get to work on the new stable!"

When not monotone, Larry's voice was relatively high-pitched, though not to a grating extent. He sent his eyes skyward, "All right, all right," and scampered off before Mr. Zarzerous could say anything else.

His mother sat on the plumper side of the spectrum, but not by much. From her personality to looks, she was easy on the eyes and heart. It was a misstep in fate that brought her and Mr. Zarzerous together. He had a liking for short brunettes. She was lonely and trapped in a dead-end home. Sin imposed itself from there.

Waiting at the kitchen table for her husband, all she could do to satiate paranoia was tap her fingers and hum. When Mr. Zarzerous entered, she took a sudden breath. "I know you're busy, but can we talk about something?"

He squinted at her, "What's going on, Maude?"

Maude was quiet and rubbed a purple mark on her left cheek. She sighed, "You're too hard on him."

He pursed his lips, "That's how my father treated me." The aggression he spoke with amplified. "I know what this is *really* about. I was Larry's age when my Pa pulled me outta school, and I turned out fine. Quit goin' on about it! God," he clenched his fist, "Damned if you do, damned if you don't."

"Times have changed, Grey!" More energy came to her, "Teenagers need time to relax and learn. If Larry spends his entire youth working, what will he have to look back on?"

"The fact that I raised him right. **What!**" Grey slammed his fist on the table.

Maude nearly flinched out of her seat.

"You think it's up to *him*? The boy doesn't have a choice."

"But you do!" She pressed her fingers into her temple. "Could you at least stop calling him *boy*? It's like you don't even know his name."

His expression was desolate. "Don't you dare get that way with me. You're acting like a character in one of his damn books!"

Larry, upper lip raised, burst through the backdoor. His unrefined voice squealed like a pig in a burning building, "QUIT FIGHTING!"

Maude's mouth fell. "Oh, God."

The lad's father was furious. "What did I say about eavesdropping, you little shit!?"

Maude shot him a grimace.

"Don't look at me like that. Your son is spying on us!"

Larry's pupils were wide. "It's not spying when I can hear you halfway across the property."

Mr. Zarzerous cut in before Maude could say anything. "What me and your mother discuss is none of your business."

The lad advanced toward him, his expression fierce, "Well, I'm sorry, but when you're shouting at my Ma, I happen to get a little concerned."

Without hesitation, he struck Larry, who collapsed to the floor.

Maude clasped her mouth.

His father scolded him through gritted teeth, "You do *not* talk to me like that! Show me some goddamn respect."

Larry wheezed and struggled to push himself up. "What are you going to do? Beat it out of me?" He spat near his steel-toed boot.

Grey geared up to kick the lad, but Maude snatched a plate and smashed it over his head, rendering him unconscious.

She helped Larry stand, her face solemn, "Son, you shouldn't have done that."

He stepped away, "Shouldn't have what? Stood up for you? To think, I almost expected a thank you."

Larry ignored her further comments. He walked to his room and slammed the door, collapsing face-first onto his bed.

Only a few minutes passed before something told him to open his eyes. He turned on his television and stared at the luxury shown on the screen.

Channel surfing brought him to a book review show called *Casanovella*. It showcased the opinions of two overly expressive gentlemen "dialoguing" in a green-screen bookshop. The presentation's musty aesthetic reeked of antiquated eighties vibes.

"This week's book *killed* me, I have to say," a portly gentleman introduced after a snazzy intro. "A novelized gritty reboot of *Three Men and a Baby* is just... you know, missing something."

Larry squinted, "Is this real?"

"Same here," concurred the other, speaking with more personality but fewer brain cells. Before their banter could continue, Larry's television began shorting out. Confused, he opened his window and was caught off guard by the wind. No storm clouds were overhead, just a handful of red leaves floating through the breeze. Then, as though seizing an opportunity, the wind accelerated, knocking him down. It twisted his TV antenna, frying the signal. Larry felt frozen but could still hear the TV as it zeroed back in on a distorted version of *Casanovella*.

The critics' conversation began playing out of order, Frankensteined together by sudden cuts. **"Who asked** *for* <u>your</u> HELP? *The only* **function** *YOU HAVE IS* RIPPING **<u>the heart</u>** *OUT OF YOUR* **source material**. Do you know what I mean? ***<u>The kid</u>*** forgets what HE is. **With** *that kind of* **source material**, you're limited on *what* *you* CAN AND CAN'T **DO.** You have *NO CHOICE* **but** <u>*you act*</u> anyway.

You make everything <u>so much worse</u>. *The kid serves as an excuse* for everyone to *YELL AND SCREAM* at each other. **Words like** *worthwhile* <u>imply that</u> SOMETHING HAPPENS ***<u>as a result</u>***, BUT NOTHING ***does when you act***. ***<u>Sorry, but this has to happen</u>***."

Then, Mother Nature flipped a switch, and the wind stopped. Larry's television returned to normal, but he was too dazed to notice. His current circumstance manipulated the credence he lent this anomaly, and his hands began quaking.

~

With determination acting as his alarm, Larry woke at dawn and set off. Cars were a rarity on the long stretch of road he walked. Despite the thin fog, the sun was warm, so he chose not to bring a jacket. In another act of wisdom, he only packed two bottles of water, three apples, and a ham sandwich. Books from John Steinbeck and various playwrights filled the remaining space. He also brought three hundred dollars. That, a social security card, and a driving permit fit snugly in his velcro wallet. Though he lacked a plan, the lad was confident things would work out.

After three hours of hiking through warm mist, Larry flopped against a road sign. The fog grew thicker and made recognizing his surroundings difficult. He pulled off his dusty, drawstring bag and grabbed an apple. Halfway around the apple's core, a red pickup truck drove past him and suddenly stopped. The cargo bed was filled with cardboard boxes. A generic sneaker stepped out, and a young man eventually became visible through the fog. The details were fuzzy, but he was clearly a few inches taller than Larry. He was also older, if only by about six or so years. When walking, the man kept his shoulders and back aligned, with hands pocketed.

He stopped a reasonable distance away. His voice was amicable. "Howdy!"

Larry studied him. The man's bright red hair caught his attention first. A purple bandage was around his left cheek. Besides that, his slim face was clear of blemishes.

Larry raised an eyebrow, "Who're you?"

"Oh!" He chuckled, "I should've led with that. I'm Jared, Jared Solano. My friends call me Red." He extended his cold left hand.

Larry squinted at it and looked up at him. "Isn't that the wrong hand?"

Red pulled it back and presented the other. "Right, sorry. I promise I'm not that big of a scatterbrain."

After a brief handshake, Larry stepped back. "So, why do they call ya Red?"

"It's short for Jared. And a beautiful color."

Larry glanced up at his hair and nodded. Having never seen dyed hair in person before, he couldn't help but study it.

Red rocked on his feet and kept his hands at his back. "So, uh, what are you up to?"

Larry lowered his eyebrows, "I could ask you the same thing."

"We needed some odds and ends. Scarwood doesn't have a hard-ware store, so I'm a glorified delivery boy." He chuckled again.

Larry smirked. "Ain't you full of laughs."

Red remained pleasant, "I'd like to think so. And you're thinking of the word 'aren't,' by the way, not ain't."

"Oh great. You're a grammar Nazi too."

He smiled and scratched the back of his head. "Ha, sorry. I'm kind of known for that."

A tumbleweed crossed the road behind them, and Mother Nature pulled back the fog.

Larry looked up at the more visible sky. "I don't mind. Everyone's got a pet peeve."

"Right?" Red shielded his eyes from the sun. His expression underwent a more solemn transition, "Why are you out here again? It's not safe to walk through this fog so early in the morning."

Larry spoke dryly, "It's not any of your business, is it? I'm just trying to find somewhere to stay."

"Sorry, I'm not trying to lecture you or creep you out." Red surveyed the empty scenery, "But where are you gonna find a place to stay out here? I haven't seen anything in miles."

"Miles?" Larry looked up and realized that he didn't recognize his surroundings. "Huh. Look, I'm not asking you to poke holes in my story, man."

"I'm only asking because, if you're telling the truth," he raised his eyebrows and hands, "I might be able to help you."

A pinch of relief hit Larry, but he remained skeptical. "How?"

"I come from one of the most welcoming groups ever. You'd fit right in."

Larry looked up the road. He couldn't remember the last time he had seen another car. "The Manson family was pretty welcoming too, you know."

Red laughed. "You're funny." He shook his smile away in favor of a more professional expression. "No no, trust me, we're not terrorists. I can't believe I just said that. You'll be doing community service with us, basically. And we'll be able to help you build your future if I'm right in guessing that's something you need."

His prayers were being answered, yet he wasn't jumping with joy. His eyes pierced Red. "Is this a place with a warm bed and a roof?"

Red nodded.

Larry whistled. "Well, if I'm miles away from anything, I guess I have no choice." He shrugged, "Sure, I'll go with you."

Red smiled and rubbed his hands together, "Awesome! Well, there's no reason to stand around." They both walked to his truck and climbed in.

The car was impressively neat. There wasn't so much as a crumb on the floors, and although it had over one hundred and twenty thousand miles, it still smelled like new. The latest issue of Rolling Stone was rolled up into a pocket behind the passenger seat.

Larry clicked his seatbelt and turned to Red, his eyes more examining than ever, "Why'd you stop? As personable as you seem, this is pretty shady."

Red pondered. When he finally answered, respect drove his voice. "I know words mean nothing, but I promise that you're not in danger. You don't have to do anything you don't want to." He paused and began fiddling with his fingers. His voice was soft. "You just... remind me of someone I know." As though saying that removed a leech from his chest, confidence returned to him. "Listen, it's good that you're cautious. Being alone can be scary without a plan, but I know you have no reason to trust me so I won't ask. Just know that I get it."

"You do?" His stomach then growled over thoughts and spoken words alike.

Red grinned. "How about this? Before we decide anything, let's get something to eat. Then, I can take you home, or you can meet my friends."

"Well," he looked to the stars for validation before returning to Earth, "Before any of that, I'm gonna try getting some sleep." He yawned and stretched out his arms, "I'd try staying awake, but these leather seats are so cozy."

"Yep," Red patted the steering wheel, "Everyone loves Joe's truck. I'll slam on the brakes when I find something." He paused. "Kidding, of course." He glanced at Larry and found him already engulfed in a comatose sleep.

Thirty minutes of driving and nodding along with the sixties station followed before a sign for Cain's Diner appeared through the mist. Red missed the entrance. He stuck out his lips like a pouting child and turned onto the crunchy grass. The truck rattled and shook from the uneven ground, waking Larry. The impromptu shortcut led back to the parking lot.

"I-uh," Red inhaled through clenched teeth. "I'm sorry about the noise."

In a brief search for his bearings, Larry found the diner. "Eat time," he announced, pulling open the lock and exiting the vehicle.

The two sat down and began digging through a sparse menu. Red didn't take his eyes off the specials, "Breakfast is on me, buddy."

After ordering, they made small talk about the weather and animals. Food arrived fifteen minutes later.

"Oh boy," Larry eagerly examined his steak and eggs, "Time to eat up some muscle mass."

Red smirked and spread butter across his toast, "Good luck with that. If you don't play sports in high school, you're screwed."

Larry looked at him, bewildered. "I think you're just lazy."

He scoffed, amused. "Hey, I'm stronger than you think." The man's arms weren't thin, and his shoulders were broad.

Larry, however, wasn't swayed by the surface level. "Okay, sure. I'd have an easier time believing you if... I don't know. Do you have any notable athletic achievements?"

He whistled a stagnant tone while jogging his memory. "Well, in my first year of high school, I swam a fifteen-hundred-meter freestyle in twenty-four minutes. That's the closest I ever got to doing sports. I was planning to join the team, but..." he trailed off, "something came up."

"Oh, that's cool. Fun fact, I don't know how to swim. So, that's one thing you have over me."

Though shocked, he remained polite, "That's not good. What if your family took a trip to the beach or something?"

He almost choked on his orange juice. "My family?"

Red's eyes darted from side to side. "Yeah?"

"Well, I'd stay in the sand. Build some castles, perform some Shakespeare. You know, cool stuff."

He chuckled. "Oh yeah. I hear the competition for a role in beachside Hamlet is intense."

Larry watched the young servers feverishly run around with food and notepads. "Honestly, I wouldn't be surprised with some of those weirdos on the West Coast."

"You have to get in the water eventually. I mean, imagine if someone threw you in the water. What are you going to do then, Moses? Part the seas? I don't mean to get smart with you, but you have to think about that."

Larry raised his hands like a man on trial. "I grew up on a farm, dude. What am I gonna do? Go swimming in a trough?"

"What about PE?"

He shrugged. "Didn't take it. But even if it did, I doubt I'd care. I was too busy lining up my schedule with English classes and easy As."

Red's eyes wandered toward the Elvis shrine above their booth. "I wish my Mom would've let me put whatever I wanted on my schedule. Then, I definitely would've joined the Men's chorus. The only fun classes she signed off on were English, so those were my bread and butter. You probably already guessed that."

"Yeah, you're kind of a geek."

Red laughed. "Well, you too!"

Larry's face lit up. A faint glimpse of his dimples became clear. "Nah, I'm just smart." A sincere sigh overtook his words. "I liked school. Sure, it doesn't teach you how to be a good person or finance a home, but at least it tells you," he stammered for a moment, "You know, human culture! The weight of the world! Since I dropped out, I don't know as much as I could and have to rely on my parents for everything." Larry slammed his palm on his mouth.

Red glanced down at his coffee and tapped the cup a few times. "Judging by the mark on your cheek," he looked up, "leaving was the best decision."

Larry was caught off-guard. He rubbed the bruise.

"It's really not my place to judge. Honestly, I-I shouldn't have said that." Red released a long, nasal exhale. "We all have our reasons for leaving home. I left because I finally found someone who believed in me as much as I believed in them. Do you know what you believe, Larry?"

He shrugged, "Something along the lines of if you care, nothing will go wrong. I mean, why wouldn't things work out if you care?"

Red pulled at his collar and sat back. "You say that now, but—"

"Call it whatever you want. Any way you cut it, my parents don't care, and neither do I. So, I left."

"I-um..." Red had stepped on an all too familiar landmine. Although he knew the score and wished to change it, his feet were frozen. The fiddling in his fingers intensified. "Oh boy. Care can take many forms, Larry. It changes with time, it..." He examined Larry's bruise again, and his expression saddened. "No. It's tricky, but I won't try rewriting your interpretation. I'm sorry for confusing you."

As Larry swirled his straw around his cup, he put less effort into maintaining a careless front and spoke monotone and somber to Red for the first time. "I'm just tired of feeling alone."

Red gasped quietly. "Buddy..." Deja vu ran through his body like a rat in the wall. A twinkle entered his eyes. Red was so engrossed in his optimism that he almost didn't see Larry. "You aren't alone, and you're not running away. At a certain point, it's not running. It's not selfish to search for a better life. That's all Jury and I wanted to know when we were your age."

"Jury? What kind of a name is that?"

He examined the lad's bruise again, and his smile dissipated into resolve, "Want to find out? Come with me to Scarwood, and maybe you'll find whatever it is you're looking for." He reached into his wallet and set some money under a salt shaker. "Ready to hit the road, man?"

"Sure!" Larry got up. "Where are we goin'?"

"Scarwood." Red put his hand on the lad's back and led him out.

POWER

On the outskirts of Scarwood, just before the Golgotha desert, was the base of *Robust Before Lunch, America:* a low-budget news outlet that had been broadcasting for three years. Rising ratings (for less than noble reasons) caused the budget to increase over time. Preston Epalit, RBLA's founder and lead reporter, retained high hopes despite mediocre ratings and a small, apathetic staff.

From his build to his manners, Preston was more like a grizzly bear than a human being. Crumbs were always abundant in his black mustache and white beard. Around the corners of his lips, the colors aligned to form something that looked like television static. The man was formidable in size and stature. Despite being in his early sixties, being six foot six and round like a glob of gum afforded him troves of personal satisfaction and intimidation tactics. One detail, however, halted Preston from becoming a standard thug: his voice. Resonant and authoritative, the confidence in his inflection always gave the impression that he had a plan and a point. People——like moths attracted to flames——couldn't help but listen.

The sun rose on a new day, but RBLA received no such luxury. The outside was coated in darkness when Preston began broadcasting.

He straightened the papers in front of him before aiming his dark but not lifeless eyes toward the camera. His beautiful voice made his words pop. "Robust Before Lunch, America. RBLA CEO Preston Epalit here. No doubt rising from the ashes of Jim Jones and David Koresh, a new cult has had all of Texas talking these past few days. This is old, useless news, but I have received multiple calls asking why I quote-on-quote *chose* to ignore it. So, here goes. If you did not know, the signal belonging to numerous shows and news outlets..." he gritted his teeth, "*excluding* our own, was seized three nights ago by someone known as Mister Chessjurist." Although Preston's eyes were fiery, his tone remained cool. "Without a single flub, he delivered what many are calling the most bizarre and jarring speech in television history. People are also calling him relaxing, personable, and a moron. I bet you can already guess which one I call him. Decide for yourself."

The sermon played in an unedited but grainy state. Preston chuckled before continuing. "What a funny little man. It pains me that I had to contact another station for this recording, but—" he rubbed his temple and sighed. "No one knows this man's true identity or how he got on the air. This *Mingugular* character he uses as a substitute for God is believed to be completely original. Their first little get-together is today, but do *not* expect me to show up. I refuse to waste my time on whatever pretentious crap he has lined up. I plead the fifth, all right? I honestly have no idea why you people are so intrigued by this dime-store hippie. Yeah, you have your freedom of speech and religion, but when you start criticizing America, I have a problem. Alien and sedition laws: they existed for a reason... other than to invent the term alien. Patriotism, pride, and faith in your country is important above all else. Everything falls into place from there."

While most of his staff cringed uncontrollably, Preston marched on. Mockery invaded his tone. "Next thing you know, Chessjurist will come on screen telling us how Mailugula wants us to *raise* the minimum wage even more or get the government involved with healthcare." He smirked but maintained a severe lack of irony, "This whole thing reeks of overblown, leftist propaganda. If Chessie has so many problems with America, he should move to Russia. I bet the Soviets would eat up that Mailugu*lar* crap. It is best I stop before I get political, though. If you have any information regarding Chessie or the cult which serves him, call the number on the screen. In other news, Scarwood tourist attraction Mary's General Store faces more financial trouble as–" *Click.* Most viewers turned him off and went about their daily business.

Thirty minutes later, RBLA's morning broadcast ended. The staff sat in the breakroom, enjoying a break. Upbeat jazz music played softly in the background. The smell of donuts and coffee complemented the congenial atmosphere. Everything was peaceful until Preston stomped in, throwing open the door and creating an explosion of noise. "What is it with that bastard?!"

Everyone in the room walked out or ignored him except Jude Ariotics, Preston's right-hand man. Thick blonde hair reached his shoulders. Rosy cheeks, bushy eyebrows, and ice-blue eyes adorned his slim face.

Through his personable manner, Jude managed to capture the love of his co-workers. He was as meticulous in his relationships as he was in his work. Everyone knew he was more than fit to run RBLA. But Jude was loyal. Although never blindingly so, it was obvious something was off. Even when Preston was at his most offensive, Jude never left his side. For whatever reason, he cared in a way no one else did.

Jude trailed behind him, "It could have been worse, Boss. At least it only lasted a few minutes."

Preston threw his hands up, "Who the hell does he think he is!? Giving our rivals crazy publicity but leaving us to *rot*. Talk about a crock. What a *incredibly* conceited and *protentious* man!" He became so desperate and bitter that he didn't notice he had stopped breathing. "If we are going to become the biggest news channel in Texas, we need every scandal we can get. How else are we supposed to expand?" Having pushed his lungs to their paltry limit, he leaned against a wall and fought valiantly to catch his breath.

"Calm down," Jude's tone reflected this suggestion, "You're wasting so much time being angry that you're forgetting how big of an opportunity this is for us."

Preston peered at him with an open-mouth glare as he reached for a chocolate eclair, "Oh?"

"Scarwood is barely three miles from here. In that sense, we can get exclusive coverage. All we have to worry about is manpower."

"I knew from the moment we became neighbors that you were a gift from God. Moving next to you was the best thing I ever did." He glanced around the room. "Speaking of, I see our manpower." He eyed three employees, trying to avoid his glare. "Hey, you three: Take a trip down to Jonestown and see Chessie speak. Mailugula's first little get-together is today, as you all know. Take detailed notes, and I will have an extra fifteen bucks waiting for each of you on top of your usual pay."

"Absolutely, Mr. Epalit!" they blurted in near unison. They may not have respected him, but they feared his power.

A few hours later, the men returned. Preston exited his office to greet them. "Good lord!" he checked his watch. "What took so long?"

One of them piped up, "To start, we found this flier posted on a telephone pole."

Preston read off the flier. "Everything was unknown. My ability to live became a question." He facepalmed. "What in the name of chick flick Hell am I reading?" He looked again, and confusion seized him. "Wait, what is a Sturdy?"

"That's what they call their churches, sir," one named Fin responded. He was wearing a Mustang hat and a baggy t-shirt.

Preston ran his hand through his hair and spoke with weariness, "Lord, the world is losing its marbles. I assume you went to the discount chapel after finding this, right?"

Fin spoke as though enlightened. "Oh, it's much more than that, sir."

Preston squinted but said nothing. At the very least, Fin's words captured his attention.

Fin continued. "When we walked inside, this weird discussion thing was goin' on. I didn't want to interrupt, but Chessjurist interacted with us and answered our questions better than I expected him to. The whole thing was relaxing, to be honest. It was a very good experience."

"Uh-huh. Interesting." Preston's voice lightened. "How many people were there?"

"About... three hundred, I assume," another employee answered.

Preston peered toward the ceiling and sighed aloud, "I do not care about what you assume. In fact, I doubt it." He released a long exhale. "All right, I have one more question, which is great because I tire of asking questions. What was he going on about for so goddamn long?"

Impulse seized Fin, "Things that made sense."

"Now, what is that supposed to mean?"

"Just... you should've been there."

Preston frowned and shrugged. "Give me your notes." He grabbed notebooks from the first two employees, but Fin gave him nothing. Preston narrowed his eyes and lowered his brows. He exhaled through his nose like a steam engine going into overdrive. Despite this, he managed to chill out. "Whatever. You gave me good answers, so I will let this slide. At least I'll have enough money to buy myself a good bottle of vodka." He reached into his wallet and pulled out two twenties and a five. "Take it before I change my mind."

The three shared immense frustration. "How are we supposed to split this evenly?"

Preston began walking away, "I do not know, and I do not care. I have to focus on writing a script for tonight." He smirked and went into his office. Cackling erupted from behind the closed door.

"Piece of human garbage, I tell you."

Preston suddenly opened his door and leaned out of it, using the doorknob as support. "How hard is it to ask someone for change? Morons! Ever heard of a bank?" He slammed the door, and after a moment, his cackling reclaimed the air.

That night, RBLA reported on all things Mailugula. Although Preston's signature style tainted it, influential news outlets from around the world repeated his information and cited him as the source. Robust Before Lunch, America received record publicity. The producers keeping the doors open were ecstatic. All Preston wanted was to keep the attention flowing. He immediately began brainstorming ways to milk his new prize mule.

ALL THEIR PEOPLE

The Morning of the First Session.

Jury's office was plain, save for a Kurt Russel poster that said *Read!* and a stack of VHS tapes on the floor below it. Only three videos had a case: *The Thing, Phantom of the Opera*, and *Halloween 3: Season of the Witch*. Everything else was tidy except for his atrocious desk. The only thing of note was a copy of Fangoria magazine buried under flyers.

Jury multitasked between cleaning his desk and talking with Larry, who sat across from him.

"I don't see what you mean," asserted Jury, confused, "Yeah, Patrick Swayze may be a hunk, but have you *seen* Kurt Russell?"

Larry rolled his eyes and pointed at the poster, "How can I not? But Patrick Swayze has just stuck in my head more."

"How?! They're both great, okay? But has Patrick Swayze saved Chinatown from a sorcerer? Has Patrick Swayze outsmarted a parasitic, man-exploding alien? No! He just taught Jennifer Gray some dance moves." He paused, "He *does* look immaculate in drag, now that I think about it."

"What do you expect? I haven't seen most of Kurt Russell's best work because I haven't been old enough!"

"Someday, we'll fix that." Jury smiled and sat. "You're a good kid, Larry. Hard to believe you've been here for three months. Do you miss it back home?"

Larry exhaled, "I don't know. I just can't believe I actually left. I never even thought about it before." With an inquisitive expression, he turned to Jury, "What was it like when you left?"

Jury patted his shoulder and relayed an uneasy grin, "You were more mature about it than I was. I didn't have the courtesy to leave a note." He laughed and shook his head. "I even stole my Dad's Corvette. I had friends to lean on if things went sideways, though. And I want you to know that you also have friends you can count on, substantially less shady friends."

"I don't know. You're still kind of weird." He smirked. "You're rambling. Don't tell me you're nervous about your big day."

An edge of Jury's lip lifted, "Woah woah. Today is *our* big day! It's what we've all been preparing for."

He chuckled, expression dead, "Nice try. You'll never convince me that you're humble."

Red barged into the room, "Hey, Jury?"

Jury's tone softened, "Uh, hey. What's up?"

Red was fiddling with his fingers right off the bat. "How do you plan on tackling today?"

Unconsciously, he mimicked Red's gestures, "What do you mean?"

"Have you planned what you're going to say?"

"Why would I do that? I mean, you understand Mailugulism."

Red pulled up a chair, "I know everything usually falls into place for you, but this is different. We need to find a way to endear this to people so they keep coming."

Larry lowered his eyebrows. "No one will ever wanna come back if we sound like robots."

"True," elaborated Jury. "If we try to make a checklist, we'll start forgetting things and lose our flow. You know I come up with my best material on the spot, so don't be so paranoid, Red."

"Took the words right outta my mouth," muttered Larry.

Red grunted and eyed him. "I'm allowed to worry!"

Jury faintly blushed, "And we appreciate it. Your concern always makes me smile."

Red remained calm, "I just think somewhat of a safety net is a good idea. Even if it's just something to bail us out if things are slow."

"Okay," Jury answered. "If it makes you feel better, I'll do it."

Old Aceo's Chapel was the only part of the building that crackheads and teens hadn't completely ruined. As a result, transitioning the Chapel from Old Aceo to The Sturdy was simple. The oak rows of seats were embroidered with red cushions. The ceiling and floor were neatly patched.

The only significant new addition was a stage for the podium to sit on. The podium was smooth and slightly curved, with an appealing, wood grain pattern.

Everyone got to work preparing the Sturdy for its first Session. The Speakers sprayed Febreeze across the building, dusted seats, and filled pitchers with water. A personable doorman sat outside the entrance, greeting passersby and guests. A vase of freshly bloomed hydrangeas sat near the door. It acted as a second greeting for the people gradually entering. Even with all this, the Sturdy still smelled like a musty, old church.

Old Aceo had no shortage of seats, but after fifteen minutes, even the extras were filled. Those without a seat lined the walls. Talk among folk ranged from curious to contemptuous.

When traffic stopped piling in, Michael Fredrickson, a new recruit, took the podium. He was an artist, yet hadn't painted anything for the Sturdy.

He tapped the microphone, "Hello, everyone. My name is Michael. Welcome to the first Session. We appreciate all of you coming on such short notice." He sounded less invested with each sentence. "Certain details may be a lot to take in. But remember, we ask for nothing but your time and an open mind. But don't let me explain it. It's time you all meet the uh... *charmer* yourselves," he cringed before continuing. "Thank you all, and please keep the big picture in mind. Here's the man himself, Mr. Chessjurist!" He bowed and limply shook Jury's hand. The crowd lightly clapped.

Jury was exploding with enthusiasm. "I must express thanks again, both to my Speakers and you. Everything Michael said was on point, except that, although I may be the man himself, I am not today's focus. After all, I am a mere man gifted with the understanding of something greater than myself." Three men bumbled into the Sturdy. "Come in, come in. You guys are right on time! Anyw–"

One of the fashionably late men raised their hand shortly after finding a spot against the room's side. "Mr. Chessjurist, sir?"

Jury remained polite. "What's your name and question, bud?"

His oversized t-shirt further amplified his dull appearance. His face was long and thin, with small, piercing eyes. He adjusted his Mustang hat and stepped forward, "My name is Fin Eisenhower. I'm with RBLA. Can I ask you a few questions?"

He stroked his chin, "Preston Epalit's channel, huh? Ask away if it's about Mailugulism, but nothing regarding why I ignored your channel."

Fin was about to speak when one of his coworkers stole the baton, "How did you broadcast your message, and why did you ignore RBLA?"

Jury clenched his fist, "What did I just say?" he stifled himself, "*Not now, Chessjurist.*" His grip around the podium tightened. "Look, nothing was lost in the six minutes our message lasted. The episode of *Seinfeld* we interrupted will air another thirty times in the next year alone, I promise. And Preston? Well, I understand how he treats publicity. That's all I have to say." He gestured toward Fin, "It's rude to interrupt. Please, Fin, go ahead."

Fin appeared blessed, "Thank you!" Sincerity lingered. "What do you believe in, sir?"

"That people shouldn't have to fight for their freedoms. Our world is bent on convincing us that outside parties, and not ourselves, know what we need. It's unnatural. Mailugula is a way to reclaim stolen freedom."

Fin tapped a pencil's eraser against his bottom lip, "How does Mailugula do that?"

"Mailugulism can combat uncertainty and feelings of inadequacy. When the limits and memories tying us down fade, the road to a better life can be built. A lot of times, we can't do that alone. By being there in an undemanding yet limitless capacity, Mailugula helps break those barriers. Limits differ from person to person, hence why Mailugulism zeroes in on interpretations."

Journalists feverishly scribbled down each line. Fin kept asking questions. "So, how do you overcome any problems you face?"

Jury shrugged "No higher power outright does anything for you. Mailugula, in particular, prioritizes independence."

"Is Mailugula like a therapist, then?"

He leaned his head toward his shoulder and thought for a moment, "I believe the idea of Mailugula transcends perceivable labels because their values are yours."

Unrelated to the reporters, a woman in a dark green skirt rose from her seat, "Excuse me, my name is Ann. I may be stupid, but I've read about you in the paper, and I'm not sure how to pronounce Mai...."

"There's nothing stupid about your question, Ann." He smiled. "I like to imagine that the pronunciation of Mailugula is whatever you want it to be. That would mirror the philosophy. But to avoid confusion, *I* pronounce it as *My-loog-you-luh*. Does that answer your question?"

Ann nodded and sat.

Another visitor quickly rose. "I'm still not sure what Mailugula is supposed to be."

Jury clasped his hands together. "If you ask me, Mailugula is what brings us home every night. But the key phrase is, 'if you ask me.' Mailugulism is a way of thinking you can design in your own image. For instance, it could be identical to any mainstream religion, just with the additional tolerance you need to express yourself. You can be who you want, love who you wish, anything."

With that example, a small portion of the crowd became alienated. Leaving flyers of the meeting and the group's newsletters behind, some headed for the double doors, but others sat with their brains turned off, arms crossed.

Jury stared at those leaving, but his voice contained the light lacking in his eyes. "Mailugula is a figurehead for what you value most. You make every decision without any pressure or major time commitments. How you live is not our decision. We are only speakers. What reason is there to pressure and prod when every action we take is up to interpretation? Higher powers should be no different. In that sense, Mailugula is the start of a revolution."

Certain audience members nodded along, taking Jury more seriously.

A smooth, authoritative voice seized the air. It was cold, like a blade sculpting ice. "You said Mailugula isn't a major time commitment, but coming here five times a week sounds like a big one."

"Ah, yes! Thank you for reminding me, Miss?"

"Akila, Akila Hatem." She lit a cigarette and inhaled through her plump, peach-colored lips. Ash fell on the pants of her gray suit. A hint of blush in her prominent cheeks made them shine a tint brighter than her copper skin. Her dark mascara and eyeliner made her lapis lazuli eyes pop. Their gaze was fierce and analytical, capturing Jury's attention from afar.

After a staged pause, Jury straightened the microphone and his posture. His voice was strong, but he struggled not to stare at Akila's cigarette. "Thanks, Akila. We encourage everyone to visit whenever they want rather than at a strict circadian rhythm. And, on that subject, those already committed to another religion can still benefit from Mailuguilsm. I am not suggesting polytheism, either. Look at Mailugula through a different lens. It can be anything from a sole power to a minor source of strength."

Everyone in the rows turned to face Akila.

She crossed her legs and leaned against her seat. "But are your doors always open in case someone needs you?"

"Of course. With Mailugula, helping someone at a moment's notice is simple. Circumstances determine their need, but their imagination determines how Mailugula can help."

"Hm." Although Akila's attention was captured, her tone was sharp. "Okay. And what would you say, then, to the accusation that you're worshiping false idols?"

Jury struggled to hide a gradually emerging frown. "Mailugulism promotes belief in oneself, above faith in me or a higher power. That's what separates us from cults and other religions. To answer your question more directly, though, the image of Mailugula is not a universal one. Everyone who chooses to believe will believe to different extents. So, Mailugula is too broad an idea to deserve the label of a false idol. It's even a stretch to define Mailugula as an idol in the first place."

"There has to be some set of boundaries. I-" A slightly aggravated exhale overtook Akila's sentence. The palm of her hand wrapped around her mouth and slim cheeks. Her eyes proved she was pondering.

Before Jury or Akila could speak, another RBLA crony stepped in front. "So, what's the difference between your Mailugula and my God?"

Jury spent a moment processing the question before chuckling and shaking his head. "I'm not trying to get people to dump their thing for mine. The higher power in peoples' lives means much more than that. With Mailugula, you can be anything. You can be your true self without judgment."

"Wait a minute," Fin piped up, "What's against the rules?"

His expression and tone intensified, "Nothing. Why should we care if something contributes to your happiness and doesn't harm a soul?" The crowd murmured, just as Jury had hoped. He struggled to hide the pride on his face. "Your surprise is disturbing. Think about it! The trivial restrictions placed by multiple, common sets of values are absurd." The passion in him multiplied with each sentence. "This is why we need Mailugula! People do wonderful things when they're content and open-minded. Acceptance that broad isn't common. We're fighting to fix that!"

A brief silence followed. To Jury's surprise, Fin clapped, and many people in the crowd followed. It wasn't a standing ovation, but people were impressed. The Speakers, especially Larry and Red, beamed.

One woman in her mid-fifties clashed with the clapping, "I remember Aceo, all right? This isn't how a church should be functioning!"

He didn't attempt to shelter his loss of patience, "That's because this is no longer a church."

"I wouldn't be so sure about that! Mailugulism is your twisted version of what many people have worshiped for centuries. Only you're teaching everyone not to care about how they act, that consequences have no meaning! I'm done with this cult!" she exclaimed as she stormed out of the Sturdy, slamming the door.

"Cult," he sighed, "What exactly makes something cultish? And how are we an example? No wars were fought over Mailugulism. No lives have been lost. We aren't a cult simply because we offer a new set of values. The Cold War's over. We don't have to fear our neighbor. We have the luxury of trying something new. So, I implore you all to try and understand us. We'll return the favor, I promise."

A member of a different news station raised her pen, "Look, this is all well and good, but where does Mailugula come from?"

Red leaned over to Larry, "I was worried someone would ask that."

Jury stared back at Red, trying to recall something dear in his eyes.

VISION OF LUSTER

Jim was as isolated as the land he wandered. Though blistering sand pelted him, he noticed nothing. Amidst the desert's monochromatic color palette, a purple luster flickered in the horizon. Pursuing it was the only thing he could bring himself to do.

Trekking toward it brought him to a ghost town. All of the houses were identical. From afar, they looked dilapidated. As Jim approached them, however, they came alive. In each house, the same child sat alone with his eyes glued to the TV. The child aged with each place, but the light behind his eyes dimmed while the television shined brighter.

The last house called to him, but he couldn't bring himself to see how the story ended. He kept meandering toward the purple light, still unsure why.

An occupied ward materialized through a mist. A woman lay on her side, facing away from Jim. He recognized her black, puffy hair and the hospital gown that fluttered over her ankles. The bed spun around, and he saw her reading to a young boy. Her gentle eyes were weary, but her smile radiated joy.

Time began accelerating. He rushed toward the bed but watched, helpless, as the woman disintegrated. Black dust rose from the empty bed. It was too late, but the lingering luster told him otherwise.

The sun made him feel like he was under a spotlight. It burned. All of Jim's thoughts and senses became muted. Sand loaded his shoes, making each step heavier. He lost his sense of time altogether, and his legs grew weak. He crashed to the ground but felt a surge of determination strong enough to dig into the sand and pull himself forward. After an eternity of crawling, he reached the source of the purple light: a giant, cylindrical sinkhole. On instinct, he flung himself in and was finally illuminated.

Jim found himself trapped in a perpetual freefall. When he accepted his fate, a colossal hand pulled him out. He kept jumping, but he was saved every time. He felt compelled to jump forever, but a nostalgic force seized his will. The black-haired matron, no longer confined by illness, stood statuesque on the other side of the rabbit hole. The purple light danced around her. She smiled as the wind tossed around her gray dress. With watery eyes, the beating of Jim's heart eased.

"Live for those who can't," she urged in the motherly tone he could barely live without. "Believe in what makes you happy. Believe in, believe in..."

He became stricken with exhaustion. With his final ounce of strength, he reached for her, "Ma, ma..." and passed out.

The question of salvation remained, but from there, answers were conceived, and Jim was reborn as Jury.

"It was what I needed to start living again. It's a miracle: when no one else would give me relief, Mailugula did," Jury checked his watch and gasped, "Woah! Who knew I'd go on that long?"

Red smirked.

Jury looked around the crowd and couldn't hide his pride. "I'm flattered you all listened to that. Bottom line: I know what my senses picked up, and I perceived it as I saw fit. You may disagree with my interpretation, and I welcome that. It's the nature of the world and Mailugula." He peered into the crowd and smiled wide.

Ninety minutes later, the first Session ended. Jury approached Fin as everyone left, "Did you get what Epalit needed?"

Fin stared vacantly at the notebook in his lap, fearing what Preston would turn it into. "I-I think you should keep this," he handed Jury the notebook, "Think of it as a memento." His peers retained their notes, but the gesture was not lost on Jury.

He beamed, "Thanks, Fin. You're a good egg in a rotten cart."

Fin nodded and left, empty-handed but fulfilled.

~

The first Session brought exhaustion to all but Jury. Energized by the day's events, amplifying pre-existing insomnia, he sat upright in bed, flashlight in one hand, novel in the other. Red's snoring had yet to tear him away from the world of Dairy, Maine, but a strange *rattle* did.

"*ScroOoOoOoge*," he vocalized with the metallic rhythm, "Heh, probably just the fridge."

Before long, however, the noise evolved. It sounded like iron chains were being swung against the back door. It boomed through the halls. Jury stepped out of bed, grabbed his pocket knife, and investigated. On his way, he stopped in front of a security camera and waved at it.

It took a moment, but eventually, it blinked back. Jury gave a thumbs-up and continued, slightly more confident.

The Sturdy's dumpster was right outside the back door. Jury assumed the noise was coming from a raccoon. Knife in hand, he kicked open the door. Nothing! The sound ceased immediately. The only thing of note was a large, heavy box sitting beside the door.

He hauled the package into his office and hurled it on the desk. No writing adorned it. There wasn't even a return address. Jury cut through the packing tape.

Someone knocked. Jury stood in front of the box, doing an awful job hiding it, "Uh, come in!"

Red entered the office. "I heard the back door. You better not be smoking behind my back again!" He saw that Jury was hiding something, and his tone became terrifying. "I know I'm soft and timid, but if that's a pack of Newports behind you, you're *dead*."

Jury blushed. "Love the assertiveness, but no, I don't have cigarettes. Mailugula, they'd be gone in a heartbeat if I did."

Red cringed.

Jury revealed the package, "I found this out back. No identification or anything."

"You..." Red's blinked rapidly. "You're telling me you opened it even though you had no idea what it was? What if it was a bomb?! You have to be more careful!"

"Well, it hasn't exploded *yet*. I think it's fine. Look yourself if you don't believe me." He handed the box to Red, who wasn't anticipating the weight and dropped it.

Stacks of money blew through the flaps.

"Sweet lord," Red placed his hands on his head, "I hope there wasn't a mix-up or something. The mafia is the last thing we need on our backs. Preston Epalit's enough. We should pack this up and let Joe handle it."

"The mafia? Life's not a Martin Scorsese movie." Jury furrowed his eyebrows. "And what would Joe know about this? Last time I checked, he's not clairvoyant. He won't even come out of the basement." Jury pulled out an opaque plastic sheet from the money pile and noticed a slip of paper inside with a typed message printed across it.

You'd be surprised what can 'harm' another person. That itself is an idea of interpretation. Interpret your vision how you see fit, but be wary of the consequences. Keep up the work. -Progenitor

Jury furrowed his eyebrows, "Huh, how ambiguous."

Red turned to him, perplexed. "Do you know someone named Progenitor?"

"No," he looked toward the cash, "but I know I'm grateful for them."

MURAL MURAL

Two months later. September 3rd, 2000

Preston glared at himself in the bathroom mirror and clasped his hands around the sink. He breathed as though trapped in a trance. Rinsing his face did nothing to alleviate a feeling of decay. His malformed beard diluted the water into something less essential. The static between his mustache and beard had spread around his lips. He tossed some pills down his throat.

An intern knocked. "Mr. Epalit?"

"What is it?" He grumbled, flushing red-tinted piss and drying his face.

The intern cleared his throat. "It's Donald and Fin, sir. They still haven't called in or shown up."

"Oh. Was there not a third guy?" His tone suddenly shifted, "N-not that it matters or anything. I am just curious."

A glimmer of personality shone through, "Sure. You fired him because he wouldn't, and I quote, 'shut up about comic book gibberish or Nic Cage.'"

Preston swung open the bathroom door and dug his index finger into the intern's chest, "I tire of your sass! Riddle me this: how are you supposed to work when all you think about are chronic over-actors and nonexistent fluff?"

The intern stared at Preston's finger, "Please tell me you washed your hands."

He scoffed. "Regardless of what has touched my hands, I assure you they are *clean*. Now, *intern*, tell Jude to meet me in my office."

He tightened his lips and flared his nostrils, "Did you forget my name?"

Preston sent his eyes skyward, "Well... of course not. I do not need to tell you your name, right? Ha!" He sighed. "Just get Jude in my office, Innie."

Jude entered fifteen minutes later.

"Took your time, I see," Preston remarked, finishing a game of solitaire. "How would you like to take a trip down to the Sturdy with me?"

"Wouldn't be my first visit. Sure." Jude cocked his head to the side. "What's taken you so long to visit?"

"When you are *soooo* busy," Preston turned his head and viewed a barren calendar, "...like me, you barely have time. But you saw yesterday's package. We have a mystery investor to satisfy, and I have a strict no-dollar-left-behind policy. It is a matter of honor."

Jude laughed and shook his head.

Preston glared at him, confused.

"You're bizarre, you know that?"

Preston chuckled. "All right, big hoss. You know what's weird? Your last name. *Ariotics*? What country is your family from? Looney Tune land?"

Jude shook his heart. "You'd already know me if I was from Looney Tune land." Preston opened his mouth but Jude silenced him. "Are we bringing cameras?"

He brandished his sausage finger in the air, "Uh. What? Oh. Right! No. We can record them later. This is just to see if that cult took my workers."

Jude struggled to read Preston, "Why would they do that?"

"It's a hunch. Chessjurist and his minions have been close to their hearts lately. Catch my drift?"

"Outside of Epalit land, no one does." He sighed. "Why do you hate the Mailugians so much?"

Preston growled, "We were not good enough for them before, right? As Chessie said, 'oLd MaN ePaLiT dOeSn'T hAnDlE pUbLiCiTy WeLl.' Talk about a crock! He is afraid of me, plain and simple." He turned to Jude. His eyes and tone hardened, "As *everyone* should be."

Jude scoffed. "Everyone except me." He stood up and traveled to the doorway, "We should probably get going." He motioned for Preston to get up.

"I will not be rushed!" Pushing against the chair's arms, he shakily rose.

Jude furrowed his eyebrows. "You've been getting slower every week. Are you okay?"

"Uhhhhh, what?" Preston's eyes were racing. "Am I okay? Of course! I cannot help how comfy this chair is. It is like I am sitting on Catherine Zeta Jones's lap, even though, in a perfect world, it would be the other way around. Heheh. Ehhh, sorry. I will meet you there. I need to piss again."

~

Jude was sitting on the hood of his Firebird when Preston parked.

Preston leaned against his baby blue 1956 Chevrolet Task Force and eyed the Sturdy. Constructional magic oozed through its pores.

For most of the last month, the Sturdy was closed for large-scale renovations. Since donations were never collected during Sessions, no one outside of the Sturdy knew how the operation was being funded. Many reporters tried sneaking into the construction sites to probe Speakers and laborers for answers to no avail. The parasitic press soon stopped gossiping, and after three weeks, the Sturdy re-opened.

No attention was called to the improvements, although many were noticeable. The Session area had undergone a three-hundred-foot expansion. Gone was the weird, out-of-place office area, and in its place was a large refectory with plenty of space to eat, cook, and socialize. A new and colorful playground added personability to the property's front lawn. Most impressive yet, a second floor was erected for bedrooms. The roof was completely flattened to make room for future renovations.

Expansion had greeted more than Mailugula. RBLA was picked up for a morning and evening news block by a Southern-based, MeTV rip-off network seeking to diversify its avenues. An increase in staff and scale followed. Preston had never seen such notoriety, and it massaged the Hell back into his ego.

Jude looked up at the Sturdy, "Huh. And I thought we were doing well."

Preston scrunched up his face. "So what? They got a playground and an extra floor. OoOoOoO," he twiddled his fingers like a witch casting spells. "Growing like goddamn tumors."

They walked to the front and were greeted by an old man wearing the attire of an early twentieth-century doorman. His red velvet coat was royal and fit like a flowing but well-fitting gown. It was held together by gold buttons. A gold watch hung around his right sleeve.

The Doorman delivered a hearty salute, "Good to see you again, Jude!"

Jude tipped his hat, "Doorman."

Doorman was in his elder years and quite rotund. Muttonchops covered his full cheeks and flowed into a thick mustache, more than compensating for the bald spot sheltered by his fancy sailor cap. He turned to Preston, a hint of sarcasm contradicting his friendly expression, "Oh, I know you! You're the RBLA CEO, right?"

"Preston Epalit, in the flesh." He grinned, the subtleties lost on him, "I am he, but I like to think of myself more as a creator. Pleasure to meet you."

The Doorman could barely keep a straight face, "The pleasure is all mine, good sir! My name is Emil, but most folks call me Doorman." They shook hands.

Preston waved his hands around as if he owned the place, "I bet you are wondering what brings me here. The answer, quite simply, is nothing much. Just," he licked his lips, "woke up and felt like it."

Emil laughed and held open the door, "And we're all better off because of it. Please, come in and make yourselves known. You've been on Jury's radar for a while, Mr. Epalit."

Preston flipped his hand, "Oh please. Call me... actually, that will do. You have yourself a good day, Emmet."

The Session room was mostly unoccupied. The hydrangeas persisted, and the walls were lined with pictures of Speakers. Michael was busy planning a mural behind the podium.

Preston cupped his hands around his lips and shouted, "Howdy!"

Michael turned around. "No way!" He descended the podium and approached him. "How can I help you?"

"Point me to where Chessjurist is."

Jude stepped forward, trying to cover for Preston's bad manners, "We're wondering if he knows anything about some missing employees of ours."

"Oh, let me get him."

Michael found Jury in his office, writing with an antiquated typewriter. Jury threw a new box of cigarettes and its receipt on the floor just before Michael could see.

"Hey," Michael started giggling, "You will never believe who showed up just now."

Jury flew out of his seat, "Oh my gosh! Kurt Russell?!?! Here!?"

"What? No! What! It's Preston Epalit from RB–"

"Since when does that man make house calls?"

He rolled his eyes, "Can I tell Epalit you're on the way?"

"Absolutely!" He wrapped his hand around his chin. "Huh, he took his time getting here."

When Michael returned, he found Preston on the stage inspecting his planning materials, which were different figures sketched on separate sheets of paper. They ranged from humanoid husks to inanimate objects. No central details tied them together. He pointed at one that resembled a simple mist, "What in God's name am I looking at?"

Michael sounded weary, "Someone's interpretation of Mailugula."

"Excuse me? This crap counts as Mailugula?"

He sighed, "Think about it, Mailugula doesn't have one universal appearance to represent on a canvas. So, I asked some regulars to draw their interpretation of Mailugula. These are the results so far."

Preston eyed him. His tone was light. "And what are *you* doing to help?"

"At the moment," he began, grinning and bearing the frustration, "I'm creating my own Mailugula. Once I get more submissions, I'll develop a detail that ties everything together."

Preston laughed. "Yeah, I wish I had your job. Pf, drawing a fart in the wind."

Michael was on the verge of snapping, but Jury ascended the podium with Red behind him. "Good to see you again, Jude, and I see you *finally* brought your boss." He turned to Preston and extended his hand, "I'm Jury Chessjurist."

"Is that seriously your real name?" Preston cut through Jury's attempt to interject with a shrieking laugh. "I thought that was a stage name. I mean, it sounds straight out of a comic book." He chuckled a few more times and wiped his eyes. "My name is Preston Epalit." He nudged Jude. "You know, maybe I can have a religion, if I start calling myself Prestonaphous Epalitte."

Jury chuckled, "*What?*"

"Yeah, I'm funny. Anywho." He motioned toward Red. "Who is this?"

Jury answered before Red could. "This is my associate, Red Solano."

Red shook hands with Preston. "Hi. Can I ask you something, Preston?"

His brain fixated on the lack of an honorific, "I guess."

"Sorry, but this has always bothered me. Why would a channel with 'before lunch' in its title broadcast after dinner, too?"

Preston puckered his lips, disgusted. "Stow the *Gremlins* logic, will you? What you should be focusing on is that limp grip you got there, sport."

Red furrowed his eyebrows, "I'm sorry, what?"

Jude mouthed an apology.

Jury's eye twitched. He appeared energized, "Oh! Mister Invalid-"

"Epalit! Ee-puh-lit."

"Ope, my apologies. As I was saying, I heard you admiring Michael's latest work. Any thoughts or criticisms?"

He groaned, "Obviously. Everything I come across here confuses me more. Why are there no guidelines for what your followers are worshiping? Is Mailugula white or yellow or lizard or what?"

"Worshiping is not the right word choice."

"I won't be able to get a word in edgewise," Jude rubbed his forehead.

Red agreed, "Why don't I give you a tour of the construction while we wait?"

The two men walked away from the upcoming trainwreck.

Preston rubbed a persistent back pain, "Now that the filler people and Jude are gone, can you educate me on what this goofy operation is accomplishing?"

"To put it simply, we are encouraging people to be more independent and self-trusting in how they handle higher powers. People sometimes cannot express themselves, and Mailugula aims to return that power."

"Be more specific."

Jury radiated passive-aggressive energy. "Ask more specific questions."

Preston frowned, "I did not ask what you *want* to accomplish. I asked what you are *already* accomplishing because, to be frank, I see no point in what you are doing."

Jury lowered his eyebrows, "Closed-minded people like you wouldn't."

Preston stepped toward him. "What's that supposed to mean?"

"You would never see the point of what we do because you only judge others by your own standards. For instance, I wouldn't kill someone for a million dollars, but someone else would. *You* would. You may not see it, but a cold beer and some fearmongering won't take the stress away for everyone. The world can't fit the image of one thing, no matter how large and powerful it is." Jury shrugged. "People should choose how they live."

He raised his hands to the sky and proclaimed his words with an absurd amount of pazazz. "Why, people are just infallible! Their values would never fail or lead them down a dark path." He pointed at him. "What a crock. Cut the flowery crap and answer the essential questions. What does this man do, what role does he play in my life, and why should I give a shit?! There is no base for Mailugula, and that is nonsensical."

He kept his poker face and continued, "Man? When have I ever applied a gender to Mailugula? You give me the impression you haven't paid attention to our ideas. The way you interpret Mailugula is up to you, not Mailugula. I don't see what's so hard to understand about that."

Preston glared at Jury, mouth faintly open, "Someone as dense as a goddamn brick wouldn't. Freedom to worship what you see fit as you see fit, I get it. But what are the guidelines? Why would people change their lives for something so unclear? This whole ego trip you're on is RIDICULOUS!"

Meanwhile, Michael was showing Jude and Red concept drawings. When they heard the yelling, they halted their conversation.

Jury was satisfied and lost his poker face. "Yeah? The most ridiculous thing I can think of right now is the lack of respect you show your workers."

Red gasped, "What are you doing Jury?!"

Preston planted his index finger in Jury's pectoral, outrage live in his face, "Take that back, you hippie!"

He persisted, "Stop wasting my time. You came here for something, right? Get to the point."

"Fine! WHAT DID YOU DO WITH MY WORKERS!?"

Jury crossed his arms, leaned forward, and grinned in Preston's face. "All I know is that Fin is happy, probably because he doesn't have to see you anymore. I bet no one will find happiness in your own little Sturdy. News network, church, what's the difference when it's run by someone like *you*?" he gritted his teeth, "Good day!" and returned to his office.

Preston went to follow Jury but was held back by Jude. "I WILL *NOT* BE TALKED TO LIKE THAT!" He brushed off Jude's arm and straightened out his shirt. "Fine! We will settle this, Chessjurist! Someday, I'll show the world what a prick you are!" He extended his arm and pointer finger and tried to follow him again. "AND THEN I WILL KICK YOUR ASS!" Jude's grip proved stronger, and he managed to strong-arm Preston down the hall and through the exit as he shouted, "NO ONE IS INVINCIBLE!"

Red followed Jury into his office and closed the door. He folded his arms, "What was that?"

"A grand slam." He shrugged. "I may not plan Sessions, but I do plan for disaster. Don't worry."

Red scratched the back of his hair, "Phew, okay then. Just be careful. Not that I don't think you could handle yourself. I just don't want it to come to that."

"No need to fear. Everything is fine." He patted the side of Red's arm. "And look, you heard the way he spoke to you. How could I not rip him a new one? No one talks that way to my Red."

Red turned away, his cheeks living up to his name.

~

Optimism was unwavering in Michael's tone, "So, what do you think?"

"Uh," Jury scratched his head, "I'm a little confused."

"What do you mean? It's brilliant!" Inspiration struck quickly. The second Epalit left, the painter found his symbolic cherry on top. An azure jellyfish now hovered over the podium. It had a neon outline that made it glow like the sign of a Bourbon Street tattoo parlor. It popped out of the wall, creating a three-dimensional facade. Its tentacles stretched around the walls of the Sturdy. "All I have to do now is add the concept sketches at the end of the tentacles."

Jury hesitated before answering, "Although jellyfish are my favorite animal, what you have here worries me. I thought you'd bring me a plan before making something final."

"Well," Michael's pride started leaking, "When inspiration strikes, sometimes all you can do is create. You should understand that more than anyone."

"That I do. As stumped as I am, I'm open to an explanation."

"Jellyfish don't have a brain or a heart. Therefore, any emotion or motivation we perceive from them is just personification. They leave nothing behind and serve only to fuel the greater organisms of their ecosystem. They represent flexibility and beauty, but they also have the potential to kill. Draw the parallel to Mailugulism from there."

Jury tightened his lips and spoke sternly, "I appreciate the symbolism and artistic integrity. What concerns me are the impressions this can give at first glance. The jellyfish has a cultish vibe to it. People may start seeing jellyfish as the central figure of our ideology when the whole point is that we don't have one. I don't want anyone judging our book by its cover."

"You're looking too closely into it, but whatever, Chessjurist. Whatever."

Before Jury could try salvaging Michael's pride, he again heard the high-pitched, metallic clink of chains against the back door. Whatever bond remained between Michael and Jury swayed beneath it.

Jury put his hand out, "No need to fear. I'll be right back."

Michael did not react.

Upon entering the backlot, he saw a man with greasy, blonde hair rounding the corner. "HEY!" He tried running after him but tripped over a box. By the time Jury picked himself up and peered around the corner, blondie was missing in action. "Of all the *damn* places that box could've been!" He muttered obscenities under his breath while bending over to read the note.

You're clever. But remember, even the mightiest of forts can crumble at any time, and with little warning. Only time can tell whether it's caused by an earthquake, or a loss of loyalty. -Progenitor

Once again, there were no markings on the box. Diving into its contents revealed more of the same. No ill will crept toward him. Jury lugged it back to his office and hollered for Red.

Red glanced over the note, "I feel like there shouldn't be a comma after earthquake, but that's just the grammar Nazi in me." They stored the box in the closet and returned to the jellyfish. Michael no longer stood by his piece. Painting supplies were strewn about the floor, and Larry—with the help of other Speakers—was tidying up.

Looking at the jellyfish from afar brought with it a new perspective. Jury snapped, "It's an enhancer, not the main figure! I'm beginning to see Michael's point." He scratched his chin. "I think I'll call it The Jellyfish Principle!"

They grabbed paintbrushes and etched his terminology above the jellyfish. In the spur of the moment, Red painted a visual flourish surrounding it. A unifying urge flowed through the air, and each nearby Speaker grabbed a brush and started lining the walls with whatever resided in their hearts. Jury kept splashing Red and Larry with paint. Many others were similarly playful. Art graced the Sturdy, although its main artist was nowhere to be found.

THE FERRYMAN

September 12th, 2000

Unseen forces dictate the world in ways few can comprehend before it's too late. Whether they be prophetic in warning or conflicted with intentions, the strangest things lie beneath us. Though shrouded in mystery, what's below is always more apparent than what sits atop Jacob's ladder.

Red stood at the kitchen counter, making a sandwich at Jury's request.

Michael walked past and stopped. Raising an eyebrow, he leaned over the counter, "If that sandwich is for who I think it is, then you'll be sorry."

"What do you mean?"

"The basement dweller doesn't like peanut butter. I see it's chunky, too, so you're extra screwed."

He lowered the knife and turned toward him, "What's wrong with peanut butter?"

"Nothing... unless you want to be a murderer. Besides, who the Hell likes chunky peanut butter in the first place? Just eat peanuts."

Unless you want to be a murderer, echoed in his mind. Red abruptly jolted in place. "I'm sorry. Can you just... *please* tell me what you're getting at?"

Jury entered the kitchen and wrapped an arm around Red's shoulder, "It's okay, Red. Joe's allergic to peanuts, remember? I'll make another one." He peered at Micheal. "Our friend and I can handle it."

After a brief but unconvincing protest, Red left.

Jury started affably, "Michael, I know you disapprove of how we're using the basement. You're entitled to that opinion, but you *can't* bug people about it. The questions we get from the public are already annoying enough."

He pointed at the basement door. "That guy is a major creep, and you refuse to confront him. But as usual, no one listens to me. Everything I do is misinterpreted!"

Jury's lips quivered. "**Hey!** That *creep* is managing the work no one else can." He moved toward Michael and dug his index finger into his chest. "And don't change the subject. You have no right to push that angle when you're the one who goes out of their way to bother people. That's what you were doing with Red just now, and I better *never* see you doing it again." Michael opened his mouth, but Jury extended his palm and spoke louder. "Ope! I know what you're going to say, and there's a difference between having a personality and being a dick. I apologize for not appreciating the jellyfish the way you wanted me to. Still, there's no reason to go down this apathetic rabbit hole as a result. Take some criticism and grow up!" Jury huffed and puffed before quieting.

Michael sounded hollow. "Jesus, you really echo Epalit with your temper." He began walking away.

Jury stabilized himself. "Oh, come on, Michael. I lost my temper, and I apologize. That is the only thing worth being offended by. I interpreted your art the way I did for Mailugulism's sake." Michael stopped in the doorway. "Using the foundation you built–"

"I don't care!" He gritted his teeth, "You don't respect me or my creations. I see your game, and it's not working. Use the jellyfish however you want. I'm done with *them*."

After that, Jury had every intention of letting him walk away.

One ham and cheese sandwich later, he approached the basement door. The doorknob squeaked with the screams of a thousand mice, and for all he knew, those same mice awaited him beneath the final step. Darkness lingered across the cellar. Flipping the light switch over and over did nothing, and neither did punching it. "You know what?!" He released a pent-up breath. "I don't care. If I die, I die!"

Step by step, Jury trekked into the abyss. Upon hearing his foot tap against the terracotta floor, he whispered, "I'm alive," astounded and grateful. Plate in hand, he turned the corner. Blue light from a computer illuminated a mysterious figure reading at the desk.

Many details set Joe apart from the average Speaker, the most significant being his age. Though over fifty years older than Larry, he was the opposite of feeble. He was built like a tall bat. Streaks of gray ran through his buzzed hair, complimenting his black skin. His sky-blue eyes carried an authority that ascended past his reading glasses. His voice was smoother than the touch of marble against callused hands. No one knew if its sonority rang for angelic deeds or devilish acts. The only way to tell would be to see his wings.

Joe didn't glance away from the horror novel in his hands. His demeanor was dark but welcoming, like a ferryman waiting on the Styx river. "There a reason you have to shine that in my face?"

"Oh." He lowered his flashlight, flicked on the downstairs light, and handed him the plate, "The lightbulb for the stairs died again, Joe."

"Yep." Joe lowered his book and nodded at Jury's flashlight. The beauty of his voice made the most benign exchanges resonate like an aria. "One of those works fine. I don't see why anyone but you would come down, anyhow. Hell, you shouldn't need a flashlight. Why don't ya pull from that infinite supply of faith?"

"It wouldn't be an issue if that computer screen wasn't the only light you had on." He paced his words like a Woody Allen impersonator. "I know I'm nagging, but there's a difference between Gothic and unhealthy."

His laugh altered how he enunciated his words, "I'm goin' for relaxation, you idiot."

"Whatever you say," Jury clasped his hands together. "To business! Have you heard anything from Larry's parents?"

He shook his head. His eyes narrowed. "Why?"

"I like Larry and all, but," he scratched his arm, "I can tell he misses them. He should really go home eventually."

"Nice idea," Joe lowered his glasses to his nose, "But it's none of our business."

"So? I've seen you–"

"Enough. We mean well, but it's selfish as Hell."

The light above Jury flickered as he spoke. "Is there a problem with that?"

"Yeah, who needs a moral compass?" Joe rolled his eyes. "Some of the crap ya say makes me wanna slap you."

Jury pinched his lips and turned his attention to some pictures on the wall of Joe and his granddaughter. "Mm." He shook his head. "Anyway, how's F–"

"He's asleep. So, let's not wake him with any dumb arguments about art."

He rubbed his forehead, "Ugh, that whole Michael thing is a trainwreck. Wait, how do you already know?"

"Hey," Joe put his hands up, "New kitchen, new cameras."

"Well, I apologize you had to hear that."

"The cameras are vision only. Rest assured, I was still annoyed."

Jury wasn't amused. "Look, audio or not, don't go too far. No cameras in bedrooms or bathrooms."

"I'd be more interested in stalkin' people around here if they were actually interestin'. Heh heh." Joe looked at the silent Jury with an edge of contempt. "Not even a chuckle? Don't be a stone wall. I was jokin'. Anyhow, things borin' as usual?"

"With all those cameras, don't you already know?"

Joe rolled his eyes. "Askin' for conversation sake."

"Oh." Jury gave a thumbs-up and slyly grinned. "Well, besides the obvious, I think things have been awesome. If anything, I should be asking you."

Joe remained infectiously casual. "I've been busier than usual."

"All you do is sit on the roof and stargaze like a drunken sailor."

"I prefer to think of myself as a ferryman, not a sailor. But no. I've been out these last few nights diggin' around."

He raised an eyebrow, "Ohhhhhh, so that's your code for finding a prostitute. I didn't know they had those in Scarwood."

Joe narrowed his eyes. "Very funny, ya prick. Don't belittle the man who got you on nearly every TV channel in Texas! You were raised better."

Jury crossed his arms and spoke harshly, "Past age six, no. You never did tell me how you managed that, by the way."

"And I never will." Joe's expression became shifty, "Did you know I was *also* behind the Max Headroom incidents?"

He rolled his eyes and smirked, "No, you were not."

"Okay, I wasn't. But that would've been cool."

"Some dude getting spanked by a fly swatter isn't my idea of cool."

A loud squeak erupted from under the stairs. Jury turned and was confronted head-on by a bat careening towards him. After ducking, he glared at Joe, shocked, "Do bats even *live* in Texas?"

"No, Jury, they just spend all year migratin' from one Denny's to another." Joe pressed his fingers into his temple. "Damn place was a sauna one night, so I opened that tiny window in the corner. Somehow, he flew in. Bastard's been good company. Real tender guy, ya know? I named him Hue."

Hue landed on the lamp's stem. Joe ripped off a piece of bread and threw it under the stairs. The bat followed and stayed put.

Jury couldn't take his eyes off it, "You... you named it. How long has he been here?"

Joe pursed his lips like a pondering scholar. "When was the first Session?"

Jury somehow kept his rant confined to a single breath. Even the clenching of his teeth didn't halt a significant rise in volume. "WE'VE HAD A BAT INFESTATION FOR THREE MONTHS?! If that bat escapes upstairs and terrorizes so much as one person, the city would shut us down if the satanic implications hadn't already."

Joe spoke casually. "Infestation? Satanic implications? Don't be so neurotic. This is the last place we need to worry about findin' the Devil."

"Okay, okay—" admiration slid into his tone as he simmered down, "Although I respect your sneakiness, this is still a little frustrating."

"I'm not here for pest control."

Jury chuckled. "Well, I'm letting you live here for free. The least you could do is take care of the place."

"I wouldn't consider it free."

"Look, your past," he paused, struggling to find a proper term, "*services* are not why I let you stay. You needed help and I had the room.

It's nothing you wouldn't do for me. Just be more courteous. You feel me?"

Joe couldn't help but be suspicious, "I *feel* like ya want somethin'."

Jury smiled. "You know me well. I need information on Preston Epalit's past. Stuff I can use."

"Preston Epalit? Hmmm…" He scratched his chin, "Oh! You mean Daffy Duck on lard?"

"I prefer to think of him as the stranger PSAs warn children about."

"We all have our descriptions."

He grinned. "That's my 'idea of interpretation' bit at work!"

Joe visibly winced. "Ech, movin' on. You're in luck. I already did some pokin' around."

Joe approached a dusty cabinet with sheets of paper protruding from each drawer. He rummaged through it and removed a thick series of articles held together by a blue paperclip. One firm breath freed most of the dust.

Some ancient particles remained, but Jury didn't care. He clapped and rubbed his hands together, "Oh boy! Old, grimy, and just what I needed! Thanks, as always. Well, I'll leave you to whatever it is you do. Good day, Joe." He grabbed the file with his thumb and index finger and left the basement.

Just as Jury was about to enter his office, he heard someone vomiting nearby. He tossed the file onto his desk and ran to the source. Emil was bent over a toilet in the Sturdy's restroom.

He knelt at Emil's level, "Are you okay?"

Keeping his hands planted on the toilet seat, he turned to face Jury. Blood was smeared across Emil's chin and the corners of his lips. The water resembled a grotesque pool of melted flesh. Emil breathed frantically, struggling to retain consciousness, before shaking his head.

The file would have to wait.

FAULT LINES

After a stomach-churning ride, Jury and Emil arrived at Pontifex Catholic Hospital. It was the largest medical facility within one hundred and fifty miles and attracted staff from across the Bible Belt. Whereas many hospitals were infamous for shady billing practices or rude staff, Pontifex was idolized for a lack thereof.

Staff rushed Emil to surgery. Jury was ushered into a waiting room. He sat leg over knee and skimmed through Teen Weekly, baffled. Half an hour later, his desire to read had drained, and he had no choice but to stare at a television missing its remote, forever trapped on the Travel Channel. His eyes drifted to the main hallway. Amidst a sea of everyday joes and nuns, a familiar, staticky beard caught his eye. It protruded from a large man dressed like a detective in a snowstorm. The man stopped and spun his head. Through orange-tinted sunglasses, he returned Jury's stare.

The voice which erupted from him was irreplaceable. "Mailugulism dulled your senses yet? Or just sight?"

Jury smirked. "Howdy, Press! Not having a soul is now considered a diagnosable disease, huh?" He smacked his lips. "I'm so sorry. I'll be sure to send some flowers."

Preston made a strange gurgling noise, "Good luck burying your dead," he snickered, "Jury Chessjurist," and continued down the hall.

Another hour passed before he could visit Emil. His condition was stable. At Emil's request, Jury sat in for the doctor's prognosis. The two braced themselves, but not hard enough. She told them everything Mailugula feared most. When the doctor left, and things seemed their bleakest, Jury rested his hand on Emil's shoulder and smiled, "No need to fear. We're here for you."

Jury spent every second he could with Emil. Larry and Red often tagged along. Joe arranged a beautiful array of flowers and listened to him reminisce about days gone by. Even Jude set aside time to visit. Speakers who hadn't formally introduced themselves would stay and play poker into the night's farthest reaches. Bonds were forged despite the curtain closing. Emil told many, "Being one headstone in a sea of many scares me." In response, Jury decided to bury Emil on the Sturdy grounds. Jury announced these plans at a Session. No one objected, but word spread to Pontifex Catholic and met the ears of some who did.

From there, Jury requested a court order. Once it was granted, everyone felt relieved Emil wouldn't rot in the morgue.

In Emil's final moments, a massive crowd from the Sturdy filled the room to the brim. Some brought flowers, little stuffed animals, and heart-shaped balloons.

Each of Red's jagged breaths spawned a tear.

Larry handed him a tissue, "Stay strong, dude."

Jude wiped his eyes with a handkerchief, "It always gets me when others start crying."

With a calm, collected grin, Emil glanced from face to face, "Why so down, everyone? It won't be hard to find another doorman."

Jury frowned, "But we'll never find another Emil."

Peace came flowing to him. With his voice fading, he clutched Jury's hand, "Thank you, Jury. And everyone, for saving me." His breathing slowed from a crawl to nothing.

~

The following morning, Jury, Red, Joe, and Larry arrived at Pontifex Catholic's morgue. A worker led them to Emil and helped place the body into a temporary casket. Before any further actions could be taken, a priest jogged toward them, hands raised. "Hold on!" He turned to Jury, "You're Chessjurist, right?"

"Who's asking?" Jury responded.

"Abraham Wingjer." He stooped for a moment to catch his breath. "You could say I'm involved with many affairs here. I stop you because I'm worried about this man."

Joe shared Jury's confusion. "Why?"

The priest shook his head. Despite his thinning hairline and portly size, he spoke with more conviction than any of them. "I speak of the afterlife, sirs. It's already concerning enough that you plan to hold his ceremony in your facility, but burying him on those same grounds is asking for damnation."

Jury sounded more upset than enraged, "Don't act like you know what's best when you have no idea what we do. Emil signed the papers and helped plan everything himself. Mailugula would never let him suffer."

"Have faith in something besides your own creation." Abraham pressed his hands into his chest, "Have faith in *me*, at least. I have only the best intentions. We at Pontifex follow a moral, religious doctrine."

Larry didn't hesitate becoming confrontational, "And we follow the *law*. We have every right to do this, so mind your business."

With a subtle cringe, Red pulled Larry back, vocalizing nothing but a sigh under his breath.

A sly hint of pride came to Joe.

The worker assisting them stayed silent. His empty gaze sang an undervalued, underpaid melody.

Jury leaned toward Abraham. Cruel sarcasm dripped over his words like blood on a knife. "Get out of my way so I can damn this man for all eternity. That's what I'm doing, right? Exercising my judgment over your nonsense is clearly against your poorly defined *religion*, right?" His tone snapped back to reality. "That's just your interpretation. You may be entitled to it, but it is still a problem."

Everyone standing around the casket was ready to lift when Abraham finally muttered, "Such a disgrace."

Jury removed his hand and turned toward him, "What was that?"

Fervor overtook him, "I said that you are a disgrace! Cults and tricksters have no place on Planet Earth."

Jury seized Abraham's clerical collar, taking him with, "Call us a cult one more time, I dare you!"

"Ah... ah," he groaned, "Security!"

Jury dropped him and scraped the pious germs off on his pants, "It's always the same with you guys: starting fights, but then calling on someone beneath you to finish them. Disgrace," he scoffed, "My father took the words of people like you and made me kneel on rice until my knees bled." He clenched his teeth. "*That* is a disgrace."

Red squeezed between the two. "*Jury!* How do you think people will react if this comes out?" He reached into his pocket and handed the priest and morgue worker three hundred dollars, "Please just forget this ever happened, okay? We're *very* sorry."

Joe's frown intensified.

Jury refused to look at Red. "Let's just get the damn casket out of here."

Abraham's face grew redder every second. He plucked the money from the morgue worker's hands and threw it back at Red. "Take it back and get out!"

Joe, Red, Larry, and Jury lifted the casket and walked out of the hospital. As soon as they placed it in the hearse, Jury stormed off. Red turned to everyone, his face downcast. "I'm sorry you all had to see that. If we aren't back in a few minutes, please leave. Don't worry about us."

Fifteen minutes came and went.

The next day, Jury gathered the Speakers to begin planning Emil's funeral. He ascended the stage stairs and took a deep breath. There was a hunch in his shoulders and a squeak in his voice. "Hi, everyone. I'll be quick." He identified a plan, materials, and budget. The only person absent was Red.

Everyone felt motivated to start as soon as possible, and within the hour, work began. The only people who looked like they were preparing for a funeral were Red and Jury. Among a group of people cleaning and setting up, Red seemed distant. The glint in his eyes, though still present, was dim. He couldn't hold much of a conversation, either. Jury similarly conducted himself. He remained locked away in his office like a princess in a tower. Some gossip sparked, but most passed it off as grief. Larry suspected something more, however. He took a break to speak with the only person he thought was more honest than him.

Joe snored sonnets at his computer desk. Larry tapped him awake, "Earth to Mr. Aphasiac."

He jumped and, hand over heart, turned to face the lad, "What the hell, kid! You tryin' to make this a double funeral?"

"That'd save money, but no. I need advice."

Joe yawned, "Why? I may be old, but I lost my touch centuries ago."

Larry chuckled, "I feel like you'll speak your mind no matter what." He paused and took the silence as permission to continue. "I'm worried about Jury and Red. They've been distant since we got Emil's body."

"Go easy on 'em, kid. They're grievin'."

"I don't know. Things were already tense between Jury and Red at the hospital, but they've been giving each other space. Nonstop. And that's just the obvious. Red's been distant, and Jury's locked himself in his office. For crying out loud, man's acting like–"

"A princess in a castle? Yeah, that's Jury for ya." Joe mused for a moment before looking back at Larry. "So, what do ya think? That they had some confrontation at the hospital?"

Larry was silent for a moment. "Good thought! Thanks, Mr. Aphasiac." He walked to the stairs.

"Hold on, kid! Why fix their problem? It's not your responsibility."

As he looked back at Joe, a flood of optimism entered his tone and expression. "But I can, so I should. Anyway, thanks again!"

"Don't mention it. And ease up with the Mr. Aphasiac crap. Just call me Joe, capisce?"

Larry nodded and went upstairs.

Joe turned back to his computer and chuckled. "*I can, so I should.* Heh heh. Good kid." He put the camera from Jury's office on the monitor and watched intently.

Larry rested his hand on Jury's office door and took a deep breath before knocking.

A few seconds of dead air followed. "Who is it?"

"Larry. Do you have time to talk?"

The following pause felt like lag in a simulation. "Fine."

Scrunching his face, Larry opened the door, "Fine? A little aggressive, don't you think? You haven't been yourself lately, Jury. I'm worried about you."

Jury didn't look up from his typewriter, "A Speaker has passed away, Larry. I'm grieving. We all are."

"Well, all of us haven't been so lifeless." He sat on Jury's desk and emoted like an interrogator. "Look, I'm just trying to help. Don't lie to me."

Jury's attention was captured. "Huh. What's your goal, exactly?"

"I wanna know what happened between you and Red at the hospital."

"A stupid argument. That's it. All I wanted was to smoke in peace."

Larry frowned, "Come on, cut the crap, Jury."

"Hey!" He stood up. "Don't you dare talk to me like that!"

Memories of his father frazzled him, but Larry persisted. "Handle this with some honor! You're acting like my Dad."

Jury stammered over a few syllables before falling silent.

"I'll ask you an easier question." He grabbed Jury's arm. "What was the fight about? What did Red say that pissed you off?"

Jury stammered. Highlights of Red's words echoed in his mind. *Hey! You told me you stopped smoking!*

Jury snapped out of it and pulled away from him, "Enough! You saw how Red handled the situation, right? I'd rather burn the money than give it to a slanderous reptile like Abraham. Everything compounded, and I couldn't take it. Then, when I wanted to be alone, he fought me."

Larry's tone was stern. "No, he was trying to make you learn."

Memory flashed in Jury's mind once more, *Why are you being so mean? I'm just trying to help you understand where I'm coming from.*

Jury ran his hand through his hair and sighed. "I just don't get it. Why turn against innocent, hard-working people just because they believe something different? It's so selfish! This is why I never listened to my Dad when he—"

"You weren't talking to your Dad or Abraham! You were talking to your friend. Someone who'd do anything for you."

Jury began breathing unevenly. His bottom lip lowered. The memory of Red's words once again pierced his bitter exterior. *We've stuck it out through thick and thin for nine years. Please don't push me away because you're angry. I can't watch you take everything for granted!*

Larry leaned forward. "You put everything at risk, and for what? As rude as Abraham was, you were out of line."

"I KNOW!" He stopped to catch his breath, "*I know*. Abraham didn't even try to understand us before starting a fight. I just—What in Mailugula's name is the problem with wanting to give Emil the meaningful send-off he asked for?"

Larry's voice and the memory repeating inside Jury's head became one, "*Nothing at all!*" Larry took a deep breath and calmed his voice. "The problem is that you threatened someone that can destroy everything you've built. We may have money, but that doesn't give us a license to be careless. Now, judging by how Red's been acting, something worse happened. Can you tell me what that something is?"

Jury hung his head. *"You gave that vindictive, crooked man real money from the Speakers' funds. That's the real disgrace, Jared. You."*

His tone solidified, "This is unbecoming of a leader, and you know it! You're acting like Red encouraged the priest's behavior when he was just covering your ass! I care about you, man, but stop behaving like a brat. I know things are building up, but don't let it distract you from what matters. Red deserves better!"

"If anyone knows that, it's me. It's not Red's fault. I blamed—"

He stuck his palm out, "Save it for Red. Have faith. If you truly believe in what you're doing, then you have to take criticism in stride."

He smiled, "I wouldn't suggest I don't believe, but I see your point. Red said the same thing."

"And Red was right."

FOR THE VAULT

September 19th, 2000

After days of hard work, the Sturdy was ready for Emil's funeral. The hardwood floor glimmered, as did the seats. A gray rug stretched across the center aisle and led to the casket. It was a calm shade of burgundy that complemented Emil's velvet coat. Even in death, his mustache was still a powerful sight. Flower arrangements of different sizes and colors surrounded the coffin. Pictures were hung everywhere, showing recent and ancient history. There was a table at the back with refreshments and snacks.

The Speakers were all dressed in suits and dresses. Larry acted as a doorman at Emil's request, greeting guests and distributing programs. Joe stayed downstairs to monitor the cameras. Jury was the only Speaker wearing a tie and offered a friendly face while drifting between crowds. Red acted similarly but avoided Jury. The visitor turnout was stronger than expected, so everyone kept busy. People fluttered in and out, but the Sturdy was still packed when the ceremony began.

Jury rehearsed endlessly the night before, but he now spoke with a foreign melancholy. He leaned over the podium. "Your generosity brings our hearts great solace in these trying times. I assure you all that our Doorman is smiling upon us, wherever he may be." He cleared his throat and straightened his tie. "Our first memory of Emil was one of great confusion. It was January, and a rare batch of snow had fallen.

One of my Speakers looked out a window and saw Emil making snow angels on our front lawn." He chuckled and spoke like warmth from a fire. "It was charming, but when he passed out from the cold, we picked and propped him up. The rest is history," he took a breath, "Fate led him to the figurative yet welcoming arms of Mailugula. Things happen that way, after all. Life is full of blind luck and hopeless gambles, but eventually, something good *will* happen to you. That's the logic in this frankly illogical situation."

Jury captured even those who didn't believe in Mailugula. Pain splintered across his eyes. "The way my Speakers and I see it, Mother Nature smiled upon Emil when he found us. Every Speaker shares some bond with him. He was here before we could open our doors without walking into cobwebs... before we could walk around without seeing ghosts. But as I look into the audience, I have no doubt you are all more than familiar with either the grin on Emil's face or the majesty of his mustache. Though he could've held the door and said nothing, Emil contributed in the largest capacity he could because that's the kind of person he was and forever will be. There will always be a hole in this Sturdy, and in our hearts, once filled by his warm smile and charismatic salutes. One that will never be filled again."

Jury's body stiffened. Although he still sounded charismatic, it felt like he was reading off a script. "In situations like these, we must take time to appreciate life rather than curse it. Every breath we take and every word we speak *matters*. We all fear that we won't be ready when our time arrives. We count our moments instead of making them matter. It's frightening. In a way, that silent phobia unites us all. That's why death should not be an individual struggle, which is a realization even I struggle with." He inhaled deeply. Nervousness flickered in and out of his emerald eyes. "Just as it tears the fabric of life from our bodies, death often tears the love from our relationships, which is odd when you realize death should bring us together, not tear us apart. It's up to us to ensure we remain united and in love through all conflict. Though sometimes we find ourselves lost in grief, let us be found in the eyes of those around us," he looked at Red and smiled hopefully, "and the embrace of Mailugula. Thank you all. We are forever indebted to your generosity." Jury floated over the podium for a few seconds and surrendered it.

Red was sitting at the end of an aisle. Jury moved a chair next to him and rested his hand atop Red's knee. A mutual smile emerged.

Within forty-five minutes, memorials finished. The final Speaker announced Emil would be laid to rest in fifteen minutes. The Speakers spread out to comfort and network. Though many people filled the place, only one surprised Jury. He finished a brief conversation with one of his regulars when he saw Mallory approaching him.

He lit up, "I never thought I'd see you again!"

She side-hugged him, "Howdy, Mr. Chessjurist."

He hugged her back. "It's so great to see you! How's it feel to come in through the door?"

Mallory was silent for a few seconds and stared off to the side, "Good."

"Uh, what's up?"

She tried but failed to stifle a smile. "I'll just come out and say it." With a wide grin, she grabbed his hands. "I'm pregnant!"

Jury's mouth hung open. "Ummm, oh."

Those within earshot threw glances of shock at Jury and Mallory.

Jury shook away his surprise and leveled his tone. "That's…" he inhaled through clenched teeth and shrugged, "Incredible? You said you wanted a family, but I didn't think you'd try so *soon*."

"I didn't." Mallory wrapped her hand around her stomach and smiled.

"Well, I'm glad you're happy. How have you and the father been preparing for the little stranger's arrival?"

"Oh," she chuckled sheepishly, "He doesn't know. He's fun but not exactly reliable."

"Oh boy." He squinted at her. It took every ounce of self-control to conceal his concern. "Does this mean you've decided to retire?"

"Mm…" Mallory looked down. "Not exactly. I stopped leaving the card after you caught me, though."

Jury latched onto her eyes, his look fiercer and more examining than ever. "You took nothing I said to heart. I am very disappointed in you."

Mallory scoffed and turned away from him. "I took your words to heart, Mr. Chessjurist, but I disagree. People like me can't change. That's my truth, and in a way, embracing it with Mailugula is setting me free. Mailugula has given me the confidence I've been lacking my entire life."

Something caught Jury's attention. The basement door crept open, and out of it stumbled Joe. He wore dark slacks with a matching shirt and tie. Jury didn't take his eyes off him. "Getting an actual job is the first step to living a clean, honest life. It's not a scary road to travel down. The sooner you start, the better."

"I reckon I am clean. As long as I'm careful and always learning from my mistakes, I don't see the harm in what I'm doing."

"Then why did you put the money back in the desk?" Mallory stared at him like a shopper caught with stuffed pockets. His voice was cold. "That's what I thought. I will not tolerate you using Mailugula as an excuse. Anyway, I'm afraid I have other matters to pursue. Don't forget what I said this time. Put your behavior into question before it's too late." His eyes hardened, "for you and the little stranger's sake. I know you're happy, but this can change on a dime." He walked away.

She shook her head and left.

Jury approached Joe and hunched his back in a goofy manner, "Do my eyes deceive me? Is that Joe Aphasiac in a crowd, dressed in something other than sweats?"

Joe furrowed his eyebrows, "Did ya forget you're hostin' a funeral? I appreciate the lightheartedness, but this isn't the time to screw around."

Jury didn't look sorry. "I meant nothing by it. My apologies." He cleared his throat. "Cameras show anything worthwhile?"

"Your speech was fine. Otherwise, nothin'. I figure it's safe for me to visit."

"Good." Curiosity overtook him, "If this is inappropriate, shut me down, but why don't you ever join the Speakers?"

"Because I'm not one."

"Oh, come on. You care more than Michael, but he still attends Sessions. What's keeping you from the spotlight?"

Joe lowered his voice and leaned toward him, *"You know why I'm cautious."*

"Mm." Jury's face tightened. "Your secret's safe with me, and you're safe here. You *know* that. After all this time, do you still not believe?"

He groaned and rubbed his hand across his hair, "I can't do this now, Jury. The only person I relate to here is dead. Cut me some slack."

"Yeah..." Jury snapped out of a trance. "Yeah. I'm sorry. I can't help but get a little distracted sometimes. I'll leave you be." He disappeared into the crowd.

Joe approached Emil's body.

Larry stood next to the casket. Stranded in his thoughts, he didn't notice Joe.

After a few seconds of dead air, Joe snapped in front of Larry's eyes. "Earth to Mr. Zarzerous."

He flinched, "Ah! Oh, sorry," and jutted his head forward, "Joe!?"

"Come on, kid. I'm not a celebrity."

"I don't think I've ever seen you and sunlight in the same place."

"Heh heh." Joe noticed a tear in the lad's eye. He furrowed his eyebrows. "You're takin' it hard."

"I miss him. I know we didn't talk much, but that makes me feel worse." Larry shifted his gaze from the casket to the people around him. "I've never really thought about death before. Now that I see it right in front of me..."

Joe leaned against the casket and brushed his fist against Larry's shoulder. "You've got a long way to go, kid."

Larry's frown tightened. "I'm not thinking about me." he looked up at Joe with puppy-dog eyes. "Maybe I was too hard on my parents. What if I never see them again? I would never be able to set things straight."

Joe frowned. "Emil would hate to see ya talkin' that way." An unfamiliar twinkle struck his eye, and all anguish became pep. "You know, at any moment, ya could be hit by lightnin', a bus. You could be stabbed, caught in a fire, shot, anythin'! Then, it's over, and you are none the wiser! You're lucky to be livin'. So, ya know, live well because," he slowed down and started speaking into the ether, "who knows when you won't be able to enjoy it?"

His words reached both of them. Larry smiled and patted him on the shoulder, "Looks like we both got some livin' to do, old man."

Larry looked away, but Joe stared at him. His smile faded into cold resolve.

At that moment, the doors slammed open. Preston Epalit and his cronies busted into the Sturdy, barraging the place with cameras and microphones. Preston accosted a random guest. "Do you feel the events taking place here are unholy?"

The guest stared at him, "What?"

Jury rushed up and pressed his hand against one of the cameras, "Do you people have *any* decency? Get away from my guests and GET OUT!"

The snotty intern behind the camera hollered and pushed his glasses up his nose. "Excuse me! You can't touch my camera."

"This is a funeral! Do you know how much disrespect you're showing me, my Speakers, my guests, and Emil?"

"I could give a sh-"

Jury punched the camera, sending it careening to the floor. Debris launched across the center aisle. Shards of glass landed on the intern's shoes. "You're paying for that."

"Send me the bill, I dare you," Jury was right in his face, "Send me the bill the same way RBLA sends away women who aren't willing to show six inches of cleavage on live TV. Huh? That why you have no female staff?"

Preston pushed Jury away, "Get your hands off my property! Me and my assistants can film wherever we please. We aren't harming anyone. The only person we could hurt is already dead."

Red squeezed into the conflict. "Do you have any idea how unreasonable you're being? A man loved by this community is lying in a coffin fifteen feet away from you. *Please* show some respect."

Preston erupted in laughter, "I hate to break it to you, but Chessie here is not worthy of this town's respect."

Joe leaned against the wall, "He means the man in the coffin, ya dolt. This is a funeral."

"Oh yeah?" Preston's Cheshire smile stretched further across his face than many thought possible. "Since when can cults hold funerals?"

Jury grabbed Preston by the lapels, pulling the two face-to-face. "CALL US A CULT ONE MORE TIME, YOU JEALOUS BAS-TARD!"

The doors swung open once more. Jude, unkempt and sweating, raced toward the commotion. Upon seeing Preston and the cameras, his hopes were steamrolled, "Dear lord. I'm so sorry, everyone. Robust Before Lunch is on their way out," he nudged Preston to the door but got resistance.

Preston gritted his teeth and dug his pointer finger into Jude's pectoral. His voice rained quiet hellfire. "*What* are you doing?"

"WHAT ARE *YOU* DOING!" screeched Jude, pushed to the brink. "SOMEONE NEAR AND DEAR TO THESE PEOPLE IS DEAD, AND ALL YOU CARE ABOUT IS GETTING RAT-INGS!"

"Thank you!" Red chimed in.

Everyone stood in silence as Preston gave Jude the evil eye. "You know what? I got all the footage I need." He gathered his crew and cruised out of the Sturdy, leaving shattered glass in the aisle.

No one looked away from the door. Jury released a pent-up exhale and scraped Preston's remaining germs onto his pants.

By this point, many guests had left for fear of being caught in the crosshairs, but those who remained walked outside. Jury, Red, Michael, Joe, Larry, and Jude carried the casket outdoors. The grave had been dug in the same spot Emil was discovered.

Before lowering the coffin, Jury stepped in front of the gravestone. He spoke with tender sentimentality, "We all view the idea of an afterlife in different lights, but we can all agree that everyone goes somewhere. Mailugula celebrates the autonomy in our hearts and shapes the afterlife in our image, whether it be a dark abyss or a splen-dorous life in the clouds. If we deserve it or not is irrelevant, however, for the man we celebrate today deserves far more than anything our imaginations could muster. Let's not despair, ladies and gentlemen, but rejoice. Our snow angel, we can all agree, is where he belongs. Farewell, Emil Drehermund. May you rest in peace." After the casket was lowered, the crowd dispersed. The headstone's inscription became visible.

"Through our altruism and struggles, we live on. The man insistent on holding the door has finally been let inside."

Jury said little after his closing remarks and went upstairs with Red. No clean-up orders were given. Exhaustion spread past Jury and convinced everyone to retire early. The Sturdy was assumed empty.

Joe remained outside. He blinked away the tear in his eye. "What a corny inscription. Heh heh." He shook his head and basked in the sunlight surrounding him. "Thank you for everything you've sacrificed, old man. Watch the stars for me, will ya?"

~

Instead of returning to Jury after using the restroom, Red gave into his stomach's demands. En route to the refectory, he noticed Jude reading alone in the Session area. Red called out to him from the stairwell, "I'm surprised you didn't follow Epalit home."

Jude didn't glance up from his book, "I can leave if it's a problem. I just figured this was the most peaceful place I could be right now. Preston's probably blowing up my answering machine as we speak."

Red sat in the row behind him, "Why didn't you find out about his plan sooner?"

"One of my friends from Oklahoma State was in town, so we met for a late lunch. I came back and saw that Preston had left me a note." He half-frowned, "I'm sorry I couldn't stop him."

"No one's blaming you, Jude. It's okay. I'm just shocked that all RBLA employees aren't caricatures. You actually have a conscience."

He chuckled, "I may be on Preston's payroll, but that doesn't mean I lack basic morals."

A light bulb exploded in Red's mind. He put his hands together and leaned toward Jude. "Would you ever consider switching payrolls?"

Jude laughed, but after turning around and seeing the determination in Red's eyes, his perception changed. Jude peered off into the distance and closed his book.

~

Midnight

The shaking in Jury's hands had intensified since Emil passed away. Though the stench in his clothes had disappeared and his appetite returned, he felt worse off. All he could think about was taking a puff of his Newports, like a reward for making it through the day. Relapse appeared inevitable when he snuck away from a sleeping Red. On his way out, Jury came across some leftover shards of glass. "An excuse!" he whispered, sweeping some into his palm. No mysterious auras or metallic rhythms were present as he walked to the dumpster. All appeared normal until he went through the back door, tripped over a package, and fell, lodging the glass into his palm.

A crashing sound echoed. Jury exhaled through gritted teeth and groaned while trying to ignore the blood gushing from his hand. As though enough noise hadn't been created, Red, bite-sized emergency kit in hand, slammed open the door.

"Jury? *JURY!*" He rushed toward him, speaking without taking a single breath, "Are you okay? What happened? Did someone do this to you? Sit down, sit down! Let's wrap you up."

Jury couldn't help but smile, "Glad to see we're on good terms again, dear. No need to fear. I'm okay. No big deal."

"No big deal?! Imagine what would've happened if that glass went anywhere else, and I can only imagine the effect this'll have on your hands."

"I understand. You don't have to talk to me like I'm six. You're not my Dad, thank Mailugula."

He rolled his eyes. "Ugh, hold your breath for me, goober."

Jury complied and flinched as Red pulled out each shard of glass. Tiny spurts of blood exited his palm in tandem with the shards. No amount of squirming or lip-biting could stop tears from filling Jury's eyes.

"Okay?" Red looked up at him and patted his leg.

Jury gave him a thumbs-up.

Red grinned. "Good job! We're almost done." He looked back at his hand. "Hey, why are you out here so late, anyway?"

"Oh, you know..." He looked away and scratched the back of his head. "I just went to get some water and saw this glass lying in the center aisle. Like any good samaritan, I picked it up and went to safely dispose of it. I tripped over this box on my way out. Nothing more."

The wound had been cleaned and patched. Red was monotone, "Oh. We'll take a look at that tomorrow, then. I'll head back to bed. Will you be there soon?"

Jury widened his eyes and spoke with excess enthusiasm. "Uh, of course!"

When Red went back inside, Jury grabbed a cigarette from his stash behind the dumpster. However, the quivering in his hands became so intense that holding the cigarette became a feat, and lighting it proved impossible. He frowned and flicked the monster away. Only then did the tremoring rest.

Jury began reading the package's note.

Cameras: they're just one way of controlling land. But don't think about what your land is. To rise above, think about what your land could become, and how you plan on getting it there. -Progenitor

P.S: STOP SMOKING! Just seeing you people do it depresses me.

The box was Progenitor's largest by far. Before Jury could lift it, Red burst through the back door.

"Ah-hah!" he exclaimed, pointer finger extended. Red looked around and, after a moment, the tension left him. "You really aren't smoking?"

Jury stood for a few seconds, aimless, "No, I... I was. You're right, as always. Can you help me find another way to relieve my anger? I can't do it without you."

Red embraced him, "Of course, Jury. Of course." He was one step away from tears.

"I'm sorry. I'll do my best to listen to you more. I don't know how I'd function if you ever left." His tone became more unstable and desperate. "Please never leave me. Promise to stay forever."

"I promise."

They hugged for a few seconds before Jury pulled away. "Hey, Red?"

"Yeah?"

"How much do you know about community service?"

With that, the Sturdy went quiet for the first time in a week. One detail escaped everyone's mind, however: Preston had captured a temper only Speakers were familiar with, and he wasn't content to let it rot in a vault.

ACT 2: PROOF OF CONCEPT

Six months prior to The Sturdy's opening.

Boxes were strewn across the floor: some partway unpacked, others sealed. Besides a microwave and a chair, the only thing set up was a television. The deafening sound of *Gunsmoke* filled the air, as did Preston's open-mouth chewing. Insects rode the soft breeze traveling through an open window and passed by the thunderous sound waves from the TV. It was so obnoxiously loud that a fly landed on the speakers and exploded. The neighbors already had choice words for him, but Preston remained indolent and free. The sounds of MeTV were paltry, however, compared to the encroaching roar of an engine racing down the street.

Preston sighed and rose from his reclining chair. "Goddamn hoodlum. Day one, and I have already found someone with enough gall to interrupt my programs."

He peeked through a window and watched a 1977 Firebird drive off-road and park halfway on his lawn and halfway on his neighbor's. The driver dashed to the neighboring home and threw open the door, leaving the vehicle running. Preston caught a glimpse of his face and noticed the man was on edge: his breathing was rapid, and his face dripped with sweat.

"What kind of parking job is *that*?" He rolled up his sleeves and walked next door. The introduction to Rolling Stones' *Sympathy for the Devil* boomed through the Firebird's speakers as he crept through the front entrance. "Hello? I'm looking for the owner of the Fire*brand* trodding on my sod." The lack of a response angered him. His voice became gravelly. "Move the car before I move it into a river."

In the absence of a pursuable noise, Preston turned his head. He noticed a shelf adorned with trophies and family photos. He soon realized that one face tied them all together. It belonged to an initially young boy. One particular display of images originated from what Preston assumed to be a yearly family reunion. The boy grew and matured in each photo, but the family surrounding him gradually decreased. He connected the face from the latest image to that of the mystery driver.

The shelf below was devoted to trophies of varying sizes and colors. He read the label belonging to the largest and identified the name Jude Ariotics.

Sounds of glass shattering overtook him. He ran toward the sound and discovered an older, skinnier Jude. Before any interrogation, Preston noticed him pressing a knife into his wrist. On instinct, he jumped forward and slapped it out of the man's grasp.

"WHAT THE HELL ARE YOU DOING?!" Preston smacked him and dug his finger into his pectoral, "Get a hold of yourself!"

Jude regained focus and replied through jagged breaths, "Wh——who are you?"

The singing of Mick Jagger loomed in the distance as Preston extended his hand. "Name's Preston Epalit." He draped Jude's arm over his shoulder and took him to the emergency room. Lucky for both of them, Pontifex Catholic had access to MeTV.

POKER FACE

Present day. Three Days After Emil's Funeral.

After a brief hiatus, Jude returned to RBLA headquarters. He approached his office and flipped the light switch. Where light should have been let, there was none. Then, Preston's withered hand pulled the desk lamp's tassel, illuminating the room.

Preston's skin appeared washed out, like a cross between Nosferatu and a wendigo. The static in his beard had overtaken his mustache. Despite a receding stomach and less energetic movements, his voice remained golden, "Consider yourself lucky I was able to Frankenstein my footage into something worthwhile." He ground his teeth. "Tell me why you pulled that stunt."

Jude pointed at the ceiling, "Is there a reason my light's not working?"

"I smashed the bulb. Be thankful it was not over your head." Preston clenched his fists, "Answer me, Jude."

"I don't want to talk about this, Boss. It'll rile you up, and the last thing we need is your heart finally giving out."

He scoffed, "Too bad!" and slowly stood. "You will *not* have that wish after you put my plan at risk." His index finger found a home in Jude's sternum.

Jude maintained a low, stern tone, "What is it with you and impaling people with that finger? Look, I know we've done some immoral things in the past, but defiling funerals?"

Preston was exasperated. "Defiling?! We are not *talking* about assault, Jude! Get over yourself and listen to me. You must be committed to the RBLA, not to some fairy and his fables."

"What does that even mean?"

"*Your* interests, whether you like it or not, are aligned with mine. So what if I offended a few people? Yeah, it was selfish, but not nearly as selfish as that Mailugula crap. We actually have a cause!"

Jude's temper rose, "What is our cause: slamming hard workers?"

A cruel giddiness danced across his delivery, "And people say *I* exaggerate. *Chessie* is not a hard worker. He is a prissy, Union bastard with prissy, northern values."

"Northern values?" Jude put his head in his hands. "Do you hear yourself right now? I understand you come from a different time, but—"

"That is *not* what this is about!"

"Then what? Are you jealous that people like Jury more than you?"

Preston squinted and lowered his voice, "What are you saying?"

"You think the Mailugians led Fin and Donald away from you, right?"

"Away, no. *Astray*, yes. I do not even remember Don, but Fin? Fin was weak. The bastard should have faced me like a *man*. At the very least, he should have known I never would have killed *him*," his eyes widened, and he froze.

"What are you talking about?" Silence followed, and Jude had a frightening realization. "What did you do to him?"

Preston's pupils shook as they never had. An unrecognizable expression of terror entered his face. "Now listen, Jude. Listen to me good." He held up his index finger, and his voice trembled, "*Once.* I let a few things and a few drinks get to me, and I... I..." he couldn't come to terms with his following words. They visibly rattled him.

Jude spoke with conviction, "You know what? You may have saved me once, but this is too much." He tried walking out.

"Ah!" He blocked the doorway, "That is exactly right. *I* saved *you*. Anna Fitzgerald would have driven you into the grave had it not been for me. You had a knife pressed into your wrist, Jude! You want to prove her wrong, right? Don't you want her to see how much you matter in the eyes of influential people like me?"

"I don't appreciate being manipulated by my past. My family was shrinking, and I was depressed. How things ended between Anna and I sent me over the edge. I realize that now. But I also realize your intentions have always been slimy. I don't owe you for what you did! You aren't upstanding."

He laughed, "And you think Mailugula is?"

"See? There you go again, off-topic and completely missing the point."

"Is there a point for me to miss, or do I have to make that up too?" He took a deep breath and abruptly calmed down, "Okay, okay. We are getting too riled up." Preston slowly approached him and spoke like a negotiator leveling with an armed lunatic, "We can debate ethics all day, but *you* need to simmer down, partner."

Jude's temper flared. "I'm not your damn partner, all right?!" He pushed Preston off and backed away. "I may be angry, but I will *not* stoop to your level, and I will not dignify this unprofessional bullshit with a response. I'm gonna go somewhere where I can actually help people. Stay away from me, Preston." He opened the door and left.

Those working in the building could only stare, Preston included. He imagined chasing after Jude, foaming at the mouth with rage and obscenities, but he couldn't move. All Preston could muster, after minutes of standing in the hallway, was, "You've never owed me any thing..."

Then, all threads of self-awareness were numbed by fury. Preston shook violently and lumbered into Jude's office. Nothing was safe from Preston's explosive path. Fire brimmed from his lips, and earthquakes spawned with each step. Staplers and office supplies cowered below him. Sixty seconds of destruction followed until heartburn struck. He clutched his chest and slumped against the wall. As the night ended, Preston filled a trash can with vomit and empty pill bottles. The roar of an ambulance grew closer.

~

The Next Day, 6:00 PM

RBLA broadcast an edited, dramatized cut of the funeral footage. Interspersed with Jury's rage were interviews of RBLA workers, who expressed disdain and fright for their treatment and suggested the Speakers endured worse daily. Towards the spotlight's end, a particularly stiff Preston appeared before an obvious green screen and described abuse not documented on camera. "We would have been able to show you proof had my men not been afraid to do their duty." Scents of deception were strong, but the spotlight still garnered attention from across the Bible Belt states.

A group of Speakers crowded around a television while Jury flipped through news stations and talk shows. Between each channel, a burst of static rang out.

Chhh.

"What gives Chessjurist the right to deny press coverage of a funeral, or even host–" *chhh.*

"RBLA managed to disrespect even the dead earlier this week when–" *chhh.*

"No matter whose side you're on, Chessjurist should have handled the situation–" *chhh*.

"Sexist remarks were made by–" *chhh*.

"You have to wonder. Does Chessjurist treat his staff with the same–" *chhh*.

"Are we really gonna debate morality? Chessjurist was attacked. I'd have done the same–" *chhh*.

The crowd surrounding him dissipated. Larry, Michael, Jude, and Red remained.

Jury turned off the TV and buried his face in his hands. "This is going to ruin us."

Jude put his hand on Jury's shoulder. "I wouldn't worry. There's always a way to turn around bad press."

A strange sense of authority was burned into Michael's tone. "You must give Preston some credit. This whole stunt is quite clever."

No one responded. Red adopted a more supportive tone, "Don't worry, Jury. It'll be okay."

"Okay?" Jury lowered his hands and peered at the ceiling, "The whole world is doubting our intentions, regardless of if we're in their favor or not."

"Sheesh," started Larry, tone light, "How can we win back their favor?" His eyes lit up, "I have had an epiphany. If my extended family has taught me one thing, it's that love can be bought."

"I'm sorry," chuckled Jude, "But does this have a point?"

Larry raised an eyebrow and leaned forward. "Uh, yeah. It does. I actually know something besides Preston Epalit's belt size."

Red, wide-eyed, turned to Jury. Neither could stifle their smirks.

Jude remained stone-faced.

"As I was saying," Larry continued, "What if we proved ourselves by helping small businesses or doing fundraisers? Gestures of good-will, ya know?"

"Yeah, good thinking," answered Jude. "We buy back the county's support figuratively with events and actions that show–"

Larry spoke in a mocking falsetto, "Sorry, but does this have a point?"

"That was rude of me, and I apologize," Jude said, looking contrite. "Can we move on?"

Larry nodded.

"All right, then. I'm not trying to sound selfish, but Preston is reeling from my departure, and he'll do anything within his power to make us look like assholes. And I hope he does. He's too frustrated to realize that letting the pot sizzle is the smartest choice. So, if *we* let the pot sizzle, we'll be the better men."

Jury tilted his head, "And prove how much we care in the process. What an excellent idea! I've been entertaining similar concepts myself."

"See!" exclaimed Jude. "This is our first step in building up the Sturdy. Preston's just a careless idiot without me by his side, and you're giving him way too much credit anyway."

Michael crossed his arms. "Yeah, chances are he's doing the same thing with you too, Jude."

Jury stared at Michael with a blank expression.

Jude furrowed his eyebrows, "So, Larry, you gonna ask him for his point?"

Michael rolled his eyes. "Who asked you to join the Speakers, again? Just one person? Wow, what a welcome addition." Without another word, he walked upstairs.

Larry shrugged, "Maybe it's Michael we should retaliate against."

"Funny." Jury rose. Hints of his usual vitality returned. "I've had enough drama for one night. Thank you all for your support, and Jude: I'm glad to have you here. Tomorrow, we start proving that we care. Until then, get some rest, you guys." He started walking up the stairs but turned around midway. "Hey, Larry?"

"Yeah?"

"Isn't your birthday on the 30th?"

"Yeah."

Jury's charisma was now flowing like normal. "Well, happy early birthday. Can you join me, Red? We only have eight days. We gotta start planning."

"Of course," he smiled and wished everyone a good night.

Something new crept through Jude's mind. "Hey, Larry?" Caution entered his tone, "Where are your parents?"

The bags under Larry's eyes became more apparent. He found himself unable to answer, and it troubled him greatly.

Jury watched the sun set from outside his room. His eyes followed the top of the sun as it faded into the horizon, leading Jury to the sight of Michael standing by the dumpster. Suitcases sat beside him. The two made eye contact as Michael looked up. He lit a cigarette and began walking away from the Sturdy.

Jury shrugged. "Good riddance."

PHOBIA

Jury ignored the drama, and session attendance remained strong. Jude appeared to be acclimating well, but one crypt dweller was unconvinced. At Joe's request, they started having lunch together. After their latest meal, Joe and Jude walked to the basement door.

"You know," began Jude, arms crossed, "I've always wondered why this door is different from the others."

"Oh yeah," Joe spoke with vigor and personality. "I uh... *joined* Jury a month or so after he bought the place. Back then, it was gross. The paint was chippin'. The bedrooms were infested with cockroaches. And there was a bunch of *crack*."

Jude stared at him, eyes wide. "A bunch of *what*?"

"It was in my tomb, in the office, under the stage. Everywhere!" A sly look came to him. "And without that crack, we never would have been able to clean this shithole."

Jude's mouth was hanging open.

Joe smirked. "I'm messin' with ya. Jury turned it over to the police."

"After the place was clean?"

He gulped. "So about the door." His energy remained jovial. "One night, I saw this huge wheel bug on that door. Now, I didn't know what a wheel bug was. Well, I did, but I mixed it up with somethin' more poisonous and painful. It's a freaky lookin' thing. I'd call it a cryptid, but that word doesn't mean much since there's proof of everythin' if ya know where to look." He took a deep breath. "Anyhow, I only saw a sledgehammer, and it's not like I had time to investigate."

Jude released a soft chuckle. "Did you get him?"

Joe flashed a mischievous smirk. "Her, actually. And yeah, but I overreacted."

Jude's tone was light. "Well, my ex had a bug phobia, so I understand. I admire what you did. You took action in the moment. So what if you didn't stop to think?"

He batted his hand and began sounding tired. "Eh. It sounds great on paper, but havin' guts doesn't mean anythin' if ya don't know how to use 'em. I either go all the way or not at all. It's kicked me in the ass far more than ya think." His tone went from worn to despondent. "Nothin' I can do, though. It's the way I am."

Jude meant well. "You sound pretty self-aware to me. Are you sure you're not making excuses?"

Joe scoffed. A hint of vexation lied in his softened voice. "I don't make excuses. I can talk about my problems all I want, but when the time comes, I won't rise above 'em. I won't even think to. Besides, when I look at the door, I feel a certain," he snapped a few times, "I don't wanna say warmth, but ya know what I'm gettin' at. It's nice to know I've made one thing that's gonna last."

Jude smirked, "Not any friendships?"

"Larry's a good kid, but besides that, it's entertainin' around here. That's enough."

"I've always wondered: how do you know Jury?"

Joe chuckled nervously and avoided eye contact. "Uh, ya see, Jury was my intern after he graduated high school. We stayed in contact after his apprenticeship."

A dog's feverish bark erupted near the distance and rang through the halls.

Jude narrowed his eyes. "Apprenticeship or internship? And for what? All you've done is sit downstairs and play on the computer."

Before he could defend himself, the sound of someone clearing their throat and wheezing exploded from the basement.

Jude furrowed his eyebrows, "I thought you were the only one who lived down there."

"Oh!" Joe stepped in front of the door, "Every so often, someone brings me food. Some dust probably got in their throat. Nothin' to worry about."

"Doesn't everyone know by now that we have lunch together?" The coughing escalated in volume and intensity. Sounds of objects crashing to the floor then erupted and echoed through the Sturdy. "They need help!" He squeezed past Joe and raced downstairs.

Although Joe was alarmed, he stood back, allowing Jude a head start.

Jude found the victim facing away from him, desperately pressing their stomach against the back of a chair. On instinct, Jude sprung forward and performed the Heimlich maneuver. A chunk of food launched out of the man's mouth. He turned around, and Jude identified him. His eyes widened immediately, and he shouted, "FIN?"

About three weeks had passed since the outside world had seen Fin. The man was already skinny, but now, he looked vampiric. With pale skin and long, greasy hair, the color in his eyes had dulled. Emptiness filled him as air returned to his pores.

Joe rounded the corner.

Jury jumped over the final step. "What's going on? It sounds like..." He saw Fin catching his breath and Jude staring at him, arms crossed.

He addressed Jury plainly, "My friend here was choking, but I managed to save him."

Fin leaned on Jude and caught his breath. "I'm fine. I was eating and... heard something familiar. Thank you, Jude. I really can't say that enough."

"No problem, but uh—" He sighed. "You disappeared out of thin air, man. I thought you ditched this shitty town, but why are you here?"

"A while ago, something horrible happened, and I freaked out. I've been staying here ever since."

"What—"

Fin was desperate. "Please don't ask me what happened. Please."

Joe re-entered the conversation, "Outta the blue one night, he burst in, screamin', panic attack, the works."

"It was blood-curdling," shuddered Jury. "One thing was weird about the whole situation, though. Fin kept muttering Preston's name when we calmed him down. We tried pushing but got nowhere. Since then, he's developed a phobia of him."

Jude, from his tone to expression, was bewildered. "A phobia?"

Joe tightened his lips. "Yeah, bad word choice, but he won't even go outside because he's afraid Preston'll see him."

Jude growled quietly and turned to Jury. "You should've told me when this first happened. I may have been on Preston's payroll, but I still had basic morals! Do you not trust me?"

Fin opened his mouth, but Jude silenced him. "I'm sorry, Fin, but I want to hear this from Jury."

Jury blew off Jude's accusations with an angry breath. "It's not personal. Don't dive into that abyss. Some things are best kept under the table, and we wanted to wait until Fin was emotionally ready."

Jude scoffed, "Emotionally ready for me? Is that all you have to say?"

A wave of compassion surged through Jury's irritated veins, "Don't look at this situation in a negative light. Fin led himself here during his greatest hour of need. Why on Earth would we turn him away? What kind of people would we be if we ignored a call for help?"

Jude maintained a reasonable, albeit entitled, timbre, "And I appreciate that. I'm not mad that you've been sheltering him. I'm mad that you hid him from me! I could've helped."

Jury's response was instantaneous. "Everyone here is perfectly trustworthy, and that goes double for you. I think saving Fin makes you just as trustworthy as me and at least twice as trustworthy as Michael."

"Guys!" Fin smiled and stepped between them. His weak voice sheltered a firm resolve, "Jury is not like Preston. If y'all have a problem, you can work through it."

Jude sighed, "I want this to be different from RBLA. I want to help people, but before that can even start, we need to address the elephant in the room." He turned to Fin. "I know this might be quick, but we need to talk about whatever's hurting you, Fin. If you don't, this paranoia will never stop."

Fin sat at Joe's computer chair and took a deep breath.

"No need to fear. We're all here for you," encouraged Jury.

Joe nodded at him.

Fin glanced from face to face, eye to eye. Though he felt cursed, a part of him realized he was lucky. "Just give me some space."

~

September 6th, 2000

Shrouded in shadow, Preston slouched, fiddling with the phone's handset cord, "*Come ooooon*! I fire people all the time. I do not always mean it."

Fin's eyes were downcast. "Would I get a raise?"

"A raise!? The nerve!" Fin stayed silent, but Preston refused to wait, "Uh, hello!? Fin? Fin! Answer me, ya Muppet!"

Fin slammed the phone on its hook.

His dog, a middle-aged golden retriever, trotted up to him. He was smiling and panting steadily.

Fin's eyes lit up. "You wanna play outside, Spark? Let's go!"

Another day, another restless night. As Fin tossed and turned, Preston's voice—garbled through the answering machine—claimed the halls, slurring through endless rambles. The only intelligible phrase was Preston mumbling, "I am famous. You can not do this to a famous person," over and over. Although he wanted to rip the phone from the wall and smash it against the floor, Fin calmly unplugged it and set it aside. Spark was fast asleep on the couch, which soothed him.

The next day, he decided to invest in a mobile phone. It wasn't cheap, but he didn't care. The day passed without much noise, a welcome change to his routine. That night, Spark slept with him, and Fin was at ease.

Since he was between jobs, Fin had a good deal of time on his hands. The following day, he decided to attend a Session. Worried about how Spark would react to the crowd, Fin left him home.

Spark was gone. "It's not like him to run away," Fin repeated, tearing his house and backyard apart. To his horror, he found a hole in the backyard fence large enough for Spark to squeeze through. Nighttime had already encroached. Fin returned home, resolving to search town tomorrow. He created a few signs and fell asleep over the kitchen table.

When the clock struck three, Fin was battered awake by the ear-piercing sound of glass shattering in his living room and tires screeching away. He turned around and saw just in time. A giant blob encased in newspaper plummeted to the floor. The newspaper had begun to unravel, and dark red splotches covered it. Through his sleepy haze, it looked like a sack of rotting meat. A tattered note written in black sharpie was stapled to it, the words almost illegible:

"I T*I*RE OF B*e*ING *i*GNO*r*ED. PLUG IN UR D*A*MN PHONE!"

The words were clear, but his thoughts were not. An idea crept through Fin's mind, "Wuh... what? *No...*" He reluctantly unwrapped a portion of the mysterious object. Its contents caused him to wail and fling himself back.

"It's all my fault," he repeated to himself, the words taking precedence over breathing.

His willpower and purpose disintegrated. Without grabbing anything, Fin left his life behind for the one place he felt safe.

~

A few days later. The Sturdy Basement
"No matter what happpens... I will be free."
Joe inhaled sharply and rose from his slumber like a zombie. After wiping drool from his lips and desk, he noticed Fin's light was on.

He peeked through the doorway and noticed a peanut butter and jelly sandwich on a plate sitting at his bedside.

Fin didn't look up, "Leave me alone. Why do you care if I eat?"

He stepped into the room, "You raise a good point. But if ya don't eat, ya die. That makes more work for me. I also set my pet free for you. So eat."

A glint quickly flashed across his eye, "Guess you'll have to hook me up to a tube, then."

"Oh," he chuckled, "Ya think I'd give you the easy way out? All I'm givin' you is a knife and a fork. Then, I'll wait for your survival instincts to kick in. Well, in that case, hopefully, ya'd eat the food and not me, idiot." He delivered idiot as one would a term of endearment. "You know what? I'm gonna sit and watch you eat." True to his word, he plopped beside Fin and motioned to the sandwich.

"I hate peanut butter."

"Same here! I'm allergic, so biased, but what do ya like?"

He shrugged. "Mayo and turkey."

"I'll see what I can do," Joe walked towards the stairs, "HEY! ANY-BODY LISTENIN' UP THERE?"

Everybody was listening, but only Larry responded. He opened the basement door, "What's up?"

"TURKEY SANDWICH WITH MAYO?"

He scowled, "Dude, I'm like, fifteen feet away from you. And… what? Is that a statement or a question? Do you want me to make—"

"Exactly, kid!"

Larry sighed and closed the door.

Joe put his fists against his hips and turned back to Fin, "See? Efficiency."

Fin chuckled and shook his head. He looked more attentively at Joe. "What is it you *do* here?"

"I, uh, advise Jury. I don't know? I'm mostly an observer."

The basement door opened. Instead of hearing footsteps, they heard a loud smack against the floor. A sandwich was contained in a plastic bag. The note attached to it read:

"My legs are sore, sorry."

Joe frowned and snatched the bag by its zipper, "Damn kid. Eh, it's edible." he tossed it at Fin.

He failed to catch it, and it flopped against the floor. "Thanks," he smirked. While eating, the two discovered a shared love for many things: old autobiographies, ABBA, and Mash, to name a few. After a bit, a curious expression came to Fin. "Can I ask you something?"

He leaned his head to the side. "Shoot."

"Why don't you go to Sessions?"

Joe rolled his eyes, "This again? Look, I am busy."

"Whenever I catch you working, it never revolves around the Sturdy." He narrowed his eyes, "Why are you here?"

Joe was silent for a few seconds. "Mm." He ground his teeth and looked up. His tone loosened. "I used to work for the government. I'm too intrigued by anythin' human-made to resist. Durin' the last ten years of my career, I pulled some strings for Jury. We went our separate ways a while ago, but I always kept an eye on him. Well, then my life fell apart and I had to hide. I needed a favor and Jury answered."

"That sounds intense. Can I ask you to be more specific?"

He smirked, "No."

"That's fair. I have one more thing I'm curious about."

Joe hung his head and sighed. "One more."

His voice was calm and polite. "Since you aren't staying here for Mailugulism, what're your thoughts on it?"

He hesitated. A loose strand of hope entered his voice. "Maybe Mailugulism can change the world. I'm not sure. For now, I'm waitin'. Whether or not I believe in it doesn't matter."

Each sentence further electrified Fin, "Isn't it impossible to say you don't believe if we're the ones with the power to make Mailugula?"

Joe spoke modestly, "I don't know, but maybe some people shouldn't have that power." He put his hand on Fin's shoulder. "People do crazy things when they lose what they love. That silent phobia is the only thing that unites us all."

PARENT FUNCTION

September 30th, 2000

Speakers huddled in the refectory, waiting in darkness for Larry to arrive.

Jude whispered to Jury and Red. "I don't mean to sound like a dick, but shouldn't we be focusing on our public image?"

"We still have priorities!" replied Red, irked.

Jury leaned in, "If we want to convince Scarwood we care, we have to convince each other first."

"**SHHHHHH!**" barked Joe, "Kid's gonna be–"

Larry opened the door and flipped the light switch, revealing the hidden crowd.

"SURPRISE!" they shouted in broken unison.

Larry grinned ear to ear.

They blew their party horns, threw confetti, and ate cake. After the initial spectacle, everyone sat around and made small talk. Hefty subjects were on the menu, ranging from Kurt Russell's filmography to Preston Epalit's belt size. Everyone was social, except for a certain crypt dweller.

Joe stood behind the crowd, observing. A casual smile livened up his gloomy eyes.

Larry's party also doubled as an introduction to Fin. Recently, he and Jude created a small newsletter for the Sturdy. Fin was relieved to do something news related. Strangers and acquaintances alike happily made discussion. He was adjusting well, but for whatever reason, Jude seemed to be having a more difficult time. He spent a good portion of the party starring quietly, lost in thought and unsure what to say.

It seemed like mere moments. But tragically, the cake disappeared. Love is fleeting. Loss is inevitable. The tragedy of consumption reigns again.

Before anyone could grieve, Jury wobbled through the doorway, balancing a stack of presents with both hands.

Larry's grin said everything his inflection lacked. "This keeps getting better and better!"

"I have no doubt things are boring around here," Jury set the presents at the lad's feet, "So, we decided to give you something to liven things up a bit."

Larry clawed through the wrapping like a tiger tearing through a child. "Game Boy but with color, huh? I'm movin' up in the world!" He gazed at the box from each possible angle. "I always wanted one, but Pa hated anything that made me happy."

Red was relieved. "Glad you like it, buddy! It was Joe's idea, actually."

Larry turned to Joe. "Thanks, old man! This is pretty cool."

Joe nodded at him and raised his drink. Watching Larry, Joe's face grew brighter and brighter until he was beaming. "Don't make us wait, kid. Open the others!"

He ripped the wrapping to shreds. Three games revealed themselves.

"We didn't know what you'd like," explained Jury, "So we bought what the clerk recommended."

"Now, you shouldn't play it all the time," Red cut in. "I'd try limiting yourself to an hour a day. Video games can rot your brain."

Larry chuckled, "My brain melted a long time ago, man." Though he was now an adult, the joy of his party rekindled flames of yore. He looked away from his gifts and into the eyes of his friends, "Thank you, everyone. This has been the best birthday ever."

Red smiled wide. "You're welcome, buddy."

"Wait!" exclaimed Jury, arms extended, "We need to sing happy birthday!"

On the count of three, the group began singing. Larry glanced from grin to grin and noticed two empty chairs in the corner. He couldn't help but imagine his parents occupying them and silently waving on. An uncanny feeling possessed him. He noticed Joe examining the same two seats with a similar melancholy. Then, his gaze shifted, and the two met eyes. They stared for a moment until Joe snapped away.

After the song, Joe went up to Jury and Red and whispered something Larry couldn't make out. Jury and Red's expressions stiffened, but the party still ended on a positive note. Unfortunately, in all the commotion, Larry forgot to make a wish.

When the celebration ended, the birthday boy retreated to his room. He spent the remainder of the day multitasking between gaming and spacing off. He had difficulty relaxing because something he couldn't spell out was gnawing at his mind.

The clock struck nine. Larry was drifting into slumber as some murmuring on the other side of the door woke him.

"How do you plan to do this, Jury? You're not exactly–"

"I'm not exactly what? Subtle? I may be a little eccentric, but I can still be tender when the moment calls for it."

"Tender? Well, I guess, but I was thinking tactful."

"Tact?! ...Should I knock again, or–"

Larry opened the door and smiled. His voice was energetic, if a little tired. "Y'all need whispering lessons. Come in!"

Red's wired energy was overstimulating, "What's up, Larry? I bet you're tired after your big day."

Larry furrowed his eyebrows. "I'm exhausted, yeah. I was just about to go to bed."

"Cool." Jury's expression and tone tightened, "So, listen. Red and I have something we'd like to talk to you about."

Larry couldn't help but think something was wrong, and that anxiety grew by the moment. "What? Are you upset that Kurt Russell didn't jump out the cake?"

"Always," Jury snickered and cleared his throat, "But no." They sat on the bed. "I'll cut to the chase. When you first came, no one anticipated you'd be staying with us for so long."

"Which isn't bad!" exclaimed Red. The fidgeting in his fingers intensified. "We just thought that, well…"

With a smile, Jury placed his hand atop Red's knee. "What my neurotic partner wants to say is that, as much as we like having you here, there has to be a point where you stop running."

Red ripped his hand from Jury's grasp and looked at him with an astonished expression. "Jury! No!" He sighed into his palm. "Larry, we know that you miss your parents. It's none of our business, but trust me when I say that you should confront them while you can. We will absolutely stand by your side for that, and if they turn you away, you can come back with us." He released a tense breath. "Not to judge your life by mine, but *I* wish I confronted my mother. I think about it every day."

Larry was overwhelmed with confusion. "I don't think they want me back. If they did, they would've reached out by now."

Jury put his finger up and spoke in a more pretentious voice. "It doesn't matter what *they* want. Like Red said, this is something that needs to happen eventually."

Larry rolled his eyes and laughed. "Yeah, take it from you guys, two grown men with crippling mommy issues."

Red stared at him, in total shock, before bursting into hysterics.

Jury frowned. "Very funny. So, what do you say? Wanna make a little welfare check tomorrow?"

Larry thought for a second, and the more he considered it, the more the idea quelled his heart. "Okay. It could be our last rodeo, though."

Red's chest tightened. "That'd be the best possible way for this to end."

Jury stared at him with furrowed eyebrows.

~

As long as we're careful and quiet.
Come on, talk to me!
We aren't opening any doors, Red. Okay?
Dead air followed.

Slow and steady, Jury awoke from his dream. He ignored the details, and they turned to ash. Larry was already waiting. With that, the three piled into Jury's car and grabbed breakfast to go.

Larry's heartbeat accelerated by the mile. The further they drove, the more he recognized. The anxious nostalgia reached its height when Jury pulled into Cain's Diner.

Red exited the car, "Only about thirty minutes away, now. I'm just gonna run in and use the restroom."

Jury watched him go inside and pivoted toward Larry. "You okay?"

He was quiet, "For now."

Jury sounded hopeful, "It's okay to be nervous. My advice is uh, don't plan what to say because you'll forget every word the second you see your parents."

Larry gulped. "I appreciate that, thanks."

Jury turned back. The supportive expression he carried while reassuring Larry dissipated into something number.

Red returned. "Here we go," he exhaled, "Make sure you're watching for the farm, buddy."

Over sixty minutes, the grass grew from a pinch to a jungle. The clouds progressed from tufts to scrambles. Then, they parted altogether, revealing Bethany within their gap. Larry shakily pointed.

Jury made a sudden turn onto the gravel drive. Except for his blue Corvette rocking and rattling from the uneven terrain, all was silent. No birds chirped, and no wind blew. The wheels smushed wild grass and dead dandelions.

Jury turned back, "Unless you grow weeds here, Larry, I'd say this place is abandoned."

Red gave him a dirty look.

They pulled up to the house and parked. Getting out of the car, through the corner of his eye, Larry could have sworn he saw a jellyfish float across the attic window. Before he could comment, he caught a glimpse of something more concerning.

Larry rushed to a flowerbed in front of the house. Every flower had shriveled. He raced through his words, "These were the same flowers from when I left! Ma changes them every season."

Red crouched and examined the flowers. "Hm, marigolds and dahlias. These *are* out of season."

Larry crossed his arms. A muffled sigh emerged from his clamped lips.

Jury remained quiet and at a distance.

Red stayed positive and put his hand on Larry's shoulder. "Hey, don't worry. Let's just knock. You'll be able to ask Mom yourself."

Larry and Red ascended the stairs to the front door. Larry knocked three times. They waited for an eternal minute, and Red knocked louder. Larry hoped and prayed for anyone to answer, but the other side was silent. He started jiggling the doorknob. Though it was locked, he kept trying relentlessly. Red pulled him away. "Why don't we go check the back?"

Larry's breathing was deep. After snapping out of a trance, he nodded.

Jury's eyes wandered as he walked. "Did you raise animals here?"

"We did. Mostly for slaughter, but we stopped doing that last year. We had horses, though." They were finally in the backyard, and Larry caught a glimpse of what remained of the new stable.

The once eighteen-foot structure was now a cesspool of unusable materials. Mounds of clay, mud, and clumps of grass made the ground invisible. It was the kind of mess you'd get tetanus just from looking at.

Larry was frozen. "But, but where are the—"

Jury dashed to Larry's side. "Larry, listen. Let's drive to a pay phone and call the police. *They* can make this welfare check, you know?"

Larry's eyes were wide. Before he could speak, his attention was seized by a slamming sound from behind him. Although the wind was absent, the back door swayed open and closed, beckoning him. From afar, he realized no knob was attached and sprinted toward it.

Red grabbed him before he could get anywhere, "Hey! It's okay. It's okay! You don't have to charge ahead. We'll go together."

"Okay," Larry nodded, "I'm sorry." With Red and Jury behind him, Larry went inside.

The only sound was the rhythmic dripping of the kitchen sink. Each drop splattered upon a pile of dishes coated with dirt and smeared food. Flies surrounded the moldy, softened fruit in the pantry. Multiple items of furniture in the living room were flipped over. Roaches scurried through holes in the sofa. Jury grabbed a flashlight from his pocket and illuminated one of them. He wasn't arachnophobic, but what he saw still repulsed him.

Dust bunnies hopped between Jury's feet as he stepped over busted floorboards. "Watch your step."

Red's heart rate fiercely increased, "Jury, we should go."

"NO!" shouted Larry, "We need to see if they're here."

"As long as we're careful and quiet." Jury held Red's hand and led them down the nearest hallway.

The garage was next, but the door wouldn't budge.

"Did you bring your pocket knife, Jury?" asked Red.

"Always."

After picking the lock, they entered. A black GMC Syclone and routine tools extended no welcome. The truck sat above huge wheels, with its hood against the garage door.

Larry took a few steps and froze. A pungent stench instantly prevailed.

Jury sounded stilted, "Seems fine to me. Let's move on." He and Red tried nudging Larry toward the door, but he refused to move; his eyes were latched onto something.

Red put his hands on his shoulders, "Larry? Larry!" Fret overcame him, "Come on, talk to me!!"

Jury followed Larry's line of sight. Dried blood was splattered across the truck's bumper in the shape of a parenthesis. Locks of brown hair were on the floor behind the wheels. By the hood, a bruised, pale leg became visible. Jury was fixated on it. "*Red?*"

Larry, without blinking, lumbered toward it. Except for head trauma, her body remained intact, for no pest dared skitter across Maude. Her head tilted back, and her mouth hung open. An open suitcase was beside her. Clothes and toiletries were strewn around it. A baseball bat, bloodied like a dried rose, sat among the mess.

Larry's breathing intensified with each step until he collapsed, upon his knees, in front of Maude. While his eyes were wet and bright, hers were dim and dry. Larry stroked her icy cheek. "What do I do?" he muttered through fits of grief, "What *did* I do?"

Jury and Red both knelt to him. Before they could comfort Larry, he buried his face between them.

Red wrapped his arms around him and helped him stand, "We need to call the police, buddy." His voice was strong, but his eyes kept welling up.

Larry was one step away from hyperventilating but nodded. With Red's assistance, he was able to walk.

Jury led them. "We aren't opening any doors, Red. Okay?" Deja vu struck Jury, but he set his superstitions aside.

On their way to the front door, Red caught a glimpse into a nearby room and froze. His hand cracked off Larry's shoulder and snapped over his agape mouth. Larry broke from his haze and followed Red's eyes.

All Jury could hear was a buzzing sound coming from the room. He tried ignoring it, but when he noticed Red and Larry weren't behind him, he turned around and noticed they had stopped.

Jury growled. "Red! What's wrong with you!? Keep moving!"

With a blank expression on his face, Larry stepped into the room.

Jury rushed toward him, but it was too late.

Grey slumped against a wall with half of his brain and scalp splattered across it. The only thing clearer than blood was the chatter of the flies feeding on it. A filthy shotgun laid across his chest. He was covered in dirt as though given an advance on his burial. Apparently, the damned rot quicker.

Jury was mortified.

Red began hyperventilating and started sobbing.

Larry's pupils hopped from corner to corner and did the talking he couldn't. Without warning, he collapsed.

~

Larry's slumber was growing lighter and lighter. As his consciousness fought its way back, Jury had just finished catching Joe up on the situation. Red was sitting in the corner, silent. They were back at the Sturdy by Larry's bedside.

Joe set his head in his hands. "If I'd have known, for even a second, that our luck would spread to Larry, I never woulda let him stay. This. Is. *Horrible.*" His voice was weak and wobbly. "You're sure someone else didn't do it?"

Disbelief permeated Jury's tone. "The wall was absolutely covered, Joe. From that angle, it has to be suicide. He killed her because she was trying to leave and then killed himself."

"This can't be happening." Joe ran his hand across his hair and rested it on his neck. He peered up at Larry. "I *knew* I needed to check on 'em."

Jury sighed and sat down next to him. "Don't blame yourself."

Joe's tone underwent a frightening transition. "*Don't* tell me how to feel!" Joe wasn't crying, but his voice made it sound like he was nearly there. "We need to bury them."

Jury spoke without any emotion. "A funeral is going to be tricky. The family is going to find us, and then what? If Larry's family starts poking around, then the news will start poking around. We still have to focus on the little things, too. There's a lot of legality stuff I'm–"

"THE NEWS?" Red quickly rose to his feet. His tone was incendiary. "IS THAT ALL YOU CARE ABOUT RIGHT NOW?!" He released an explosive sigh and lowered his voice. "This whole time, Jury, you've been so insensitive and apathetic! It's like this doesn't affect you!"

"I can't *let* it."

Red gasped and looked from him to Joe. "Are you hearing this? It's like Mailugulism is the only thing in the world to him."

Jury scoffed and began intruding on Red's personal space. "Hey, *I'm* not the one who opened the door, *Jared*. Your mother was a teacher, right? Guess it's my fault for thinking she taught you how to follow some simple damn instructions!"

Red stood quietly, holding his clenched fists at his side, and started shaking. His lips quivered and quivered until they exploded. He burst into tears and ran out of the room.

Joe shoved Jury. "What the Hell is wrong with you?" His deep, resonant voice scratched rock bottom, causing Jury's spine to tingle. "Larry has lost the two most important people in his life, and you start bullyin' *Red*? I get you're tryin' to see all perspectives, and I know he doesn't need us." He pointed at Larry. "But we *can* help him, so we should!" Determination bolstered with each word. "I will *not* abandon his family, and I will not let another good soul go down the wrong path!" He caught a glimpse of Larry waking up and gasped. He quickly composed himself and smiled. "*Heeey*, kid. How ya feelin'?"

Larry looked around the room absently. "Where's Red?"

Joe looked at Jury with an edge of contempt.

Jury chuckled and scratched the back of his head. "Oh, heh heh, probably mad at me."

Joe sighed and wrapped his hand around Larry's shoulder. "Do ya remember what happened?"

It all shot through Larry at once. "I left them behind." His head sank into his chest, and he rolled over, pulling away from Joe.

Before Jury could respond, a sudden pang of guilt overtook Joe. He approached the bed and held his hat between his hands. "I'm sorry. Things are gonna be tough, but if you give it time, you *will* make it through, even if it doesn't feel like it. I'm always in the crypt if ya need to talk. We're in this together, kid, even if ya wanna leave and never come back." He chuckled, and a lighter side shone through him, "Anyhow, I'll give you some privacy. You should too, Jury."

Tears glided down Larry's cheeks. "Thanks, Joe, but I want company."

The two looked at each other and nodded. "Sure!" sat Joe.

"Of course," reassured Jury, his voice soft.

Larry's voice was quiet. "Jury, I meant to ask you this a while ago, but what was your dad like?"

A long silence followed. Jury was pondering. Pain filled his eyes as memories flooded him.

Joe's face drooped like a tired dog. "Ugh."

THE FISHING BUSINESS

Nebraska. Summer, 1991. Midnight.

The sleeves of an oversized bomber jacket drooped over Jury's knuckles as he clenched the steering wheel. Ripped jeans and a black shirt outlined his skinny figure. Excluding a purple mark around one eye, his face was as symmetrical as ever. He flipped his long, fluffy hair in rhythm to the deafening glam rock on the radio.

Cigarette in one hand, steering wheel in the other, mountainous hills surrounded Jury. The stretch of road he traveled was more path than pavement. Its sporadic, rollercoaster-like topography carried the speedometer to heights even heaven would envy. Thankfully, no soul was in sight, but Jury had no way of knowing. Overwhelming darkness obscured the sides of the road, but his foot remained glued to the gas. His light blue Corvette's roar echoed through the valley, filling the space his mind couldn't vacate.

Jury tapped his fingers to a Queen cassette and searched for somewhere to ask directions. Forty-five minutes passed before he stumbled across a three-story house. Calling it gothic or secluded would be an understatement. The navy-colored wood dominating its infrastructure had begun to decay. Tiles from the slate, patchy roof were scattered among bushes and tracts of dirt. Yet, the house was whole and fit for life, albeit one only an Addams would cherish.

Jury and Freddie's voices coalesced as he turned onto the dirt driveway. Light streamed through the edges of an opaque, first-floor window. He noticed this, along with a trashcan near the mailbox. He reached into the glove compartment and retrieved an Indiana license plate. After triple-checking the locks, he disposed of the plate and approached the door. The steps to it croaked and bellowed, nearly snapping with each minuscule display of force.

After a deep breath, he knocked.

A sky-blue iris popped into the peephole. An older gentleman with a white beard opened the door as much as its security chain would allow. His voice and legs were wobbly, "Hello, young man. Anythin' I can do for ya?"

Jury tried to cough over the ambiguity plaguing him. "Sorry to bother you so late, but do you know a way out of these mountains?"

"Mountains? Heh heh, those are hardly mountains, sonny." He smiled and unlocked the door. "Name's Phil. I'd be happy to help." Phil listed off a lengthy series of directions to the nearest town. Instead of affirmation, Jury stared at him like an ant beneath a lawnmower. Phil smiled. "I can write it down. Come in."

"Thank you! I'm so sorry for any inconvenience. My name's Jury."

Phil led him inside. "Jury? Never heard that name before. Is it Russian?"

"No, it's an epithet."

"OoOo, exotic. You don't look like one-a those."

"An *epithet*. It's a nick–"

"Wait here while I write your directions." He hobbled into the kitchen with his cane firmly in hand.

Phil's living room was dusty but aesthetically pleasing. Isolated from furniture and knick-knacks was a vase of thriving anemones, which infused the house with a vitality its outward appearance lacked.

Jury zeroed in on a box of records, not noticing the lack of family photos. Upon returning from the kitchen, Phil saw him holding a mint copy of Queen's *A Night at the Opera.*

"Be careful with that, please."

Jury lifted the record, "I see you're a man of good taste, Phil."

He chuckled. "Very simple taste."

"I prefer the term 'old fashioned.' As a lover of all things *Queen,* I–" Before Jury could be crowned king of "Did I ask?", the record slid out of the packaging's torn bottom. Jury leapt out of his skin and managed to secure the record before disaster. He exhaled and put it back. "My God, Phil, I am so sorry."

Phil grinned, "If anyone should apologize, it's me. I should've told ya about the packagin'. Anyhow, here's how ya get to town." He handed Jury an envelope with writing on its back. The two met eye-to-eye, and Phil noticed the bruise around Jury's right. He spoke slowly. "That's a mean shiner."

Jury turned away. The energy immediately left his voice. "I was standing too close to my car door when I opened it earlier. No big deal."

Phil pointed down the hall. "I-I got medicine if it hurts."

"No thanks. I should be going. Thanks again." He walked toward the door.

"Son," his voice deepened, "I know a black eye when I see one. Look, things can get tough, but ya should go back home before ya hurt yourself worse. Runnin' won't get you anywhere."

Jury froze with his hand on the knob. "People have been telling me that my whole life, but I don't consider it running anymore."

"It's okay to be confused. Just don't forget what you're riskin' by doin' this." He approached Jury and reached out.

Jury resisted the man's touch and eye contact. His voice was strong, if a tad bitter. "I've been ostracized my whole life. For the first time, I'm standing up for myself. Who said I'm confused? If anything, I'm enlightened." He turned toward the door and opened it. "Goodbye, Phil."

Phil frowned, but his tone was still bright, "Goodbye, Jury. Please try takin' my words to heart."

Jury slammed the door behind him. Soon after, he trekked into the distance, one less obstacle between him and his fast-approaching freedom.

~

Six hours earlier

Dishes clanged together as a middle-aged woman scrubbed them. She was tall but skinny, so much so that her ribs poked out of her black tank top, and her legs looked like chicken bones. Her jet-black locks were tucked into a hair net, and her long, slender hands were in yellow gloves. Dye stains resided beneath her hairline. The bags under her eyes were heavy. She shared her hazel peepers and copper skin with the seventeen-year-old sitting at the table behind her. Despite the racket, he remained engrossed in the latest issue of *Rolling Stone*.

The woman cleared her throat. "Was your day okay, Jared?" Her high-pitched voice was grating to those unaccustomed to it.

Red remained glued to the Madonna section, "Yeah. How was yours?"

"My students won't stop calling me Barb, and it pisses me off." She began scrubbing harder. "The first thing you learn in school is to respect your teacher. It's ridiculous how your generation regresses."

"I'm sorry."

"*T*ch. Nothing a good run can't fix, I guess." She wrapped her hands around the sink and peered at him through the corner of her eye. "Another thing that's been bothering me is Jade's diary."

Maintaining eye contact was difficult for him. "Huh, weird."

She examined his outfit—an unbuttoned, red flannel over a tucked-in R.E.M. tee—and squinted. "You look like you have some-where to be."

"Mm-mm," he cleared his throat, "Yeah. The boys and I are going fishing."

"It's six in the afternoon, Jared."

"So? I'm eighteen. I can protect myself."

Barb crossed her arms, "*So?* That's not what I was getting a*t*." She slammed on that T sound like she was stomping on a roach. "You need to look at colleges. It's been a month since you graduated."

"I will later."

"Hm." Her eyes hardened. "Then you don't need to go tonight."

Red stood up and pushed his chair in. "I guess I'll go to sleep, then." He walked down the hall.

Barb shook her head and threw her gloves into the sink.

The house's lone hallway contained all three bedrooms. Red's was the furthest down. His mother always left the door open, so there was no way to avoid Jade's room and the memories it immortalized. Every decorating choice was a cliché: **JADE** spelled in stars along the wall, pink everywhere, a *Full House* poster on the door and a spread of Rob Lowe from *The Outsiders* pinned above the bed. Her half-deflated birthday balloon sank into the floor, the "13" staring at him. Each glimpse filled him with equal parts cringe and nostalgia. He stopped in front of the Rob Lowe banner and nodded at it.

Fifteen minutes passed before twiddling thumbs overtook all thought. After staring at photos of a once-full family, Red decided to turn on the radio. As soon as Rainbow's "Since You've Been Gone" blared through the speakers, he switched it off and sat up. After climbing through the window, he reached into his pocket and pulled out a slip of paper. Written on it were an address and a signature from an "Emily Rosie."

"Let's see how the waters are tonight."

From outside, Emily's house resembled the stage of a Skittles rock concert. Red found himself reluctant to attend. After weighing his alternatives, he quickly walked inside.

He passed by drunken acquaintances before plopping onto the end of a couch. The other cushions were under the occupation of his passed-out history teacher. One of his friends offered him a beer. Red declined initially but conceded to shut him up. Disgust poured through him upon sniffing it. After ensuring the coast was clear, he tucked it under the teacher's arm. "Operation successful," he declared, having fun at last.

"NOT YOUR THING, HUH?" shouted a woman across the room as she approached him. She was a short tomboy with huge green eyes and light brown hair that fell below her shoulders.

"I'm surprised you found me so fast, Em." The music conquered his words.

"WHAT?"

Red rubbed his forehead, "Why did I come here?"

"SPEAK UP!"

"I ASKED MYSELF WHY I CAME HERE! IT WAS A JOKE... kind of."

"OH. HA! THAT'S FUNNY!" The two stared at each other for a beat. "Uh, WANNA FIND SOMEWHERE QUIET TO TALK?"

"GREAT IDEA!"

Emily led him outside. "How's this?"

He shrugged. It was just a regular backyard. Nothing stuck out to him. "I mean, yeah. It's fine."

"Hm," she rubbed her chin, "I have a better idea: let's go on the roof!"

"That's a little dangerous, isn't it?"

Her voice and mannerisms were infectiously peppy. "Come on, live a little!"

His lips loosened into a slight grin. "Okay. How are we getting up there?"

"Give me *ooone* second." She walked behind the house and returned with a ladder. "This'll probably make it less *dangerous*."

They set it down together and climbed up. Red went first, and Emily stared at his butt all the way to the roof.

The sky surrounding them was ethereal and reflected the color of Red's denim. He closed his eyes and imagined his sister's smiling face. Emily sat beside him at the roof's edge as she too became lost in the stars. After a benign exchange about astrology, their conversation screeched to a halt.

"So..." Emily's feet hung over the roof and swayed back and forth. "What were ya talking about downstairs?"

Red crossed his legs. "Oh, uh, I was just wondering why I came here."

"Because I invited you. Aren't you having fun?"

Red smiled at her, "Now that we've ascended past the drunks, yeah. Since when do you invite teachers to your parties?"

Emily's laugh was unnaturally long, "Are you talking about couch guy?"

"Mr. Scroggins? Yeah. The man of the hour."

"To be honest, I don't even know how he got in," she burst into laughter, which Red uncomfortably reciprocated.

"Anyway," Red glanced away from her. "How're you?"

Emily smiled. Her wide eyes sparkled as she checked him out. "Same old crap, you know? What about you?"

"I'm fine. I've been getting out more, which actually feels nice. If it was up to my Mom, I'd be home every day with her. I've been telling her that I'm going fishing with some friends, but I've actually just been walking around, enjoying the fresh air again."

"Yeah! It's good to see you," her expression turned grim, "you haven't been around much since..." she trailed off.

"I'm sorry about that. Really, I am."

"We all have important people that aren't in our lives anymore. It's gonna be okay." She began stroking his wrist. "I promise."

The two gazed at each other. Emily leaned in for a kiss. Red lurched away from her. His voice was quick and panicky. "Uh, sorry. Oh God."

"What!?" she raised her voice. "Was the only girl in your life your sister? Start living for something and get over it!"

Red's growing ease deflated. He sounded like he was six feet under. "Does telling me to get over it suddenly erase the fact that Jade drowned in my backyard while I was supposed to be watching her? Is getting rid of the pool going to get rid of the grief? No, it's not. The seizure wasn't my fault, but not being there was."

"You weren't always like this," Emily stated, monotone, "You used to be chill and cool."

"You know what?" He stood up, confidence mounting, "I hate to break it to you, but my sister wasn't always dead. I'm a bummer right now, but I'm not boring just because I don't love you. Heck, I don't even like you. How can I have a relationship with someone who lives to get them and their friends drunk? Let alone someone so insensitive. Look, I'm not saying you're a bad person. I just really think you should reevaluate your life." He stood up and started stepping down the ladder.

She yelled after him as he descended, "I KNEW INVITING A SPINELESS BASTARD LIKE YOU WAS A MISTAKE! STAY AWAY FROM ME!"

Red whistled and kicked the ladder down. He waltzed away with his hands in his pockets, hearing Emily's screeches switch from anger to panic.

"An angel like her has to have wings," he quipped, some of his anxieties clearing.

Red's mother confronted him moments after climbing in. She sat at his desk and swayed Jade's diary between her fingers. Her breathing was loud, and her nostrils were flared.

"You thought I'd never find this?" Her tone flatlined, "Where were you?"

He looked away. His voice was quiet. "A party."

Her voice quivered with wrath. "A party *where*?"

"Emily's."

"Have you been at Emily's a lot lately?"

"No."

"Oh yeah?" Barb reached behind the chair she was sitting in and pulled out Red's fishing rod. "Then why is this thing as dry as a bone?!"

"I... shouldn't it be?"

"Don't get smart with me! It's dusty. You've been lying." She swayed the diary with her fingers, "And this is just more proof."

The problems he illuminated earlier became shrouded by sorrow. His posture weakened. "I had my reasons. You don't understand."

"Oh, I do. Dancing around whatever problem you think I'm going to have won't solve shit! Did you think I'd never find out that my thirteen-year-old daughter thought I was a–" Barb paused and flipped to a bookmarked page, "selfish bitch? Or a rotten whore?"

"Mom... I..."

She eyed him. "I didn't raise her that way, you know."

Her words pierced his heart. "You... can't do that to me. I know what you're suggesting, and it's–it's awful."

"Well, excuse me for not knowing where she learned such behavior."

Red shook his head, "Why are you doing this to me?" He looked up at her. "*Why* have you been so mean?"

Barb slammed the diary shut. *"You're trying to abandon me, Jared."*

Red's posture straightened. "I don't want to be constantly stared at by you. I can't live like that, especially with Jade's accident in the back of my mind. Dad was the same way. That's why he's gone."

Her delivery didn't contain a hint of comfort. "Don't bring your father into this. It wasn't your fault."

Red's eyes moistened. "You don't believe that. The way you're looking at me now is all the proof I need." He turned away and wiped his eyes. "Can I just go to bed?"

Barb sighed, "Sure, we've talked enough for one night." She hugged Red but received nothing in return. "I love you, you know. There's a lot I wouldn't put up with if I didn't." She returned to her room, taking the diary with her.

A new feeling overcame him. It was strong enough to keep idle thoughts at bay and gave him the will to wait. After an hour of silence, Red stuffed a bag with clothes and toiletries but no pictures. With a heavy melancholy, he crawled out his window and left without looking back.

He stopped for a bathroom break at the nearest gas station. On his way in, a reckless driver sped over a large puddle. The resulting tsunami rendered Red a wet dog. He repeatedly said "dang-it" under his breath while trying to wring out his clothes.

A man in a bomber jacket holding a credit card, caramel candy bar, and car keys walked out of the gas station. He looked Red over and chuckled lightly. "Don't tell me you were out fishing."

Red couldn't see. "Huh? What?" After clearing his eyes, he saw a man with emerald eyes staring back, a personable smile stapled to his face. The smell of smoke on him was nauseating.

He spoke while chewing the candy, "It was a joke," and noticed Red's backpack, "You got a dry outfit in there, I assume?"

"Yeah. I MEAN," he slapped himself on the head, "Yeah... that's not weird. Sorry."

The man laughed and lowered his eyebrows, "Sheesh. You're jumpier than me! Don't tell me. Are you a runaway too?"

Red released a large, pent-up breath. "Yeah. Hearing that probably shouldn't put my mind at ease, but here we are."

He laughed again and pushed the candy in his direction, "Would a candy bar make you feel easier?"

A glint of light flashed across his eyes. Maybe it was the man's fluffy hair or beautiful eyes, but an enamored smile exploded onto Red's face. His tone changed completely. "If I was a kid and you were a stranger, yes." He grabbed the candy bar. After getting a good grip, he consumed the thing in one bite. "Where are you headed?"

He shrugged. "Away from Indiana."

"You've already done that, you know. This is Nebraska."

"I can still go farther. What about you?"

"What about me?"

The man furrowed his eyebrows. "Where are you headed?"

His tone hadn't been this steady and energetic in months, "Away from here, too. I-I'm Red. What's your name?"

The man hesitated, "My Dad called me Jim, but I'd love it if you called me Jury." He stuck out his hand, and Red spared no time in shaking it. He never asked a single question.

Discontent is a magnet.

THE MAILUGIAN TIMES

Mary's and Mailugula

Written by Fin Eisenhower

Jury Chessjurist's charitable donation to Scarwood tourist attraction Mary's was finalized earlier this week. Mary's General Store opened nearly one hundred and fifty years ago and found massive success during the Gold Rush. The store continues to operate and serves as a reminder of Scarwood's tenacity.

Mary's was named after the wife of founder Aron Verbinski. In recent years, it has been expanded to include a museum containing historic pictures of the town's early years and antiques, such as some old materials from the original building. One of the standout souvenirs among tourists is a novel chronicling a brief history of the shop, along with other interesting, local content.

Three years have passed since ownership changed hands from the late Terrence Verbinski to Robert Verbinski. The period following this has been marred with a series of financial woes. Mary's was on the verge of shutting its doors when Mr. Chessjurist approached Terrence with a donation.

When asked about this business venture, Mr. Chessjurist had this to say: "It's immensely important to my associates and I that we preserve the history and culture of Scarwood. Mary's casts light on our legacy as a people, and highlights that our past never truly fades. It's one of many things Scarwood and Pontifex County residents should be proud of." In addition to Mary's, Chessjurist plans to donate to, and volunteer with a variety of local businesses. Though no specific plans have been announced, this Speaker is more than happy to see the Sturdy finally reaching out to the community.

Speaker of the Month with Jude Ariotics

His favorite movie is *Grease*, his favorite food is Caesar salad, and his favorite novel is *To Kill a Mockingbird*. Ladies and gentlemen, I am of course talking about none other than Red Solano: Mailugian advisor and resident moral orel. He's been a Speaker since the beginning, as he was drawn to Mailugulism early in its lifetime. His enthusiastic, kind nature brightens every room he walks into. However, the untimely death of his sister changed the course of his life dramatically. He remembers feeling abandoned. He has gone on record saying that following the principles of Mailugula saved him. Though he misses his sister, Red feels like he has been given a second chance. Red is dedicated to helping other people in any way he can. That is one of the many reasons why we at *The Mailugian Times* decided to award him with the coveted, first-ever "Speaker of the Month" award. He deserves this, and all the praise that may get thrown his way. Thank you for your support, Red, and we look forward to your future at the Sturdy and your future with Mailugula.

Upcoming Events:

- On October sixth, during our regular Session, Mr. Chessjurist will be hosting a separate function for younger children and their parents. Children will learn the value of empathy and the importance of engaging in complex topics of discussion.

Preston slammed down the newsletter. "*This* is what Fin and Jude left me for?!? Talk about a crock." Some air got lodged in his throat, and he coughed like a possessed goat.

Preston's desk was teeming with loose papers and fast food trash. Empty Jack Daniels shooters and pill bottles poked out of his drawers. The only clear thing was his computer screen. He played solitaire so much that it was practically a screen saver.

Preston's new sidekick, Akila Hatem, sat across from him, legs crossed. She picked up the newsletter and examined its design, trying very hard to ignore the clutter surrounding her. "Usually, I try to be positive, but this is one of the most mediocre things I've ever read."

Preston finally regained control of his breathing and chuckled throughout his response. "You are being too civil. It. Is. **Awful**. It looks like a menu at a retirement home and reads like a middle school newspaper."

Akila raised her eyebrows. "Well then, I'll throw it away for you."

Preston quickly snatched it from her. "No! I can keep it."

"Why?"

"Never mind that! This is a simple memento, nothing more." He lowered the newsletter from Akila's sight and broke off Jude's article, folding and setting it in his pocket.

"Why would you be so harsh toward something you wanna keep? Are you jealous Jude is working for Chessjurist and not for you?"

Preston extended his boney pointer finger. His voice scratched frightening new depths. "You have been here three weeks. Far as I'm concerned, your *balls* haven't dropped yet, so don't go thinking we stand toe-to-toe. You saw Jude's writing. It was horrible. I..." he took a deep breath. "Am lucky I lost him, and if you do not play smart, I will lose you too."

Akila bit her tongue. "Sorry, Boss."

"That's Mr. Epalit to you!" He clutched his stomach and groaned. "Ugh, why did you show me that crap in the first place? Mailugula is old news."

"Well, *Mr.* Epalit. I thought it would be good to do a story on the family event tomorrow."

"Why should I care?"

Akila shrugged. "I'm curious what Chessjurist has planned. He's an interesting man, you know. We should get him down here for an interview sometime."

Preston leaned back in his chair and scoffed. "I would sooner interview Satan himself... or that guy who shot Ronald Reagan. As long as the producers are content with my usual schtick, that Antichrist will not step foot in my office. Trust me, the less publicity we give *Mailorderla*, the better."

"*Mailorderla*? It sounds like you're saying it wrong on purpose."

His tone was immensely casual. "You have one Hell of an attitude today. Would you rather be on the other side of me or the other side of the border? Pick."

Akila bit her tongue harder. "Sir, *again*, I'm Egyptian, not–"

"Hold on!" A light bulb exploded in his brain, no doubt impaling his frontal lobe. "I think the Lord himself just sent me an idea. We do not want to give *Mailugula* publicity, but what about ourselves?"

"Publicity is a good thing, yes."

Preston spent a moment processing her remark, "Thanks for the input, brainiac. Just do me a favor and ask what my idea is."

She sighed. "What's your idea, sir?"

Preston leaned in, "Tonight, on air, I am going to highlight Chessie's little preschool."

"Wait, wouldn't that accomplish the opposite of what–"

"You are not thinking chaotically enough! The controversy with the funeral is dying down. That is where I come in. Tonight, we inform and incite some potential voices of protest about the discount Sunday school. From there, they rile others up." He wiggled his fingers in the air like a chef sprinkling salt. "We will drop a *hint* of protest but leave the rest to them."

"As long as you don't steal the spotlight from our other stories, do as you please."

"I do not need your approval." Preston yawned, "Get me some coffee, will you?" Akila left without another word.

Akila tapped her fingers against the roof of the coffee maker. "Just you wait, invalid," she muttered, lips pursed. "Someday, it'll be me in charge. I just need a little more time." Her rambling was interrupted by the greetings of a few coworkers.

While Preston's heart remained locked behind iron bars, his employees paraded theirs around like diamond rings. Akila could read them well and soon figured out how to appease them. Soon into her employment, after subtle pushes and buzzwords aplenty, a wider variety of stories from across Pontifex County began airing. With Preston's tirades becoming less common, this stabler direction was precisely what RBLA needed. Profit and ratings were rising at a steady pace.

Tonight's broadcast was tame until Preston took center stage. He spun a yarn about "Mailugula super soldier training" and the "teaching of radical, over-throwing beliefs."

Preston slammed his fist against the table and imagined the National Anthem playing behind him, "First, the attack on my workers, and now this? The Mailugians are out of control in their conceitedness! We must stand against this new generation of communism before *they* stand on *us*!" Whether or not he spoke from the heart was unclear, but the fervor was no fabrication.

The Speakers laughed it off.

Although the target placed on Jury's back was rudimentary, suddenly, every nearby, anti-Mailugian zealot took aim.

MATTERS OF INTERPRETATION

The Following Night.

To say Red was scattered would be an understatement. With each tick of the clock, he leaned or sat in a new way outside Larry's room. His fist hovered over the door but never knocked. Instead, he laid his palm against it.

Down the hall, Jury was staring at the space beside him. His dreams manipulated his loneliness, disturbing him more than ever.

After many arduous nights, Jury's family event arrived. Tables in the refectory were pushed aside, creating plenty of space for families. Among the crowd of about thirty sat Akila Hatem and her six-year-old son: Timmy. He was busy pushing his *Tiny Toons* Hot Wheels back and forth.

Jury entered the kitchen and flashed a smile. "Hello, everyone!"

"Hi!" some of the children replied with varying enunciations. Their ages ranged from six to nine.

From there, the kids were sorted into a circle. Jury instructed them to introduce themselves and state their favorite and least favorite colors.

"My name is Sam, not Samuel! My favorite color is orange, like my shirt, but I hate green 'cuz I'm colorblind and just see a weird blue."

The next child rocked back and forth. "My name is Steven, and I like all of them."

"Emmi. Um, I don't have a least favorite, but I love green."

Jury rose. "Thank you, Emmi! If I can interrupt, I have a question for Sam. Can you repeat your least favorite color?"

Sam sucked his thumb, "Green!"

He exchanged his usual fanatic energy for a Mr. Rogers-style gentleness. "If you believe that, then what do you have to say to Emmi?"

Sam stared at him, "I don't know."

"Do you like Emily less because she likes green?" Jury asked.

Sam pulled his finger out of his mouth and shrugged. "No. She can still be my friend. The only thing we couldn't do is watch the Grinch."

Jury pointed at him. "A terrible fate, but that's right! Her opinion is different from yours, but you still respect her. In life, opinions differ from person to person. Do any of you know what an opinion is?" He waited a moment but received no response. "An opinion is a belief wholly unique to you." He began speaking with a suit rather than a cardigan and looked solely at the parents. "Many different words mean that same thing. My favorite is *interpretation*. Now, interpretation itself is not evil. Even people with very different interpretations can become lifelong friends with proper communication. But it's not as simple as it sounds. Emotions drive everything, and understanding the emotion behind interpretations is a difficult beast."

One child pinched his cheek and cowered. "That sounds scary."

His voice remained light. "It's not scary at all. The only thing you need is empathy."

Confused, the children looked up at their parents. Sam raised his hand but didn't wait to be called on. "What's *a* epiphany?"

Jury smirked. "*Empathy* is understanding and accepting another person's feelings, even though they differ from yours. It's much like what you exercised with Emily." He paused for a moment. "Does that make sense?"

Sam stared at him, puzzled. *"I'm six."*

Jury widened his eyes and raised his brows. "O-kay. Anyway, there will come a time in your life when your parents tell you to be more empathetic. It's natural but confusing. Why would they ask you to do that, and what do they mean?"

Sam gasped. He sounded enlightened. "That it's time to join the army!"

Jury did a double take. "No. *No!* They're *trying* to say that you're placing how you feel above how others feel, which is the opposite of empathy."

Most children stared blankly out the window, likely wanting to jump out of it.

Jury read the room and leaned toward them. A fun expression came to him. "Would it help if I told you guys a story?"

The children eagerly nodded, their attention snapping back to him.

Jury sat. "When I was young, I knew a woman named Mary." His eyes passed from child to child. "Now, everyone in town loved Mary, but there was something different about her." He noticed that Sam wasn't paying attention. "And it's not that her favorite color was green, *Sam.* She was adopted. That means her Mom and Dad couldn't take care of her, so they gave her to another *couple* who could. Do any of you know someone who's adopted?" No response. "Mm. When Mary learned she was adopted, it made her feel very sad because she felt unwanted. However, even with this sadness, she lived a great life. She was a loving wife, mother, and an undeniable free spirit, who made those around her very happy." His tone underwent a somber, wistful transition. "But that discontent in the back of her mind caused her to make mistakes. And because of those mistakes, she..." he gulped, *"left* two people who needed her very much. It's been twenty-one years, and I still feel her absence every day."

A familiar voice from the back of the room spoke. "Kind of a negative way to look at things for such an undeniable, free spirit. Why do you think Mary didn't appreciate being chosen?" Jury peered up and saw Akila staring back.

The children couldn't care less.

Jury frowned. His voice was weirdly distraught. "That's just the way she interpreted it." Energy returned to him. "Some of us may not understand or support her beliefs, but they were still important to her. As long as an interpretation has value to another person, it must be considered and accepted, not bullied or ignored." He noticed Sam dozing off. "Oh, Sam?"

He shot upright. "YES?"

"Does green matter even though you don't like it?"

"Yes!"

"Mary's views on color differ from yours, but that doesn't offend or hurt you, right?"

"Uh-huh."

Jury raised his eyebrows, "Then, why would her views on being adopted? None of you know Mary, but we still have to respect how she thought. The power of interpretation is one of the brightest beauties of this world, not one of its principal sins. I hope you guys remember that during your next disagreement."

Emmi raised her hand. "Do you ever have a hard time with inter-per*ata*tions?"

"You mean interpretations, honey. And, yes. Of course. Everyone does."

"Well," Sam became more interested. "What do you do?"

"What do I do?" He chuckled, "Well, I..." He couldn't think of anything. The first thing to come to mind were all the horrible things he said to Red. His eyes widened. He thought about every conflict he could remember and only saw how he handled them.

That's the real disgrace, Jared. You.

Red! What's wrong with you!? Keep. Moving!

Hey, I'm not the one who opened the door, Jared.

Jury didn't realize he was thinking aloud. "I assume I'm the only one that matters. I yell... and lash out at the person who cares most about me. When faced with extreme circumstances, people come apart... while others come alive." An image of Red bandaging his hand came to mind. *"My Mailugula, I'm a hypocrite!"*

Children and parents alike were bewildered. Then, a small voice came from the back of the circle. "Is that why my parents got divorced?"

Jury snapped out of it. "All right! That's where we'll end, today and forever."

Akila put her head in her hands. "If I knew this would turn into the Chessjurist trauma hour, I would have brought the cameras."

Suddenly, the technological hiss of a roaring megaphone controlled the air from outside the Sturdy. Multiple voices began chanting, in broken unison, "RADICAL, WRONG, AND A SIN. WE WILL NOT LET YOU RUIN OUR KIDS!" Jury raced to the window and saw about seventy-five protesters outside the Sturdy. A wide variety of people comprised the cattle, although only a third of their voices could be heard. Most of them carried a sign, a few of which read "mai-GHOUL-ula will NOT overthrow GOD!" and, "MAILUGULISM = COMMUNISM!" Another sign was a repurposed "live, laugh, love" sign that read "hate, lie, gaslight."

Jury spoke with equal parts sarcasm and rage. "Communism?! Have people forgotten that we're not living in the fifties? The Cold War's over!"

Parents had turned to each other for answers by the time Jury addressed them. His eyes were aflame, but he spoke like nothing was wrong. "So… yeah. Thanks for your time." He stepped out of the room before anyone else could. "LARRY!"

It was Fin who answered him. "Hey, he and Joe are–"

"Oh. That's right. Can you lead these people to the back exit, then?"

"Sh-sure. Are you going to take care of the mess out there? I don't want Preston to—"

"I will. I just need a minute." He exhaled. "Follow this young man, everybody!" He pointed at Fin. He waved like a child who had heard of waving but never actually done it.

Everyone filtered out in a uniform march. When Jury thought the room was empty, he let out a huge huff and broadened his chest as though about to explode. Out of the corner of his eye, he saw a cigarette on the floor. It was something he saw every day, just not in this way. For the first time, he realized how small they were. Yet, despite their size, they completely controlled him. He released the tension from his body. With this thought in mind, he approached the window and gazed at the protesters from a new angle. "It's my fault that they're here. Maybe we wouldn't be in this mess if I controlled myself better."

"You okay?" inquired Akila, eyebrows lowered. She had been sitting there the entire time.

Jury pointed at her, "You know what I just realized? You and I have the same problem, and it would end altogether if Preston left RBLA."

She smirked. "Sure, but I've tried. He's harder to crack than you'd think."

"Well, why don't *I* try? Could you see if you can get him to agree to an interview?"

"I've been thinking about that, too, actually. But are you sure?"

Confidence fueled him. "I'm positive. All it'll take is a little pushing to get Preston to show his true colors, and I have a feeling I know which buttons to press. All people care about is that golden voice. Once they see him for the brute he is, they'll change the channel. Then, the producers will have no choice."

Akila gave a thumbs-up. "Great idea, Jury! I'll do that tonight."

Jury gave her a thumbs-up, saluted, and walked away.

She waited until Jury was out of sight and grinned from ear to ear. "Expose Preston for *'the brute he is?'* Ha! Like the people don't know that already? What he should be thinking about is that man's temper." She knelt down to Timmy. "Mommy's gonna get that promotion soon!"

At the same time, Red was leading a Session. He was already distracted, but when the commotion interrupted them, he stammered and froze, failing to recoup his footing and the crowd's attention. Jury saw this and sprinted on stage.

Red didn't turn to face Jury and spoke through the side of his mouth. "What the heck is going on?"

"Don't worry. I have an idea." Time froze around them. Jury grabbed his hand, "I'm so sorry for the horrible things I've said to you. I've been making every problem we've run into worse. And I'm sorry for smoking behind your back, disappointing you, and having this ridiculous temper that blinds me to how you feel. I will get better, I promise. As long as you stay by my side, I can do anything. *Please* never leave."

Red smiled and hugged him. Joy overcame him, "I never thought you could be so direct."

He broke away from Red's embrace. "Ladies and gentlemen," Jury announced, taking the microphone. "In no good conscience can I sit here and accept protest from people who have no idea what Mailugula stands for! They barely know what they're protesting. So, do any of you think they'll stick around through an ounce of inconvenience?"

Multiple voices rang throughout the room.

"Probably not."

"Meh, nah."

"I could see it going either way."

The apathy didn't faze Jury. He laughed. "No! From this day forward, we, unlike the husks outside, will no longer be tools of Epalit's oppression!" He pumped his fist into the air. The cheesiness of his gestures and the crowd's indifference were also lost on Red, who smiled while wiping a tear from his eye. "Now," Jury continued, lowering his fist, "We will win by doing nothing. Please continue with your regularly scheduled Session."

Everyone in the crowd shrugged and began talking amongst each other as Jury walked off stage. Red followed close behind him, "Nothing? What do you mean, nothing?"

"They're expecting us to do something, right? Press may have thrown them a bone, but it won't take them long to realize there's no meat on it. The ultimate inconvenience is being bored."

True to his word, Jury sat near the window and stared at the crowd. His empty gaze drifted from eye to eye and sign to sign. Over the next thirty minutes, the crowd's vigor waned, and their arms became sore under the weight of the signs.

One of the protesters, exasperated, threw his sign against the ground. "I'm missing *Jeopardy*? For *this*?"

Another man checked his watch, "*Damn!* Happy hour's almost over," and rushed off, leaving his sign on the ground.

"Why am I here again?"

Within minutes, the crowd faded, and Jury went outside to pick up the signs and aggressively wave at those who remained.

~

Later that night

Upon hearing of his parents' passing, Larry's estranged family dropped everything and flew to Scarwood. After seeing the bodies, they decided on cremation. With Joe's help, Larry and his family planned a small ceremony. They convened at Bethany days later.

Larry remained glued to Joe, who did most of the talking. Larry's uncle, a pastor, spoke a dour eulogy and scattered Grey and Maude's ashes. Mother Nature swept them up before they hit the floor and spread Maude to the stable and Grey across his wife's flowerbed, which was now brimming with life.

Bethany would remain abandoned. The family was too intimidated to indulge their greed. Instead, they burnt the decrepit home to the ground. The smoke filled Larry's eyes. Within it, he could've sworn he saw his father's gaze piercing him. Although the smoke eventually evaporated into the sky, it never left Larry's pupils. Even on the way home, his eyes didn't brighten.

Joe bought fast food and parked in a field with a great view of the sky. They spent the rest of the evening quietly watching the sunset over the flat plains until Larry leaned back and closed his eyes. Confident that Larry was asleep, inspired by the stars now surrounding them, Joe regaled him with memory after memory of times past through. Yet, Larry wasn't sleeping. He only pretended, afraid Joe would stop if he opened his darkened eyes.

BEHIND CLOSED DOORS

Later that Night.

From a television in his doctor's office, Preston discovered how short his scheme had fallen. Most news stations took Jury's side, mainly focusing on Preston's failed attempt to incite a riot.

In the past month, he had lost fifteen pounds. While his stomach thinned, his beard thickened. The static plague within it had extended into his nostrils and around his chin. The bags under his eyes looked like upside-down parachutes.

His doctor put her hand on his shoulder. "Mr. Epalit?"

"Huh?" he pivoted toward her. "Oh."

"Were you listening to me at all?"

He shook his head.

She spoke to him like a toddler. "We're almost done, so please bear with me. Have you been eating okay lately?"

"No."

She grabbed a pen and a clipboard. "Can you elaborate?"

Preston checked the time on his watch, which no longer fit snugly and rolled under his arm. He threw his hands into the air, "UGH! I can't feel hungry, stand for more than a minute, or find a single shirt in my closet that doesn't fit like a goddamn dress! And that doesn't even touch my nightmares." He took a moment to breathe. "Look! I, of all people, know how badly I'm doing. Why am I here?"

Gloom weighed down her energetic brogue. "Mr. Epalit, we both know you've progressed to the point where-"

"The point where what?!" Preston pointed at her. "I'm *not* a bank! You're not gonna cash me out just so I can die slower." His tone became more sincere. "Just tell me how long I got."

"Six months. But if you retire and start taking care of yourself-"

"Stop." His voice was pensive. "What can I say? I'm dying."

Any adept runner could conquer two miles in the time it took Preston to walk from the doctor's office to his truck. Each step weighed on him, and he frequently stopped to wipe the sweat from his brow. He unlocked his truck and hurled himself into the driver's seat. After blasting his air conditioning for five minutes, the weight in Preston's chest became bearable, and he drove away.

The road was abandoned. While driving home, he focused on the scenery surrounding him and wondered if similar sights awaited in the afterlife. Trying to sleep spawned similar musings. Jude's car was still absent from his driveway. Only one other place soothed him. So, at three AM, Preston drove to work.

Around noon, Akila, posture straight and head high, walked into Preston's office, "Mr. Epalit? There's something I need to talk to you about."

Preston fidgeted with a newspaper. The cover photo was an image of the Sturdy, and the headline was about the protest. His voice lacked vitality. "How in God's name did Chessie scare off that crowd without doing a thing?"

"They were bored, Mr. Epalit. And they didn't care in the first place."

He growled. "Next, you're going to tell me that Chessie's kiddie boot camp went well, too."

"Well," Akila hesitated. "Not really. The kids were bored out of their minds. It was more for the parents, even though I think the message was only clear to Chessjurist."

Preston wrapped his hand around his chin. "Always a silver lining, huh?" He cast his glance to the side, "Times are changing. I need to do this while I have the chance. Get famous or die trying," vigor returned to him. "Get me an interview with Chessie. Make it next Saturday at three. I will be less depressed by then."

"Oh!" Akila almost had no clue how to respond. "That's great! I'll tell him right away. Don't worry. You're doing the right thing. I mean, what would people think if you refused to take on a snake like Jury?"

"Jury? Since when are you on a nickname basis with... oh, never mind. Get me some coffee before I reconsider."

"Of course." Akila walked out and shut the door behind her. After ensuring she was alone, she rubbed her hands together and spoke quietly, "I didn't even have to say anything, *again*! Still, snake?" she shuddered. *"What was I thinking?"*

~

With their conflict resolved, Red could finally sleep. Jury's brain was too fried for reading, so he turned on the radio. Static surfed through the speakers. Bit by bit, it morphed into the gentle sound of ocean waves. Jury sat up and listened closer. The remaining strands of static coalesced into a feeble, elderly voice that he didn't recognize, *"Come home, Jim."*

Red opened his eyes, and the radio switched back to static. "Are you having the dream again?"

Jury was speechless.

Red groggily pushed himself up, "Oh, I didn't realize I fell asleep. We still have stuff to talk about."

Jury shook away his shock and looked into Red's eyes. "Like what?"

Red peered into the distance and sighed, "I needed you to have my back at Larry's. I'm not saying what happened is your fault, but you weren't careful, and you weren't kind." His voice deepened. "For you to call me Jared like that." His words came out with an occasional quiver. "You know me, and you know what happened the night we met. The *way* my mother said my name with all the contempt and none of the love *scarred* me, as silly as *I* sound. You do the same thing when you get angry, even though you know *how it makes me feel*. You never apologize, either. I just forgive you, and we ignore it. That has to stop." His breathing became unsteady.

Jury scooted toward him, "Breathe. It's okay." He lowered his voice and wrapped his palm around his neck, "I've always been drawn to your sensitivity, and I'm sorry for not respecting it."

"It's okay. This might be hard for you to hear and even harder for me to say, but for our relationship to go any further, this has to stop. I mean it." His watery eyes gazed into Jury's. "It's been *nine* years."

Jury blinked every second. He expelled his response like blood through a punctured vein. "Okay." He put his hand atop Red's knee, "Okay," he repeated more reassuringly. Jury leaned toward Red and kissed him.

At that moment, Jude stormed into the room and saw everything. "Whoa-ho." He backed out.

Jury jumped out of bed. "GET BACK HERE!"

Red flinched and wiped his eyes.

Jude crept into the room. "I didn't know you both had a thing going on. My bad."

Jury's rage returned once more. "HOW DARE YOU ENTER MY ROOM WITHOUT KNOCKING!? State your business and get out!"

"Right, right." Jude was pale and had a hard time looking at Jury. "I just got off the phone with Akila. She said that Preston wants to interview you next Saturday."

With a smug grin, Jury wrapped his hand around his chin. "Oh. Oh! Well, consider me caught off guard."

Red paced his words like a confused parent. "The Fourteenth?"

"Yeah, and Akila said it was Preston's idea, too."

"That doesn't sound like him," replied Red.

Jude agreed.

"Well," Jury shrugged. "It's a date."

Jude's tone shifted. "Wait, you actually want to do it?"

Condescending undertones permeated Jury's disbelief. "Yeah, why wouldn't I?"

Upon reading the writing on the wall, Red rolled his eyes and left the room.

"Because it's a terrible idea," replied Jude, "It's exactly what Preston wants."

Jury's tone evoked an immediate annoyance. "Well, yeah. He stands to gain an ego boost if it goes well. Even if it doesn't, the ratings will be good. Dynamite, I bet. He doesn't realize that I have even more to gain, so I just have to bring my A-game."

"This isn't a performance, Jury. And besides, that's not the most moral perspective"

"Ach." Jury swatted his hand. "Have a little faith. It'll be fine! Besides, did you and Preston always do the 'moral' thing? No."

"But that's why I came here."

Jury laughed on his face. "What do you want me to say? Sorry you feel that way. There's nothing we can do about the way the world works."

Jude stuck up his nose, "If that's what you believe, then what's the point of Mailugulism?"

MOTHER NATURE

Dig, inhale, repeat. Larry breathed in but not out. The soil behind his house was like a combination of sand and ash. His hair unraveled each time he struck the Earth. He dug past decaying bones and worms until the shovel hit something it couldn't pierce. Dropping to his knees and clearing the dirt by hand revealed a casket.

The lid burst open, throwing him backward. Grey crawled out. The veins in his hands popped out of his clubbed fingers. Smoke filled his eyes. He lumbered toward his son, dead but not brainless. "Why now, Larry?"

Grey repeated himself and returned to the room where he met his maker. Larry followed, trying to avert his eyes from the hole in the back of his head and the centipedes skittering out of it. Grey lumbered toward the wall and sat with his back against it.

Light entered the room. The shadow it cast resembled a jellyfish, and it swam from the floor to the wall above Grey, taking the place of the brain matter and blood.

Grey's eyes became blue. They focused on Larry, "No one wins the blame game, kid."

Larry bolted upright. Sweat filled his pores as he struggled to regain oxygen. The clock read six AM. Even with the burial done and his family gone, anxiety still haunted him. His disheveled room, with clothes and trash lining the floor, only exacerbated this. Larry awoke from one nightmare only to be consumed by another. So, he let slumber reclaim him.

Six hours followed before consciousness returned. To his delight, Larry noticed a Game Boy game, manual, and box had been slid under his door. The smile it created creaked like rusty tin. Under the video game stuff was a copy of The Mailugian Times. He flipped through and noticed Speaker of the Month had been highlighted. Skimming it helped him understand why.

After reading the article, a wave of motivation washed over Larry. He threw together an outfit and showered for the first time in three days. The bathroom light highlighted the enormous bags under his eyes and the paleness of his skin. After staring at the stranger in the mirror, he went to consult the Speaker of the Month.

Red spent his mornings feeding birds from a bench on the playground. Larry decided to start there. Upon stepping outside, a soft breeze flipped his wet hair back and forth. Mother Nature welcomed his return. He regretted not wearing a coat, but the chill lost meaning when he saw the bench's current occupant.

Joe assumed Red's role, pelting each pigeon with feed rather than sprinkling it at their feet. His roaming eyes soon met Larry's. He sounded relieved, "Howdy, kid! Steppin' out of your comfort zone, I see."

Larry sounded spaced out. "I could say the same to you."

The two shared a moment of silence until Joe looked up at him and smiled. "I'm glad you decided to stay with us, kid. That's all I'll say." Larry's stomach rumbled, seizing Joe's attention. He pinched his lips. "You eatin'?"

"Oh, I didn't even notice I was hungry until now."

He chuckled to himself. "I got some birdseed if ya want it." No response. Joe rolled his eyes but retained a grin.

Larry glanced around and caught a view of crisp autumn magic. "I can't believe it's already fall."

Joe dumped the birdseed and shoved the bag in his pocket, "Me neither. It's depressin' how time flies, but at least winter is close."

"Winter's your favorite season?"

"It's peaceful. Besides, fall has too many memories."

Larry looked at Joe more attentively.

Joe leaned forward. "Hey, since you're here, can you help me up?" Joe did most of the work, but Larry's grasp was steady and firm.

He let go of Joe's hand. "I don't remember you being old."

"Oh, ha ha. I'm just sore. It's weird, though. I-I knew this was comin', but it still caught me by surprise."

"What do you mean?"

"Oh, uh, nothin' much." He paused for a moment, struggling to find a transition. "Uh... speakin' of cold, I know it ain't the best weather for it, but—" he shrugged, "Wanna get some ice cream?"

"Sure."

They walked to Joe's crimson Chevy Scottsdale and drove to a local ice cream shop, Jeri & Co's. It was a family-owned joint much more in line with something from the Midwest than rural Texas. From the drive-thru, Joe pulled into a spot at the back of the parking lot. A decent-sized forest sat behind them. He pointed at a trail leading in. "Wanna sightsee while we eat?"

"I don't care," Larry's tone lightened, but not by much, "as long as you aren't taking me back there like Old Yeller."

"Hey, if you start nippin' at my ice cream, no promises."

Small talk took a backseat to appreciating the landscape. Joe, entranced, gathered red leaves and tossed what he didn't crumble into the wind. Larry was drawn to the sky. A quaint stream, no wider than a foot, flowed beside them. Sunlight glimmered fantastically through the trees, casting a menagerie of shadows that bounced from one tree to the next.

Larry threw away his trash and turned to Joe. "I love ice cream as much as the next guy, but why is that the first thing you thought of?"

His tone was gentle. "Ice cream helps me relax. I usually come two or three times a week, usually in the middle of the night. Some weeks, I spend every night here. Your circumstances are more extreme, but we still thought it could do ya some good. Truth be told, though, I've–" he looked at Larry and sighed. "I've been real worried about you, kid."

He sounded more robotic than ever. "Thanks, means a lot."

Joe smirked and rolled his eyes. "Never mind me. Did you get what I slid under your door?"

Larry's face regained some color. "I did! I haven't been playing much recently, but I appreciate it."

"It's nothin'. I..." His tone and expression darkened. "I owe you after what I did."

A leaf floated in front of Larry's face, and he blew it out of his way. "What?"

Joe clenched his teeth. "I should've gone to Bethany. That way, you wouldn't have seen 'em in that state." He bit his cheek to maintain his tone. "There's so much I could've done, and I am *sorry*."

His tone was grim. "Don't apologize. You're not the one who killed my parents."

Joe's voice had more pep than ever. "And neither are you! I can only imagine all the rabbit holes you're leadin' yourself down." He put his hand on Larry's shoulder. "Ya know we're all here for ya, right?"

His eyes glistened. "But my parents aren't."

They walked a little further down the path. Larry picked up a long branch to use as a walking stick, then handed it to Joe after realizing it would help.

After grabbing the stick, Joe gathered his words. He spoke with intense confidence. "Realizin' you're not alone is the first step to the fourth step of grief."

Larry shot Joe with a confused, borderline repulsed expression.

Joe looked down. "Yeah, I didn't think before I said that."

Despite his bewilderment, he was slightly more interested in Joe's words. "Since when do you know so much about grief?"

"Fair question," he stopped and leaned on his stick. "Keep this between us, capisce?" He extended his hand.

Larry instantly shook it. He looked at Joe with a new wave of attentiveness.

Joe bit his lip and took a deep breath. "My granddaughter was born around nineteen eighty. *I* wanted to name her Gaia, but my son chose Ariel. That was the name of his mother, my late wife. I didn't raise the most responsible kids, so I usually watched her when I wasn't workin'. And let me tell ya. That girl was a prodigy. They didn't understand her like I did. That's why we got along so well. *Looooong* story short, I took custody of Ariel when she was six. After we adjusted to each other, it was a dream come true. There was one season we loved in particular: fall." He stopped and pointed at him. "Everyone becomes a poet in fall, ya know." They paused to admire the red and yellow leaves on the ground. They almost made the path look like a living mosaic.

Joe wrapped his hand around Larry's shoulder. Visions rushed through his mind. Despite knowing nothing about her appearance, Larry could now see transparent figments of a young Ariel and Joe walking ahead, re-enacting the story.

Joe's tone and mannerisms showed a side of him that Larry had never seen. His voice was nostalgic, and his expression oozed warmth. "It was our favorite time of the year! I remember she and I would walk 'round town every day, pickin' up more red leaves than we could carry. 'Grandpa! It's the apple one! The apple one!' she'd say to me." Joe's eyes glistened in the luster. His tone underwent a meditative transition. "It was adorable how emotional she'd get whenever they started to wilt. Ariel would try everythin' to keep 'em alive. She'd hide 'em in plastic bags, freezers. She even stuffed 'em in my suit pockets. Good surprise that was durin' an interrogation." He laughed. "Anyhow, freezin' seemed to work the best. She did this with three or four leaves every year until third grade, when one morning, she woke up, took her leaves out of the freezer, and set them outside. I thought she was just growin' up. But as usual, I wasn't thinkin' big enough. She told me, 'If I get to go home and see my Grandpa at the end of the day, these leaves should too.' It was sweet, but I still didn't understand why those leaves meant so much to her. So, I asked, and I'll never forget what she told me," His voice broke and faltered. "'Because we pick them together, Grandpa!'" He smiled and bit his lip. "Even now, I can see how beautifully her red hair shined." He blinked away tears. "She was my little Mother Nature. Whenever it starts to get cold outside, I miss her more."

Larry was engrossed by the painting Joe had created, but he spoke cautiously. "Is that because Ariel…"

"She got the chance to grow up," he began choking on his words, "but was *killed* before she could use it. She was studyin' to be a teacher." Before Joe's fantasy could become reality again, the imaginary Ariel disintegrated like sand in the wind, leaving Joe alone. "You two would've been good friends. That's why I was quiet at your party. It was all I could think about." A tear broke through his tough facade. He stopped in front of Larry. "Listen. The people we love wilt away. Don't waste your time preparin' for it because you'll never be ready. Focus on livin' for those who can't. The only way ya can honor their memory is by livin' on. There's always another way. You *have* to believe that." Joe put his hand on Larry's shoulder and pulled him in for a hug, "It'll be okay, kid. I promise."

He couldn't help but cry with Joe. "I'm sorry about Ariel. I can't imagine how hard it must've been."

"And I can't imagine how hard this is for *you*. This world can be an awful place, but no matter what, you'll *always* have me."

Larry nodded, and the two remained quiet. They chose to bask in their new companionship, which was almost warmer than anything they had ever known.

After a bit of leaf-watching, an odd degree of caution entered Larry's manner. "Joe, can I ask you something kind of intense?"

Joe nodded.

Larry breathed nervously. "When whatever happened... happened, did you feel forsaken by what you thought should have been protecting you?"

Joe was temporarily blinded by a sudden burst of fury. "*I* should have protected Ariel! After I failed her and acted out, I didn't have time to reflect. Everythin' happened at once, and I had to find asylum." He shook away his anger. "Let's stop flipping those stones and look at Red instead. When his sister died, he must have felt lost and weak. Now, with the Sturdy surrounding him, I bet he feels stronger than ever. Mailugula saved his life not through principle but people. It's the same people you have. All you gotta do is let them help."

"People, huh? You have a habit of talking around Mailugula. Around religion." Minor uneasiness underscored Larry's rising voice. "What exactly *do* you believe?"

He smiled, "Good to see you're back and cynical as ever. I believe you should always try to give, but in times like these..." he sighed, "It can be better to take. That's never how it should be done, but it's always in the back of our minds."

Larry's eyes were slightly wide, but he didn't wholly discount Joe's answer. "That's... a little dark."

"Jury should have a better answer." He checked his watch, "Let's head out. There's one more thing we have to do."

The two made their way back to the truck. "What is it?"

"We're taking a trip to the pound, kid. Come on, daylight's burnin'."

~

Sturdy Basement. A few hours later.

The rhythmic trotting of four legs against the concrete floor woke Fin. He lifted his head. A golden retriever pup was scampering around and sniffing everything it could reach. Unsure if he was dreaming, he advanced toward it. The dog yipped and wagged its tail. Fin picked it up, and color flooded back into his face.

Larry and Joe pushed the door open.

Larry beamed. "His name is Biscuit."

Fin embraced them both, "Thank you... so much! I can never repay you for this," he laughed and wiped his eyes. Biscuit jumped up and licked Fin's nose. He flinched and froze but soon became lost in a warm, familiar midst. Larry and Joe watched as Biscuit replaced Fin's tears with slobber.

Larry beamed.

Joe poked him with his elbow. "I didn't know ya had dimples, kid! Look at the size of those things!"

He kept his eye on Fin. "Like it or not, Joe, I think you just became a Speaker."

"I don't have to be a Speaker to help these people, ya know." Joe leaned toward him. "Spark's death'll always hurt, but Fin's on the right track. Just like you. All ya gotta do is keep pickin' up your feet and movin' forward, no matter how heavy the sand is. If you know where to look, you'll find a much stronger faith in kindness and companionship, not," he froze, "not—"

"Mailugula?" Larry snapped him out of it.

Joe sighed. He closed Fin's door and lowered his voice. "This whole operation makes me nervous, but keep that between us. Put yourself first. Not Mailugula. Capisce?"

He was casual and free. "Capisce."

With lowered eyebrows, he turned toward Larry. "Do you agree with me, though?"

Larry moved his lips to the side and shook his head. "I haven't thought about it, but I would never hold it against you. Anyway, I should head upstairs before it gets too late. Thanks for a great day, Joe. I'm here for you, too. I'll help make sure you don't give into your guilt."

Joe watched him walk upstairs until the surging daylight absorbed him completely.

~

Larry halted a deep cleanse of his room at the sound of a familiar murmuring outside his door.

"You know I'm not good at starting a conversation, Jury! Please come with me. I'm begging you."

"Stop thinking so much and just do it. You'll find a way, I promise." Three knocks materialized. Jury sprinted away like he was playing ding-dong ditch.

"WHERE are you *going*?! I wasn't ready!"

Larry smirked and opened the door.

"Oh!" Red noticed the color around Larry's cheeks and felt his chest loosen. "Uh, mind if I come in?"

"Hello to you too." He gestured for him to enter.

"Sorry. Uh, hi."

The two sat on Larry's bed.

Larry was lovingly suspicious. "I'm surprised to see you. Isn't the interview—"

"You're our priority, you know." The fidgeting in Red's fingers intensified, "I'm sorry if you heard us out there. I'm not good at this stuff." He lowered his head. "I've just been really worried about you," his voice broke a little. "It makes me *so* happy... how vibrant you look."

"Yeah. Talking with Joe and seeing Fin interact with Biscuit was great. But," his expression stiffened, "I can't get it out of my head. What did Joe do?"

Red frowned. His eyes ambled everywhere but Larry's direction. "Jury hasn't told me. Honestly, I think it's better that way. Joe's a good man. I would've gone with you two, but Jury thought it would be just as therapeutic for Joe. Anyway, how do you feel? Uh—in your own words."

"I mean, not great. But better." He exhaled. "A lot better."

"That makes me really happy, buddy. I know you'll be frustrated and angry about what happened for a long time, but..."

Larry tightened his lips. "Who said I was angry?"

Red looked away. "Sorry. I don't mean to put words in your mouth."

Larry's heart grew warmer. "Say what's on your mind, Red."

Red took a deep breath. "What happened isn't your fault."

"You know, after today," he nodded, "I think I believe you. At the very least, I can be grateful that I have friends like you and Joe to fall back on. I still have a reason to live... thanks to *you*."

Red beamed. Tears fell from his eyes in a delicate rhythm. "That's nice of you to say. I felt the same way when I met Jury." He wiped his eyes and cleared his throat. "Crying? Who, me? No sir."

Larry chuckled. "It's good that you express your feelings."

He laughed. "I don't know about that. I just have a lot of experience crying."

"Do you cry better with experience or worse?"

Red smirked. "That's not what I meant." He paused. "Worse, actually, now that I think about it. My teenage years really did a number on me."

Larry tilted his head, "Oh?"

"Yeesh, uh," he scratched the back of his head, "I don't want to shove another sob story down your throat, but my sister drowned in our pool when I was sixteen. I was supposed to be watching her. I wasn't. I was reading or listening to music or something. We didn't know she was prone to seizures." He bit his lip and shook his head. "I let grief take me over and my mother beat me down. My self-standards, relationships, everything I had disintegrated."

"Hm." He looked away, "I'm sorry. Is that why you're so timid?"

"Maybe. Even though I felt horrible, I knew, in my heart of hearts, that it wasn't my fault. But I was afraid to accept that truth, and my mother left me no choice but to bury it. Knowledge of the truth breaks people, but ignorance can do the same. Religion can help, but there's so much under the surface with that. I have a hard time trusting it. Making the truth with Mailugula is still hard, but it's the only thing that's worked."

Larry interlocked his hands. "How did you handle all the problems back home?"

Red smiled and placed his hand on his heart. "Jury rescued me. Ah, he was so optimistic. I never would have forgiven myself had it not been for him or Mailugula."

The look in Larry's eyes hardened. "Has Jury changed at all?"

He removed his hand from his heart and looked at him, confused. "Why do you ask that?"

"When we got back from Bethany, as I was waking up. I heard what Jury said to you."

"I—" he stopped. Larry's question mortified him. After swallowing the words he wanted to say, he continued. "N... no. He didn't mean it, so it's okay. I know he cares about me."

Larry sighed. Disappointment now controlled his tone and expression. "Listen. I used to think that care was the only thing a relationship needed. But my Dad cared. He cared a lot..." his voice faltered and shook, "and it *corrupted* him. Caring isn't enough. You have to be strong and accept reality. Ignorance only makes it harder to breathe. Do you get what I'm saying?"

Red's expression was blank. He breathed deeply. "A little." He snapped out of a weird trance and smiled. "Hey! We're supposed to be talking about you!"

"Well," Larry shrugged, "If you want to teach me that badly, I have a question. When your sister died, did you feel forsaken?"

Red's eyes widened, "I felt alone. But forsaken? Eh? I don't know. That'd be a great question for Jury."

He shrugged, "Eh. I'll ask him another time. I've got a room to clean."

Red's stomach grumbled, "And I should probably eat something. Uh, check in with Jury soon, please? He's worried about you."

Larry hesitated. "I will."

After a quick hug, Red left.

That night, even with a clean room and a clear conscience, the nightmares returned. Upon waking up, he felt chilled rather than warmed. The sound of chains bouncing away from his door slinked into his ears. A package now sat at the foot of his door. Blue moonlight illuminated his room and the note atop it.

Happy belated Birthday, Larry. I know I'm late. You'll find this useful. It's a perfect tool to learn from your past. -Progenitor

Larry tore open the package and found an antique copy of the New Testament.

LANTERN

If you ever get lost, light this lantern, and I promise I'll find you.

The only memory Preston retained of his mother was confined within that crimson, iron lantern. From the moment he laid his little eyes on it, he was enamored. He had never seen anything more beautiful. Despite its overwhelming weight, he lifted it repeatedly until his arms went numb.

He couldn't help but admire the craftsmanship again and again. On each of the lantern's four walls was a jellyfish, and as the purple flame within cast them upon the wall, they danced and swayed as if they were really swimming. Every night, Preston would sleep with the flame lit, hoping his mother would find her way back.

All it took was one thrashing from his father. The latch was broken, and the wind that managed to squeeze through always extinguished the flame. Without it, Preston knew his mother was lost. He'd sneak out every night and roam the streets. He prayed his lantern would light the way, but it never did. It was never even bright enough to make his father look up from his newspaper.

All Preston wanted was to be brighter. He began acting as a lantern, and the people around him rallied, even if they never knew why. The only exception was his father. No matter how loud he was, his home was always quiet. Years passed, and Preston grew from a helpless child into a frightened man. Instead of extinguishing his flame outright, Preston let his father fan it. It had taken his entire childhood, but he finally had the fuel to keep his lantern lit.

Soon after, Preston's father died under mysterious circumstances, and he has coasted on his inheritance ever since. His lantern remained aflame, although the jellyfish never danced as it used to, and his mother remained lost.

Whenever Preston couldn't sleep, he'd sit in front of his VHS player and watch a highlight tape from his career. Before RBLA, he worked as a storm reporter for a major Texas broadcaster. As other reporters were panicking and escaping, Preston would go deeper and deeper into the eye of the storm. Sometimes, even the cameraman would run, and Preston became director and star. Even when face to face with death, he'd still be cracking jokes. Scrapes and scratches were routine, but a constant sense of adrenaline always healed him. However, adrenaline can't reflect a stop sign, especially one hurling fifty miles an hour into your stomach.

Lawyers found a way to sue his broadcaster and secure a hefty settlement. As a result, he was blacklisted by the news industry. Although he was deteriorating, Preston still desired that high. The only way to continue working was to open his own studio. Taking only his mother's lantern and his dream, he left his life behind and moved to Scarwood.

Although the light from his TV was always brighter, his mother's lantern made him feel complete. To this day, before bed, he still made a point to light his lantern. Sometimes, he'd gaze out the window, and, unbeknownst to him, someone always gazed back.

Sitting up in bed, Jury stared out the window at a mysterious purple flame. Red's snoring broke his concentration, and he turned to him with a smile. Jury laid back down and rolled toward Red but heard something lightly scraping against the floor. There was a golden leaf twirling on the carpet like a figure skater. He was captivated by its bright, golden tint and bent down to pick it up. It shimmied and squirmed, resisting him. Then, an itch overcame him, and with one firm clutch, he crushed it. Gold dust slipped through his fingers. A light breeze scattered them across the floor, and they began shining like tiny lanterns. They tumbled down the stairs one torch at a time, illuminating a path.

Entranced, Jury followed them. All that was visible was the ground beneath him until the lanterns rose into the air, and the darkness lifted. Jury had made it downstairs, in front of an open window. The lanterns danced around it.

Jury leaned against the windowsill. Gazing through the breeze, he thought of a matron whose hair once blew through it, then another.

A tired voice came from behind him. "Jury, what are you doing?"

Jury stayed facing the window. His voice was so soft that it was almost unrecognizable. "Red, have you seen Mallory lately?"

Red thought for a moment and shook his head. "No, why?"

"This is the window she snuck through." He sighed. "I'm going to sound like you do all the time, but I'm worried. We're the reason she's still out there." For a quick moment, Jury's voice quivered. "Her and her little stranger."

Red's voice was soothing. "It's not your fault. These are all decisions that *she* made. That's the nature of interpretation and the nature of Mailugula."

Jury hung his head. "The nature *we* introduced to her." He bit his lip and shook his head. "I'm sorry. I'm just nervous. The interview is tomorrow. I don't want people thinking I'm faltering again."

Red put his hand on Jury's shoulder. "Don't put so much pressure on yourself. All you're doing is making us nervous." He wrapped his arms around him. "Everything will be okay. Life is just like that. People zig when you want them to zag. All we can do is use our hearts and try."

Jury's emerald eyes glistened. He stared at Red and hugged him tightly. "I love you so much. I know we can't have rings to show it, but know that you'll always have my heart."

Red sniffed and wiped his foggy eyes. "Oh, Jury. You have no idea how much I love you, ya cheeseball." His voice adopted an optimistic edge. "Think about tomorrow like this: we've finally broken the ice with RBLA. That's fantastic! I think the community is finally seeing our struggle."

Jury smiled, "Because we're proving that we care."

"That's right." His tone became a little sterner. "But we have to be up in a few hours, silly. I know you're worried, but you need to rest."

"I know. I know. Let's go." Jury grabbed Red's hand, and the two went back to bed.

As they slept, speculation about the interview ran rampant. For every person who hoped Jury would dominate, another secretly vied for Preston's success. Either way, someone's lantern was bound to dim.

FACT FROM FANTASY

Jury opened his eyes and rose into consciousness. This time, he retained one scrap of his dream.

"Why *did* I pick something so obscure?" He scratched his chin.

Jury's lunch consisted of bubblegum and a prayer. Moments after sitting in the refectory, Joe sat beside him.

Jury smiled. "Good morning! I never thought I'd see the day when you and Fin got out of the dungeon. It's a miracle."

A smug grin was plastered across Joe's face. "Be happy for Fin. The dog is takin' up so much of his attention that you can barely tell he's grievin'. Gotta say, I did a good job with that."

"Yeah. You did. You know, it's never too late to—"

"Uh-huh. Tell yourself whatever ya want." He looked over his shoulder and saw most of the congregation staring at him, "Hard to talk without mentionin' your big interview. It's soon, right?"

"I'm leaving in about fifteen minutes. I wanted to eat something beforehand, but..." he rotated his finger at the tables around them. People everywhere were murmuring to each other and stealing glances at Jury. A sly smile came to him. "This is all the sustenance I need."

"Selfish ass." Joe hit the table and rolled his eyes.

Out of the blue, Red pulled up a chair, "Good morning, you two."

Jury's expression lit up. "Hey! How was your morning?"

"Fair. I talked to Jude earlier."

Joe leaned in. "And?"

Red hesitated. "He's still completely against it."

"Hm." Joe stood up, "Well, good luck, Jury," and walked away.

"Uh, thanks?" Jury furrowed his eyebrows and turned to Red, "What did he say this time?"

A hint of concern popped into his energetic voice. "He still thinks this is exactly what Preston wants. I get where he's coming from, but we want this too. Preston has bullied a lot of people. It's about time someone called him out. Even if it's not our responsibility, we can, so we should."

Jury smirked. "You're sounding more like Larry every day."

The sound of dreaded footsteps halted their conversation. The noise grew closer, and before long, Jude rushed through the refectory and pressed his hands against the table. "Jury, come on. It's not too late to back out."

Jury sighed through his teeth, "It definitely is. I understand the aversion, but this needs to happen."

Concern drowned out Jude's other facial cues. "Listen! This is just a grudge match, Jury. After it's all said and done, you may look better, but you won't *be* better."

Jury shrugged. "It'll make me *feel* better."

Jude crossed his arms. "Are you *that* petty? Don't let your ego blind you."

"Lay off a little and trust me for a change. It'll all work out."

"Stop being reckless!"

Jury frowned. "You know what? Why do you need to approve everything I do? I have priorities, and like it or not, your comfort zone isn't one of them."

Jude barely moved his lips. "I just want to work with you. But if you don't, I'll gladly find someone who does." He stormed off.

Jury checked his watch. "There goes my relaxation time." He looked up. "Will you walk me out, Red?"

Light from a nearby window gradually dimmed until nothing shined upon them. "Of course."

They walked outside. When no one was looking, Red hugged Jury as if he was going off to war. "Be safe, okay?"

"No need to fear, hun. I'll make it work!"

"Just say don't be afraid." He laughed. "It's so weird how you... anyway. I know you'll make it work. That's why I love you. Did I say that I love you? Because I do. I *love* you." He kissed Jury on the cheek and pulled away, smiling sheepishly. "Sorry."

They both blushed like strawberries.

~

When Jury walked into RBLA headquarters, a group of employees bombarded him with handshake after handshake. His natural charisma flowed through each interaction he shared with them. Akila then led him to the interview.

No fanfare, greeting, or effort awaited him. Preston sat in a leather chair, and pointed at the wooden stool designated for Jury. Make-up and optimal lighting made him look sprightly.

"Good luck," muttered Akila as she closed the door and went to operate the camera. She counted down from three and relayed a thumbs-up.

Preston looked into the camera. His weight loss made him look like a meerkat with a beer gut. His movements were stiff, but his tonality remained strong. A pretentious sense of class filled him. "Robust Before Lunch, America. I am Preston Epalit, your host for today's interview and the founder, owner, and biggest creative mind of RBLA." Preston cleared his throat. "Today, we are broadcasting live with our guest, prophet of the Mailugians, Jim Chessjurist. Or, as his underlings know him, **Jury**." Impatience filled him as he looked at Jury for the first time.

Jury opted to address the camera rather than Preston. "Hello! As we've established, my name is Jury Chessjurist. I'll start with a correction: I am no prophet. I want the hearts I mend to save the world, not myself."

Preston smacked his lips. "Already not making sense, I see. Onto the questions. This is the only one I wrote myself." This was the first time Preston aggravated a portion of the one hundred and fifty thousand viewers. It was clear he was struggling to stay focused. He kept wiping sweat from his brow and sighing under his breath. "One of the many things I do not understand about your base of operations is the name. I understand church, chapel, and whatnot are probably copyrighted, but why pick something so obscure?"

Though he should have anticipated this moment, Jury was caught off-guard. "Great question! I... uh, originally wanted to call the building a Shaker. As a quick history lesson, Shakers were a restorationist religious sect that found most of their footing during the Great Awakenings. Their approach to religion and worship intrigues me. But some still remain today, so I feared we'd be lumped into that same revivalism. Sturdy has a similar ring to it. It's also an important trait people often overlook. Something sturdy doesn't outright change in the face of adversity. It evolves. It strengthens. The human body does this flawlessly while our minds struggle."

Preston gazed to the side. "Cool. Profound. Moving on." He took a deep, strained breath. "You have a lot to say about Mailugula. Where does it all come from?"

"About twelve years ago, we were on some…" he shuddered, "*horrible* church trip. We stayed at a hotel in the Golgotha desert called The Ranger. Pretty sure it's abandoned now. I don't know why they thought a hotel in the middle of a scorching hot Texas desert was a good idea, but I digress. I got lost in the desert and had a vision."

A single corner of Preston's lip lifted into a sneer. He leaned forward. "See, you use words like *vision*. Are you sure you do not mean hallucination?"

This question was another Jury had thought out numerous times. He couldn't help but smile. "Whether it's fact or fantasy doesn't matter because the ideas I extracted are strong regardless."

"So, by that logic, there is a chance Mailugula is just as fake as the values he stands for, right?"

Jury interlocked his hands. A condescending edge entered his voice. "Press, religion is a very moral concept. Any debate on my vision being fact or fiction doesn't change the fact that Mailugula's values carry weight. They strengthen resilience while encouraging independence, intertwining the goals of religion with amendments to its most common–"

"I did not ask you to advertise Mailugulism. So, moving on." Preston smiled through an aggressive sigh. "Ever since the funeral, you have been donating to small businesses across Scarwood. Why is that?"

"After my behavior at Emil's funeral, certain community members began doubting whether my intentions were as genuine as I suggested. So, I decided to ground my words in action."

Preston's response was matter-of-fact. "You used money. You bought back the love of a community that was beginning to see your cracks. If a politician would've done the same thing, they'd call him corrupt."

Jury no longer veiled his growing frustration. "I'm sorry, what is this? Because this isn't an interview."

"It is called a style, Chessie. And it is very unprofessional to–"

"UNPROFESSIONAL!?!" Jury stifled himself. After a quick breath, he continued. "You don't have a style, Press. You're one step above the paparazzi. Here's the way I see things. By saving Mary's and helping other businesses, I want everyone to understand that Mailugula—"

"Do you need to turn everything I say into a commercial for Mailugula!? Come on!" He threw down his notes. With his pointer finger aimed at Jury, he leaned out of his chair. "If Mailugulism is the people's choice, why are you shoving it down their throats?"

Jury gave him a thumbs-up. A strange sense of approval conducted him. "Interesting thought, but I'm not shoving anything down any-one's throat. I'm proud of what I'm doing, and I'm allowed to voice that."

"No one cares! Who in their right mind would listen to some hippy brag about nonsense?"

"They're watching this interview, right? And even if they don't, maybe your viewers would care," he paused, "if you reported the news as it was."

A Grinch-like simper spread across Akila's face.

Preston squinted. "What're you saying?"

Jury's voice rose. "Everything about Mailugula is portrayed in a negative and heavily biased fashion!"

Looking away from Jury, hints of disbelief undermined his calm voice. "How I see your cult isn't about bias. It is about my interpre-tation."

"Your interpretation is not news! Aren't reporters supposed to inform, free of personal bias? I may be biased, but I made Mailugulism, *not* you! And I realize I'm not perfect." He pivoted toward the camera. "I acted like a child at Emil's funeral. I'm sorry for disappointing the community. I have more self-awareness than people like Preston ever will, and I promise to improve and bring Mailugulism across the world."

Preston threw his hands into the air as far as he could. "Yeah, right! You control yourself once and automatically think you're disciplined and strong-willed? Gah! What am I doing?" With a single exhale, Preston calmed his nerves. He took a page from Jury's book and looked into the households of his viewers. "No matter how soon I will die, sitting here and arguing with this petty hippie will not help me live on. I am just playing the Mailugula game." He pointed into the camera. "And so are you. This is just another act from another hack, and it will go nowhere. Give your attention to something worthwhile, like our broadcast tonight. Thank–"

"Just look at Press." A mischievous glint flashed across Jury's eyes. "He's practically suffocating under all the lights and make-up. I can *smell* the formaldehyde." Jury chuckled. "Or maybe that's just his disgusting beard. What is that in there: static from your crappy signal or dried sour cream?"

Preston looked at Akila. "Cut! Cut the damn camera!" Akila gave him a thumbs-up. He rose as quickly as possible and stomped to Jury. Pride entered his voice. "You're right. You're not a prophet. You're a pretentious know-it-all! What would you know? What the Hell could *you*, of all people, see in this world that no one else does? You would not give a homeless man the change out of your pocket, let alone your love to the God that makes life possible. You have to give back to Him in any way He asks."

"Guess He hasn't asked you much." Jury smacked his lips and began speaking more eccentrically. "You know something, *Press*? Sometimes, the most religious people understand it the least, especially when they use it as an excuse to put others down." He shook his head. "Religion has nothing to do with our feud. You're being unfair to religion and unfair to me."

The sweat from Preston's red face boiled. "Life is unfair, and I hate how liberals like you try to walk around it."

Jury threw his hands into the air. "What are you talking about?! Why do you always bring politics into irrelevant situations?"

"I see nothing irrelevant about it. I've seen too many good men fall in the trenches hidden by snowflakes like you."

Jury scoffed. "Mailugula is not a political statement! There's nothing political about wanting a better life, about striving for change. Life is unfair, but you have to stand up and be strong. People need to realize that nothing worthwhile is won without a fight."

"Is that right?" replied Preston, deriving crooked amusement from what he planned to say, "Were you winning something worthwhile when you attacked my workers at the funeral?"

The remorse in his tone was immense. "I've lost control a few times, but my heart has always been in the right place. Your heart only cares about furthering your own standing, and you can barely stand as is."

"At least I can actually control my own emotions!"

"Oh yeah?" A sly look came to him. "Does the name *Spark* mean anything to you?"

At that line, Jude and Fin cringed.

Preston stuttered and began getting flustered. "What? How do you..." He turned away from Jury. He seemed smaller and weaker with every word. "What difference does it make? I can't take back what I did. I can't make it better." He growled. A new anger flashed across his heart. "Do *not* talk down to me when you do *not* know better. No amount of pretty words will EVER give ANYONE a purpose!" Preston was one step away from strangling Jury—and dying while trying—when he noticed the camera light still blinking. His heart sank. "I've been live this *whole* time!?"

Jury beamed.

Preston stormed toward the camera, shoved it over, and stomped on it. He approached Akila. The fire in his eyes obscured his pupils. "Why is the camera still on? I told you to cut the damn feed!"

Akila was confident. "And I told you that ratings are more important than anything. So," She grinned, ear to ear, and buried her pointer finger into his chest. "What are you gonna *do* about it?"

Preston stopped breathing. No amount of rage could reverse the hands of time. Destroying them was his only option. He bared his teeth, grabbed Akila by the neck, and slammed her against the wall, slightly denting the plaster behind her head.

Before anyone could jump into action, Akila kicked Preston as hard as she could.

Preston roared in agony. He stumbled over the camera and fell to the floor. The veins in his skull protruded like nails in a sinner's coffin. "WHAT A CROCK! YOU DO NOT TREAT ME THAT WAY! I AM PRESTON EPALIT!" He tried to stand, still shouting, but collapsed every time he pushed himself up. Then, he started grimacing and grasping at his heart. Every breath was a fight. "I'm dying." His entire demeanor turned to chaos. 'I'M DYING! Oh, *God*. It's like an elephant's sitting on my chest." He meekly uttered, and his emaciated body became limp.

Despite being in shambles, the camera chose to stop functioning at this moment.

FIGUREHEADS

Having finally pried RBLA from Preston's fingers, Akila stood taller than ever and watched the paramedics wheel him outside.

As the ambulance raced into the horizon, an intern poked Akila on the shoulder. "The producers called. They'll be here in three hours to talk."

She pressed an ice pack against her head and looked at her watch, "That's dinner time, though." A lightbulb went off. "Say, Jury. Wanna grab a celebratory late lunch?"

Jury smiled, "Sounds good. Let me call the mothership real quick and I'll be on my way."

The two met at a local barbecue restaurant and snagged a table outside. The soft wind made the parasol above their table rustle like a palm tree. Country music quietly echoed from inside the restaurant.

Jury ordered coffee and Akila showed her ID to get a margarita.

She raised her eyebrows. "You drink your coffee black?"

"And you're hitting the hard stuff before dinner?" Akila opened her mouth, but Jury stopped her. "If you're about to say, 'It's five o'clock somewhere,' I will kill you. RBLA too."

She chuckled, "Won't be RBLA for long."

"Think a name change is in order, aye? What do you have in mind?"

Akila smirked and propped her head up with her fist. "You'll have to wait and watch our upcoming broadcasts."

"Ugh. You're sounding like Preston already."

"We're here to celebrate, not scare each other." She raised her glass, "To Preston Epalit fading into obscurity."

Jury followed suit, "And to hoping we never face a similar fate." He held back his glass. "And also to Preston not dying a horrible death, now that I think about it. Empathy, ya know?"

Clink!

Food arrived quickly.

"So," Jury began, pouring cheese over his fries. "I've always wondered: what made you turn to the dark side?"

"What do you mean?"

"I remember you from the first Session. I'm just curious why, when faced with Epalit or Mailugula, you picked Epalit. I'd understand more if you picked neither."

Akila split her attention between Jury and cutting her pulled pork. "I wasn't *faced* with Mailugula. Not everyone you come across is gonna join you in the Sturdy, you know. But if you wanna talk about Mailugulism, I will." She smiled at him. "It's too vague for me. Rules help me operate. I'm not a fan of rigidly following them, mind you. I just like that they're there."

Jury shrugged, remaining casual. "I can't help but feel suffocated by rules and regulations."

Akila's strengths as a news anchor were evident in the reverence flowing through her tone. "I understand the appeal of making rules based on your own values, and I like how easily it can fit into someone's schedule. But I don't see much point, and I've tried to. There'd be a lot of uncertainty."

"We prefer to say 'responsibility.'"

Concern persisted in her light voice. "And some people are irresponsible. What if some psycho used Mailugulism as an excuse to kill people? They'd think they're in the right, and countless lives would be ruined because of it. Extreme example, but you're teaching people that they're more different than alike. That's the last thing we need."

"When you're making the rules, you should see any failure coming from a mile away. In regards to Mailugulism, ignorance goes as far as you let it."

She sprinkled pepper onto her food. "Not everyone is self-aware."

"That's not Mailugula's fault. They're not designed for everyone. Nothing is."

Akila shook her head. "Doesn't that defeat Mailugulism's point? It's designed for everyone and anyone. Sounds great on paper. But by human nature, it's doomed to fail."

Jury sighed under his breath. "You can be pessimistic all you want, but unbending rules fail people more than any combination of open-minded thoughts."

"Any combination? Any at all?" Her eyebrows lowered. She began chuckling. "There's a difference between pessimism and realism, Jury. If you're not grounded in reality, then you need to find a planet that fits your gravity. In the end, you have to decide whether or not something is worth it. Mailugulism can't be disqualified from that debate just because it's new."

The sun started to set below the parasol, blinding Jury. He covered his eyes. "Mailugulism is wholly different from any other religion. I think it should be judged on separate merits."

"Mailugulism's not a horror movie, Jury. You have to judge it somehow."

"You really don't. Not yet, at least. Mailugula helps, and all I need is time to demonstrate that."

Akila's keen eyes rooted through Jury's soul, "Demonstrate... or justify?"

Jury froze up. For a moment, he was silent. "Mailugula is new. It needs time, just like anything else. That doesn't mean it's a cult. In cults, you don't have rights. You don't have freedom. It's the complete opposite of Mailugulism."

"It may sound redundant to you, but by your line of thought, people *are* allowed to think that way."

He took a long sip of coffee. "That doesn't stop them from being ignorant. They can't use *their* freedom to restrict mine."

"When you started this, you *had* to know that some people wouldn't like it." Akila raised her eyebrows. "But they aren't stopping you. You're not afraid, so why let it bother you? You're getting upset over the very thing you're preaching, which, you have to admit, is ridiculous. I don't know what you want because religion, as a term, can't be thrown around."

"Hm." Jury tightened his lips. "Why?"

"What do you mean?"

"I'm just wondering why you think it shouldn't be thrown around."

After staring into the ether, Akila took a deep breath and returned her gaze to Jury. "There's a lot of ways you *can* define religion, but a lot of ways you can't. If you ask me, it's not just a blank slate of values. I understand that you feel like you need to reclaim your freedom, but is that really religion? Anyone can preach, Jury." Her tone skirted past condescending and settled into a groove of calm congeniality. "The word 'cult' has more versatility than you give it credit for. It's not nearly as damning as you think it is, either. It'd only be damning if it scared everyone away, and we both know that's not the case. This is just about your ego."

Jury put his palms together and moved them up and down to emphasize his words. "Cult, as a term, is always derogatory. It's used to separate our beliefs from others. Hell, I don't see the point. If corpses are any indication, then religions have more blood on their hands."

Akila double-taked. "Recently? No. In the dark ages? Yes."

"And I disagree with that." He chuckled. "Sorry!"

"Wait. You're saying that religion has more blood on its hands, but also that you want to be viewed *with* those religions?" Her face hardened. "Jury. You need to make up your mind. Do you want to be separated from other religions or viewed with them? You can't be seen in the same light while being judged on separate terms."

He rubbed his forehead and sighed. "Sorry. I don't mean to contradict myself."

Akila shrugged and crossed her arms. Her food was getting cold. "Not everyone means it offensively. I believe Mailugulism has a right to exist, and I know most people agree. Their voices just aren't as loud. Why do you fixate on hatred? There's no point. No one who already disagrees with you is going to listen unless God himself is hiding in your basement!"

Jury could barely formulate a response. He leaned back in his chair. "Uh, well. I don't mean to be arrogant. I may be critical of certain religions, but I know Mailugulism's not perfect."

"Do you?"

"I—" He blinked, hard, as if he was seeing Mailugula's corpse. "Compared to what others are forced to adhere to, it's ideal."

"I can't imagine a Mailugula, let alone how to build it. If you don't mind me asking, how did you build yours?"

"My Mailugula?"

Akila nodded. "And I'm not talking about your vision, either. What did little Jimmy go through that brought us here?"

Jury sighed. His voice was plain and sorrowful. "My mother died when I was six. In his grief, my father looked to the church and expected me to do the same." He held his head down before continuing. "How do I say this? My Mom was a free spirit, and I took after her. Mom always told me to stand up for myself. One day, I did. And my youth fell apart because of it. That's when I realized what it's all about: pressure. Pressure to be a certain person, pressure to dress a certain way, pressure to think along lines you oppose. As I grew up, though, I watched many people in the church suffer just as badly. I ha—" His eyelids popped open as though he had caught himself in a lie. "*We* had no constructive means to deal with it. That's why I created Mailugula. Anything to reclaim freedom and faith."

Akila put her fork down. "My condolences, first of all, but I feel like there's more to your situation than freedom and risk. A lot of people don't want to think your way, along your lines. To you, they may seem closed-minded. But they have every right to stick with what they're comfortable with. Do they have the right to attack you? No. And from what I've seen, they don't." She paused and looked around. "All things considered, they've gone pretty easy on you. Preston represented a very small group of people, and without him, I don't think this anti-Mailugula sentiment will grow. As is, you seem to be more preoccupied with labels than ironing out Mailugulism." She stammered with a variety of vowels before sticking with one. "I can tell how many sleepless nights you've put into this, and I understand why certain people may need Mailugulism." She tapped her fingernail on the table. "But there's something you're not considering."

"Oh?"

Akila's voice was warm and powerful. "There *can* be a balance between autonomy and religion. Mailugulism may make it clearer for some, but for others, it may just cloud that fact. To be honest," she took a deep breath, "I think that's what it's done to you." She caught Jury's chuckle. "What's so funny?"

"Your points are surprisingly well thought out."

Akila smirked. "It's a subject I care about."

"Me too." Jury began thinking. Even though his food was unfinished, he found himself antsy and unwilling to sit with Akila. "Well, it's been an adventure, but I should head back." He stood and tossed fifteen dollars on the table. "That should cover my stuff and a tip." They shook hands.

Akila nodded. "From now on, I'll make sure Mailugula is painted in an honest light." She watched Jury walk away and snickered into her palm. "Always the mothers. Tch, what a cliché."

Jury drove into the nearby outskirts of Golgotha and parked on a random hill. Akila's words echoed through his mind. *I believe Mailugulism has a right to exist, and I know most others agree. Their voices just aren't as loud.* He sank into the velvet, "Good God. I never realized. If people are truly this accommodating, do we even need Mailugulism?"

His question echoed through the valley, past abandoned buildings and roadkill galore. Validation, rather than salvation, became his priority.

~

The superiors Preston ignored towered over him and set boxes at his bedside. Even in his anesthetic stupor, he knew what filled them.

Just pull the plug.

They denied his request. Instead, a lawyer pulled up a chair and began negotiating a price for his RBLA assets.

"You'll be happy to know that Akila has chosen not to press charges. But we still need to act. Due to your fading health and spirit…"

Preston might as well have been underwater. Everything was a blur to him. Regardless, they settled. Hefty compensation, accounting for the present and future value of RBLA, flooded his bank account. Each night, however, when Akila announced, "Robust Before Lunch, America," rage consumed him.

Seventy-two hours later, Preston, skeletal as ever, was discharged into the night, leaving his RBLA belongings behind. He felt ashamed to face the world. Being forced to wobble around on a cane worsened these sentiments. He looked at his hands and still felt Akila's neck. He shivered.

Driving home, he gazed at himself in the rearview mirror and couldn't differentiate between his skin tone and the moonlight. His foot sank into the gas pedal like a tombstone on soft, exalted ground. He leaned his head back, shut his eyes, and released the steering wheel.

He waited and waited for death to take him. Yet, minutes passed without incident. He opened his eyes and realized that, somehow, he and his car had made it home. Awestruck, he crept through his house and collapsed onto the couch, leaving the front door ajar.

Sleep, to Preston, had lost its peace. He groaned and grunted like a dog left out overnight. Blinking didn't tear him away from his terrors, but the doorbell did. He rambled through a cold sweat. "Sweet Mary and Joseph, when will that dream *stop*?"

The doorbell reverberated through his eardrums once more. He opened the front door and found the boxes he had stranded at Pontifex Catholic occupying his front steps. They had stalked him. He used his cane to push the boxes over and watched the contents spill along the foundation of his house. He sighed, "Outta sight, outta mind," and hobbled back to bed.

Later that night, while channel surfing, he stumbled across RBLA, Akila framed in the center. "Thanks to all of you, my first few days in the saddle have been a breeze and a success. To celebrate this new era, my superiors and I have agreed on an important change. Many people view our name as unoriginal, and I agree. For this reason, Robust Before Lunch, America will change its name immediately to HNN, Hatem News Network."

With a gargantuan force inconsistent with his declining health, Preston hurled his cane at his TV. It pierced the glass, and minuscule shards flew into the air. White splinters and fractures formed in the glass around the entry point. Flashes of red filled the remaining space.

Preston's pupils doubled in size. He stood up and leaned against the wall. His lungs violently pulsated with each syllable. "***Hatem. News. Network?!*** How could I let this happen?! God! I was nothing more than a fiddle and a figurehead." He felt ready to topple every piece of furniture in his house.

Before his heart could palpitate, he heard a metallic echo near his patio. Despite only wearing a white robe and ripped underwear, he threw open the backdoor and found a package with a note. On instinct, he crumpled the letter and threw it outside. Diving right into the box revealed an antique Ruger Single-Six Revolver.

Preston noticed every other chamber was filled. He spun the cylinder and snapped it shut. "Three rounds, three opportunities." He pinched his lips and giggled. "Ooowee! That was ***coooool***! And I thought this wild west stuff was only in the movies." A smile returned to his sagging face. "Looks like I still have some dedicated members of the Preston Epalit fan club. Hm." He looked out his sliding glass door at the moon. "If I was Akila, I would've done the same thing. Maybe this isn't as bad as I made it out to be. I'll just have to find another legacy."

While he slept, Mother Nature slipped a now-pristine letter through his bedroom window.

In this world, whether you're right or wrong doesn't matter. It's the means and ambition that does. -Progenitor

ACT THREE: SPEAK OF THE DEVIL

Pontifex Catholic Hospital. Midnight.

Jude approached the front desk. He leaned in close and smiled, "Hi! I'm here to..." he mumbled, "see Preston Epalit."

The wrinkly, glasses-wearing receptionist squinted. "See who? Joe Piasacha?"

"No!" Jude stammered for a moment and looked around. After seeing no one in his vicinity, he returned to a normal volume. "I'm here to see Preston Epalit."

"Oh." The receptionist squinted harder at Jude. "Ohhhh, you used to work for him. I remember. Jude... *Areola*, right?"

He chuckled sheepishly. "*Ariotics*, actually. You got–"

"Oh, okay. You're out of luck, hun. Mr. Epalit is gone."

"HE'S DEAD?!"

"No! Idiot! He's alive! Why are you asking me so many questions? You're not the POA! What are you, some kind of spy?" She lowered her reading glasses. "I won't break *HIPPO*. You should visit him, though. He was talking about you."

Jude was caught off guard. He processed his shock and widened his eyes. "Okay. Thank you." He composed himself at the moment, but when he returned to his car, his face reflected the confusion rattling it.

He took the all-too-familiar trip home. The lights were off, and it was well past midnight, but Jude still felt tempted to knock at Preston's door. He sat in his idling car, words blending together in his mind. Each moment, he became more clueless about what to say and uncertain that he was doing the right thing. Impulse seized him. He put the car in gear and returned home, empty-handed and unfulfilled.

PROPHETIC IN WARNING

October 17th, 2000. Three days after the interview

Sitting at the bottom of the stairs, a bitter vapor coursed through Joe. Before he could ponder what could have been, Biscuit trotted up to him and dropped a pink rubber ball into his lap. Joe grinned. He scratched behind Biscuit's ears and around his head. Right as he was about to toss the ball, Fin approached.

He propped a suitcase against the wall and smiled. "Who'd have thought the creepy old basement dweller would be a dog whisperer?"

"They're man's best friend... after all." His eyes were heavy. "Let's not drag. It's time."

They led Biscuit into his crate and went outside. All the remaining Speakers lined up to wave Fin off.

Joe picked up Fin's bags. "I'll load up the truck for ya."

Fin nodded and began his goodbyes.

Jude saluted him. "The newsletter will live on without you, pal. I promise."

The two shook hands. "No one reads that thing, you know. But thanks."

Jury breathed deeply. "Are you certain you have to leave?"

"This is for the best, Jury," Fin said, looking at him respectfully. "It's not personal. I just have nothing to do here. Sure, taking care of the dog is something, but I could do that anywhere. I hate to think that I'm taking your space."

Jury frowned. His voice was excessively dour. "I'm sorry you feel that way."

Red rubbed Jury's back. "You don't have to apologize. Today's a special day." He turned to Fin. "We're happy for you. I promise"

"Hm." Fin smirked. "Thanks. It may not have been long, but I'll remember my time here fondly, even if we never spoke much." He suddenly looked at Jury in a new way, and his eyes hardened. "Although, I wish you hadn't used Spark as leverage during the interview."

Jury remained speechless.

After a few goodbyes, Fin climbed into Joe's truck and rode off into the distance, constellations twinkling in the evening sky.

When Fin was out of sight, Jude released an enormous sigh. He shook his head and went back inside. Everyone else followed.

~

As Joe pulled onto Fin's driveway, his grip around the steering wheel tightened. "Here, right?"

"Wasn't there a hole in the front window?" Fin asked. He exited the car and walked up to the house.

Joe followed with his hands in his pockets. "Oh, I replaced that. I also buried Spark. I would've waited till you were ready, but I didn't want him to rot."

Fin's eyes welled up, but he managed to suppress the flood. "You're a true friend, Joe. Thank you." He extended his hand.

Joe grabbed it and gave it a hearty shake. "I wish we could've talked more. But I suppose actions speak louder, as few as they may be." Joe looked from Fin to the window. "Sure you aren't gonna press charges? Some time may have passed, but I could still get proof."

Fin shrugged. A dead expression overtook his optimistic tone. "Justice for Spark sounds nice in my head, but I know Preston's dying. All he wants is to live forever, and he's gonna die without touching a soul. Honestly, that makes me feel great." He cleared his throat, and warmth came flooding back to him. "I may have thanked Jury, but you're the one who got me through it, Joe. Without you… I—"

"You would have pulled through." He looked at the sky above them. The sun was setting, and they bathed in its strawberry glow. "So, what now?"

"Hm. I think I'll call Akila. Try to get my old job back. I enjoyed what I did, you know?"

"I do. I'm sure she'll welcome you." Joe pocketed his hands and turned away from Fin. "Just do one thing for me: whenever life gets hard, no matter how heavy the sand gets, keep marching. Capisce?"

Fin nodded.

On that note, Joe left. As he drove, a disheartened look entered his face, and a single sentence echoed through his mind. *I may have thanked Jury, but you're the one who got me through it.*

Fin nudged the front door with Biscuit's crate in one hand and his suitcase in the other. He unleashed the dog into his new home and plopped onto the couch. Dust catapulted into the air, and he violently sneezed.

Watching Biscuit sprint from corner to corner reminded Fin of another dog who once did the same. After putting a leash on Biscuit, he went outside and saw the grave. The shallow plot of dirt was marked with a wooden cross that read: *Spark*. He imagined scratching the back of Spark's neck one last time. His mind filled the silence with a panting that wasn't there.

Biscuit approached the cross and pawed at a note behind it.

I'm sorry. -Progenitor

Attached to the letter was a picture of a young Fin holding Spark as a pup.

~

February 2000. 3 AM

Joe kicked open the door to an abandoned building, nearly separating it from its rusted hinges. His surroundings were illuminated only by moonlight. Glass from shattered windows lined the floor, along with debris and rotting food. Each step produced a crunch. Rats and roaches skittered beneath his feet. A faint whimper echoed from nearby.

His eyes widened. The pit in his stomach grew. *"Ariel!"*

Though quiet and unintelligible, another person was speaking through clenched teeth.

Pursuing the noises brought him face-to-face with his worst nightmare.

Ariel was unconscious. A bruise adorned her cheek. A man cloaked in darkness held her up, one hand across her neck, the other pressing a gun into her back.

Joe held his breath. "You're gonna regret that, Jeremiah."

Jeremiah stepped forward, revealing his face and the cuts around it. His greasy blonde hair was in a ponytail. His bloodshot eyes had different colored pupils: one brown and the other yellow. Muck and grime covered his eyebrows. Sewage dripped from his drenched, orange jumpsuit. Joe could smell it from across the room.

Jeremiah pursed his lips. "If you were smart, you would've snuck up on me. You're letting—"

"This isn't a game!" Though his mind raced, Joe remained down to Earth, "Put the gun down and let my granddaughter go. Do you even know her name?"

Jeremiah expelled a warm breath. "You should've quit poking around me and my family."

"That's my job, not Ariel's." His voice lost its stability. "Let. Her. Go. She's barely gotten the chance to live."

"It's fair. This way, I take from you what you took from me."

Joe advanced toward him with one arm extended, "Your family didn't have to die. It was supposed to be a regular bust! It's not my fault they started shooting."

"It's not *Ariel's*, either. I don't care. We made a deal!"

"They couldn't turn a blind eye forever." Joe's volume rose sharply. "I did all I could!"

Jeremiah caressed Ariel's hair and pinched her cheek. His lips were close to her neck. "Your Grandaddy did what he could, all right. He *could've* slaughtered each and every one of them, and that's what he did. You know what?" He looked back at Joe and eyed the red tint nearly covering his pupils. "I think he'd do it again, too."

Ariel released a muffled whimper through Jeremiah's palm.

Joe's chill demeanor was becoming worn. "They did it to themselves. I know it's hard to hear, and you miss your family, but the only way to end this cycle is to put the gun down and turn yourself in. It's the right thing—"

Jeremiah cut through his words with a fit of laughter. "You don't care about right and wrong! The only thing you give a shit about is this bitch here." An ethereal glint entered his eyes. "My family was reborn. No matter what happens, I will be free. I feel God's love in every breath I take."

Joe's eyes lost their light. "Take my word for it. How could God love someone so willing to end an innocent life?"

"That's your interpretation, but this is mine. I choose to believe that He's proud of me. I can't think of anything more inspiring than the love of something greater. One life won't change that."

Joe's hands began shaking. "You're wrong! Put the gun *down*!"

Jeremiah pressed the barrel into Ariel's temple. "What's the point? No matter what, I will be free."

Joe crept toward him. His hands were raised, but his eyes proved more piercing than a bullet. A feral growl entered his voice. "Ya think you're invincible? *You* won't be leavin' this room, not even in a body bag. But if you go one step further, your whore and the baby in her womb will *rot*. No interpretation necessary."

"How do you..." Jeremiah's pupils widened. With closed eyes and still breathing, he looked up, "No matter what, I will be free." His pointer finger tightened around the trigger.

Intense ringing in Joe's ears didn't block out the sound of Ariel collapsing against the concrete floor. For the next three days, Joe only saw red. He stayed true to his corrupted word, leaving an insurmountable trail of brutality and emotion behind.

~

The Basement. Present day.

Joe muttered himself awake. His eyes were empty, and his face sagged like a punctured balloon. His eyes wandered to a few loose pictures along the edge of his desk. Jury, Ariel, Larry, and Fin filled each panel. Though the memories triggered something, Joe stared at them without a twinkle in his eye.

Biscuit's pink ball rolled off his desk and bounced against his foot. He bent over to grab it and cradled it like one would a family heirloom.

"This is the point I'm at," he remarked, irritated and disheartened.

"It's a little cold to play catch, isn't it?" joked Larry, hands pocketed, as he approached. His voice was energetic and warm.

Joe dropped the ball and pivoted toward him. His voice lifted. "Hey, kid. How're you?"

He sounded as though this thought took the wind out of him. "I've been thinking about my future: getting a job and having money and stuff."

"Get a license first. You have your permit, right?"

Larry nodded. "Yeah. It's gonna expire soon, though."

"Then, I'll take ya to the DMV tomorrow."

Apprehension shot through him. He extended his hands. "Woah! I haven't driven since February. Shouldn't we practice?"

He batted his hand. "You'll drive my truck on the way there: that's practice."

"Why do you want me to get my license so bad?"

Joe lowered his voice and leaned in, "You need your independence. Bein' locked up here isn't healthy, let alone for someone your age. Besides, I got nothing better to do."

"If you want something to do, why not go upstairs and hang out with the Speakers? Why are you just sulking down here, alone?"

Joe drummed his fingers for a second. When he realized his answer, he hung his head. "Fin's gone, and with a license in your future, you'll be out in no time. I'm proud, don't get me wrong. But I don't have an out. No matter what I do, I'm goin' down with this ship." He pinched his lips, closed his eyes, and shook his head. "I'm sorry. I just wanna be more than a ferryman, ya know?"

"Uh," Larry rubbed the back of his head. "So what if you're a ferryman? You got me where I needed to be when no one else could. And even then, you don't have to do anything to earn your spot here. You're my friend. That's enough."

He looked at Larry with an uneasy smile. "Thanks, kid, but you had the right attitude from the start. I didn't do much."

"Well, all I did was listen."

"Exactly! I wish Jury would listen." He started chuckling. Light began shining through him. "What's he been up to, by the way? Things have been too quiet."

Larry crossed his arms. "Quiet? Jury? No!"

"You sound like you haven't talked to him."

"Since my parents died, I haven't. If I'm being honest, what you said about Mailugulism is still on my mind," Larry shrugged. "I don't want to face him without knowing where I stand. He'll convince me otherwise if I do."

"That's givin' him a lotta credit." Joe pointed at him, "I wouldn't be so sure. In a period of silence, anything can happen. Ever since the interview, it's been dead quiet."

Larry shrugged. "It's a nice change of pace."

He scoffed. "It's always quiet before a storm. I got a feeling somethin' is on the horizon." He propped up his head on his fist and stared at the wall. "Whatever it is, I'd give anything for it to happen soon."

ONE'S OWN DESIGN

October 21st, 2000. Night.

Thunder struck the Earth. Rain cascaded against the grass. Mallory looked around, threw her hood up, and approached a house shrouded in darkness. The house was one story taller than the others on the block, and the front yard was adorned with a tacky series of amphibian lawn ornaments.

Sneaking in through an unlocked window, she searched through shelves and knickknacks. With her nose buried in a drawer, a light turned on above her. She turned and saw the home's owner pointing a gun at her. Her skin turned white, and her breathing became frantic. She started crying and was too terrified to speak. Without warning, the man fired. A bullet rocketed through her left shoulder, and she collapsed to the floor.

Adrenaline surged through her, and she sprinted up the stairs. The man followed closely behind. Mallory reached the third floor and cornered herself in a room. Before she could hide, the man grabbed her by the neck. As the breath left her body, she procured a switchblade from her pocket and shoved it into his stomach. With a sharp scream, he threw her toward a window.

The brisk night air greeted Mallory when she crashed through it. Before her descent began, time slowed to a crawl. Mallory floated in place and reached for the purple moon. Glass sliced through her back, and drops of blood trickled into the sky. The shards sparkled around her, illuminating the grim fate awaiting her and her little stranger forty-two feet below.

Troves of neon blue jellyfish appeared around her, brightening the darkness as they swam into the sky. A single red leaf sat atop each of their heads. Mallory reached for each passing jellyfish, but they were always just beyond her grasp. Many passed, but none were strong enough to carry her. The stars rippled around them.

Mother Nature could no longer delay the inevitable. Time returned to normal, and the jellyfish disappeared.

It may have felt like Mallory was floating, but in reality, she plummeted to the ground immediately and landed, a blisteringly loud crack, with her leg pressed into her stomach. Blood exploded. Bones snapped. She writhed on the ground and groaned in agony.

With her adrenaline nearly depleted, she snapped out of her daze and pushed herself up. For a brief moment, she could focus on finding somewhere to hide rather than the bend in her calf or the blood running down her legs.

Only a few steps followed before the pain caught up with her. She fell to the ground and, by pushing herself up, caught a glimpse into a nearby house. The television showed a still image of Jury during the interview. She stared intently at him, unable to express her thoughts.

It was too late, but regardless, the wind became stronger. As her consciousness faded, Mother Nature assumed it.

~

Outside the Sturdy.

Mallory's legs wobbled as she leaned against the dumpster. The wind propelled her forward.

Larry tiptoed through the backdoor and saw her.

Her face relaxed. She exhaled, leaned her head back, and lost consciousness.

Larry threw open the basement door. He almost ran into Joe as he crossed the final step.

"AH! Almost gave me a heart attack. Did you forget somethin' kid? The ice cream place is–" The blood on Larry's jeans made his face drop.

Larry dragged him upstairs and caught him up. "I laid her down on the couch. She's conscious, but she's in bad shape, Joe. I just want you to be prepared."

"Don't worry about me. I'll be—" His eyes met Mallory's. Mallory's crimson hair reminded him of one person and one person alone. When combined with her battered exterior, it created a mortifying pattern. He stepped back and covered his mouth, his body violently shivering, his eyes hopelessly wide.

The hammering against their door was unlike any Jury and Red had heard. It pierced their sleepy haze like a bullet.

Red almost fell out of bed. He covered his bare chest with a blanket. "Should I hide? I don't have any—"

Jury shushed him. He hopped out of bed and answered the door.

Joe was pale. "We have a problem."

Jury grunted. "Sweet Mailugula, you look like you've seen a ghost."

"SHUT UP!" He straightened himself. "Sorry. Larry found the thief girl out back. She..." he took a deep breath. "She's in bad shape."

Mallory was sitting on the couch. Her eyelids fluttered, and she was unresponsive.

Upon seeing Mallory on the couch, Red rushed down the steps and dug his hands into his hair. "What happened!?"

Larry froze and pondered with wide eyes.

Mallory's consciousness faded once more, and she drooped over the arm of the couch.

Joe rushed up to her and dug his index finger into her palm. Relief partially washed over him. "Pulse is weak. Larry, go under the kitchen sink and get the window cleaner. The fumes should wake her."

Larry brought the bottle. Joe unscrewed the sprayer and waved the container beneath Mallory's nose.

Her eyelids snapped open. She sat up, her hands digging into the cushions for support. "How... did I get here?"

Joe practically jumped onto his knees, "Don't worry, honey. My name is Joe. I'm gonna protect you. First, you need to tell me what happened."

Mallory pressed her palm into her forehead and groaned, "I broke into a house and got attacked by the owner."

Red covered his mouth, muffling his words. "You didn't kill anyone, right?"

She began coughing up blood and red leaves. Then, her eyes cracked wide open. She wrapped her hands around her stomach. Her voice was muted and frantic. "I fell! I fell on my baby! Oh my God, oh my GOD!"

Jury, eyes wide, lurched forward. "You don't mean—"

Joe lifted Mallory to her feet. "We need to get her to a hospital *now*!"

Her cheeks then expanded. She covered her mouth with a clenched fist before vomiting into a trash can held by Larry.

Joe wrapped her arm around his shoulder. "Listen, I know someone nearby who can check you out. Okay? Jury, you're comin' with."

Jury remained speechless. His pupils were transfixed on an indeterminable point.

Red nudged him and wrapped his hands around Jury's cheeks, "Jury? Jury!"

The whites of Jury's eyes welled up with tears. The only sound he made was a scattered inhale.

Red was in awe. "I've never seen him like this."

Joe sighed through gritted teeth, "Havin' a panic attack, I bet. Larry, you come instead." He turned to Red. "I know we don't talk much, but I need you. Please get Jury upstairs and in bed. After that, clean up this room and stay quiet. Capisce?"

"Of course. Please be safe, Larry." Red hugged him.

Red had no choice but to be a pale beacon. For all he knew, Jury's heart became imbued with the same darkness that coated Joe, Larry, and Mallory as they left the Sturdy.

The clock struck midnight. Although not how intended, Progenitor's game was now past the point of no return. The boulder had grown too large. It passed over the final hump holding it in place and finally began its eternal roll.

STINGING SENSATION

October 22nd, 2000

"Finding another legacy," for Preston, meant "Do nothing and wait for a sign." Every morning at six, nightmares tossed him out of bed, and promises of a high-calorie breakfast dragged him into the kitchen. With a strip of bacon in hand, he collected the mail, squinting and hissing at the light before retreating inside. It had been three days since he changed his clothes and nearly a week since he had a conversation. The static plague in his beard extended down his chin, rendering the bread crumbs and dried peanut butter invisible.

Though his mornings stayed consistent, his afternoons depended on MeTV's programming. In just a week of retirement, he binged *Hogan's Heroes* and *O.K. Crackerby*. MeTV, in summary, became his lifestyle.

"I could get used to this." He muttered to himself, scratching the stitches in his chest while watching the leaves fly through the breeze. He was so absorbed in his indolence that he didn't realize his physical health was improving, contrary to what his doctors predicted.

Every so often, when he got tired of staring at Jude's empty driveway, Preston would surf the channels for any gossip on himself or Jury. It was the closest he ever got to a workout. He did about six reps before finding a station re-airing clips of his interview with Jury. Preston stared at himself as one would an imposter. Yet, he couldn't stop watching as he told Jury that *"No amount of pretty words will ever give anyone a purpose."*

"Why did I say that?" He scrunched his lips and wrapped his hand around his staticky chin. "My purpose *has* to be reporting. What else—"

An enormous crash interrupted him. His sliding glass door had been obliterated by a large box attached to a brick. Preston ran outside, passing over the shattered glass with his bare feet as if it was dirt in a greenhouse. The veins in his forehead writhed like a serpent on fire. "WHO DID THAT?!" He waited for a response. "Quit being a coward and terrorize me like a man! I will not hesitate to have a heart attack and DIE on top of you!" For the first time in a year, Preston didn't have to catch his breath after losing his temper.

After poking around his property and finding nothing, Preston returned to the package. He ripped off the attached note and tried throwing it into his backyard. Instead of blowing it away, however, the wind threw it in his face.

Looks like the silly little newsman lost his job. I left you a coupon for some free beer. It's from Mary's, in town. Visit their museum while you're at it, and see all the local figures who are infinitely more memorable than you ever will be. Maybe next time, Samson, make sure your rage is strong enough to topple the temple, and not just your faulty heart. -Progenitor

Preston peeled the note from his face and crushed the paper. He kicked open the package, finding a box of tissues, a coupon from 1940 for a free case of beer, and three bottles of Mary's finest liquor. Without hesitation, he created an alcohol monsoon, smashing each bottle against the wall. The sting of liquor and glass against his face chilled his body, and he stood zen-like as it washed over him.

Once Preston collected his thoughts, he felt invincible. He stood statuesque and proud. "For now, my purpose is finding this douchebag's ass and branding it with my boot!" He stepped outside, his flushed face glowing. "You hear that, Progenitor? I swear to God that I will expose you for the freak you are... AND THEN I'LL *KICK YOUR ASS!*"

~

Larry and Joe held open the Sturdy doors. It was a gloomy morning. When Mallory crutched in, no light accompanied her, only the smell of incoming rain.

Red greeted them. "Did everything go okay?"

Joe removed his coat. "Sorry for takin' so long." He turned to Larry. "Help her upstairs, kid."

Larry nodded and followed Mallory around the corner.

Joe waited to speak until they left his vision. "She insists she can make it up the stairs alone, but I ain't convinced. She's patched up, and the leg isn't broken, but she's still in rocky shape."

He shuddered. "What do you mean?"

Joe's voice was low. "She fell three stories. Landed on her stomach... with her knee pressed into it. We don't know if the baby's alive. Since we came in last minute, they didn't have time to check. But we're headin' back tomorrow for an ultrasound." He took a deep breath and sounded like he was cursing life itself. "Mallory doesn't deserve this. Not knowin' if the baby's alive is gonna torture her."

Red's positivity was overwhelming. "Well, we can help! How do you–"

"Thanks, Red. But she needs space." Joe smiled through his flustered exterior and put his hand on Red's shoulder, "I appreciate you. If ya ever need a break, let me know. You, me, and the kid'll go fishin'. It'll be fun. Anything to talk to you more."

Red returned his grin. "That sounds wonderful. Until then, you should go check on Jury. I got him talking last night. You were right, I think. He told me he was overwhelmed."

"I'm glad you could take charge when he wasn't. It's nice to see you showin' guts."

For a moment, Red sounded rehearsed, almost like a lawyer. "Oh, I wouldn't phrase it like that. Everyone freezes up sometimes. Jury's an emotional person, and he's been worried about Mallory for a while."

Joe furrowed his eyebrows. "Mallory's the one sufferin'." He hesitated for a moment but couldn't withhold his thoughts. With a weary, reluctant expression, his eyes met Red's. "I may be takin' charge, but you have no idea what I see every time I look at Mallory."

"I wish I did. I'm here to listen if you want to talk about it."

"I'm okay. Let's just say we're buddies and call it quits for now." Joe extended his hand.

Red spared no time in shaking it.

The two went upstairs and parted ways.

Joe opened Jury's door and found him sitting at the edge of the bed, facing away from him. His fingers were interlocked, and his head was down. The window was open. A subtle scent of smoke permeated the air.

"Uh," he knocked on the doorframe, "You rebootin' in there?"

Jury's head rose as he inhaled. "You're back sooner than I expected."

"Yeah." Getting acclimated to Jury proved a struggle for Joe. He sounded distant. "I see you're up and runnin'. What was last night about?"

"Don't concern yourself with it. We'll let that fade into history." His voice stiffened. "Tell me what the doctor said."

"We're not sure if the baby's alive. We're goin' back for an ultrasound tomorrow."

He pivoted his head toward Joe. "Does she know?"

"What? Why wouldn't she?"

"Well, I don't know what you told them. That could affect what they do and don't tell her. What *did* you claim your relationship was?" He fidgeted with his fingers and looked down. "And how did Larry handle it?"

Joe bit his lip. "Larry is fine, and I didn't lie. Why is that the first thing you ask?" He furrowed his eyebrows. "You know I cover my bases. I just told you the baby might be dead. Is that the only reaction you have?"

Jury barely sounded alive. "I'm worried to death. I'm also exhausted, as all of us are. I just–"

"You're not the one who's been up for thirty hours, ya prick!" Joe grabbed his collar and yanked him close. "Snap out of it! The priority is Mallory. Why are you so preoccupied with everything *but* her?"

Jury's voice suddenly became sincere. "I can't face her, not yet."

Joe drew Jury closer. "What the Hell are you talking about?"

"I told her everything would work out, and it didn't. I was wrong, and once you push a boulder down a hill, it won't stop until it–"

"Gimme a break!" Joe sighed and let go. Although each word out of Jury's mouth frustrated him further, he lowered his voice and continued, "You never told her that! She took what you said and did her own thing with it. Isn't that the value of interpretation you won't shut up about? You need to help fix this problem, not make it worse."

He released a long, stable exhale. "I should talk to Larry first. I don't think I have since that day we found his parents. Are you sure he handled himself well last night?"

"In one ear and out the other! Ugh!" He threw both hands into the air and turned away. "You stay away from Mallory. *I'll* take care of it. Just like I always do!"

Jury watched Joe storm out and slam the door behind him. He felt like a passenger in his own body as he watched himself walk to Larry's door and knock three times.

Larry opened the door. "You're alive!" He smiled. "It's been a while."

"It has." Jury widened his eyes and tried to blink away the crust surrounding them. "My apologies. I just wanted to stop by and check on you."

"Check on me?"

He closed Larry's door. "It must've been hard finding Mallory like that. Are you holding up okay?"

Larry sat on the bed. "Uh, yeah? So anyway, did you hear that I'm licensed and ready to drive?"

He sat and leaned back, awestruck, "That's right. How long has it been?"

Caution entered his voice. "Only a few days."

"That's still a big deal." Jury whistled. "Time moves so fast. I apologize for not keeping up with you better."

"No, it's fine. You have a life, too. I get it."

"Still, you know you can come to me anytime, right?"

Larry tilted his head and furrowed his eyebrows. "Sure. I could bother you more if you like."

Jury chuckled. "It's hardly a bother, Larry. You don't need to avoid me." Larry withdrew an uncomfortable breath.

Jury noticed but continued unfazed. "Heck, soon enough, you'll start working, saving. Maybe even getting your GED and going to trade school."

"Mm-hm." He clenched his fists and looked away.

Jury stared at him for a moment and, with a smirk, slapped his arm. "Hey. I'm just trying to be friendly. This whole conversation has been way too awkward. Am I interrupting something?"

"Well, I am pretty tired after—"

"Is it Mallory? Are you upset about what happened?"

Larry rubbed his heavy eyes. "I'm not six, dude. What's up with the baby talk?"

He scoffed under his breath and looked away. "I'm not *doting* on you, Larry. I just wanna know why you've been avoiding me. You're acting like we're strangers."

"I'm sorry, Jury. I shouldn't have drawn this out." He looked up at him. The twinkle in his eye flickered out. "I didn't know how to face you as a non-believer."

"As what?"

His voice became more sincere. "I'm sorry. I've just... never needed Mailugula. *You* were all there for me when I needed it."

Jury lowered his eyebrows. "You know religion is much more than an imaginary friend, right?"

Larry's mouth fell to the floor. "Come on, man. Don't be condescending. I know you're upset, but that's not what this is about."

"Oh yeah?" He pointed at Larry. "Without Mailugula, you wouldn't have a roof over your head OR your precious Joe! You owe more to Mailugula than you think. Whether they're here or not, their impact is undeniable."

Larry spoke in a more aggressive tenor. "I don't owe Mailugula anything! I don't owe *you* anything, either! Don't take this the wrong way, but I barely know you. We're friends, sure, but you don't bond with me like Joe does."

Jury sneered. "It all comes back to Joe, doesn't it?"

Larry's eye twitched, and his expression hardened. "Don't you *dare* talk about Joe like that! It's not his fault Mailugula does nothing!" He took a deep breath. "You have to be strong and accept reality. I feel like Mailugulism makes that impossible to do."

He crossed his arms and turned away from him. "That is your interpretation, and I'm sorry for making you feel guilty. I just wish you would have told me how you were feeling."

"So what? You could tell me I'm wrong? You're the one who said that opinions are one of the brightest beauties of this world, so why don't you appreciate mine?"

"It's unfounded. I think you're just bored."

"I'm not!" Larry snapped. "This is ridiculous. What do you think I'm saying? That Mailugula killed my parents? No! If anything, *I* did. But I won't think about what I could've done. There's nothing constructive in that. Just like how there's nothing constructive in what you're doing now." He stood up and glanced at Jury through the corner of his squinted eye. "Do you have any idea how hard it is to think positively? What gives you the right to come in here and derail that over your dying ego? Between the two of us, I'm not the one lying to myself." He gritted his teeth. "Now get out of my room."

Jury shook his head. Though he snickered lightly, goose pimples popped up across his arms. His blood had run cold. "Your room, heh. You're not a baby anymore, Larry. I agree. So, why don't you get a job? I bet Joe would *looooove* to write a resumé for you. While he's at it, maybe he can find you an apartment, too." He walked out, growling under his breath.

Although the cameras were silent, Joe knew what the argument had unleashed. He turned off his monitor and crushed a pop can between his fingers. While Jury's heart stopped, Joe's thumped a cacophonous symphony. He turned off his monitor and grabbed a few bottles of beer.

They might as well have been building the tower of Babel.

GOD

Later that night. The roof of the Sturdy.

Cigarette smoke lingered through the air. The tile at the roof's edge chilled Mallory's bare feet. Amidst the night sky, her poofy, crimson hair glistened. The bitter wind pushed against her stomach each time she leaned forward. Preparing for a long-awaited embrace, she closed her eyes and extended her arms. Her breathing intensified. When Mallory stepped to jump, a pinch at her shirt pulled her back. As she adjusted her footing, an empty bottle slid off the roof. She watched it shatter against the concrete.

"Isn't one fall enough?"

Mallory turned around. "Joe?! What are you doing up here?"

Joe was sitting at the back of the roof, his tired eyes staring at her. Although alcohol lingered on his breath, he wasn't remotely intoxicated. He opened another bottle of Mary's beer and flicked away the cap. His voice was soft. "Trying to get a glimpse of my favorite star." Joe smiled. "Wanna look together? Maybe you can bring me some luck."

She sat beside him.

He wrapped his arm around her shoulder. Light from the stars rained down. "Nothin' more beautiful than that."

She pulled away from him. "How could we have a normal conversation? You were just gonna watch me jump."

"I knew you wouldn't." He pointed to her stomach. "There's still hope."

Mallory stared into space, away from Joe's glance. "In what? If I actually cared, I would've stopped robbing houses the second I knew I was pregnant. I don't deserve a family." She fought a losing battle against a steady stream of tears, "And having to wait to hear what I already know makes everything so much worse."

"Ya made a mistake, Mal. We all have. But to say ya don't deserve a family? Come on."

The stars no longer shone upon them, and they bathed in a new wave of darkness. "It's my fault! *I* put everything at risk. I was selfish. But... why did he have to be so brutal!?" Her tone was emotional and erratic. She raced through her words. "I stopped when he caught me. I put my hands up, dropped everything. And he *shot* me! He chased me up the stairs, threw me out a window! Yeah, I fought, but he didn't have to put me in that position. He was obviously stronger!" Mallory shakily wiped the tears pouring from her eyes.

Joe handed her a handkerchief and spoke in a voice as desolate as the sky above them. "People are given a choice, yet they always choose the most brutal option. It's human nature. Seems like that's all I've learned in this life." Despair lingered in both of their eyes. Joe sighed. "This might sound like a copout, but everything happens for a reason. You survived because ya still need to find your truth, and only you can find it, not Jury, Mailugulism, or some idiot upstairs. All ya need is enough motivation to last till tomorrow."

She sighed. "Who am I kidding? No matter what happens, I'm stuck living in the past. How could I possibly prepare for the future?"

"Hmmm," his eyes floated to the sky. With the stars on hiatus, all that remained was the moon. Joe pointed at it. "Isn't the moon the most beautiful thing?" He paused. After realizing Mallory wouldn't respond, he continued. "Millions of people around the globe look at that same Moon every second of every day, and each person interprets it differently. Obviously, there aren't multiple moons, but if ya only look at ours in a single way, ya might miss the sheer beauty and majesty of the thing. I think," he gulped, "I think you could say the same thing about *God*."

His words rattled across her mind, and suddenly, all tension left her expression. "The moon?" Mallory raised her head, "Do you believe in Mailugula?"

"Do you?"

She sounded bitter. "Not after being scolded by Jury. I did what he asked. It's not my fault it wasn't what he wanted."

Joe raised his bottle and clinked it against the air. "That's why I stay in the basement."

"Wait," Mallory eyed him up and down. "Are you what Jury was hiding in the basement?"

He chuckled. "Did he make it sound that corny?"

"No, it sounded more like y'all were hiding a dead body."

"Eh. I'm hidin' a few-a my own." He looked at Mallory. "Everything takes time. You can experience relief if you're patient and strong. But on the other hand, downfalls don't happen overnight."

"Hmm..." she looked into the sky, struck by a realization, "Neither do upswings."

Joe winced. "Good sentiment, terrible wording." A tint entered his dark eyes. "For the record, I believe in your dream. That means more than you realize."

Mallory sighed. She laid her hand across her stomach. "I may not be in the right place, but somewhere down the line, I *do* want a family. I'm just worried that this is the only chance I'll get. Even if it does work out, with all this trauma, I'm worried I'll make a mistake."

His sonorous voice overrode all ambient sounds as it rolled across the rooftop. "The thing about sin, Mallory, is that you can atone for it. There's a balance to it. Some aren't willing to put in the effort, and some put it in the wrong places. But as long as you focus and try, you'll be better off."

She never thought to question his authority. She was in awe. "How do I atone?"

"Get a job. Save some money and find a community college. Study education. You'd be a good teacher."

"Huh. Why did I never think about that?" She looked at him with a new sense of appreciation. "You're so much more direct than Jury. How come you're not in charge?"

"I couldn't answer that without puttin' ya to sleep."

Mallory yawned and stretched her arms. "You're already doing that, old man. Do you mind if I go to bed?"

"No. Let me help you inside."

A skylight in the upstairs hallway was the only way in and out of the roof. Mallory felt like she was floating as Joe lowered her back into the Sturdy.

Before heading inside, Joe took one last look at the sky. A dark cloud passed, and behind it was an apple-red star. It was shaped like a leaf, and a straight line of light emerged from each edge. He grinned. "My little Mother Nature." His eyes welled up, but before he could shed a tear, he looked at Mallory. His expression evolved into a sense of determination, and he followed her back to her room. "Anything else?"

She crawled into bed, facing away from him. "Can you sit with me for a while? Just until—"

"Of course. Tomorrow's gonna be here before ya know it. Your dream will live. I promise." He covered her and watched her crimson hair scatter across the pillow. Sleep quickly consumed her.

"Damn," Joe whispered. "I've spent so much time lookin' in the wrong places." The twinkle in his eyes became fire. "There will be Hell to pay if that woman's dream is shattered." He stared at Mallory until the shapes and colors between her and Ariel blurred for good.

THE FERRYMAN'S TOLL

The Following Day. Pontifex Catholic Hospital.

Only a moment seemed to pass from their talk on the roof to the present moment. A part of Joe knew what was about to happen, but he still had hope, though not as much as Mallory.

Her heartbeat overpowered the hospital's ambient noise. When the doctor entered, time slowed. Her grip around Joe's hand tightened. With one sentence, her world stopped. A high-pitched ringing in her ears blocked out all attempts at comfort. If Joe hadn't been holding her, she would've collapsed. She sobbed, and yet, Jury was the only one who didn't hear it. She sank into an abyss, and he followed close behind.

During the ride back, Mallory went from sobbing to despondent. Joe relentlessly tried comforting her as they walked through the Sturdy doors. "Mal, please!" She brushed past him.

Joe followed her around the corner before realizing his power only spread so far. As he tried to walk away, the mural over the podium caught his eye in a way it hadn't before. It was a combination of circumstance and perspective. Regardless, he saw the jellyfish as it truly was, and it infuriated him. No amount of color or symbolism could sway him otherwise. Without a prayer in his head, he approached Jury, who sat against the front door.

The bags under Joe's eyes burned. Between his coarse breathing and dry voice, there was no light in him. "I'm worried, Jury. Everything is wrong, and I can't change it anymore."

Jury's glazed-over eyes sparkled like a black hole. "It hurts, right? Telling someone that they'll be okay, only to be agonizingly wrong."

Joe's voice was low and still. His eye twitched. "You know what? There's somethin' we need to talk about." He grabbed Jury's arm and dragged him into his office. "Just about every day, you're askin' me if I believe. Want my answer?"

Jury remained cautious. "I understand we've been fearing this outcome for months, but don't get so caught—"

"That's the thing. I've thought about this." His unsteady voice wavered. "Night after night. Year after year. I've *tried*." He stared Jury square in the face and took a deep breath. "I do not believe in Mailugula."

"Why tell me this now, with everything I have on my plate?" Jury asked.

"Don't act like ya don't wanna hear it. I know this keeps ya up at night." He crept toward Jury. "I've always disagreed, but I chose not to give a shit. Now that you're hurtin' people, I can't."

Jury scoffed and crossed his arms. "That explains why you never stood up for us."

"Us?" Joe threw his hands in the air. "Quit referrin' to this place like it's a country. These people aren't unified. For cryin' out loud, you divide 'em more every day!"

He batted his hand. "That is your interpretation—"

"NO! That is you bein' an asshole!"

Flustered by a wave of shock, Jury stumbled over his words. "I have had good intentions this entire—"

"Shut up!" Joe's face was growing red. "Why should I let you speak if all you do is pump out questions? It just makes it more obvious that you know *nothing*."

That slapped Jury awake. He straightened his posture and his tone. "Questions are the only thing you're leaving me with. How else am I supposed to respond to such over-the-top criticism?"

"Results!" He pounded his fist into his palm. "Mailugulism didn't support Mallory. *I* did! And honestly," His breathing became less steady, "I didn't care. I *wanted* to help. I was as selfish as you, and all I did was build her up to let her down."

Jury slouched and wrapped his palm around his neck, "That's not your fault, Joe. If anything…"

Joe's speech became frantic. "*No.* You could always argue that I'm at fault, that I *let* this happen."

"What do you—"

"It doesn't matter! I've been wearin' a false face for too long, and it's gettin' to me." Frenzied shame washed over him. "I *can't* be a ferryman forever! Larry, Fin, and now Mallory? They can still find meanin' in their lives, but they are undeniably worse off because of *us*." He hit his chest as hard as he could. "I need to step in, Jury. I need to stop people from gettin' hurt instead of tryin' to heal them after."

Jury's tone bled confidence. "If we're counting corpses, Mailugulism has helped far more than it's slaughtered. Christianity has—"

"Please." He sounded hollow. "Don't bring other religions into our mess." He sat down and put his head in his hands. "Who am I kidding? The dirt Mailugulism grew from was cursed. I don't know what to do to plug up this ship anymore."

Jury growled. "I don't *want* your help. Have you ever thought about that?"

Joe's jaw dropped.

"If you had stayed in the basement, none of this would have happened!" He threw his hands up in the air. "God! You didn't help anyone! All you did was take them away from this institution."

"I took them? I. TOOK. THEM?!" Joe's voice bounced off the walls and pierced Jury like bullets. He ruthlessly moved from one sentence to another without taking a breath. "Larry is a stranger to you, and you forgot about Fin at every turn. I had to be there for 'em when it was your decision to bring 'em in, your nonsense that struck 'em down! I did everythin' you *should've*."

Jury opened his mouth, but Joe pushed him against the wall and held him there. "You are as close to a false shepherd as it gets, and your Mailugula is toxic. Just because you think something is missin' from *your* world doesn't mean it's missin' from everyone else's! You're just dressing up self-awareness as a religion, and it's not!" The room around them began to tremble as Joe's voice rose to a crescendo. "These people are *lost*! And it's not Mailugula that's the problem. It's you, you self-indulgent, messiah *wannabe*."

He released Jury and looked at his hands. After shaking away a look of disgust, he walked to the doorway and turned his head. "And you are a terrible partner. The way you treat Jared makes me *sick*." He entered a brisk walk and passed Larry on the way.

"You okay, J—"

Joe brushed past him and ran out of the building. Larry was speechless.

Jury felt like he'd been strangled. He released short, shallow breaths and could not narrow his widened eyes. "No... I can help people. I just need to try harder." Instead of processing his feelings, he began making grand plans for the next Session.

~

Later that night.

After finishing a late shift, Akila locked up HNN headquarters. It seemed quieter than usual outside. No cicadas sang, no engines roared, and no crackheads shrieked. Before she could wonder, the sound of chains scraping against the brick exterior startled her. She could tell the sound was coming from behind the building.

"Okay, that's weird," she muttered and searched the backlot. Almost immediately, she found a package leaning against the dumpster. Given its size, the box was unexpectedly light. It was barely heavier than the note attached.

Don't overcomplicate what I'm giving you. - Progenitor

Countless cassette tapes and photographs waited for her once she sifted through the packing peanuts. She pulled out a video and examined its title: *Bribing the priest.*

She dug through the box and pulled out more: *Jury lets a thief escape; Jared crying outside of Larry's door; Jude discovers Fin; Jury rips apart a Speaker; Jury yelling at Jared; Jury and Red fighting outside hospital; Another argument with Jude.*

Without further thought, Akila brought the box home and examined its contents for the remainder of the night.

FAME

Though the alcohol faded from his wall, its impact on Preston lingered. He climbed out of the bathtub and visualized his sins drifting down the drain. He set up shop in front of his mirror. While combing his hair, he noticed the static plague had silently infested his roots. A part of him felt more masculine as a result. He shot himself with finger guns and slicked back his hair. "Is this the cover of Playgirl magazine or Preston Epalit's mirror? The world may never know."

The revolver called to Preston. Its force spoke more than its weight, like a penny falling from the Eiffel Tower. Massaging its cool exterior soothed nerves he didn't realize were frayed. He holstered it in the back of his jeans. "Meh. I am a celebrity, after all."

Ostentatious over his flimsy existence, Preston charged through the saloon-style doors of Mary's. While searching for beer, he exaggerated his movements as much as possible. A long time passed before he realized no one recognized him. "Am I dead already?"

After trudging through line after line of beer and soda, Preston's quest concluded. Countless packs of Mary's Finest sat on the bottom shelf. He grabbed one. Then another. And another.

Preston glared at the young cashier, who tried desperately to avoid returning it. "Did you find everything okay, sir?"

His tone was more inquisitive than arrogant. "Do you know who I am?"

"A customer of Mary's?"

"Preston Epalit. Jog any bells? What about the RBLA?"

She subtly shook her head. "I'm sorry, sir," and handed him the receipt. "Will that be cash or–"

Preston shoved Progenitor's coupon in her face.

She examined the coupon front to back and looked at him with a bewildered expression. "Sir, this coupon expired sixty years ago."

"Scan it anyway."

She shrugged and complied. The register made an affirmative click. Her jaw dropped.

Preston smugly grinned.

She smiled. "Your total comes to twelve dollars."

"WHAT!?"

"You bought two other packs, sir."

"Oh." Preston calmly replied, removing cash from his wallet. A realization struck him, and he put his palm on the counter. "I almost forgot. Do you have any customers named *Progenitor*? He's the one who gave me that coupon."

"Not that I know of. Okay, sir, have a nice—"

"Listen! That man challenged my reputation. His name is Progenitor. PRO. GENITOR. Maybe he goes by an assumed name. Like, Peabody or something." He slid five dollars toward her, "I bet this'll jog those bells."

She sighed and slid it back. "My condolences for your reputation, but I can't help you. Please leave."

"You know what? The manager should know. Go ahead and get him."

The customers waiting in line were growing impatient. "Hurry up!" urged one, "I'm going to miss HNN."

In an instant, Preston's eyes became bloodshot. He turned to the crowd, "Who said that?"

A feeble, old woman scrunched up her nose and raised her purse to her chest. "You already paid, you bully. Get outta here."

His voice rose with each step he took toward her, "You would not know good reporting if it slapped you across your gullet, Grandma."

She squinted. "You talk a big game for someone about as thick as a ham sandwich. Who do you think you are?"

Preston stood face to face with his geriatric rival. "Who am I? Who are you!? And when will you start aging with a little grace?"

The woman swung her handbag directly into Preston's nose. Her purse was so heavy that, had she missed Preston, she would have flown across the room. Blood spurted out of Preston's nose as his head shot back. He began preparing to tackle her. While assuming the position, his shirt moved up, and the cashier saw the gun poking out of his buttcrack. She jumped out of her skin and pointed at it.

Before Preston could move, two fed-up buff guys from the back of the line intervened. They each grabbed one arm and dragged him out the back door, the employees' cheers echoing behind them. From there, they tossed him into the dumpster. "Hope you had fun losing a fight with a Grandma," remarked one of them.

Preston's arms were stronger than their scrawniness suggested, and he pushed himself to a more comfortable position. Festering in the trash, he felt like mushrooms in a field of grass. After sitting for a moment and taking in the stench, he realized he belonged. "Christ... what am I doing?" The blood from his nose dripped onto his fingers. He stared at it. "My purpose isn't fighting the elderly. But is it even being a reporter? I did everything to be remembered, but no one cares. I guess I should have been honest instead of entertaining."

A disembodied voice pulled Preston away from his monologue. Despite being easy on the ears, it was husky and untrustworthy. Each word was elongated to an absurd degree. "Don't just sit there. Come on, take my hand."

The person behind the hand was the physical personification of a grease trap. His blonde, slicked-back hair looked wet. It complemented his sky-blue eyes and pale skin, making his stern face handsome in a Charles Bronson way. The man's hands were perfectly still, save for the occasional twitch of his massive calluses. Had Preston been vigilant, he would've noticed that the man never took a single breath. He only inhaled when he took a puff of a never-ending cigarette.

After looking him over, Preston pushed away his hand and climbed out. "Sorry, I did not mean to take your spot. I know what it looked like, but I was reflecting, not injecting. But do not let me stop you." He felt around his pants for his revolver but couldn't find it. Each pat was more frantic than the last.

The man grinned with his entire face. "Lookin' for this?" He held the revolver with his index finger and thumb like a smelly piece of cheese.

Preston gasped and grabbed it, nearly pulling the trigger. After realizing it was his, he sighed in relief, practically moaning, "Thank you. You have no idea how much I appreciate this. I promise I am not one of those weird gun people, by the way. It just..." he shrugged, "means something."

His ribs protruded through his black tank top as he laughed. "*Heh heh*. You're a character, Mr. Epalit. Name's Hyde." He extended his hand once more.

Preston now felt compelled to shake it. "Finally, a man of culture." He pointed at him with raised eyebrows and a smile. "Are you a fan of my work?"

"Sure. Listen, I'd love to sit here and listen to your best and worst hot takes, but *I* hear you're lookin' for Progenitor."

"He broke my sliding glass door. How else am I supposed to look at the deer? Go outside? Ha!" Though his words were rude, he was sincerely curious. "Hold on. Why do you care? What can you, of all people, offer me?"

The smoke billowing from Hyde's cigarette jived to the rhythm of the wind, "You have no reason to trust me, but you also don't have a reason to not trust me. What harm could supportin' a small-time entrepreneur like me do?" He rubbed his thumb and index finger together.

"You do not need to make a case for yourself." Preston looked him over, eyes squinted, "And yet, you did. I respect that." He reached into his wallet, "No meth with this money, all right? The homeless problem is the last thing I want to fuel."

"Pft." He snatched the money. "A little egotistical, aren't we? You don't know where I live, but with the spiral you're goin' down, you're bound to visit. I mean... a granny put you in your place, man. Is that how you wanna be remembered?"

Preston frowned and met Hyde's gaze with a thoughtful expression, "No. And I do not want to be remembered as an egotistical fool, either."

"Then listen." He leaned forward and lowered his voice. "I tried to steal a package from the Mailugian's doorstep a few months back. I would've taken it and ran, but I got distracted by this weird note. By the time I finished readin' it, I heard one of the Mailugula people nearby, so I bolted."

Preston rubbed his chin. "Hm. Who sent the package?"

"Some guy named Progenitor."

The grand implications of that reveal did not ruffle Preston's feathers in the slightest. All he did was grunt, unamused. "Chessie and I both got packages, huh? Interesting. Did you see if the package had a–"

"Return address? Yes, it did. But that's not–"

"For real?!" Preston nearly jumped out of his clothes. "What was it?"

"Don't you wanna know what the note said?"

"The address! What's the address?"

"It was some rundown hotel called The Ranger. It's out in Golgotha. Just drive down Parkland Avenue for a while. Ya can't miss it."

He snickered giddily. "Oh! This is wonderful." He paused for a moment. "Wait. Isn't that where Chessie had his vision?" He peered into the ether.

"You sure you don't wanna hear about the note?"

The gears turned. Preston was consumed in his thoughts.

Hyde covered his mouth with his hand. "Heh heh. Well, thanks for the money, Preston. Without people like you, snakes like me would never rise."

~

In the middle of the night, Red woke up feeling parched. While walking through the refectory doors, he stopped at the sight of Jude sitting alone in the darkness. His head was down.

Red remained in the doorway. "Jude?"

Jude rocketed up and into attentiveness. "Oh! Hey."

He turned on the light switch. "What's up?"

"Nothing. What about you?"

"Just thirsty. Want me to get you a glass of water?"

Jude nodded.

Red sat across from Jude and set a glass of water in front of him.

He grumbled, "Thanks," before slouching and sighing. "I'm sorry."

Red was genuine, as always. "For what? You don't–"

"I do, though. I do." He took a sip and looked at Red. "I've been nothing but an anchor. And I see you opening your mouth. Don't say it."

Red laughed. "I'm going to say it anyway, you know. You're not an anchor. You say what you think needs to be said, no matter what. It's admirable."

"If my heart was here, then I wouldn't care. It's just..." He scratched his neck and glanced out the window. "I should hate him."

"Preston?"

Jude sighed. "Look, I think both of us know I don't belong here. At first, I put on this passionate front, but it didn't last. Especially with the discovery of Fin and what Preston..." he ran his hand across his face and grunted. "I should hate him. I really should."

Red tilted his head. His voice was gentle and optimistic. "You *should* hate him, but you don't. You could say that about a lot of things in life. Jury may put me through a lot, but I still love him more than anything. Heck, I owe him the world, so–"

"*You don't owe that man anything.*" Jude's eyes lost all light. His stern expression bordered on frightening.

Red looked like he had been shot in the back. A terrified smile was plastered across his face. "Huh?"

His voice was gravelly and dark. "You heard what I said. You don't owe anyone anything for making your life better. Thinking that way is inhuman. The only thing you 'owe' is a thank you." He lifted his glass, "He may have pushed you up a few steps, but you're still falling."

With a pale expression, he sank into his seat. "I'm sorry."

"That's your problem. You're sorry, but you shouldn't be." Jude didn't realize the relevance of his words until they left his mouth.

Red bit his lip and glanced away from him. "Well, I think you already said what I wanted to say. So, I'll leave you be." He finally shook away his bleak expression and smiled. "Don't feel like you have to stay here, Jude. You have our support no matter what. Or, at the very least, mine."

Jude smiled back. His voice returned to its casual norm. "Thanks. And Red? It's none of my business, but will you at least consider what I was trying to say?"

"Oh..." Red looked away again and gulped. His tone remained positive. "I really appreciate you trying to help, Jude. I'm sorry you—"

"That's okay. Goodnight." Jude shook his head.

JEKYLL & HYDE

November 1st, 2000

While Preston divided everyone, Jury conquered nothing. He was so rattled that he fumbled over the slightest bit of planning. Every idea led nowhere. When he wasn't brainstorming himself into dead ends, he stared at the door, waiting for Joe to enter through it.

As Session time rolled around, he felt a lack of piety. From his messy hair to baggy eyes, the professionalism typically flowing through him was absent. The smaller than average crowd didn't help, either. Without Preston stoking the flames of outrage, fewer people were being drawn to Mailugulism as regular visitors moved on. What it lacked in size, however, it compensated for with volume. Discussions between guests were more frequent than usual. They were stirred mainly by Akila, who asked everyone their thoughts on the latest Sturdy news. Jude caught a glimpse of her, but before he could approach her, Jury ascended the podium.

The pit in his stomach grew as he addressed the audience, "It's... been a hard few days at the Sturdy."

He sounded weary and cold. "People say that it's okay if things go wrong, that failure is necessary and refreshing. But that doesn't stop it from being absolutely exhausting, especially when it happens nonstop." He chuckled and shook his head. His tone underwent a frantic, helpless transition. "Things will always get better. Mailugula will make sure of it. But... how do you know that? Sometimes it feels like Mailugula or God or whatever isn't there, but I can assure you he—" he took a deep breath. "*They... they...*"

Akila's ears perked up. She pulled out a notepad and started writing.

Jury's voice trembled. "It's hard not to know things, but eventually, you *will* sense their presence. All you need is faith that everything will work out. Things fall from the sky more than we realize. It's a question of when, a brutally helpless feeling. But if you believe you can be better, then you will. Mailugula can make things better... even if I can't." He looked up and saw that his audience was unified by confusion. A family sitting next to Akila quietly rose and left. A few individuals followed. There was a hint of worry in Akila's expression, but she continued writing.

Jury rubbed his head. "Oh, God. What am I doing? I deeply apologize for my nihilistic rambling. It's definitely time to pass the baton to another Speaker." Each Speaker either avoided his glare or shook their head from side to side. He frowned. "Apparently, no Speaker has anything to say. I shouldn't be surprised. So, is there anyone in the audience who—I don't know—needs advice or help?"

His musings garnered no response. He glanced around the room and found someone who piqued his interest. He was a heavyset, short gentleman, dressed like a stereotypical English teacher, plaid sweater vest and all. His beard burrowed into his collar as he looked at the crossword puzzle in his lap. Jury pointed at him. "You, sweater vest."

Red put his head in his hands and whispered. "What are you doing, Jury?"

Jude raised his hand. "I know you're having a bad time, Jury, but don't be rude. If we need to end early–"

"Quiet!" He gritted his teeth. "I'm *talking* to Mister Sweater Vest."

Akila feverishly wrote every word. She signaled to an HNN employee in the back, who pulled out a hidden camera and started recording.

Once someone nudged him, the man looked up. The bewilderment on his face was immeasurable. "Is there a problem, Mr. Chessjurist? "

"What's your name, professor?"

He furrowed his eyebrows. "Simon. I must ask again, is there an issue?"

Jury pursed his lips and raised his eyebrows. His tone switched from resentment to sophistication. "Not at all. I'm just wondering what brought you here today. Is there any problem I can help you work out?"

Every spectator was uncomfortable. The Speakers were unsure how to handle the situation and sat helplessly as the boulder kept rolling.

Simon adjusted his glasses. "I'm afraid not. My reason for coming here is simple. Sometimes I have little to do around my home, and listening to you speak is quite enjoyable. You're a good speaker, you know."

Jury was disgusted. "Gee, I sure hope I am. But, there's so much more going on here than just people being bored, right?" He looked at the crowd. After a moment of silence, all life vacated his expression. "That was *not* rhetorical. If there's a time to ignore me, it sure as shit isn't now."

Akila pressed the tip of her pen against the notepad and stared at Jury, shocked, as did the rest of the audience.

Jury scoffed, "I'm not here to entertain! There are people out there who are suffering! I'm here to help them, and I can't believe we have guys here just loafing around like I'm doing stand-up! I—" He sighed. His tone became despondent. "What's the point of all this? Joe was right. Go home, everyone." He walked offstage.

Silence followed. Then, *relief*. It was Larry who broke the tension. He stood up and grabbed the microphone. "I'm sorry, everyone. Jur—I mean, Mr. Chessjurist is having a very bad day. It doesn't excuse his behavior, but I'm still sorry you all had to see that. Please don't let this impact your week. I speak for my fellow Speakers when I say that a week-long break from Sessions, starting now, is a good idea. Thanks for your patronage, and I look forward to seeing you all next week!"

As the guests stood up, Akila rushed over to Jude. After quick salutations, they mixed into the crowd. Jude looked at Red, and Red gave him a nod and a smile. Then, he and Akila left.

Red didn't feel pride for Larry's maturity. Instead, he felt hope that his words would come true and that this day wouldn't mark the beginning of the end.

~

That Night.

Without Joe around, Larry had few means to distract himself. As a result, trying to find Joe became his priority. He wasn't willing to wait and decided to take a more assertive approach. For the past three nights, he had been sneaking out to investigate the parking lot of the ice cream shop. Larry banked on Joe's words ringing true.

"She told me about how they'd come here whenever they were havin' a bad day. I do the same, too, usually in the middle of the night. Some weeks, I spend just about every night here."

It was an excuse to wander around town and loiter as any youth should. It was also an opportunity to escape the Sturdy and think.

After three nights of nothing, Larry was tired of Scarwood's rural spectacle. Upon realizing Joe's truck was again absent from the ice cream shop, he didn't know what to do next. His eyes drifted to the entrance of the woods, which was illuminated by a single, flickering light. "Perfect place to be murdered," he shrugged. "If I die... oh well."

The forest wasn't as desolate as the time of day suggested. Light posts were scattered across the path. Numerous shadows were cast, none of which resembled animals. While walking, he avoided crushing red leaves.

A gruff, gravelly voice pierced through the darkness behind him. "What's a kid like you doin' out here so late?"

Larry swung his head.

Light from the tip of a cigarette illuminated the man's face. He had greasy blonde hair and wore a black tank top. He sat on a bench, legs crossed and arms outstretched.

The speech patterns were familiar, but the voice was not. Despite the circumstances, Larry's guard was down. "Just... looking for a friend."

The man took a long puff. "No one here. Go home."

"How would you know?"

"It's dangerous out here. You may not know it, but Scarwood has a big crack problem. Also, from this here bench, I've heard the roar of a *chupacabra* more times than I can count."

"That's probably just the crack."

The man's eye twitched. "Shut it, ya brat." He flicked away his cigarette and stood up. "Buncha bullshit. Just beat it already!"

Larry stood still for a moment and looked truly bewildered. "I'm sorry, who are you?"

He bit his lip. "Name's Hyde. Like the guy from the book."

"Thanks, dude. I thought you meant the verb."

"Smart ass." He began walking but stopped midway. "If searchin' for that idiot has brought you out here, then he ain't worth shit. Rip off the band-aid and quit chasin' ghosts. You're too damn young." Hyde continued walking and didn't stop until he was out of Larry's sight.

Larry, eyes wide, shook his head. "God, these crackheads are getting weirder and weirder. I wish he would've just murdered me."

DISILLUSIONMENT

Without a clear thought in his mind, Jury knocked on Mallory's door. Perhaps he intended to overturn a string of bad luck or validate a dying ideal. Still, the baggage under his eyes could only express so much.

Mallory sensed that something was wrong immediately. "Um, are you okay, Mr. Chessjurist?"

Jury was pale and in a sleepy daze. "I'm fine. Mind if I come in?"

The smell of smoke emanated from him. Mallory turned her nose up. "Sh... sure."

Jury walked inside and noticed an unopened bottle of water. Relief washed over him. "Thank God. Can I–"

"Go ahead."

He swallowed a huge drink, "Ah," and continued without taking a beat. "Excluding the obvious, how're you?"

She sat and stared into the ether. "Lost."

Jury sat in front of her and held her hands. "You shouldn't be afraid to live without your dream, Mallory. For now, you just need to find something else, which is much easier done than said. I'm not saying you need to find a new purpose right this second, but you at least need to find some hope." He visibly struggled to find his next words and looked at her through his bloodshot eyes. "Mailugula keeps our purposes vague because we have multiple callings in life. The best advice I can give you is to just live. Soon enough, you'll begin hearing different calls, and it'll be your choice which ones you answer."

Mallory tried chuckling away the growing tightness in the air. "That's nice of you to say, Mr. Chessjurist, but I don't want a different call. I just want to forget."

"I know you're upset, but don't neglect your options. If you're that desperate, you could always adopt."

Her frown grew tighter. "I don't wanna hear that. Why would you..."

"I'm doing the best I can, Mallory."

She was being as polite as she could. "I don't *want* your help. Just let me be miserable for now."

Jury's expression underwent a devastated transition. He turned away from her. "There are some things we can't do alone. Think about it. There has to be a way Mailugula can help."

"Forcing it will only make it worse. At this point, what could Mailugula do for me that I can't do alone?"

He raised his eyebrows. "People around here tend to forget this, but Mailugula did offer you shelter."

"No. That was *you*!" She scoffed and began pacing around the room. "If Mailugula is as good as you say, then why did they let this happen?"

Jury was struggling to remain congenial. "Because that's not how Mailugula works."

Mallory's bottled-up discontent exploded. "That's how I *want* it to work! You say Mailugula will always be there, but what's the point if they can never be bigger than me?" She took a deep breath. "*I'm* the one struggling. *I* lost something. Why are you making this about you, about something that obviously isn't there, when you haven't lost anything?"

Jury covered his mouth and glared around the empty room. "I can't believe you said that. You just challenged everything I stand for, and for what? I'm trying to help you come to terms with your discontent."

"And have you come to terms with your discontent, Chessjurist?"

"I…" Jury stammered for a few moments. "I lost someone once, too." He lowered his head. "That's why I can't bring myself to leave until I've uplifted you somehow."

"Okay," she sighed, "I know your mom died. But didn't that happen like ten years ago? Pain doesn't go away, I know, but you're acting like she just died yesterday."

He released a scorned chuckle. "She might as well have! But that doesn't matter. On paper, you lost something way worse than me."

"On paper, but not to you. Is that what—"

"Come on! Argh!" He pressed his hand into his temple. "You're acting like all I can do is…is…" all energy left him. His eyes popped. He weakly uttered, "Lead. Astray."

Jury's emerald irises gradually faded until all that remained were still, empty pupils. He rose, zombified, and wandered out of the room.

Mallory went downstairs to grab another water bottle. While in the refectory, she caught a glimpse of Larry. He was sitting near a window at the corner of the room, staring at nothing. From afar, he looked a bit like a chipmunk. His cheeks were full of food. His gaze remained unshaken as Mallory slowly approached.

She rapped on the table. "Whatcha lookin' at?"

Larry jolted in place and pivoted toward her. His mouth was still full. "*Whash up, Maruree?*"

Mallory burst into laughter and covered her smiling face.

He swallowed his food without chewing and grinned. "Ha. Sorry. What's going on?" He motioned toward the chair in front of him.

She sat and retained a sunny demeanor. "Not much. You're... Larry, right?"

"Yep. I'm happy that you're up and walking around! Joe would be, too."

Mallory chuckled. "If you hadn't found me out there, things would've been way worse. So, from the bottom of my heart, thank you. I've been meaning to say that."

He failed to suppress a blush. "Aw. You did most of the work, managing to get here and all. So, if anything, thank yourself."

She smirked. A hint of sarcasm shined in her voice. "You know, while I'm thinking about it, what were you doing out so late? You don't seem like the kind to sneak out."

A playful light flashed across his gray eyes. "I don't seem like the kind to want some peace and quiet? You've noticed by now that Jury's turned this place into a circus."

"Ha, yeah. He seemed so professional on TV and during Sturdy stuff, but in person? He's so... so..." She snapped her fingers.

"Man-childish?"

"Yeah!" Her quick burst of energy faded into something more sensitive. "Er, I guess. You make it sound like you don't like him."

"I mean, he's all right, just the kind of guy you need a break from." A sudden wave of somberness tore through his demeanor, "Joe must feel the same way." Larry snapped back to attentiveness. "Sorry. A depressing conversation is the last thing you need."

The joy in Mallory's face faded.

Larry began speaking more cautiously. "So, have you been sleeping okay lately?"

Mallory remained silent. She glanced away from him.

A more happy-go-lucky vibe entered his voice. "You know what? Let's get some ice cream. It's not a long walk. Some fresh air did me good when—"

"Stop." She looked at him, eyes hollow. "There's nothing anyone can do or say to make me forget what happened. Don't even try."

"Well," Larry leaned back and crossed his arms, "I won't. I definitely won't. Because I don't think you should forget."

On a surface level, Larry's words captured her. She was curious but unconvinced. "What do you mean? Why wouldn't I want to forget?"

"I'm not saying you should never move on. I'm saying that you should live for those who can't and try to learn."

"Learn? Well, I'll never rob a house again if that's what you mean."

"Mm." He thought for a moment. There was a gravitas to his words. "Even if you think what happened is your fault, it's not your responsibility to chase ghosts. You have to live in the present. As awful as this is, it can change you for the better."

"Huh," Mallory paused, letting Larry's words settle. "Chessjurist didn't word it that way."

"Because Jury has no concept of forgiveness."

Although Mallory was thinking, she sounded vaguely annoyed. "Well, what if I don't, either?"

"It's something you have to learn, but here's what I think. If you can't find what you're searching for, all you need to do is look from a new perspective. Imagine loss like a necklace always snug, not a weight to be forgotten."

In three sentences, Mallory's perception was shattered. In three sentences, Larry said more to Mallory than Jury ever had.

A burden on her heart eased. Her posture straightened. Peace came to her, yet she didn't show it. She couldn't, she thought to herself, "Because there is more to be done. I don't need to atone."

Mallory's relief rubbed off on Larry. An innocent smile was splashed across his face.

They talked for the rest of the day, regaling each other with stories of days gone by. From their memories, they found solace.

Despite the price of this lesson, Mallory was still grateful. Although wounds still persisted, she now felt motivated to heal them. She felt like she could finally grieve, and to do that, the Sturdy was the last place she could be. That night, she gathered what little she had and left.

Against all odds, Mallory experienced relief, despite her acidic perception of Mailugula. Even with this, it was hard to feel optimistic. Recovery is unpredictable, and the patch is always smaller than the wound. Her despondency may have faded, but her rage had not. Everything reminded her of what she had lost, and when she realized nothing could bring it back, her attention turned to what had taken it.

FINAL ACT:
AND HE SHALL APPEAR

THE RAGE

The Golgotha desert sat in the center of Pontifex County. It provided transport between towns while devouring whatever air its scattered vegetation produced. It was more of a parasite than a rejuvenating core. Yet, many throughout history sought to profit off of its strategic location. But no business bore fruit. Settling in Golgotha proved ruinous. Many abandoned buildings remained, serving as a warning to those who aimed to cultivate its hallowed, private grounds.

With its flashing, technicolor letters, the Ranger's sign was more appropriate for a casino. The motel itself was considerably less glamorous. Each of the two floors had six rooms. Everywhere you looked, there was a chip in the paint or a beetle on the wall. There were more cracks in the foundation than furniture in the rooms.

In recent years, the N and second R fell from their post and smashed into the ground. No one removed them, and thus, Mother Nature reclaimed them. The detail and color had been washed out by sand. The occasional spark revealed sporadically appearing red leaves.

Preston slammed on his brakes to make the entrance. He stared at the incomplete sign and lowered his sunglasses, "The Rage, huh? I would feel the same way if I had to spend a night in this dump." He turned to the vacant passenger seat, as if someone was sitting there, in search of a laugh.

Preston stopped in the middle of the empty parking lot. A pair of sky-blue eyes peered at him through a window on the first floor. When compared to the barren desert colors, they shined like headlights. The blinds closed, and Hyde emerged. His tweed suit was patchy and rustic like a bale of straw.

Preston remained in his truck. "So, is this where you like to crash?"

"Yep." Hyde put his hands in his pockets and looked down the road.

He thought for a moment and squinted. "You know Progenitor, don't you? Does he own this place?"

"You could say that."

Preston stepped out of his car and leaned over the open door. He looked at the building again. "I understand why Chessie is so traumatized. If I had to stay in a Hellhole like this, I would have visions, too. Why doesn't Progenitor fix it up?"

He yawned. "Who would stay at a hotel in the middle of the desert?"

"Well, the desert's called Golgotha, not Jericho. That already scares off your religious market."

Hyde was already sick of Preston's nonsense. "Ask Progenitor yourself. They're waitin' upstairs."

"Oh! Thank you." Preston removed his sunglasses and peered at Hyde's suit. "You clean up well. What is the occasion?"

"Today's a special day." He grabbed his lapels and thrust them forward. "Progenitor doesn't meet just anyone. You should've dressed up."

Preston looked down at his gray sweatpants and tight t-shirt from the 1984 election. He sardonically responded, "I do not care if I am meeting John Wayne or the frozen corpse of Walt Disney. Clothes do not make the man. That is a stupid expression."

"Maybe you should show a little more respect to the one who–"

"Has been lining my pockets? That does not make him better than me." He extended his pointer finger. "Do not tell him I said that, though."

Hyde gave him a long, mindful stare. "Is that so?" His voice was cold and gravelly. A chilling wind blew around them. "*Think.* Without them, Preston, ya'd never be *alive*. Let alone famous."

"Famous, ha." He put his hand on Hyde's shoulder. "Never said I wasn't thankful, Hyde. Bastard may have broken my screen door, but I am in a better place because of him. I'm in reality, albeit a romanticized version. Now, can I *please* meet him?"

With a grinding of his teeth, Hyde led Preston upstairs. He pointed down the hallway. "The big kahuna is waitin' behind door three." Before Preston turned, Hyde stopped him. "Hey. Before we never see each other again," he pulled Preston's cash out of his pocket and threw it on the floor. "I don't need this. You may be an ass, but I'm still happy I got to meet ya."

Preston grunted and picked up the money. "Okay, uhhhh... you too." He began walking, but Hyde's words resonated. He couldn't remember the last time someone had shown him kindness. Although he couldn't face Hyde, he balled his fists and gathered his words. "Th... thanks, Hyde. I have been thinking, and it was not right for me to make jokes about you doing drugs. I fade in and out whenever I speak and usually end up saying something stupid, but you made my dream a reality. So, what I'm trying to say is..." He finally gained the strength to face Hyde, but as soon as he turned, he realized Hyde had vanished. He smiled. "I'm sorry."

The door was ajar. Preston pushed it open, but before he could look inside, a blunt object smashed over his head and sent him crashing to the floor.

~

The disembodied voice of his mother rang through a dark abyss.

"If you ever get lost, light this lantern, and I promise I'll find you."

With his lantern in hand, Preston found himself stranded in a pasture of purple and white. The purple light from his lantern illuminated the area around him. Microphones with four legs grazed on newspaper grass. A familiar voice from afar whispered, "*Purpose*" repeatedly. The sound bounced from microphone to microphone, becoming louder and louder until Preston's head was ready to explode.

Then, with one clap, the darkness lifted, and Jury appeared in the distance. His body was limp, and he jumped into the horizon like a puppet grabbed by the strings.

Preston tried chasing him, but the ground began swirling back and forth like jello, making him lose balance. He dropped his lantern, but the flame remained lit.

A vivid mist appeared above him, and Preston basked in its rainbow glow. He felt nostalgic for something he never had and longed to be somewhere he had never been. He stared into the sky as the vapors aligned, forming visions of his future.

"*I should have given her more credit.*"

"*A miracle?*"

"*If anything, he betrayed you.*"

"*You broke your promise.*"

"*And I am willing to burn in Hell because of it.*"

A gunshot echoed from behind him. An unknown power held his eyelids open and pointed them at Jury. The bullet rocketed through the sky and into Jury's chest, and he disappeared in a lemon glow.

Then, the flame in Preston's lantern evaporated, taking his existence with it.

A sonorous voice echoed through a dark abyss. **"Kill him, Preston. End this game."**

Preston's eyes were snapped open. Light filtered through his eyelashes as he returned from realm wandering. The revolver somehow jumped out of his jeans and onto the ground in front of him. Except for a framed picture of Chessjurist, the room was barren. Preston looked from the revolver to Jury and gasped.

As he drove off, although The Ranger disappeared from view, the *rage* did not.

~

For the first time in months, rain fell on Scarwood. Larry still set out undeterred, even with Hyde's words ringing in his mind.

Tonight, something was different. The air felt heavy. Larry knew the way, but somehow, he couldn't regulate the tempo or direction of his steps. The breeze around his ankles just seemed stronger. Instead of the usual pitter-patter, the rain sounded like a metronome.

The make, the model, the color: Larry saw everything at once. A dead ringer for Joe's truck was parked in front of the building. Its crimson coating glistened through the storm like a lighthouse. Smoke flowed out of the exhaust, obscuring the license plate and back window.

Larry didn't feel grounded in reality. As he approached the vehicle from behind, he felt like he was floating.

The rain moved from drizzle to downpour. It was loud enough to muffle the sound of the engine thrashing alive. The truck began backing out. Larry snapped out of his trance, and his feet returned to the ground. He shouted and waved to no avail. Without knowing if the truck belonged to Joe, he ran and jumped into its bed.

Larry sat in the back of the truck. Darkness and rainfall obscured his view. He couldn't see where they were going or the silhouette behind the steering wheel.

The truck abruptly stopped on the side of the road, knocking Larry over. As he pushed himself back up, the rain stopped, and his vision cleared.

Joe eyed the house to their right. It was the tallest in the neighborhood, sitting at three stories. Amphibian lawn ornaments decorated the yard. He maintained a leather-denting grip around the wheel that made the veins in his hands squirm like drowning worms. The usual glint in his eyes was absent. He didn't breathe or blink. After a few moments, Joe grabbed something from his passenger seat and marched to the front door.

Larry peered around the side of the truck and realized that Joe was holding a silenced handgun. Mystified, he stared, searching for a semblance of Joe he recognized.

Joe pressed the barrel against the doorknob and reduced it to scrap. His breathing became more intense when he stepped inside and ascended the stairs.

Being detached from Mailugulism didn't exempt Larry from its consequences. Mother Nature latched onto him like a body snatcher. He climbed out of the truck in a daze and followed Joe inside. A tranquil melody conquered his thoughts. It reached a new crescendo with each step until he stopped just before the final flight of stairs. From his perspective, Larry could see the hallway wall and the side of a door frame. The light from the room illuminated the hall, but the inside was out of view.

Smoke clouded his pupils, and wool filled his ears. Under any other circumstance, Larry would see the truth. However, Mother Nature had different intentions.

The voice of a young female then became clear. It was firmer than a bastard's noose. Although quiet, her resolution boomed through the house louder than the gunshot that preceded it. It slithered down the steps with frightening sonority.

"You will *die* for that."

Joe's silhouette halted in the doorway. A toxic jolt ran through him. "Ariel? I MEAN—" He gasped, swinging one hand over his mouth and the other on the doorframe.

Mallory's voice was heartless. The gun in her hand was smoking. "Why are you looking at me like that? There are some things I can't forgive, Joe."

The mind-bending shock on his face was sweltering. "I... I..." The only thing keeping him upright was his grip on the doorframe. He hung his head. "I'm sorry I didn't cast judgment in time."

Just when he thought his losses were innumerable, Joe saw Larry standing at the bottom of the stairs. He rushed toward him, tripping over nearly every step.

At that moment, Larry regained consciousness. Mother Nature sent the gunshot through his ears at that very moment. Without seeing Mallory, he assumed Joe was the culprit and stumbled out of the house. The shock reached his legs, and he collapsed to the ground. He coughed up a mixture of red leaves and mucus.

Joe burst through the front door as Larry pushed himself up. He shouted over the storm. "It's not what it looks like!"

Larry staggered away, his gray, shivering eyes fixated on Joe. His tears painted lavender stains along his face.

Joe breathed heavily. "How can ya not believe me? Didn't ya hear?"

Larry ran.

The water on the ground amplified each step. Larry didn't need to look back because he could hear Joe getting closer. Street after street:

not a soul was in sight. His sobs made it impossible to keep a consistent pace. With nowhere to run, he wiped his face and grabbed a sharp piece of wood from a nearby trash heap. He turned around and, holding it with both hands, pointed it at Joe. "Stay away from me!" He lunged it toward him.

The streetlight illuminating the confrontation flickered in and out.

Joe sounded like he was about to sob. "You don't have to do this, kid." He raised his hands to shoulder level and approached Larry, who brandished the plank more aggressively the closer he came. "Words are deadlier than that. *Please* drop it."

Larry's widened, feral eyes communicated what he couldn't verbally express.

Joe's face was writhing with pleading and guilt. "Don't look at me like that! That wasn't just anyone! That was the man who threw Mallory out the window." He put his head in his hands and sat on a curb. "I needed to do something. You saw what he did to her. It's because I waited too long to act!"

Larry was shouting. "You still had options!"

"That's why it's my fault!"

As the streetlight above them dimmed, Larry became more emotional. He threw the plank down. "What happened to you? When my parents died, you told me that things could always get better. You didn't believe it, I could tell, but you still had hope." He bit his lip, trying to compose himself, but the tears kept falling. "I can't have hope for you anymore. You've been worried this entire time about the morals of Mailugulism, but in the end, you're no different than the monster under every child's bed. Dormant until provoked. God." His tears glimmered among the rainfall, and his voice broke. "As *much* as I *love* you, I can't. I—" Larry fell to his knees.

Suddenly, the streetlight above them flickered out. Larry seized the opportunity and fled.

When the light returned, Larry was gone, and Joe hadn't moved. He wiped his bloodshot eyes and covered his mouth. *Dormant until provoked,* echoed through the catacombs of his mind. He looked at his hands and realized they trembled for the wrong purposes. "I thought I was immune."

A final item remained on the list. No amount of grief could change that. After returning to his truck, he drove to a pay phone and dialed Jury's office.

The ringing woke Jury, who had passed out over his desk. He picked up the phone. "Yes!? Who is it!?"

It took him a long time to answer. "Joe."

The rain beating against the glass made it hard to hear, but Jury recognized the timbre immediately. "Oh my God. Where have you been!? Are you coming back?"

"I called to..." he sighed, "to say goodbye. And before you interrupt me, I have news. M—" Joe bit his lip and shook his head. As much as it rattled him, he knew what he had to do. "I found the man responsible for the death of Mallory's child... and I killed him. I have the right. I have *every* right. And I'm gonna start reclaiming them."

Jury dropped the phone.

Joe hung up. He took a deep breath and punched a hole through the glass booth.

THE BIG CARNIVAL

Akila straightened the papers in front of her and aimed her eyes into the camera, "Good morning, Pontifex. Recent events in Scarwood have made my peers and I realize that our usual format won't do today's subject justice. So, we decided to try something new, with exclusive coverage on an issue that has been hiding under our noses for God knows how long. Stay tuned, and stay seated." A drab, low-effort intro followed. It was a fifteen-second montage of reporters in the field, capped off with a logo reading "Reaping What They Sow with Akila Hatem." The screen faded back to Akila.

There was a hint of anguish in her voice. "Not much time has passed since the Sturdy opened its doors in Scarwood. In the early days of Mailugulism, Preston Epalit tried discrediting it and its founder, Jim Chessjurist, at every turn. These feuds and attempted scandals were mostly brushed off. But if you look past his poor choice of words, perhaps Preston wasn't as far off as we thought."

Viewers from across the Bible Belt states leaned closer toward their televisions, watching with bated breath and widened eyes.

"HNN has received a large number of tapes and photographs that show a dark side to Chessjurist. Hints of this dark side were evident during the last Session." Footage of Jury ridiculing Simon started playing. "Where Chessjurist exploded at a guest and stormed offstage, leaving the Speakers fumbling and the guests confused. But as our tapes show, this behavior is not uncommon."

Tantrums and shady-looking dealings played one after the other. Akila's voice became more business-like. "The tapes may be silent, but their contents are still clear. Many tapes show Chessjurist berating staff or document activities that we, without context, cannot explain. But one tape sticks out as being particularly shocking. It shows Chessjurist grabbing a priest by the collar and his associate attempting to bribe said priest into silence. We reached out to this man for a comment."

Abraham Wingjer appeared on screen in front of Pontifex Catholic Hospital. "He made me feel very afraid and disrespected."

The same people who watched Jury's inciting sermon with intrigue now felt cheated and stuck up their noses at the thought that Jury may have had something. Akila's words stirred countless emotions throughout the Bible Belt states, even from those who hated Jury from the start.

A smug half-grin spread across her face. "We would've had no way of knowing if any of this were true... if not for our secret witness. Our investigative reporter Jude Ariotics stayed under Chessjurist's roof. Without him, we would never have been able to legitimize the data given to us. This is what he has to say regarding the matter. Jude?"

Jude took center stage and smiled into the camera.

~

Broadcasting across the Bible Belt states, HNN's first exposé brought meteoric ratings, the likes of which Preston never fathomed. He sat in his doctor's office, transfixed on Akila's program.

"Mr. Epalit!" exclaimed his doctor. "Don't you have a television at home?" She shut it off right as Jude was about to speak and turned to him, arms crossed.

Preston snickered into his palm. "I told Akila that Jude was a snake, and she used that to her advantage." He was practically gushing. "I should have given her more credit."

"Mm-hmm. Anyway, Mr. Epalit–"

"You don't have to call me that, you know. You make twice my salary, easy."

She squinted. "Uh, thanks? Can you just tell me how you've been feeling since our last visit?"

"Uh, I no longer have the stamina of an overfed cat." He checked the time on his watch, which now fit snug. "My appetite has been decent, too. Why?"

"Well, it's interesting." An inquisitive edge entered her brogue. "The results line up with what you said. You've regained weight and color. It's significantly better than anything we expected."

Preston's face was blank, save for his eyes darting from side to side. "Okay? I beat your expectations. Now what?"

She chuckled lightly, "No, no, you don't understand. You have improved *rapidly*. What you had doesn't just disappear. I have never, in my entire career, seen such strong improvement. How'd you do it?"

"I found a purpose."

She narrowed her eyes. "Oh. Is that how it works? But I thought you loved the news."

Acceptance flowed through him. "You would think, but no. After a lifetime of searching, my purpose has been revealed to me. It... oh, let me put it like this. It is like a light from above. You suspect nothing of it, but then, you look up," he snapped his fingers, "and it overpowers you."

"Well," she closed his chart and looked at him, "You may need a mental evaluation, but physically, you're cured. It's a miracle."

Her words struck a pressure point. Preston was astonished. "A miracle?"

"That's underselling it, honestly. Oh, and about the static coloration in your beard, it's nothing to worry about. Does it itch or bother you?"

"Not at all." He stroked his chin. "It looks slick, right?"

She furrowed her eyebrows, "It looks healthy. That's what's important." She started chuckling, "I'm sorry if I sound unprofessional, but this is an anomaly. Do you mind coming back next week for some more tests?"

Preston rose steadily. "Respectfully, Ma'am, I need to spend the time I have left fulfilling my purpose. Thank you for your time." He tipped an imaginary hat and left.

Her jaw dropped.

As Preston strolled through waiting rooms and elevators, patients and visitors pointed at him with surprised murmurs. He felt untouchable, but something kept him focused. Jude's voice echoed through the halls, beckoning him from a television near the entrance. He asked for the remote and flipped through every news station he knew. Almost all of them were covering HNN's exposé. Preston felt an explosion of pride. Before long, inspiration struck.

Light streamed in through the windows around him. In a sea of sunshine, Preston glowed. "See you soon, *partner.*"

~

When Larry awoke, he was lying on a bench on the nature trail. He felt oddly well-rested and rose up while blocking out the sun with his hand. Clearing the haze from his eyes, he noticed a warm blanket of leaves wrapped around him. After a quick stretch, he brushed them off and followed a trail of cigarette butts to the Sturdy.

From a few blocks down, Larry could see a mob of reporters wanting in and Speakers wanting out. Squeezing through, he was bombarded with questions and cameras.

"Why have the Speakers been silent for so long?"

"Have you been abused, as well?"

"Does Chessjurist have any comments?"

"Are you Chessjurist's son?"

"What is your opinion of the recent news?"

Larry was about to burst. "WHAT NEWS?!"

A kind reporter dragged Larry out of the crowd. In exchange for him answering a few questions, she caught him up on the situation.

Jury peaked through his office window and sneered. "Well, look who decided to show up." He poured a tall glass of wine and sank into his chair.

Red rushed in. "It's a madhouse, Jury! People are leaving faster than I can count! I can't find Larry, Mallory—*anyone*!"

"Tch, don't worry. Larry's out there selling his soul." He took a swig of his liquor and pointed at Red. "Look, if the Speakers are this bothered by another lame RBLA scandal, *I* don't need them."

He eyed the alcohol. "Jury, we really need to talk."

Jury rolled his eyes. "The last person I need a critique from is *you*."

Larry entered the room and exhaled in relief.

"Speak of the devil." Jury took another drink.

Larry ignored him and turned to Red. "Can I talk to you?"

Red put his hands on his hips. "Where have you been? I was w—"

Larry grabbed his arm and pulled him into the hall. His voice was quiet but firm. "What has gotten into Jury? The entire Sturdy is on fire, and all he can think to do is get drunk?!"

"Is it as bad as it looks out there?"

"It's a freakshow, Red!" Red opened his mouth, but Larry shushed him. His tone was commanding and convincing. "There's more. I've been sneaking out the last few nights to look for Joe, and last night, I found him. Long story short, he ended up murdering the man who attacked Mallory. Then, he chased me around the entire subdivision. I'm lucky I escaped. It's hard to believe, but..."

Red ran his hands through his hair and began pacing aimlessly. "No, it's not. It's everything I've been afraid of." He snapped out of his paranoid stupor and turned to Larry, eyes aflame. "Did he hurt you? Was—was he coherent at all?"

A million thoughts ran through his head. "I honestly don't know. All I know is that he snapped. There's no telling what he's gonna do next."

He put his hands on Larry's shoulders. "You're right. We need to get out of here and make a plan. Go pack a bag and meet me back down here, okay?"

"Capiche. What are you gonna do?"

His determination was unwavering. "Try to bring Jury back."

EXODUS

No light shined through the window in Jury's office. The repeated flashes of cameras outside synthetically brightened what the sun refused to touch.

Red closed the blinds and turned to Jury. "We have a problem."

Jury put his feet on his desk. "Yeah, I can see that. If I listen closely, I can hear it, too."

"Will you please listen?" Red took a deep breath. "Joe found the guy who hurt Mallory and killed him. L—"

"I know."

His expression and voice stiffened. "Jury," he paused. "How do you know?"

"Joe called last night." His posture straightened, and his voice became lighter. "And you know what? I'm grateful."

"Grateful?" Although Red struggled to process Jury's words, he knew he had to stay focused. "What does it matter, Jury? We should go to the police. I know this is an emotional situation, but what Joe did was the most brutal option. You, of all people, should know it goes against everything Mailugulism stands for!"

Jury rolled his eyes. "Mailugula stands for nothing, okay? Joe rose up and took action. *He* did something that I can believe in."

"I don't know why we're talking about Mailugulism because there's something much more important." Red cleared his throat. "I don't think you're aware, but Larry saw everything because he snuck into Joe's pickup. Joe tried chasing Larry down, but he got away. Protecting Larry is the priority."

Jury lowered his legs and leaned toward Red. "He's not in any danger. He's practically a son to Joe. Now that Larry's disowned him and that he's disowned me, there's nothing left for him here. If I had to guess, Joe's gone."

Red released quick, pent-up breaths. "Think about it like this, then. What if Joe gets caught and implicates us in the crime? What if he left something behind that gets traced back here? Wouldn't it be a good idea to cover our butts and go to the police anyway?"

Jury rubbed his aching head. "Joe may be impulsive, but he's not stupid. And I know a lot has happened, but have you forgotten the whole 'Ms. M' thing? Who knows what kind of sentence Mallory'll be slapped with? Us too, for sheltering her."

"Even if we don't go to the police, we could at least leave *town*!"

"Oh no. The Sturdy would go down in flames the second I leave it. Besides, look behind me." Even through the closed blinds, flashes of light periodically broke through. "With all those cameras, we're safer than ever, but our *reputation* is not! Attaching us to a murder scandal would be the final nail in the coffin. And why would I want that when I agree with what Joe did? It was for Mallory."

Red scoffed. "Joe did *not* do this for Mallory! Tearing into her wounds isn't charitable. He's just using this as an excuse to chase ghosts, and so are you."

Jury crossed his arms and blew out his breath impatiently. "What's the point of this argument, Red? I already told you what I'm going to do."

"And what is that, Jury? Nothing?!"

He scoffed. "That's what I should've done from the start. Without the Sturdy, Larry, Mallory, and Fin would still have what they want, and we wouldn't be in this hopeless *rut*. We don't help people! All we are is a sight for tourists and idiots to gawk at."

Red was becoming increasingly concerned. "Jury, this is not about Mailugulism. Mallory was bound to get hurt. She needed a serious intervention, not to be placated by us."

"I was supposed to help her, Red. Me! Mailugula *was* the intervention."

"And Mailugulism isn't for everyone. Don't you know that by now? Don't you know that no train of thought is perfect?"

Jury bit his lip and looked away. "Mailugulism wasn't passed down through ages and eons. Everything went wrong right here, right now. I have created a parasite, nothing more. To say otherwise would just be a *crock*."

"Jury..." Red reached for Jury, but Jury pulled away.

The cramped office never felt tighter. Red felt the walls closing in on him. He started sweating, and his voice became rushed and desperate. "It all comes down to the fact that we can't save everyone, and that's *okay*. But you know who we can save?"

"Don't say Larry. Don't you *dare* say Larry. He has nothing at stake. We could go bankrupt tomorrow and nothing would happen to him. I'm struggling here, Red, and all you care about is that kid! It's ridiculous."

"I have every reason—"

"No, you don't!" Jury exclaimed, losing his temper at last. "*I* lost a mother, too. If he's so hurt, maybe he should talk to me instead of abandoning me! That's what you wanna do, too! That's all this is! And then to say something stupid like, 'we can't save everyone.' How dare you? You sound just like those assholes at my mother's funeral."

A mocking edge entered his voice. "'There was nothing we could've done.' 'Everything happens for a reason.' Yeah right! It didn't help then and it doesn't help now."

Red bit his lip and, as if that released all his anxiety, he planted his feet and stared Jury down. "Jury, I'll only say this once, and if you get offended, I'm sorry. Maybe my mother was right: dancing around the truth won't solve anything. Today's the day it stops. I–"

"Spit it out!"

The birds stopped chirping. The cameras quit snapping. Red and Jury ceased breathing. All background noise was terminated, leaving only Red's voice. "Stop using your trauma as an excuse."

Jury lowered his hand from his mouth and widened his eyes.

Though these words had been brewing for years, speaking them aloud hurt Red more than he could fathom. He held his heart and winced. "I know you're in pain *every day*, but that doesn't mean you can be a jerk. None of this is for your mother's sake, Jury. None of this even *relates* to that."

"So you're saying I'm selfish?"

"No, I'm saying you're delusional."

His words were an earthquake that shocked Jury's feeble foundation. He started shaking. "You're right." He rose from his seat and aimlessly wandered to the window. With each word, his voice became less energetic. "I don't care about Mailugulism. It only suggests change, and in a world like this, suggestions mean nothing. I just thought it would make the world care about people like us. That's how I rationalize what Joe did: justice in an unfair world."

Red rested his palms against the desk and leaned toward Jury. "We can talk and talk, but there are priorities." His voice became gracious and patient, completely losing all frustration. "I understand that this affects you, but it affects Larry more. He watched someone he looked up to *kill* someone. How is he supposed to handle that when the deaths of his parents are still fresh in his mind? There's a lot going on, but caring for the person closest to us is the priority. I've never been more worried, Jury. And I'm not ashamed of that. It's the way I am, and it's taken me a while to say this, but I'm proud of my empathy."

Jury was floored. He spent a moment brewing in anger before responding. "It's *the way you are*? Oh my God." He chuckled. "That's all you've ever cared about. The second I can't stop you from pitying yourself, you look to Larry like he's some beacon of peace and justice. The way you *pretend* to see yourself in him is sick!"

Red's jaw dropped. "I never saw myself in him." He bit his quivering lips and spoke in a soft voice. "I only saw you."

He gritted his teeth. "You can pretend all you want, but I don't care. He's no son of mine."

All life left Red in a single breath. "*He's no son of mine?*" His eyes started watering. "Well, I will not make your father's mistake. I am going to be there for my son. With or without you."

Jury could no longer look at Red. He turned his head, "No one's asking you to stay."

Those words spilled a pot that had been brewing for almost a decade. Red chuckled. A long-repressed revelation overtook him. "You know what I just realized? Nine years, and you've never been anything but an entitled, *fucking* prick!"

In the blink of an eye, the color drained from Jury's face.

Red began losing control. "Every time you say you'll get better, you don't! **I'M SICK OF IT!**"

Jury shrank into his seat and covered his mouth. "Red, I need you to calm down and lower–"

"**NO!**" Tears fell, causing his voice to break and falter. "I have been a loyal, loving partner who has done *everything* to make you happy! But what have you done in return besides break my heart? You've never changed, and you never will. It's all been a lie." His face was drowning. "**A LIE!** *I hate you.* What did I do to deserve this? *Why*?" Grief overpowered his words as his overflowing eyes met Jury's. "WHY?!"

Jury looked over his shoulder at the curtains. "You're having a panic attack, Red. Calm down! I appreciate what you're trying to do, all right? The sooner we calm down, the sooner we can move on and fix this. Okay?"

Red wiped his eyes. His voice became frighteningly calm. "I sacrificed nine years of my life for you, and I don't plan on wasting another second. Go to Hell, *Jim*." He turned around and marched out.

Jury rushed after him. "Red, wait! I can change if you give me more time! I promise!"

Blood chilled, Larry was waiting in the Session area. On instinct, he followed Red outside.

The paparazzi had tripled. They were clawing through each other to get a view of Jury chasing Larry and Red.

Jury pointed at Larry. "I can't believe you, you ungrateful snake! I took you into my home, for God's sake! The least you can do is—" Every camera flashed at once, blinding him. By the time his vision returned, Red and Larry had escaped.

Jury raised his red, sweaty hands to his face and gazed at them. Rain drops splattered against them, but he didn't feel it. He breathed in and out. He did everything he could to suppress the flood, but it wasn't enough. Jury collapsed to the wet ground.

After getting a few pity shots of Jury crying in the dirt, the news teams began trickling out.

The image of Jury sobbing on the grass spread across the news like wildfire. Whether they saw Jury as a pariah or a prophet, they now saw him as he truly was and changed the channel for good.

STIPULATION

As Preston drove home from the hospital, something warmed the blood his resolution had chilled. His plan faded into the background. He slapped his cheek lightly. "Come on, old man. Do not lose sight of—" His eyesight moved from the road to the ether.

Nothing bound Preston to his father. He accepted that as he grew up and didn't dwell on it. But looking back, he lamented how his fridge never displayed the achievements of a child. Whenever insomnia hit, he'd visualize himself sitting at the foot of his youngster's bed, reading conservative fiction aloud until they both fell asleep. It was the one thing that always made Preston smile.

Only after losing everything and moving to Scarwood did things start looking up. Soon after buying a cheap piece of real estate and meeting Jude, magnets became a daily purchase. The fridge was loaded with newspaper clippings, photos, and promotional materials. Jude was the common thread tying them together, more so than RBLA. Whenever Preston would look, no amount of conceit could wipe the prideful smile off his face.

His memories materialized Jude's Firebird. It was the first thing he noticed when turning onto his street. Not realizing he had parked on the grass, he approached the house as "Sympathy for the Devil" echoed through his ears. He couldn't stop smiling.

As Preston prepared to knock, Jude opened his door. Preston looked him over. The sight of Jude jogged a memory that seemed to originate from a different, happier version of himself. Jude looked just as he remembered. His voice was warm. "Hey... I am surprised to find you at home. Akila doesn't have you busy snitching on another criminal organization?" Jude tried shutting the door, but Preston blocked it with his foot. "I was joking. Please, *please* hear me out."

Jude's mouth subtly fell open. Legitimate concern governed his face. "Um, Preston? Are you okay?"

A grin slowly spread across his face. "Oh. You..." He shook his head rapidly, halting it. "Never mind. Sorry. You are still young, you know. You should save your worry for someone who deserves it."

"Huh. I remember you being a different kind of desperate." Jude motioned for him to come in.

Preston made himself at home, sitting in a leather chair and stretching his legs across a table. The house was nearly identical to the one Preston remembered. A sweet aroma of cinnamon adorned the air. Light trickled in through the closed blinds. A candle was lit on the table beside him, and he put his cold hands over the wavering flame.

Jude sat across from him and sipped a cup of coffee. "What do you need?"

Preston almost got whiplash. "Slow down! This is the perfect excuse to catch up. How have you been?"

"Fine." Jude stood up and opened the blinds beside Preston, illuminating Preston's improved health. "Wow, you look great! Did you finally—"

"Nope. I recovered my health through good faith. *Au naturel*, as they say."

"Well, I'm happy for you." Maybe it was how the light struck Preston, but to Jude, he looked like a new person. He was in awe. "You were half dead the last time I saw you. It feels like *years* since we've talked."

Preston raised his eyebrows. "I'm glad that all the shock with Chessie and Fin's dog didn't make you forget that, at one time, we were good partners." His hands started shaking, and his tone became serious. "No matter what you think of me, I hope you know that... I am honored to have saved your life. I am proud of how far you've come." His eyes were moist. "I mean that."

Jude's face was branded with shock and awe. "You were always an enigma, but this self-aware, apologetic act is completely out of left field."

"It is no act! I—"

"I know," Jude smirked. "You mean it. I like the thought that you do, at least. I'm glad you're owning your mistakes, but... I can't forgive you for Spark."

Preston frowned. "Not an hour goes by where I do not regret what I did to Fin. It is awful. But although I will never forgive myself, I feel that the world can. I just have to earn it. Does that make sense?"

"Not even slightly." Jude set his coffee down and gazed at him more attentively. "You plan to atone? Is that what you're getting at?"

"Funny you brought that up. To be blunt, that is why I'm here. I need your help. To atone, but also to hold up my end of a bargain. First, though, tell me about your relationship with Chessie. Will he listen to anything you say?"

He exhaled a long gust of air. "I'm not sure. Even before the exposé, we were on rough terms."

"Oh?"

"I..." he sighed and ran his hand through his hair, "I walked into Jury's bedroom without knocking and saw him and Red kissing. They were mad I invaded their privacy. But it's not like I didn't know. I mean…" his hand made frantic circles in the air, "Come on."

Preston released an extremely loud laugh and tried too hard to sound like he understood. "*Yeahhhhhh*! Right. We've all been there after a good football game." He cleared his throat. "A-anywho. How did walking in on that ruin your relationship? Chessie couldn't have been *that* mad."

Jude crossed his legs and leaned back. "I didn't want my old life to intersect with the new one I was trying to build, so I… shut myself out. My heart was never in it." He paused. "As disappointed as I am in Jury, I still like him. My expectations were just high."

Preston leaned forward. His dancing hands exemplified his confusion. "Wait, sorry. Did the Mailugula people hate you after that? Is that why you blew the whistle?"

"Did they hate me?" Jude reflected on his experiences and couldn't shake the image of Red's face. "No. It was the right thing to do. Even though bad things have happened because of the exposé, I'm sure some good can come out of it."

"Huh. I feel like I am missing something, but okay. I will say, though," Preston raised his eyebrows and spoke gently, "Do not feel bad. Being self-aware is great, but success doesn't always feel good."

Jude glared at him.

Preston put his hands up and laughed. "What would I know, right? Just take my word on this one thing. You did not betray Jury. If anything, he betrayed you. The man is losing it, and… I want to help. And, to do that, I need you."

"What?"

Preston leaned forward. "I have a proposition. For half of my savings," he flashed his checkbook, "which I can exchange right now, I would like you to make a call for me."

"To Jury?"

"Yes!" He stroked his staticky beard. "Tell him you need help thinking things over and want him to meet you at The Ranger tomorrow at noon. It will not be you showing up, of course."

"The Ranger?"

Preston was so wrapped up in his pitch that he didn't realize he was being condescending. "It's a motel in Golgotha. There's a big sign and everything. It's where Chessie had his vision."

Jude scratched the back of his head. "Why would he meet me, especially now? It would be pointless for him."

"He will see this as an opportunity to save Mailugulism while also atoning for the cruelty he showed you."

"I still don't understand. For one, why not use the Sturdy? It's abandoned as is."

"The Sturdy may be empty, but the area around it is not. The last thing I need is a bunch of paparazzi breathing down my neck. On the other hand, there is nothing outside The Ranger but sand and ghosts."

Jude was struggling to wrap his head around Preston's plan. "What exactly do you plan on doing?"

"A *real* interview that will culminate in the end of our rivalry. It is the only way for us and this world to move on. I will be recording everything, so one day, you can see it. Confusing, I know, but you'll understand one day."

With a slight turn of Jude's head, his eyelids slowly moved into a squint. "I won't pry, Preston, but whatever you plan on doing with Jury, I hope you know that nothing will change the mistakes you two have made. This seems like a vanity project."

A jolt of worry energized Preston's voice. "And that is very fair and reasonable of you to say, but also, I have finally found my purpose, a—a way to live forever! I know I sound like one of those crazies, but you *have* to believe me. The packages, my recovery, the exposé: everything has aligned for this moment. This is the only chance I have to end the Mailugian game."

Jude was quizzical. "And what if you don't? What's riding on this?"

Preston's manner became more chaotic. He jumped from the chair, "Listen to me! Nothing hurts worse than falling short of your fate. I know you are skeptical and confused, but trust me, this is my purpose. And without you, I will not be able to reach it. All you have to do is make a phone call. And it is for a good cause. Society as a whole would benefit if—"

"If I make that call," Jude rose to his feet, "I want your word that you will *never* speak to me again."

Preston widened his eyes and peered at Jude.

"Even after a miracle, you're still the most self-righteous and shameless person I know. If I had nothing to offer, you'd ignore me. I don't care about your purpose. You distracted me from mine. Why should I help you reach yours?"

Preston pinched his lips, and his heart sank. "You are wrong, Jude. This is a two-bird-one-stone type deal. I had a feeling this might be the last time we talked, so I wanted to get a few things off my chest. I am sorry if I offended you. I just hope you know that I see you as a–"

"Stop." Jude looked like the wind had been knocked out of him, "Stay here while I make the call."

He left the room and came back a minute later. An air of shock blew through him. "That didn't take any convincing at all. He agreed to everything immediately."

Preston sighed in relief. "Thanks."

Jude scratched the back of his head. His voice was warm. "I don't know what you're doing, but chances are, it'll help you move on, and I want that for both of you."

"Okay, enough of the sappy stuff." He pulled out his checkbook and started writing.

Jude extended his palm. "No thanks. You helped me once, so I'll help you."

Preston pressed his pen against his checkbook and pondered. A few fond moments and thoughts flashed across his mind, and after realizing he felt more value in their friendship than his bank account, he nodded and put the checkbook in his pocket.

As he walked out the front door, Jude stopped him. "Hey, there's one more thing I'm curious about."

Preston put his hands in his pockets. "Shoot."

"Do you miss working in the news?"

His face lost its light as he turned away from Jude. "All I miss is the power. People listen to reporters in a way celebrities can't compete with. *It. Is. Intoxicating.*" He looked at Jude and shrugged. "It was a good feeling while it lasted."

Jude chuckled softly. "While it lasted? I had the bargaining power back there, but you still managed to control the conversation."

Preston smirked. "Heh. I *did* get you to make that call. Uh," he interlocked his hands and started fidgeting with his thumbs, "Since you got a final question, I think it's only fair I get one too."

"Fine, one final question for one final—"

"Did you ever see me as a father?" The hopeful aura around his face was nearly impenetrable.

From his face to tone, Jude was pensive. "I'm not the son you never had. I'm your friend, even though you're a pretty bad person. I can't ignore that, no matter how much you've changed. I'll admit, though, I haven't seen you act like this since we first opened RBLA, back when Mailugulism was only a twinkle in God's eye." He looked into the sky and smiled before looking back to Preston. "That's why I say good luck and goodbye with a smile and a wave."

Preston chuckled and shook his head. "Who am I kidding? I never saved your life. I was just in the right place at the right time. But I can assure you that you saved mine in more ways than I can count. So.... thanks." He put his hands on his hips and released a calm, motivated exhale. "Good luck, Jude. You have a bright future ahead. I hope I get to see it." He walked off.

Jude smiled and wiped a tear from his eye. "Always gotta have the last word, *boss*."

Preston may have been motivated, but there was a bizarre sense of finality to their conversation that irked Jude. Though, even in his wildest dreams, he could never have anticipated the climactic event beyond the horizon.

REBOOT

If I were the one with the gun, wouldn't you want a chance to atone?
He was overcome with pain, and yet, he persisted.
It could've been any number of bones that broke, but it didn't matter.
They watched over everything, their message unheard.

Jury shot upright. He struggled to catch his breath and felt pain in his palms and chest. He threw on the same outfit from yesterday and grabbed his wallet and keys. As he tried to leave the room, he stared at the empty space in his bed.

When Jury sat in his car, he realized that he had forgotten his pocket knife but shrugged it off. Jude's call was the only thing stopping him from abandoning Scarwood, and the thought of putting his car in gear eased his pounding heart.

Even though it had been twelve years, he still knew the way. Palm branches littered the side of the road. Assorted shrubberies were scattered in small clumps, and a wake of vultures preyed on decaying gazelles. As Jury drove by, however, they seemed more interested in his car than the meat in front of them.

Alarm bells rang when Jury saw The Ranger's dilapidated welcome sign. He got out of his car and lit a cigarette, but before he could take a drag, he felt a cold sting in his back.

"Welcome home."

Jury slowly lifted his hands while turning around. Upon seeing Preston and his revolver, he jumped out of his skin. "WHAT ARE YOU DOING?!"

"Taking you to set." He grabbed Jury by the collar and dragged him upstairs.

Upon entering the room, Jury stared out an open window. It overlooked the vast desert, and a warm breeze radiated through. Then, he looked at the furniture and got déja vu. Room three had been transformed into RBLA's old interview studio. Everything was accounted for, from Preston's leather chair to Jury's wooden stool. All that differed was their placement. The chairs now sat across from each other with a table between them. A camera was set up along the wall, giving a perfect side view of the two chairs. A line of wooden letter blocks sat atop end tables beside them, arranged at the edge facing the camera. The one near Jury's chair spelled "Chessjurist," and the one near Preston's "Epalit."

Jury examined the C block.

"You know how, on TV, they have the names in the bottom corner of the screen? This is the best I could do." Preston paused to let the sensation settle. "Now that I have made an impression, let me get your real chair." He pointed the gun at him. "Walk to the other side of the room."

Jury nervously complied.

Preston threw the stool out the window and whipped a leather chair in its place. He wiped the sweat from his brow and plopped into his seat. He waved the revolver in the air. "Pretend this isn't here. You and I are going to have a discussion. Imagine this as a second interview, one just for you and I. I can help you fulfill your destiny, which will fulfill mine in the process. I think you can learn from this," his tone became remorseful, "although it can only end one way."

Jury remained standing. His eyes were wide. "What are you talking about?"

"Sorry, I should not have thrown all that at you at once." He motioned toward Jury's chair.

Jury sat at the edge of it. With shaking hands, he pointed at the gun. "Are you gonna kill me?"

Preston aimed it at Jury's chest and gazed into his eyes. "You broke your promise."

Jury scooted back. Though perplexed, he was fascinated by Preston's words.

Preston spoke in a high-pitched falsetto and waved his hands like a lost princess. Everytime he moved the gun, Jury flinched. "'*I have more self-awareness than people like Preston ever will, and I promise to improve and bring Mailugulism across the world.*'" His tone stabilized. "I throw around the term 'crock' a lot, but that takes the cake."

"I... I, ugh." His lips quivered. Hints of embarrassment fluttered between his words. "It's *obvious* that I haven't been true to my word, but there's nothing I can do about that now."

Preston rolled his eyes. "Is that seriously how you want to word it?"

"Ah, yes. Let me make a formal statement about every mistake I've made since the interview." His eyes narrowed. "Do your producers need me to look at the camera while I say it?"

"Oh," he grinned. "You think that, since I am better, I have signed a deal with another company."

Jury examined Preston more closely. "Now that you mention it, either your make-up skills have improved, or you're actually cured." His eyes narrowed. "How'd you do it?"

"Wouldn't you like to know?"

"Yeah, that's why I—"

"How I have been helped by the same power which has forsaken you?" Preston was so consumed in his theatrics that he didn't realize he cut Jury off. "We could quip all we want, but this can only end one way." He waved the revolver in the air again. "We need to get serious."

Jury looked from the gun to Preston and burst into hysterics. Although his giggles were boisterous and loud, he clutched the armrests tightly. "Ridiculous. Sure, Press. Make your point and get this over with."

He raised his pointer finger. "First things first, I am no monster. This is what Progenitor commanded me to do."

Jury lurched forward, nearly tipping over his chair. "Progenitor?! Have you been getting packages from them, too?"

After a brief pause, Preston bit his lip and snickered. "I do not know why, but hearing that from you tickles me. It is not surprising when you think about it. It just paints a bigger picture."

"So... you found them?"

His voice was mystical. "Progenitor lured me here and granted me a vision. The hypocrisy is not lost on me, but regardless, he commanded me to end this Mailugian game." He sighed. The energy briefly left him. "He told me to kill you and gave me this revolver to do it."

Jury stared at him. He blinked a few times. "To be honest, I'm surprised you didn't come after me sooner."

Preston moved his head back and looked disgusted. "I may not have been the best person, but I am far from a maniac."

Jury clenched his lip. "Fin's got a dead dog that proves otherwise."

His head sank. After a moment, confidence slowly bolstered his will, and it grew with each sentence as his head raised. "Even with all I've done, Progenitor still chose me. I believe in his justice, but I also believe that *you* can change. That's why I want to help you redeem yourself before it's too late. That and..." He looked off to the side.

"I think your blood is the stipulation behind my recovery. It's my purpose. If I do not do this, I picture my health reversing on a dime."

"Killing me?" He looked at Preston, enraged. "You think that killing *me* is your purpose!?" He crossed his arms and turned away. "Why talk, then? Do me a favor and get it over with."

Preston sighed. His voice became gentle. "Progenitor has put your life in my hands. *He* wants me to kill you, but *I* believe I can reach you. Besides, I can not condemn a man without first—"

"I get it." Jury pressed the top of his nose and clenched his eyes shut. "First, I'm a ticket to fame. Now, I'm a ticket to salvation. Let's just get started."

Preston sat back and nodded. He smacked his lips. "Starting off, I'd like to look at you and, specifically, how Mailugulism began."

Jury hesitated. "Y-you know how Mailugulism began."

"No. I'm talking about how it began for everyone else." Preston smiled. He addressed Jury with gravitas, as if he were a lifelong friend. "You attracted people to Mailugulism with a televised speech that was mysterious and theatrical. Even if your words were vague, people saw meaning. So, they made the trip and saw you speak."

Jury clung to Preston's words as if they were a rope to salvation.

Preston's grim voice made his words sting. "It didn't happen overnight, but, one by one, people stopped caring. Maybe it was because they couldn't find meaning in something so open-ended, or maybe Mailugula wasn't as exciting in person as it was on TV." He frowned and glanced away. "With my exploitation of Mailugula, I played a role in that, and I'm sorry. But it was your faking of intelligence and knowledge that–" He looked at Jury and noticed that he was becoming frustrated. He stuck out his palm. "Now, listen–"

"Don't accuse me of faking intelligence when *you're* the one who refuses to use contractions!"

A smile slowly spread across his face, "I am surprised you picked up on that. *You're* a little more perceptive than I thought." His tone became less rehearsed. "When I say that people stopped caring about Mailugula, do you agree with me? And, if you do, why do you think they did?"

Jury laughed. The revolver was still pointed at him, but he was so consumed in the conversation that he didn't notice. "I'm different, okay? That may sound dumb to you and to..." he motioned toward the camera, "...whoever's watching, but people have always feared what they don't understand."

Preston furrowed his eyebrows, "Then, why did they come to you to start?"

Jury's resolute exterior broke for a brief moment. His mind raced. "Because... of the speech I did on TV, right?"

He chuckled. "According to you, people are afraid of the unknown, which is why Mailugulism faded from their minds. *Right?* If that's true, then why did so many people come to the first Session? Morbid curiosity? Irony? No. *They were curious.* So, what happened to them? Did they hate Mailugula? Well, they must have, right? Unless..." Preston looked at Jury. "*You* lost those people. Not Mailugula."

"Bold statement." Despite the harsh criticism, he genuinely mulled over Preston's words. "Maybe you're right. To be honest, I just don't know." Jury looked out the window, probing the empty sky for an answer. "I had my moments, and because of that, I'm certain I lost followers. But there was more to Mailugulism than me. My Speakers were the rocks of Mailugula. They were always doing good!" Jury's eyes widened, "Even if I was *awful*." He looked at the gun in Preston's lap.

"What difference can a movement make without a strong leader? But still, awful?" Preston squinted. He eyed him up and down. "Awful is not standing by your creation. Awful is disregarding those who helped you build everything. A few moments of anger from a young man under a lot of pressure? *That* is not awful. You simply blamed Mailugula instead of yourself, which snowballed. But you used to be passionate. If that passion persisted, I don't know if we'd even be here. I can't ignore that. That's why I have to know. What made you lose your faith?"

Jury spoke inquisitively. An occasional chuckle popped up in his voice. "Why bother? How will you be able to kill me if you start seeing me as a real person?"

"I'm hesitating for a reason, Chessie. I *do* see you as a real person. Why else would I give you this chance?"

"That's what you've convinced yourself of, but I can't shake the feeling that there's a little more to this discussion."

They shared a moment of silence. It was evident from Preston's expression that he wasn't catching on.

"Whatever." Although Jury's voice lost stability, his posture remained sturdy and strong. "Remember Ms. M? Well, the night before the first Session, I caught her trying to rob us. She was young, stupid. I tried to convince her to abandon her life of crime and adopt Mailugulism. To my surprise, she embraced Mailugulism but used it to rationalize her dangerous habits. I admit I was harsh on her, but I knew she would get hurt if she continued." He ran his hand through his hair. "I should've called the police. I thought I could help her before it was too late. But she got hurt, and her life will never be the same."

Preston said nothing. He looked at the floor as if the devil's hand was reaching out of it.

"What?" Jury asked. "Were you expecting a mustache-twirling villain story?

"Sorta." After thinking, he shook away his anxiety. The darkness in Preston's eyes was piercing. "You tried to help, and sometimes, that backfires. It is not your fault and only as relevant as you let it be. All things considered, doubt is not sinful."

"I'll tell you what is: *Killing.* You can change this, Preston!"

"I won't." Preston's pupils, for a second, faded into the white abyss of his eyes. "And I am willing to burn in Hell because of it. I could sit here and say Progenitor this and Progenitor that, but there must be a point where you hold yourself accountable."

Jury squinted. "Who are you, then, to elongate Progenitor's judgment on *your* behalf? So what if they gave you a gun? That doesn't make you important. It doesn't give this conversation any meaning."

"You're not listening. Obviously, there is something they see that I don't. That's why Progenitor *told* me to do this. And because he made me judge, jury, and executioner, I will finally die for something!" His eyes widened for a moment, as if he was caught in a lie. "Er—*we* will finally die for something!"

Something irked Jury about Preston's words, but he couldn't put his finger on it. He was confused, almost exasperated. "All you're doing is finding ways to absolve yourself of fault. Killing me is just another way to do that."

"I could point the gun at my head, but I'm *pointing* it at you. It *is* my choice."

"There's a difference. You had no choice when being thrown out of RBLA, right?"

Preston shrugged and nodded.

"This conversation, however, *is* by choice. You didn't *want* to leave RBLA, but you *want* to talk to me. So, do you want to kill me? Or do you have to? And, in that case, what's making you?"

Preston blinked quickly. "Uhhh," He looked at the revolver as if it would explain itself. "I guess divine intervention."

"Divine intervention?" Jury leaned toward him, eyes wide, and lowered his voice. "Are you saying that Progenitor is a God?"

"That is not the point of this conversation," Preston said, still looking at the weapon. He broke into a sweat. "But you have answered my questions, so I will answer yours." Confidence returned to him as he looked back at Jury. "Progenitor *is* God. Think about it. How else could I have improved so rapidly? Who else could've given me that sign?"

Jury's expression underwent a wistful transition. "Visions don't validate everything. Whatever you saw was etched into your mind from the beginning. Claiming divine intervention is just your way of pushing the responsibility onto Progenitor. Viewing this conversation as a responsibility doesn't change that."

It was clear from his blank expression that Jury was losing Preston. "Progenitor may have delegated this to me, but it's ultimately my action. I don't know. Maybe I thought that if I could reach you... then I wouldn't have to."

Jury saw the lack of interest in Preston's voice and tone and became frustrated. "That has *never* been on the table! From the beginning, it's been 'this can only end one way,' over and over again." He facepalmed. "I think you're trying to rationalize murdering me, and whenever I start to convince you otherwise, you hide behind Progenitor. Well, I am *done* indulging you. When will you give them what they want?" He pointed behind his chair and stood up. "When will my blood DRIP down that wall?!"

Preston scoffed repeatedly and sounded incredibly bitter. "I don't appreciate you trying to get inside my head. I know why I'm doing this."

"I don't think you do!"

"If all you're gonna do is try to plant seeds of doubt in my mind, then I only have one thing left to say." He pointed the revolver at Jury's chest. "Any last words?"

Jury felt a tug on his leg and slipped down into the chair. Once he sat, he felt his pocket knife poke him back. It nearly shocked him out of his seat. He didn't realize he was speaking aloud. "Wait, but I forgot it. I *know* I forgot it." He looked at Preston with a frightened expression. Although he had a last resort in mind, his voice became more desperate than ever. "Preston, *think. Do you want this?*"

Preston avoided eye contact. "It's…"

"If I were the one with the gun, wouldn't you want a chance to atone?"

He hung his head and sighed despondently, "I wish it did not have to end like this." His pointer finger wrapped around the trigger. "I'm sorry."

Jury raised his hands in front of his face, "No, **DON'T!**" In a fit of overwhelming emotion, he flinched and knocked the table next to him to the floor, taking the letter blocks with it. Preston glanced in their direction and froze. Somehow, the letters from Jury's last name had rearranged themselves into two words. Jury quickly read them. This was Mother Nature's queue. Before he could pull out his pocket knife, a vision jolted through him. The shock forced his spirit out of his body and made him relive last night's dream, fully conscious and struggling to process what the letter blocks had revealed.

REVELATION

Jury, trapped in an out-of-body experience, relived his dream from last night.

Adrenaline flashed across Jury's eyes. With Preston distracted, he wrapped his hand around the hilt of his knife. Thinking of nothing but himself, he threw it as hard as he could, lodging it in Preston's stomach. As Preston struggled to register the sensation of blood dripping down his fingers, Jury grabbed the table and rushed toward him.

His hand trembling, Preston lifted the revolver. He rose and backed against the wall. Just before they collided, Preston fired, launching a bullet through Jury's palm.

Jury was overcome with pain, and yet, he persisted. With his last ounce of strength, he tackled Preston. They crashed through the wall behind them into the open air. With nothing to catch their fall and Mother Nature revolted, they could only plummet from the second floor to the cold, hard sand.

While falling, Jury held his rival beneath him but was helpless as Preston shoved the revolver into his heart. A deafening gunshot overpowered the sound of Preston's bones shattering against the sand. All Jury could do was blink and die, wondering what could have been.

The letter blocks watched over everything, their message unheard.

From the ashes of his dream, Jury assembled a puzzle. A gunshot in the air snapped Jury's spirit back to his body, and reality became normal once again.

Jury frantically looked around. There was no hole in the wall or bullet in his chest. Preston sat in front of him unharmed.

Preston's face had gone red. "ANSWER ME, GODDAMMIT! How did you do that? *How* did you get the blocks to fall like that!?"

Confidence flowed through his calm demeanor. "I didn't do anything to the blocks, Press."

"Then why do they say that? WHY DO THE BLOCKS SAY THAT?!" He sounded like he was about to burst into tears. "To live and to die. Two signs that you are far from the God you pretend to be!!!"

"I'm not a God." His breath suddenly left him. "I'm a prophet. You were right. I lost myself along the way, but if this is any indication..." He smiled. "It's not too late!"

His pupils shrank into tiny, quivering dots. "I won't let you get inside my head! You cannot change fate!"

As Preston straightened his aim, Jury wrapped his hand around the hilt of his knife... and tossed it onto the floor. "Kill me if you wish, Preston. Either way, I'm going home."

The tranquility in Jury stirred Preston. When combined with the blocks and the knife, he felt incapable of accomplishing Progenitor's task. He released the tension in his body and allowed air to refill his lungs. With a deep breath, he set the gun on the table and slumped into the chair. At that moment, Jury's prophecy faded.

Mother Nature smiled. Her message was finally realized. "JESUS CHRIST," the letter blocks on the floor read, surrounded by red leaves.

"I can't believe it. Your name is actually an anagram." Preston ran his hand through his hair. "This *can't* be my purpose. Why would I wanna be remembered for killing a prophet?"

Jury's tone was sympathetic. "You were right. All I'm doing is pushing the blame. *My* failure led us here. Mailugulism doesn't represent humanity's true dreams and desires. It's just what's missing from *my* world." He looked at Preston's letter blocks again, and his smile broadened.

"Look at you, having a spiritual awakening." He gagged. "To think, I thought you could actually change. But *everything* is a steroid for your ego, even a damn gun in your face!"

The energy he once poured into his sermons coursed through his veins. Jury came alive. "You said that doubt is not sinful, and you meant it more than you realize. There was always a part of you that was never sold on Progenitor's plan. Why else would you try helping me before killing me? You stalled because you knew it was wrong. That's why I say that, although you've changed yourself, something *else* has changed your fate. You've been on an adventure instead of in the ground. Tell me, and for once, be honest. Why must it end with my death?"

Preston's voice was barely audible. "Fine. I'll be honest. Maybe that'll get these butterflies out of my stomach." He took a deep breath. "People say that they accept their mortality, but I do not believe that. Those who seem most in tune with their fate are not the ones who go peacefully. They scream. They sob. They suffer. All their *fear* explodes at once." Tears fluttered down his cheeks. "I've been afraid my entire life. Afraid of death, afraid of being forgotten. I've let everything be defined by that: my career, my relationships, even my hatred for you." He bit his lip. "You may have made your own mistakes, but it's my fault that we're here. I invented the Mailugian game to help me and me alone. How could I kill it without killing myself?"

Jury leaned forward and extended a hand to Preston. "Killing yourself won't end anything. What even is the game? Have you ever thought about that? It seems like everything that happened in Scarwood was meant to bring us together. Have you ever wondered why Progenitor sent those packages or how it set us up for this moment?"

"No…" Preston wrapped his hand around his chin. He was hesitant to speak, and when he gathered the courage, he was quiet. "Did it even start with the packages? Hell, failing algebra led me to be a reporter and not an astronaut. Are you saying Progenitor rigged my exams, too?"

"This is more than the butterfly effect, Press. If you wanna go there, then you could say that I would've been dead if some guy didn't wake up a hundred years ago and print the alphabet on wooden blocks."

"But I'm the one who failed my math test."

Jury scrunched up his face. "Could we please stop talking about your math test?"

Preston smirked and nodded.

Jury lightened up. "Progenitor may be guiding us, but this *situation* is our fault. We always had a choice and interpreted everything ourselves. But we can't bend any longer! As long as we remain ignorant of history's pull, we are doomed to repeat it." Jury eyed the letter blocks beside Preston's chair.

"History's pull?" Preston turned toward his letter blocks and looked back at him. "What are you implying?"

Jury walked over to Preston. He pressed the letter blocks together and laid them flat. One by one, he rearranged the letters from EPALIT to spell out PILATE.

It took a moment, but when everything clicked, Preston's breathing intensified. He raced through emotions and expressions. "Power…

I have *no* power!" His tone became frantic. "I need to take my fate into my own hands. A pig-headed hypocrite like me doesn't deserve to live!" He grabbed the revolver and pulled back the hammer.

Although Jury's prophecy was gone, parallels remained. With the barrel of the gun inches away from Preston's chin, Jury had no time. At the last moment, he wrapped his left hand around the muzzle and ripped it away. Unable to process the turn of events, Preston still pulled the trigger. With an eruption far louder than the previous shot, the bullet exploded from its chamber and drilled through Jury's palm.

Preston's ears rang as he stood up and rushed toward him. "Why would you *do* that?!"

Blood immediately coated Jury's wrist and forearm. He was slightly dazed and extended his oozing hand toward Preston. "We face our fate together, or not at all."

With this, Preston finally understood his circumstance and intercepted Jury's handshake with a hug.

Jury could feel Preston's heart beating out of his chest.

Preston could barely breathe. "You know, now that it's all said and done, I almost wish we could've talked more."

"Almost." Jury grinned through the now overwhelming pain. "Let's go."

"Yeah, sounds—" He froze for a moment and began swaying erratically. He slammed his palms on his head and collapsed to the floor. He writhed around like a bug on a windshield.

As Jury watched, every improvement to Preston's health reversed. His gut receded entirely, as did the pigment in his skin. His heart and lungs shrank. Catching his breath became impossible. He started vomiting.

Jury grabbed him by the shoulders and, without meaning to, lifted him like a ragdoll. The blood from his hand dripped onto his shoulder. "Press? *Press!* What's happening?"

Preston coughed up a mixture of red leaves and dried blood. "I didn't meet the stipulation behind my recovery."

The pain in his hand lost all significance. Imbued with a reverent strength, Jury effortlessly wrapped Preston's arm around his shoulder.

Preston couldn't feel his legs, yet, while connected to Jury, he could move them. He shakily pointed at the camera.

Jury grabbed it and kicked open the door.

Jury and Preston left room three behind and descended the stairs. Upon making contact with the Earth for the first time in a lifetime, the sun began beating down on them. It exacerbated their wounds and left them both within an inch of death. Jury dropped the camera in the sand and fought to maintain consciousness. He slipped away for just a moment. When he came to, something in the desert greeted him. Amid the airborne sand, Jury saw a nostalgic sight in the distance.

The look in her eyes said everything she could not. Her voice echoed, *"Come home, Jim."*

Jury was speechless. Years of nightmares had distorted his perception of the days which bore Mailugulism. He now saw his mother as he never could: old. Even in death, age had taken its toll. He took one step toward her.

Preston shared his vision, but as he stared, it started to wane. With his final ounce of strength, he planted his feet and held Jury back. "Come on." He coughed and clutched his stomach. "Stop being so gullible."

That statement echoed through his mind, establishing reason in the place of nonsense. Then, he felt a phantom force clutch his wounded hand. *"Are you okay? What happened? Did someone do this to you? Sit down, sit down! Let's wrap you up."*

Jury's eyes widened. Memories poured through him.

"I believe Mailugulism has a right to exist, and I know most others agree."

"I wouldn't worry. There's always a way to turn around bad press."

"You haven't been yourself lately, Jury. I'm worried about you."

"That's my truth, and in a way, embracing it with Mailugula is setting me free."

"That's why I love you."

"Why don't ya pull from that infinite supply of faith?"

Jury only realized he was smiling because he felt it fade from his face. He looked to the sky. "They were my heart... and soul."

With that, the magic had run its course. Preston's legs gave out, and Jury could no longer support his weight. Preston collapsed to the sand.

Kneeling beside him, the reality of Preston's condition sank in. Among the blistering desert, the water in Jury's eyes was no mirage.

"You're... crying." Preston released a hollow chuckle. "Stop that. I'm getting what I deserve."

Jury rested his palm across Preston's chest. "I'm so sorry. I thought I understood you. But I wasn't there for you when you—"

"**Shut up.** Just. *Listen*!" Preston coughed and clutched Jury's hand. "Without you, I never would have had the opportunity to change. You're a *good* man. I would've been proud to have a son like you." His eyes welled up. "I mean that, *Jury*."

Jury bit his lip. "Thank you."

"See? That's all you had to say." A gentle smile crossed Preston's face. "So," he looked at the desert beside him. "My fate was to meet you. Honestly, I'm... I'm..." A raspy breath overtook his final words.

A ghostly shade of white replaced the static coloration in Preston's hair and beard one strand at a time. His pupils went from black to gray, though, even in death, they were not lifeless. They carried an unwavering light that vividly reminded Jury of the voice their glance once accompanied.

Jury wept.

The hole in his hand continued to bleed and ooze, soaking Preston's shirt. But Jury didn't care. Through crippling thirst and intense heat, he remained on his knees and held Preston close, afraid the vultures were watching.

Everything was a blur when an HNN van arrived, and Akila and Jude stepped out of it.

Jude dropped his camera and sprinted toward them. "Boss? Boss!" He turned to Jury. "What *happened*!?"

Jury's gaze was transfixed on the point where his mother once stood. His dry throat croaked. "The climax of our stories."

"What!? What happened to Preston?"

Akila nudged him. "Look at his hand. He's probably in shock. We need to get them both to the emergency room."

"See? I told you yesterday that something wasn't right with him." Jude hoisted Preston's limp body onto his shoulders. "God, how is he so cold? It's a hundred degrees out here!"

Jude and Akila laid Preston in the backseat and checked everywhere for a pulse. After pounding on Preston's chest and realizing the truth, Jude broke down. "Why? Why didn't I stop you?!" He hit his chest once more, cracking a couple ribs. "Why couldn't I have talked some sense into you before you tried to fulfill this *stupid* purpose?"

Akila hung her head.

"You're wrong." Jury appeared behind them, barely standing straight. He was pale and shivering. "Preston broke free. It's not your fault. The narrator of our stories has been acting out of place."

Akila led Jury into the backseat. "You've lost a lot of blood, Jury." She ripped off her sleeve and wrapped it around Jury's palm. "We need to get you to a hospital."

Jude shot him a pained look. "I *need* to know what happened."

Jury turned to the camera in the sand, which chose to stop recording at this moment.

The van raced to Pontifex Catholic. Jury held the camera in his lap. As his eyelids became heavier and heavier, he looked to the heavens.

"We're still missing something, aren't we, Progenitor..." His voice faded in tandem with his consciousness.

RAPTURE

After the breakup, Red drove two hundred miles in one sitting. Although his emotions were frayed, he never once exceeded the speed limit. During a stop for gas, Larry spotted a hotel and convinced Red to check-in. They stayed that night and the following day. Still lacking a plan, they rose the next morning and decided to pack their bags and get breakfast at a diner.

Larry salted his steak while Red spread butter across his toast. The two made innocent small talk, managing to distract their thoughts from the obvious until a waitress turned the TV to HNN.

Akila's hair was messy. A few strands of white fell beside her baggy eyes. "It's a sad day at HNN. Yesterday—"

The waitress rolled her eyes. "This again?" She turned the channel to another news station and saw that it was covering the same story, so she decided to leave it.

Red lifted his coffee and glanced at the screen. With a sharp gasp, he dropped his cup. He listened to the rest of the report and ran out of the cafe. Larry chased after him.

As Red drove, the words of the broadcast bounced across his mind.

Larry saw that the speedometer exceeded the speed limit and turned to Red. "What are we doing?"

"What are we *doing*?" Red didn't take his eyes off the road. "Jury's hurt. I can't let him be alone."

"Even with all the crap he's put you through? You *just* got away from him. It's not good to be crawling back like this."

"What?!" He cleared his throat and maintained a still voice. "I know you're coming from a good place, Larry, but you shouldn't worry about that. Jury's the one who's *actually* hurt."

Although his intentions were pure, Larry couldn't help but be annoyed. "You say that, but I'm afraid you're gonna see his injuries and be all over him again. Jury needs to face the music."

"This is a little more important than karma, Larry. Besides, I've been running all my life, which needs to stop. That's why..." His grip around the steering wheel tightened. "I don't plan on staying. After this is settled, buddy, I..."

Larry peered at him strangely. "You what?"

He sighed, releasing all the air and tension from his body. "I need to go home." Although saying this took a weight off his chest, he sounded somber. "I know I have nothing to prove to my Mother, but it just feels like something I have to do." Red bit his lip. "And I need to go alone. I promise I'll help you settle. I'll give you a couple weeks to think about what you want to do, but Jury and I can't control your life."

Larry bit his lip. His head sank. "I understand. I just don't know what I'll do."

Red's expression was filled with worry. "You'll find something!"

"I don't know if I want to. Every time something bad happens, I just... freeze." His manner reflected his words, and he didn't speak for the rest of the drive.

When they passed the "Welcome to Scarwood" sign, Larry crossed his arms and turned toward the window. "Drop me off at the Sturdy. I have nothing to say to Jury."

Red opened his mouth, but nothing came out. It took him a moment, but he shook away a frown for a smile. "Sure, buddy. I understand."

Five minutes later, they arrived at the Sturdy. "I'll be back soon, okay?"

Larry exited the car and went inside. When he heard Red drive away, he dug his hands into his shaggy hair and crashed against the wall. He lightly pulled on his hair while trying to fight tears.

Thinking only brought anxiety, so he indulged himself in a final stroll around the Sturdy. It looked as abandoned as it did before Mailugula. Dust and trash lined the floor. All the food in the kitchen had rotted. About half of the chairs from the refectory and session area had been stolen.

The basement was last. As he opened the door, however, something felt off. Dread lingered in the air. The poisonous ambiance only heightened as he headed down the stairs.

Light slowly flickered across the basement. The terracotta floor popped with each step. Scraps of burnt clothes, shredded documents, and horror novels were strewn across the floor. A sledgehammer was lodged halfway through the computer. Larry looked at Joe's desk and noticed that the picture of him was missing. He wanted to explore further, but a bitter smell of smoke and a pit in his chest told him otherwise.

After grabbing a suitcase from the supply closet, Larry went to his room. On the way there, he noticed that the skylight was open, and a few empty bottles of Mary's beer were lying on the floor.

Larry narrowed his eyes. As he stared at the skylight, another bottle rolled in, almost knocking him out. He dropped the suitcase and climbed up.

Sitting with a slouch at the edge of the roof was Joe. Although the sun was directly above him, he was shrouded in shadow. He wore a tuscany-colored cloak over a burgundy, long-sleeved shirt. The cloak was silky like a kimono and ancestral, as though it had been weaved from the skin of a dove. It was tied together at the neck by a golden cross. A few tiny jewels were embroidered into the fabric that twinkled like stars over a hollow forest. He finished another bottle and tossed it behind him without looking.

Larry raised his eyebrows. "How many lambs did you sacrifice to get *that* outfit?"

Joe flinched and, for a moment, could only fester in his shock. He pivoted slightly. "That's the first thing you think about. Heh heh." He stared at him, unable to suppress a genuine smile. "I missed you, kid. Weird as it sounds, I never thought I'd see ya again." He patted the space beside him. "Will ya sit with me?"

Hearing his sonorous voice almost threw Larry off his feet, but he kept his distance. "I'm good."

"Hm. I don't blame ya."

Larry sighed. "I just don't get it. You never seemed like the kind to snap like that."

"With Mallory's attacker?"

Larry nodded.

Joe smiled sorrowfully. "If only ya knew the half of it. But for now, I'll just say that I usually punish those who deserve to be punished." Joe hesitated before continuing. He sounded abnormally cognizant. "I know how it sounds. Who am I to decide, right? But I did the same thing when Ariel... ya know. Never said it was right. In fact, I resent myself for doin' those things. I almost regret it. At the same time, though, it's not quite a 'mountain outta molehill' situation, if ya get my meanin'."

"Hm." Larry made a grim expression and shook his head. "What brings you back, then? Are you here to burn the Sturdy or sit around and mope?"

Joe laughed. "Wouldn't matter if I burnt the Sturdy. Faith doesn't live on through a building. It lives on through its people," he gritted his teeth, "A people who rebound when you least expect 'em to."

Larry stared at him like a fly beneath a swatter.

Joe pinched his lips and shook his head. "Who am I kiddin'? I came here to end everything where it all began."

"Joe!" Larry stumbled over a bunch of consonants before picking one. "Don't talk like that!! You still have so much to live for!"

Joe furrowed his eyebrows and turned to Larry with an inquisitive grin. "You always find new ways to baffle me. After everything you've seen, you're tryin' to save me. Like nothin' changed. It's…freein'." His eyes latched onto Larry, but his mind was elsewhere. "No, I can't do that," he mumbled to himself, "But what if—"

"Uh," Larry waved his hand in the air. "Earth to Mr. Aphasiac. What are you talking about? You don't need to be saved. You may have made some mistakes, but there's still good in you."

"You say good, but I know you mean *guilt*." A nostalgic twinkle struck his eye. "Let's face it: humanity's time is drawin' near. No one can talk their way outta judgment, but I'll offer ya a deal. Come with me. You're the one thing in my life that hasn't gone cold."

"I can't go on the run with you, Joe." Larry shook his head. "You're lucky you're not in prison. *You* should be on the run, not back here chasing ghosts."

"I can't run." Joe's voice faltered. "With so many bodies behind me, you *know* I can't." He kept trying to chuckle away the discord plaguing him. He was one step from hysterical. "I'm sorry. I'm so sorry! I thought I knew the wish of the people. I wanted to bring that wish to LIFE! But I got corrupted at every turn."

Larry's tone and expressions were solemn. He said the one thing he thought could comfort him. "I understand, Joe."

"No, you don't. I *know* you don't." His hands began shaking. "I don't wanna blow up again, but if I left it alone, it would never stop. It'd just spiral into another disaster."

"Joe..." Larry sat next to him and patted his back. "You're too hard on yourself. Your guilt will only become heavier if you don't believe you can make things better."

"How can I believe anymore?" Joe rolled his eyes and began speaking in a lighter tone. "You gotta understand, kid. I'm trapped. Mailugulism should be dead. Jury dealt a major blow to it, but I thought I killed it. That it would then lead Jury to his demise. But with all the Preston business, he's more famous than ever."

"Wait," he pointed at him, "you killed it? Didn't HNN's exposé do that?"

"By using—" Joe froze. His heart thumped faster and faster, like a wasp ready to sting. Although hesitant, he continued in a cautious baritone. "Hear me out, kid. Don't reject what I'm sayin' because it's not what you're expectin'." He took a deep breath. "Without the footage from my cameras, HNN's exposé never would've happened. Without me, Preston never would've visited the Sturdy. And without my support, Mailugulism never would've grown."

Larry stood up and glared down at Joe. "Wait, does that mean–"

"*I am Progenitor,*" he revealed with a twinkle of showmanship.

Larry's jaw dropped.

"Heh heh. Come on. Not that surprisin' when ya think about it."

"Why!? What would you gain? You deliberately told me to not believe—"

"Respectfully, ya shouldn't say that until ya know where I'm comin' from." His voice was easy-going and free. "I told ya not to bother with it because I knew it wasn't for you. Yeah, I disagree with Mailugulism, but I thought it could change the world. It was just a way of demonstratin' my love for the people, but they rejected it, and they rejected me." He looked up at Larry and smiled. "All but you. That's why I want ya to come with me."

"I–" Larry was struggling. "You gotta be fair to yourself first. And saying things like, 'They rejected me,' isn't helping. It'd be fairer to say they rejected Jury."

Joe sighed. All remaining traces of hope left him. "You're good, Larry, but ya don't get it. I saw and experienced why people were miserable, and then I let it corrupt me. Jury and I are no different in that regard. Yet, after all this, Jury thinks there's hope in Mailugulism again, and he wants to atone." He clenched his fists and teeth. "Everything has gone wrong, but even then, I can't be that disappointed. It led me to you! Instead of all this talkin', ya could just come with me. I've become a ferryman, and I need to accept that. I can take you to a perfect life. Red too, if that's what it takes."

Larry pondered. Although he had nothing in mind and nowhere to go, something about Joe's proposition disturbed him.

Joe stuck out his hands. "Confusin', right? You'll understand once you agree."

He rubbed his aching head. "Why would I agree? I won't go with you until I know you're thinking clearly."

"Clearly?" A dark glint struck Joe's eye. "You'll never take my deal, then. If I was thinking clearly, I never would've launched this game to start, let alone cherry-pick Jury to bring it to fruition."

"Still, that doesn't really make sense." Larry shook his head. "I'm sorry, but something just doesn't seem right about this."

His tone and expressions became more energetic. "I may not seem like a people person, but trust me when I say that I care about them and the world they live in."

"Okay, then stop wasting your time here. Spend the rest of your life traveling the world."

Joe chuckled and shook his head. "People are sufferin'. Mailugulism can't fix that. Mailugulism never had a *hope* of fixin' that. That's why I can't *just* watch. But before I act," He interlocked his fingers and looked at Larry, "I need you by my side, kid."

Larry gritted his teeth. "Quit lying to me." His fists began shaking. "You only want me at your side because you're afraid Ariel will reject you!"

His words stabbed Joe. He scoffed and fought viciously against the water bubbling in his eyes.

Larry belted out each word. "I am not your whole life! I'm my own person, and *Ariel* was her own person. Why can't you remember that? Why does everything good in your life have to be drowned out by her death?"

Joe could no longer withhold his frustration. He stood up and began choking on each word. "It's my fault! I thought I could reason with Ariel's killer. I could've done anything, but I was so consumed in preservin' my pride that I didn't. That's when I realized I had fallen to temptation! And *that* is a *terrifying* thing." His voice became a mixture of fury and anguish. "I can't help but be jealous of enigmas like you. I mean, for cryin' out loud. In three sentences, you said more to Mallory than Jury and I ever could. More evidence that–"

"Wait, three sentences? How do you know that?"

Joe batted his hand. "Camera caught it, and I watched it. It doesn't matter where I am. I can see them from anywhere."

"No, Joe. That's not what I meant. Unless you got a new camera system, something's wrong."

Joe's eyes slowly widened.

Larry was in disbelief. "You've shown me recordings from those cameras in the past, and they've never had audio. Even the recordings that HNN used were silent. Akila said so herself." He squinted. "What're you hiding?"

Joe clenched his fists. He lifted his head, closed his eyes, and breathed in, consuming every ounce of air around them. All ambient noise went with, as did the color in the scenery. Larry almost suffocated in a sea of white light and dust.

"*I am more than Progenitor.*" He exhaled, releasing the world back to normal.

Larry dropped to his knees and struggled to catch his breath. Bugs hopped off their backs and flew onward. Heat returned to the air.

Joe put His hand on Larry's shoulder. "You were right to say that I'm dormant until provoked."

Larry held his head down, mystified and unable to look at Joe. "Words are deadlier." He paused for a moment, and it hit him all at once. "Oh my G–" his eyes widened further. He started panicking. "I don't believe you. I can't!"

A hint of fear permeated Joe's shaky voice. "I'm still *me*, kid. I've always been me. Names come and go over eons, but I try to keep it consistent: from one three-letter word to another."

He became more desperate and erratic. "But if you're... how could Ariel have died?"

Although Joe was standing the same way He was before, He now seemed more powerful. He pocketed His hands and gazed at Larry. "I already told you. I thought I could reason with Jeremiah. I created him, just as I've created all of you. Isn't it natural to believe in your own creation?"

Contempt drove Larry's squinted eyes and agape mouth. "It's not natural to *toy* with it! Does anything that's happened here have a purpose? What was Mailugulism even for? To get Jury and Preston to kill each other?!"

Joe shook His head. Larry's words didn't faze Him. "I wanted Preston to inspire Jury to be what he needed to be, but when that failed..."

"You mean the man *you* needed him to be! Do you have any idea how unfair that is?" Larry bit his lip and pointed at Him. "*You* TOOK his mother!"

A reverent duty entered His voice. "Jury's mother made her choice. Just as I have made mine." His posture straightened. "It's time for the game to end."

"Does that mean..." Larry looked up, meeting Joe's eyes with a mind-bending stare, uttering his words with a mixture of horror and awe. *"The final judgment."*

"I can't believe how far I've sunk. Validatin' these wrathful ideologies." Joe nodded. "Good people, regardless of their beliefs, deserve salvation. With the world bein' what it is, I can't give that to them. I never intended for it to come to this. I never *wanted* it." His voice became utterly emotionless. "But I suppose all I can say now is that you will neither know the day nor the hour."

Larry was hypnotized by Joe. "How can you even do that? Do you really think you have the right?"

"Humanity once filled me with the hope that they would rule the world with love. Not the love of me, but the love of each other!" His tone dropped an octave. "I think we need a new type of human. Dark cannot cast out dark, so I will light this world aflame, starting with the Sturdy beneath our feet."

A misty flame oozed from beneath Joe's feet and swirled around Him like a serpent. His tuscany-colored cloak hovered, scattering the dust on the roof. The jewels glowed, and the cross around His neck glimmered like a lighthouse.

His prophetic voice resonated through the air like a choir. "Ariel died for nothing. She didn't absolve the world of its sin. She was just another reminder of how far it had fallen. But I've learned. If you come with me, I *promise* I'll make your death worth more than you can possibly imagine."

The fire around Joe spread across the roof like fog. With a snap of Joe's fingers, the flame intensified into a jungle. It covered the skylight and traced the outer edges of the roof before sprouting up like walls and trapping Larry. It slowly worked its way down the building.

Joe stretched out His arms and gazed into the sky. The pain in his face faded away as he basked in the fire's glow. "Only one thing's for certain. Whether you accept or refuse, my work is just beginning."

JUDGE, JURY, EXECUTIONER

Although the flames nearly touched the stars, no smoke billowed from them. A bitter wind filled the silence that should've been occupied by roaring crackles and pops. For the moment, no heat radiated from its humble glow. The color of the flames flickered from red to azure to gold.

The only thing the fire could melt was Larry's optimism. "There has to be another way, Joe. Life still has value. Not just the world's but yours. There's still..." his eyes darted from corner to corner, "so much..."

Joe's resolve couldn't help but wane. "Kid... people are sufferin', and it may evolve, but it'll never get better. I've tried!" His grim tone danced with the trembling flame. "I can't explain why bad things happen, and all I ask is that ya trust me instead of tryin' to reason with me. Our friendship may be real, but there's nothin' you can say."

Before the flame could thicken, an otherworldly, violet light flashed over the Sturdy. With Mother Nature's final stand, the light hit them from all directions, blinding them. Then, the season of autumn slipped away, and spring took its place. Within the spotlight, grass sprouted. Dandelions germinated. Empty trees became reanimated. Cherry blossoms replaced dying leaves and fluttered through a warm breeze. All that remained of fall were heaps of leaves, which lined the foundation of the Sturdy. Four arrows of yellow flame began circling Joe's wall.

Joe turned from side to side, the color draining from His face. Larry watched, mesmerized and calm. Flower buds rose around him, and a patch of grass spread from the skylight across the entire roof. The roof became a garden, and as the first flower bloomed, each arrow of the yellow flame rocketed into the air and exploded, causing Joe's wall to crumble.

As the fire rolled down the Sturdy like a wave, Jury appeared from the skylight. Flames erupted in the shape of a jellyfish behind him. His emerald eyes glistened through the blistering heat until the sky cleared.

Despite having braved the fires of Hell, Jury appeared at ease. "Joe," A gentle, mature smile crossed his face, "You are forgiven."

Larry ran over to Jury, shouting his name with a grin.

Joe bit His lip, but even that couldn't halt its quivering.

Jury rubbed Larry's hair with his bandaged palm. His smile was infectious. "I never thought I'd see you guys again! It's such a relief. Things can finally start getting better."

Warmth washed over Joe. "You idiot." The flood could no longer be suppressed. Joe fell to His knees and wept. The forgiveness of billions and billions of sinners was too much to bear.

Jury and Larry watched with bleak faces.

They noticed the garden and the sudden glimpse of spring that had arrived. Even with the beauty surrounding them, Jury wasn't satisfied. He still had one more miracle to fulfill. He approached Joe, knelt down, and wrapped his arms around Him.

Joe turned His head and was transfixed by the sagacious gleam in Jury's eyes.

Jury tucked his head into His cheek. "You don't need to take re- sponsibility for the faults and interpretations of others. It's not your fault that my father and many people like him focus on a religion without grace or love. You can't always be what people need. Some visions are just too strong."

"That's why I thought Mailugulism could work." He gently re- moved Jury's hands and stood, wiping snot from His flushed face. "I'm sorry, Jury. I just couldn't face my people knowin' what they were goin' through. I thought Mailugulism could fix that."

"I'm sorry it didn't." Jury's tone remained optimistic. "Sure, Mailugulism was a failure, but that doesn't render your life pointless."

Energy returned to Joe's voice. "Heh, don't let it blow up your ego. I wanted to steer Mailugulism, but that wasn't my reason for livin' this life."

Larry furrowed his eyebrows. "Then, what was?"

He slouched, and a wince of pain entered His soft eyes and voice. "I was tired of livin' vicariously. I wanna give people the help they deserve, but I can't help what has moved away from me... what I don't understand. So, I gave myself a life like any other. That way, I could thread two needles."

Jury remained earnest and comforting. "Don't let my failure distort your view. You act like everything you touched in this life is worse off. You're letting your disillusionment speak for you, just like I did. It's unnatural."

"Unnatural?" Joe released a hollow chuckle. "You bein' here's un- natural. As much as I wanna forgive ya, Jury, I can't. I—" He point- ed at him. There was genuine kindness behind His harsh words. "I shouldn't have had to control ya! All ya had to do was keep an open mind, but more often than not, you only thought of yourself. I see my role and how my attempts to guide Mailugulism corrupted it. Even with that, I can't help but think most blame falls on you."

"Most?" Larry scoffed. "Stop bringing yourself into this and listen!"

Jury nodded. "We *don't* share the blame. You made your own mistakes, but good intentions were your foundation. I can't say the same for myself."

"Good intentions? I tried gettin' Preston to kill you!"

Jury's tone remained pleading and sympathetic. "I know. I'm sorry that I left you with no other options. I'm sorry that I couldn't control myself, that I was blind to my own disillusionment."

"But—" interjected Larry. "If this prick can change, then so can this world. It may not be how you expect–"

"Don't gimme that!" He turned to Jury. "Outta nowhere, it hits ya all at once because of some damn letters? *Bullshit.*" He looked toward the stars. "How did the blocks even fall like that? That's the luckiest shit in the world."

"Luck?" Jury's eyes widened in an instant. "Luck had nothing to do with it!" An analytical glint flashed across his eyes, "or you coming to live here. It was all Mother Nature."

Joe tilted His head and narrowed His eyes.

Jury raised his eyebrows. "Did you really come here because you had nowhere else to go? Nothing stopped you from taking another form and living the rest of your life in peace. But after Ariel's tragedy, you retained your identity and hid here."

"I kept this form because I owed it to Ariel, and it was convenient that ya already knew me. I thought that was obvious."

Jury extended his palms. "*And it is.* But you wanted Mailugula to get rid of your guilt. It's my fault that I couldn't help you confront your discontent. My fault that you were repeatedly left with no other option but to act alone. But you aren't alone. Enacting the final judgment won't take away your guilt, but more importantly, the saints of this world don't deserve it. Whether they believe in you or not, they still have their own miracles to perform." Conviction exuded through Jury's statuesque posture. "That being said, *I* believe in you, and I believe in your justice. That's why I want to atone."

Larry quickly turned to Jury and stared at him in disbelief.

Jury's tone was a mixture of prophecy and relief. He was practically levitating. "I am the only one who deserves your wrath. I misused your gifts at every turn, and I will atone with my life." He lowered himself to his knees. "On the condition you spare this world and live in my stead."

Joe's jaw dropped. "How can ya possibly be willin' to lay down your life? You're not even proud of how ya lived!"

"If I set things right, then I will be." Peace flowed through Jury. His pupils dilated. "All you wanted was a normal life. It'd be wrong to rob yourself and this world of that opportunity."

There was a genuine inquisitiveness to Joe's words. His eyes sparkled. "What do I owe the world?"

"Nothing," Jury looked up and smiled. "But you owe Ariel. She doesn't hate you. If I can forgive you, then so can she."

Joe stared into the stars for proof of Jury's words. The sun was beginning to set, and the air was fragrant with flowers. Just on the horizon, Joe's favorite star appeared. He basked in its purple glow, and a tired smile appeared through the grief.

Larry covered his mouth. Hundreds of words blurred together, rendering him speechless.

Jury released a comfortable exhale. "A life like any other should end with a death like any other. It's what Ariel would want. Bottom line: There must be another way."

"There must be another way..." repeated Larry into the ether. A resonating emptiness in his voice captured Joe and Jury's attention. *"No."*

Joe's face treaded a middle ground between shocked and moved.

Larry choked over his grief. "Jury said it himself. Ariel misses you." Larry walked toward him, each step spawning a ripple of light around it. He put his hand on Joe's shoulder, "You don't have to suppress the flames anymore, Joe." He released an unsteady, emotional exhale, "It's okay. You need your star."

"Yeah." With that, Joe was reached. It hit Him all at once, and suddenly, Jury's release didn't seem so unbelievable. "Yeah..." He began laughing, each chuckle spawning a tear. He turned to Jury. "Get up, will ya?"

Jury rose. "Don't talk. Just listen." He repeated to himself, astounded.

"Some of us do it naturally." Joe released all the tension from His body and let His head go limp for a moment. He turned to Larry. "Kid," He scrunched His lips and did everything within His vast power to stop tears from falling. "We did so much together in such a short time. I only wish... that we could walk that trail one last time. Maybe then, I'd be able to express how much ya mean to me." After shaking His head and wiping His eyes, Joe pulled him in for a hug.

Larry clung to Him like a rope to salvation. His voice was muffled by Joe's shoulder. "I don't want you to go."

With the knowledge that He was finally needed, regardless of whether or not Ariel had forgiven him, Joe smiled. "You were my light when no one else was. I'll be waitin' for ya." Joe let go and shifted to Jury. "You too, idiot." He smirked and extended His hand.

Jury stared at it. He had experienced death within his arms, a relationship going down in flames, and a childhood of longing. But despite all that, withholding his tears proved impossible. He spared no time and shook Joe's hand.

With the sun nearly behind the horizon, a technicolor glow illuminated Larry and Jury from behind. The light caused the tears in Joe's eyes to glisten. "My sons," He proclaimed.

Jury wiped his eyes and turned away. "Come on, Larry." He wrapped an arm around him and began walking.

As they approached the skylight, Larry stopped and turned his head. "Joe, I just want you to know that... that..." insurmountable grief halted his words. He tried running to Joe, but a sudden wall of flame stopped his advance.

Joe turned away. His tears evaporated from His stiff face. "I know. I love you, too, *son*."

After staring at Joe and realizing he had no more miracles to perform, Larry turned around and disappeared into the skylight with Jury.

When Joe knew they were safe, His expression relaxed. He reached into His back pocket and removed a picture of Larry. After brushing His thumb across his cheek, He released it into the wind.

The breeze bowed to the will of the picture. It fluttered around the building, etching a foundation along the leaves for the fire to rise again.

As the photo inscribed its flame around the Sturdy, Autumn reinstated its reign. Flower petals no longer controlled the air, but in their place, a scalding fire grew upward. It passed over the roof and seeped toward Joe like fog, erasing the garden. As He knelt, the photo flew in front of Him and hovered over the skylight.

Joe pursued it into the Sturdy. The fire followed behind as He descended the stairs. It consumed everything, including the purple lilies that sprouted with each step He took. His right hand glided along the wall, and the fire twisted into the shape of a double helix around it. The picture flew through the twists before leaving the stairs and turning into the Session area.

The art along the walls faded behind smoke. Withered flowers dissolved. The floorboards snapped and screamed. Smog billowed off the walls and twisted together, forming figments of the past.

Joe walked down the aisle and watched the rose-tinted flame reanimate Jury delivering Emil's eulogy, and the Speakers jumping out and surprising Larry. He looked down the crumbling rows and could even see Himself introducing Biscuit to Fin, comforting Larry on the trail, and convincing Mallory to stay on the ground.

When He passed the last row, the chairs, the podium, and the stage disintegrated. All that remained was the mural, but Joe's gaze acted as gasoline. With a single flick, the picture ignited it. Each stroke of Michael's brush burned, starting from the tentacles, then spiraling into the middle. The fire switched colors every moment before exploding in a sea of black and gray, collapsing the ceiling with it. Dust and debris blew past Him, blocking everything except the basement door.

Although the fire illuminated each step, the basement beyond it was caked in darkness. One step at a time, Joe descended into the abyss. Through the sepia-tone smoke, His human form flickered and waned.

Upon feeling His foot tap against the terracotta floor, Joe whispered, "I'm alive," astounded and grateful. He turned around and saw that the stairs were no more. Jacob's ladder had been reduced to ash.

On all sides, the fire crept toward Joe. The photo of Larry finally accepted its fate. It danced proudly through the flame, and before long, its exterior shriveled away, revealing its true form: a red leaf.

With this, Joe went deaf to the roars of the fire. Millennia spent worrying now seemed like wasted time. Instead of bitterness, He felt relief. "I'm ready."

Eager to be cleansed, Joe closed His eyes and opened His arms. As He leaned back, the fire coiled around Him and lowered Him to the ground. When His back finally struck the Earth, each flame pierced Him like a bullet. Pressure built in his lungs as the oxygen was choked from him. The blisters and boils forming along His body were no fabrication. It burned like the first sunrise after rapture, yet He didn't scream.

As His consciousness faded, the ashes of the leaf floated toward Him and rested beside His cheek. Joe turned His head. His boiling tears splattered against the floor. "To live... and to die."

Joe didn't realize He was smiling until He felt it burn away from His face, and He vanished in a soothing, lemon glow. The boat finally sank, and as any good ferryman would, Joe went down with the ship.

The Sturdy's remains collapsed to the ground, and Red reunited with Larry and Jury outside. The remaining fire violently rocketed into the air like a spire. Leaves materialized around it, and the moment they fluttered to the ground, the fire disappeared. All that remained, sticking up through mountains of ash, was Larry's copy of the New Testament.

The Sturdy, for all the hopes and dreams it encapsulated, was anything but.

LIFE AFTER A DREAM

The media went rabid over Preston's death and the Sturdy's annihilation, but Jury refused to stoke the flames, and interest died out. He prioritized preserving Preston's legacy and keeping Joe's existence a secret.

Joe's funeral was a private ceremony consisting of Red, Larry, Jude, Fin, and Jury. White clouds covered the sun. A rustic smell blanketed the air and warmed their bodies as they inhaled. Since Joe's physical form perished in the fire, they buried every picture they owned and some knick knacks from His truck. Only Joe's first name and the day of the Sturdy's destruction were written on the tombstone. As the others grieved, Jury and Larry nodded at each other, confirming a silent pact.

A few days later, Jude asked Jury to help plan Preston's funeral. Without hesitation, Jury agreed. Starting the next day, he poured newfound heart and soul into the preparations. Then, late at night, he returned to The Ranger. He'd sit upright in a lumpy cot and stare into the desert until the purple light lulled him to sleep.

Red and Larry, meanwhile, moved into an apartment in downtown Scarwood. They immediately busied themselves with preparations for their impending futures.

The day before Preston's funeral, Jury spoke on HNN. He revealed that Preston's ceremony would be his last day in town and that his eulogy would double as a farewell. That same night, he visited Red and Larry to disclose his intentions. He learned they also planned to go their separate ways after the funeral.

The following day, with their futures in mind, they each set out for Preston's funeral.

The services took place entirely outdoors at Scarwood's only cemetery. The grave was pre-dug and sat only about twenty yards from Joe.

Preston's open casket was in front of a speaking podium. Although there were undeniable similarities, the body inside didn't look like Preston. It seemed more like an uncanny wax statue.

Jude struggled to look at his boss, let alone recognize him. The pale, empty sky highlighted the bags under Jude's eyes and the heavy wrinkles around his face.

Jury soon approached him, hands in the pockets of his black suit. His champagne vest and tie sparkled among the dull cemetery and winter hues. He smiled and waved with his bandaged hand. "Hello, Jude!"

"Hey…" Although the two were on good terms, Jude's eyes were always grim at the sight of Jury. "Listen. I know I've had a lot of time to do this, but…" he paused and glanced at Preston's corpse. Instead of seeing the casket and grass around him, he saw the Golgotha desert and Jury's bleeding palm. He sighed. "There's something I need to get off my chest."

Jury raised an eyebrow. "That doesn't sound suspicious at all. What's—"

Noticing the cars already parked behind him, Jude cut him off.

The crowd was nearly quadruple what Emil's funeral had generated. Although moved by the attendance, Jude couldn't ditch the feeling that the group was missing something. Amidst the mass, no one from Preston's family was present.

Nearly every attendee showed Jude empathy. On the other hand, those same people swarmed Jury with questions every chance they got. He shrugged most of them off and searched the crowd for Red.

Larry sat on the hood of Joe's truck, which he now owned. His eyes drifted toward Joe's headstone as Red pulled up.

Red's car was packed to the brim, but there was a perfect space in the back to see the road behind him.

Larry peeked inside Red's car while greeting him. "You weren't kiddin'."

Red lightly scoffed. "I told you I was going back. Come heck or high water."

"Heck," he snickered. "As far as your Mom knows, you're dead. What if she turns you away? There's a big chance she's moved, ya know."

"I'll find her." Red's expression stiffened. An air of hesitation and guilt entered his voice. "Hey, I'm really sorry about how I brought it up."

"Whaddaya mean?"

He looked away from Larry and into the crowd. It seemed like he was searching for something. "About me going off on my own. I sprung it on you out of nowhere. Charting your own course is scary, especially with what we've had to go through, but you've done a really good job. I'm proud of you."

"Well, I knew it was comin' eventually. I was overwhelmed, but... His death changed my perspective." Larry's steely eyes tiptoed toward Joe's headstone.

Through the visible worry on his face, Red managed to flash a supportive smile. "Are you doing okay, buddy?"

Larry tore his eyes off Joe's grave and straightened his back. "Mm-hm. I'm great!"

Red leaned toward him, "You nervous for your interview, buddy?"

"Oh! Uh, yeah. Sure."

Red raised his eyebrows. "It's really inconvenient to have it right after the funeral, but the sooner, the better." His cheeks glowed. "Joe would be proud of you. If there's anything you want to tell me, I'd be glad to listen. I mean, it's my turn to help you, after all."

Through his world of grief, Larry looked up and smiled at him. True light entered his voice. "You're thinkin' too much. Havin' you at my side through all this has been more helpful than you could imagine."

Sentimentality entered Red's stomach, but before he could address it, Jude ascended the podium, and the two rushed to their seats.

After a heartfelt—if excessively sentimental—speech, Jude sat. The crowd's silence pierced him with each step. Had his seat been an inch farther, he would've fainted.

Once Jude sat, Jury rose. He could feel every eye in the cemetery examining him. Despite this, he refused to rush and whistled softly to the podium. After clearing his throat and tapping the microphone, he looked up and beamed. "Good afternoon, everyone. I'd introduce myself, but most of you were talking to me as though you knew me, so there's no point."

Amidst the annoyed crowd, Red, Jude, Akila, and Larry snickered. Jury batted his hand. "Oh, lighten up. Preston's probably getting a kick outta your humorless faces."

Joe's words echoed through his mind. *Did ya forget you're hostin' a funeral? I appreciate the lightheartedness, but this isn't the time to screw around.*

Jury peered at Joe's headstone before turning back to the crowd. "I'm sorry. I didn't mean to be insensitive." His tone and mannerisms became imbued with formality and warmth. "Preston was born on

September 1st, 1939, to Albert and Gertrude Epalit. The Preston we know from RBLA is not the man I wish to honor today. I hope to instill in you an image of a man who took his rocky start and triumphantly made it his strength. The same Preston who, in his final moments, stopped being afraid and spent his last breath drying my tears."

The wind around him became more intense, and his soft, silky hair swirled. "We need to remember how Preston succeeded, not the fact that he's no longer here. And for now, perhaps our grief will interfere with our ability to do so, and we may struggle to remain positive. I once said that all we must do to overcome grief is stay united and in love, but that's not enough. Death, be it a loved one's or our own, is the only fact of life. Nothing lasts forever, and some things never even begin. There's power in realizing that, someday, all things must end: dreams, rivalries," wistfulness passed through him like a ghost. "Even relationships."

Jury desired more than anything to look at Red, but he avoided it and tossed that passion back into his tone. "Although changing your fate may be impossible, you can always change yourself and your outlook. You must be self-aware, in spite of your own suffering and service. Preston helped me realize that. Without him, I never could have learned that people can redeem themselves and change."

His voice slowed and deepened. "Life itself will change, but for most, it's never that seamless or definitive. People shift from one mask to another until, eventually, one molds to them. And what speaks louder about a person than the moment they rip that mask to shreds? As Preston's life and death have shown us, there's meaning behind everything, just as there's life after a dream." He leaned closely into the microphone, "Thank you," and promptly walked off stage.

Much of the crowd admired the eloquence of Jury's words but were confused by his message. Those closest to Preston and Jury, however, were moved. Jude's grief was more in line with a widow's, but through the tears, his face radiated joy. It was the pain of relief. A pain that Red hadn't yet felt. His trembling hands shook beyond recognition.

Jude tottered to the podium once more, nearly stumbling over his tears. He called for anyone else to speak, but no one volunteered.

Services soon concluded, and Preston was laid to rest.

With everyone trying to leave at once, Jury, Larry, and Red disappeared in the mob. Only Jude was clear, standing right in front of Preston's headstone. His gaze was cast downward. He couldn't stop staring at the inscription.

"I died? What a crock."

"Hey," Akila put her hand on his shoulder, "You doing okay?" She peered at the headstone and looked back at him, bewildered. "What's up with that inscription?"

"Preston picked it himself." He laughed. "The bastard." Jude turned around and was caught off guard by the soothing smile on Akila's face. For a moment, his expression lost its tranquility. "I'll always remember Preston. Wherever he is, I hope that's enough for him." He closed his eyes and sighed. His voice quivered. "I just wish I could've stopped him."

A familiar, Hoosier accent appeared behind them. "You can't stop everything, Jude."

They turned around and saw Jury, hands comfortably resting in his suit pockets. He extended a champagne-colored handkerchief toward Jude.

He grabbed it and blew his nose. "Look at me, the weeping widow."

Akila eyed Jury up and down. "Always nice to see you, Jury. That's a beautiful tux, even if it's a bit spiffy for a funeral."

Jury's eyes were virtually dead. "Gee, thanks." He turned to Jude and loosened his expression. "I thought it was only fair to make a good lasting impression on the town I tried playing God in."

Jude scrunched up his face. "I wouldn't say–"

"I'm trying to say that I've been a piece of shit," Jury flashed a playful smirk, "And I'm sorry."

"You know," light flashed across Akila's eyes, "With all the publicity, re-building Mailugulism would be easy. Hell, with that insurance payout from the fire, you could probably build four more Sturdys."

With a humble grin, Jury batted his hand. "It's plenty for Red and Larry to start a new life. I'd just waste it." He zoned out and found his eyes drifting to Larry and Red. They were sitting in front of Joe's headstone, heads tilted toward the sky.

"I still can't believe it." Akila turned away from them and looked into the sky. "So much death in so little time. Scarwood has never been like that."

"All it takes is one prophet." Jury checked his watch and inhaled through clenched teeth. "Larry's interview starts soon, so I need to get going." He shook Akila's hand. "Thank you for everything you've done. I'm in a much better place because of it." He then moved to Jude's. "Thank you for reaching out. I have no doubt it's been hard." He gripped Jude's hand tighter and alternated eye contact between him and Akila, "I appreciate not being asked about the contents of that camera. By the way, Jude, what did you want to talk about earlier?"

"Oh, um." Jude's face relaxed. "Nothing you need to re-live."

"I appreciate that." Jury finally released Jude's hand and walked off.

Jury approached Red and Larry and noticed they were still looking into the sky. Their eyes sparkled. "What?" Jury smirked. "Are you guys trying to catch him staring back?"

Red was so deep in thought that he didn't bother questioning Jury. His tone was wondrous. "It looks so peaceful up there, doesn't it?"

Jury furrowed his eyebrows and looked. All he saw were mobs of emotionless clouds. Still, he laboriously studied every inch.

His deep breathing became a distraction. Larry's voice emitted hints of hope. "If you're lookin' for a jellyfish, join the club. I haven't seen one since Joe died."

"Hm." Jury chuckled. Although he was free, the bags under his eyes had never been heavier.

That's what Red thought, at least. He didn't realize he was biting the side of his lip. "Are you *sure* about this, Jury?"

After processing Red's expression and words, Jury looked the other way. "Of course. Are you?"

"Mm-hm."

The two struggled to look at each other.

Larry cocked his head and raised his eyebrows. "Damn, you two are seriously beatin' around the bush here." He stood up and brushed off his khakis. "This is the last time we'll ever be together. Say somethin' more meaningful for Chr–" he looked at Jury, shook his head, and regained control of his voice, "Cryin' out loud."

"Technically," began Jury, "Since it's on his way, Red's accompanying me to Golgotha. Our goodbyes get to wait."

Larry wrinkled his nose and stared, his eyes comically wide. "I bet that'll be painful. I wish I could see you off, but–"

"Your interview. Now, that's for..." Jury tilted his head, "Sheet metal, you said?"

Larry's resulting smile almost reached his eyes. His dimples had never been clearer. "About that, I have no desire to work a boring nine to five. Joe wouldn't want that. I'm in the prime of my youth, ya know? He gave me that truck for a reason." He looked into the bright sun and closed his eyes as the rays washed over him. "So, I'm gonna drive through every state. See the sights. Follow the signs. See the world. There are going to be times where I struggle, financially and emotionally, but I know I'll find a way. Joe would want me to see the world. And honestly?" He chuckled. "I really want to. I know you may not approve, Red, but—"

"All I want you to do is be careful. Well, Larry," despite his moist eyes, Red beamed. Still, he couldn't keep up with the tears racing down his face. "Ugh, I promised myself I wouldn't do this." He squeezed his eyes shut over and over again to no avail. He opened his arms and embraced Larry, who returned the gesture and buried his face into Red's jacket.

Red managed to spit out his words through his trembling chin. "I'm so proud of you."

A single tear fell from Larry's eye. He smiled. "Be proud of yourself! You're doin' the right thing."

Red released Larry from his grasp and stepped back. He wiped his eyes and grinned.

Jury exhaled through enlarged nostrils and quivering lips. "You've become a real poet, Larry."

Larry's eyes shined. "You know what they say, everyone becomes a poet in Fall. See you l–" he stumbled over that syllable. He tightened his lips and turned away. "Good luck, guys. I'll never forget you both, for better and for worse." He rocked back and forth on his feet before walking into the horizon.

Jury and Red waved long after Larry couldn't see them. Even Mother Nature spoke her parting words through swirling clouds and dancing red leaves. The sun's pink rays grew brighter and brighter until Larry faded over the hill entirely.

Red wiped his eyes one last time. The trembling of his hands finally ceased. "It's time to go, isn't it?"

"Yeah... um. This is going to sound weird, but–" Jury scratched the back of his head, "Do you mind giving me some privacy?"

Red raised his hands. "Take your time." He walked to the car, swirling the key ring around his finger.

Jury gave him a thumbs-up and turned to Joe's headstone. It was unclear whether he was staring at his feet or the ground beneath him. His voice was soft. "I'm sorry for everything. I'll make it up to you, I promise. But if you don't like what I'm about to do, then I guess this is goodbye."

Jury turned around and high-tailed it to Golgotha.

A committee of vultures sat on the roof of The Ranger and watched Jury pull in.

Jury was enamored by the majesty of the never-ending desert. He was convinced he could faintly see a purple light beyond the horizon. After a few deep breaths, he exited the vehicle, leaving his belongings in the trunk, his jacket in the passenger seat, and the keys in the ignition.

Red jumped out of his car and race-walked toward him. "*This* is how you've been living!?"

Jury smirked and folded his arms. "I prefer to say *where*."

Red pointed at the disintegrated, sparking sign letters and looked back at him. "Jury! You see that electric waste, right? Ugh!" He took a deep breath and chilled out. "Sorry. I just don't get it. Out of every building in Golgotha, why pick the most dilapidated one?"

"You know why."

He tilted his head and stammered. "If this place has that meaning to you, then why—" He violently exhaled and hung his head. "Never mind. Sorry."

A brutal gust of wind tore through Red and Jury as though filling the silence. Red's light jacket was barely thicker than a paper towel. Without his mittens, he'd have turned into a block of ice.

Jury's face lightened up. "Want my coat? It's in my passenger seat."

Red extended a shivering palm and stuttered, "N... no. I'm good."

"You sure?"

His voice lacked its usual tenderness. "Thanks, but the one I'm wearing is fine. And can you please stop asking me if I'm sure about everything? There are other ways you can word it."

Jury cleared his throat. He placed one hand on his chest and spoke in a posh falsetto. "My dearest Red, on account of your shivering exterior, I assume you are cold. Yet, although my jacket would shield you–"

"I get it, Jury." Red pouted and lowered his eyebrows. "I'd rather not make a big production out of this."

A sudden glint of pain shot through Jury's eyes. His voice became grounded and grim. "Sorry, Red. I'm just trying to lighten the mood." He sighed. "I don't want to be wasteful, you know?"

Despite the humor of the situation, Red was weirdly aggressive. "Shouldn't you be more worried about the car? You can't just pick it up and throw it away like that coat."

"Throw it away?! My *jacket* has way more application than that piece of crap car. It guzzles gas, slips on everything, and can barely fit my fat ass! I hope some crackhead wanders out here and takes it for a joy ride. That's the only afterlife I see it having."

"So," he scratched his chin, "There's life after everything for humans and jackets, but not cars?" Red facepalmed and began speaking in a lighter tone. "Good God. How have we been taking this seriously? After everything we've been through," he inhaled through clenched teeth, "All we can do is talk about a coat and a car. Mom was right to say I dance around everything."

"And also a bitch."

His posture straightened. "All the more reason to confront her."

Jury smiled and patted him on the back. They were standing side-by-side, facing the vast desert. The nearly setting sun warmed them and their voices. Its red light made the sand look gray. "I'm proud of you."

"I wish I could say the same, to be honest." He paused. "I'm sorry. I shouldn't have said that."

Jury was caught off guard but not heartbroken. In a way, hearing that motivated him more. "It's okay. That's why I want to confront everything once and for all, just like you."

Red broke away from Jury. His tone now fully utilized the aggression that had loomed over their earlier words. "You know what? Since we're being transparent, what on Earth are you confronting? Confronting my *mother* is perfectly reasonable, even after all these years. But... ugh, what are you thinking?" He extended his arm to the desert, and his voice slightly broke. "It's a death trap out there, Jury!"

His voice was lifeless. "I think it's beautiful. When I think about death traps, your mother's house is the first place to come to mind. Not Golgotha."

"Don't make a joke out of this! What else do you see out there besides death?" He sighed and held his head down. "I'm sorry I've been snippy, but even though we're not together, I still care about you." He looked up at Jury, eyes glistening. His words were quiet and delicate. "I don't want you to die."

Jury frowned and lowered his eyebrows. He put his hand on Red's shoulder. "Hey... it's okay. I was prepared to die with Preston anyway."

His voice remained soft. "You're telling me you were willing to die without saying goodbye?"

"Goodbyes weren't even on my mind. I mean, honestly, I don't deserve to say goodbye." The kindness of Red's words struck him at once. He stumbled over his following few words. "But... *you* do. Hm. Don't you deserve a little more than a crappy goodbye from someone like me?"

"What else would I deserve?"

Jury pounded his fist into his palm. "To move on. You'll always be my dream, and now that I can't make you happy, giving you peace is my priority."

Red tilted his head and moved his eyes toward the sky. "How do you know you'll find your fate out there? I'm not trying to gaslight you, but if you saw something out here with Preston when you were *literally running* out of blood, chances are that it was just a hallucination."

Although he was filled with resolve, Jury remained perfectly calm. "All my other prophecies came true. I've been waiting on this one for *twelve... years!* Maybe it'll never come to me unless I go to it."

Red crossed his arms and tightened his lips. He didn't blink once and kept his eyes trained on Jury. "Prophecy or not, your mother is gone. Weren't you just preaching about how we must accept death to live fully?"

Jury's expression tightened. His reliably unstable eyes danced from corner to corner. "I wish I could live by those words, Red." He pivoted toward the desert. "I know there's something out there. I'll find her, and if I don't, I'll finally be ready to move on."

Red was running out of things to say but not the desire to say them. "There's a difference between moving on and becoming numb. Jury, you can't..."

For a moment, Jury became intense, almost bursting at his seams. "This is the first time in twenty-one years that I've felt in control!" His face and tone became dire at the sight of Red's distress. "I mean that. I feel closer now than I've ever been."

Red winced. "I've heard so many variations of that phrase." He crossed his arms and tapped his foot against the gray sand. "This must be going great by your logic, right?"

Jury tilted his head. He looked despaired and confused by Red's words.

Red's hardened eyes were wide and still. "The crazier you sound, the more easily I should be able to move on. It's just that simple. Like I could ever forget you!" A sudden burst of sincerity and strength entered his tone. "Fine. I'll let you go... since that's what you want."

"You have every reason to go home, Red. I'm sorry." Jury delicately took off one of Red's gloves and sandwiched Red's hand between his. He smiled. "You know, it's ironic for a man with such cold hands to have such a warm heart."

A symphony of words floated through his mind, but Red turned away and retracted his hands.

Fear shot through Jury, then resolve. He sounded like he was about to cry. "I miss your smile. I hope I get to see it again someday. Until then, it's time we make Larry proud." He suddenly threw his arms around Red. "Goodbye, my love."

Red's hands quivered for a moment, but soon he wrapped his hands around Jury's. The setting sun illuminated them. "How do you expect me to move on if you aren't even safe?"

"Please, have some faith. It's the only thing keeping me going, but you have so much more." After they released, Jury looked him in the eyes, registering every detail to memory one final time. He wiped a tear and started walking toward the desert. Before he could keep walking, he was distracted by Red's stammering and turned around.

Red looked up at him, balled his hands, and yelled. "*Why!??*"

Jury smiled. His voice was delicate. "Do you remember my favorite animal, Red?"

Red, lost in tears, stumbled over his words. "J-j-"

"Jellyfish. You were right." The sand surrounding them danced with Jury's words, and a soothing melody of wind passed between them. "I think we all wish for the life of a jellyfish. You would see everything yet feel nothing besides the waves carrying you to meals, family. In some cases, you'd even live forever. And all you'd have to do is go where you're pulled." He straightened his posture and took a deep breath. "They say life can never be that simple, but I've never tried living like that, so I will. I'll go to the first place I'm pulled and never look back. That's what you're doing, after all. There's a lot of love in your heart, and I'm praying you find someone who deserves it. You'll be okay, Red. After all, our memories are what's giving me the strength to do this." Without waiting for a reply, Jury turned back to Golgotha.

Red sniffled. Brush after brush couldn't clear the tears. Yet, through the grief, he managed a quick chuckle and a smile.

Although their attention was captured, the vultures on the roof kept their distance. The gazelles looked up from their shrubbery and peered in their direction.

Red was in awe. The way the sunlight glimmered around Jury was unlike anything he had ever seen. Breathtaking, as Red finally had the breath to give. His hands refused to tremble, and his still eyes remained fixated on Jury, their gaze not broken by a single blink. Then, even with Jury still in view, Red turned around and walked back to the parking lot.

Red begrudgingly grabbed Jury's jacket. He then sat in his own car, keys unturned. Between the death of his closest bond and the resurrection of his most essential, he was overwhelmed. He clutched Jury's jacket and wondered what he would do if Jury returned, be it in four days or four decades. He tightened his grip around Jury's jacket, but as he drew it closer, a scent of cigarette smoke slapped him. He tossed it into the passenger seat, knocking a loose cigarette out of its pocket.

He smiled and chuckled. "Asshole." He held the cigarette and thought about his memories again. Even in the days he'd rather forget, there were moments he'd treasure. Moments that define him, even when his backbone had yet to form. A warmer look came to him as he turned the keys and shifted into reverse. "Jesus, I should've done this a long time ago."

After flicking the loose cigarette out of his car window, Red released the brake and cruised out of The Ranger and Golgotha without a second thought.

Jury looked back. Fog blocked his final view of Red. With this, he filled in the blanks and grinned for the first time in a lifetime. He was so touched by his delusion that he almost cried. Yet, one final illusion awaited him, so he kept moving.

At first, the sand was more like a red carpet. As he closed the gap between himself and the epicenter of Golgotha, the wind began resisting him, and the sand became paste. His smile faded into resolve.

Directly challenged, the elements launched a counterattack. The desert heat rose. Jury felt the weight of Preston's body on his shoulders, but he still dug deep with each step. A gust of wind slapped him, removing the color from his sight. The only color that remained, shining like headlights, was that of his emerald eyes.

Over minutes or days, his mind cleared, and his consciousness be-came no thicker than the dust assaulting him from all angles. Despite the burn, his pupils never wavered or watered. Motivation remained even as his body went numb. His eyelids drooped more and more, and his footsteps became fierce and primal. Centuries passed, and he could no longer tell whether he was trudging through snow, sand, or something far thicker. Each step required more force until their demands were barely within Jury's rapidly diminishing reach.

He kept breathing in and out, but air wouldn't fill his lungs. He slowed down and leaned on his knees. After catching his breath, he looked around him and caught a glimpse of his fingers. Only then did the sensation of the sand filling his nails register. He raised his hand to his eyes and studied it.

Reaching below him, he picked up a handful of sand and let it run through his fingers. The particles that didn't flow under his hand gilded upward like seeds blowing through the wind. They sparkled like stars. Focusing on them rather than the excruciating heat made the pain fade. His hand still extended, he lifted his head, closed his eyes, and breathed. Although the air stinged and his eyes were shut, he felt more connected to the world than ever before.

When he gazed upon the Earth again, Jury found himself trans-ported to an area nestled between dream and reality. His shirt fluttered through a warm breeze as he stared upon the same ghost town from his vision. The small houses around him flickered in and out as though sputtering through an old projector. The only building he could see inside contained a hospital bed and an open window, looking out at a purple light no more than a mile away. It would have taken his breath away had there been any to spare.

Only one thing remained visible through the blazing, airborne sand. He collapsed to his knees.

The sands rolled and crashed against each other like waves on a coastline. They carried him toward the purple light. The delusion of his mother was nowhere to be found, and her questions faded entirely. Instead, he thought one final time of Red, Larry, Preston, and all the other people who inspired him. He thought of them as miracles of their own design. He smiled at the thought that the world's fate wasn't dependent on his limitless potential, but instead the kindness of those around him.

Through his flickering, nearly vacant eyes, Jury Chessjurist watched as the purple light faded, and a colossal hand emerged from a cylindrical tomb of parting sand.

Red knocks on his mother's door. Larry puts his truck in gear. At the same time, wind scatters ashes on the ground, revealing a Mailugula pamphlet to a passing stranger.

Mailugula *lives*.

About the author

Hi! I'm John Gross! I'm a nurse, writer, and husband. I grew up as an only child, entertaining myself and always thinking about what I could have said. My imagination and video games kept me company. I love *Dead Rising, Devil May Cry*, and the music of Queen. Freddie Mercury and Fred Rogers are my two biggest inspirations. I'm also a huge horror fan; some of my favorites being *Society*, *The Thing*, and 1989's *Phantom of the Opera* starring Robert Englund.

Professional Inquiries, please email johnbgrossnovels@gmail.com, Follow me on tiktok and/or instagram!

Want to know when my next project releases? Join the email list at this link: https://dashboard.mailerlite.com/forms/1594085/157229905 103292194/share

FREE FIRST CHAPTER OF MY NEXT NOVEL: THE ICK

My girlfriend calls it the ick. That immovable pit in your stomach when you're so uncomfortable you could throw up. Whenever I park my car and look into someone's house, I get that feeling. I'm supposed to be taking care of people, but that feeling never goes away. Even when I'm inside and acquainted, that discomfort persists. It's uncomfortable being in someone else's home. It's an immediate boundary break. Understandably, it's just as awkward for the tenants to let this stranger enter their lives. You think that would establish common ground. More often than not, it just breeds contempt.

This house is beautiful. It's about a mile to the beach. The echoes of the crashing waves reach it. From the front, it only looks like a handful of small rooms. I can't see anything through the nearly opaque windows. I stare at the door and gather my courage to enter. I wish I could see what was going on. Any behind-the-scenes info would ease my mind, but I have nothing. The sound of the waves does that instead.

The door opens as I'm texting my girlfriend that I made it. I jump out of the car with my backpack in hand. What type of first impression would it be if I left someone waiting at the door? I rush up to the front. My scrubs are bright red and my shoes are white. I toss my head back to knock my blonde bangs out of my eyes.

A woman is holding open the screen door for me. She grins through her thin, pink lips. The bags under her rose eyes are enormous. They expand past her nostrils and are so puffy that her pupils only poke out about halfway. She doesn't look like she's squinting. She just looks tired. Her hair is a rich, oak-brown color and appears silky to the touch. A few strands fall in front of her red, blushed cheeks. She reminds me of the actress Catherine Keener.

She extends her hand. "Nice to meet you! I'm Chondra."

I reach for her hand, and she gives me a limp, dainty shake. I exhale. I'm almost out of breath as I speak and walk past her into the house. "I'm so sorry about the texts. I started panicking because it told me there's an hour time gap, and I didn't want to be late, and–"

"It's okay!" She cuts in. "We ignore that. We use central time, like anyone who matters."

Like anyone who matters? I shake away that sentence and keep talking. "I even forgot my phone charger and water bottle, man. Do you guys have any water, by chance?"

"Yeah-yeah-yeah." She eyes me up and down. "How old are you, Billy? Twelve?"

Everyone has always told me I have a soft face. "Twenty-two. Just had a birthday a week ago today."

"So then... August fifteenth, 2001?"

I nod.

"22 in 23, nice!"

I chuckle and extend my hands, "It's probably a surprise. I know I look twelve. Those are my Mom's genes." I lightly slap my belly. "Nursing school has given me back that baby fat, too."

Chondra laughs. Right when I think she finished, she snickers again. "Oh, you're just short. If anything, you're a—" she snaps, "What's the word for it?"

"A twink?"

"I was thinking a herb, but you definitely wouldn't be a bear, so... yeah."

I shrug. "I'm five foot six with dopey Justin Bieber hair and a blue-eyed stare. I'm a twink."

"Lucky you're not in prison. That's a movie I'd love to watch. You'd be—heh heh, anyway. My apologies." She clears her throat and stares into my eyes. "Oh, Billy! Your eyes are *beautiful!*"

My lips tighten. I need to tone it back a bit. "Yeah... thanks." I get that a lot. My eyes are glossy like marble and piercing, ocean water levels of blue.

Watching Chondra gaze into them makes me uneasy. A chill runs down my spine. Or maybe it's sweat. It is so *hot* in here. I wait for her to say something, but she just keeps staring.

"Mm!" She violently shakes her head, as if snapping out of a trance. "So, this is your... *second* time with my mother?"

"I was with her Sunday. Ope! Today is Sunday. I meant Wednesday." I put my chin in my hand. "Or was it Thursday? She was in the hospital. That much I know for sure. I promise I have a better grasp on my care than what day of the week it is."

"Sure you do. You were there for fourteen hours, right?"

With a sigh, I nod. "Yeah. 7 P to 9 A. Don't worry. I stayed awake then. I can stay awake now. Even though it is ruthlessly long."

"Meh. Tomato, to*motto*." She crosses her arms and eyes me up. "How was she?"

Immediately, flashes of her mother screaming, crying, peeing on the floor, and throwing herself out of bed come to mind. "Oh, you know." I widen my eyes. "A little agitated."

"I bet!"

I nudge her arm. "But I understand. How would you feel if somebody zapped your memory, you had no idea where you were, and some stranger in red was sitting next to you?"

Chondra points at me. "Right! RIGHT!!" She's pumping me up like I'm her frat bro. "She probably thought you were the Devil herself. Exactly! We just gotta think about it from their perspective." She shakes her head. "You probably just had a bad night with her. They've doubled her medicine, so she's much more stable. Those stupid nurses. Tch. Each of them did something different!"

I remember the nurse I was with that night as a hard worker. Most nurses I know are hard workers. I furrow my eyebrows and nod. "Right. When I was with her, the nurse only gave her Tylenol."

She slaps my arm. I now regret the friendly nudge from before. "Right! RIGHT!! We're lucky we have a doctor who cares. You know he found out she was in the hospital and immediately called us? Isn't that sweet? We were able to get the narcotics like they were nothing."

I nod. I see a wheelchair in the corner, but her mother is nowhere to be found. Usually, family members in this business are either rich and apathetic or weird and overinvolved. They typically give me a tour. I stand quietly for a few seconds, but Chondra gives me nothing. She watches me look around.

I catch a glimpse of the interior. The room is shrouded in darkness, but I can still make out the furniture in the living room. I see no lamps or candles. The only light illuminating the room is from the moon, shining through the gaps in the boarded-up windows.

I point at them. "Uh, why?"

Chondra bats her hand. "Pf, you know. Mommy kept trying to–"

"*Ohhhh*, get out?"

She squints at me. "*No*. Break them and stab me."

My eyes widen. The windows are shoddily boarded up. I can still see the glass. "Oh, but... okay."

There isn't a ton of furniture, but what's here is enormous. The couch could fit at least twelve, the TV is seventy-five inches, and the table between them is the longest thing in the room. There's a roaming counter in the kitchen that doesn't even fit. It's taller than the stove. The furniture looks new. There's not a stray hair on anything. The floor is clean and clear. The whole place almost looks like an empty model home. I don't even see any family photos.

About twenty seconds have passed, and Chondra still hasn't said anything. She's staring down the hall.

I point in the direction and furrow my eyebrows. "Is Irene down there?"

"Oh!" She snaps out of a trance. "Okay. Yeah. She's over here." She leads me down the hallway. It is the only area in the house so far that has a light.

Standing in the doorway, Chondra turns to me. "That's the bathroom down there." She points down the hall and to the left. "Oh, and we have a dog. Did your boss tell you that?"

"No. But that's not a problem."

"Wonderful! He's a big boy."

At this moment, I hear a deep, ferocious couple of barks.

"Pf." Chondra bats her hand. "Ignore him. He's just mad that we gave him a tub bath today. You know dogs hate that tubby time."

"Uh," I step back, "Aren't you thinking of cats?"

She slugs me on the arm again. "Right! RIGHT!!"

Chondra's mother, Irene, is lying in a bed in the middle of the room. Side rails box her in. The bed is only five feet long, but her toes don't touch the end of it. The lamp in the corner is overwhelmingly bright. There's a bizarre, cyan tint to it. My eyes scrunch up as I struggle to adjust. Bottles of pills and uncapped needles obscure the tiny TV. At the sight of these syringes, goosebumps visibly run down my arm. I shiver.

Either Irene is so frail that she's tiny, or so tiny that she's frail. Her face is incredibly slim. Turquoise casts cover her wrists. Her skin is healthy. Her fingers and toes aren't folded over each other. Her gray hair is beautiful and full. It's like her body sends all the energy to her pores instead of her brain. A blanket is wadded up at the foot of her bed, and her heels float over a teal pillow. Her blue nightgown barely goes past her pelvis.

After setting my bag by a brown recliner, I walk up to her and smile. A warmth and energy that were previously absent from my voice now fill it. "Hi, Irene! It's great to see you again. How're you feeling?"

Chondra glares in my direction.

Irene doesn't even look at me. Her eyes are half open, and there's a dazed expression on her face.

A young woman approaches me. She's short, portly, and wearing black scrubs. "Hi, Billy!"

I recognize this woman from the last time I took care of Irene. "Howdy, Chance. How is she?"

"Eh," she wiggles her hand in the air. "Tired now."

As Chance gives me a basic report, I see Chondra glaring at me from the doorway.

"Uh, is there something wrong?"

Chondra's eyes glaze over. "Huh? Oh, sorry." She sounds more curious than offended. "I was just wondering what happened to your voice. So warm when talking to my mother, but so robotic with every-thing else."

I smirk. "I may be young, but I've been in healthcare so long that the customer service voice is just a switch that I flip."

Chondra's face crumples. "Customer service voice?"

Chance clears her throat. "Anyway." She shows me the gray bedside commode that Irene uses and describes how she transfers to it. She walks toward the door. "Irene has right-sided weakness. So, she only sits up on the left side of the bed. I usually put a pad on the floor just in case she pees. Make sure you raise the bed a bit when you transfer her. It kills my back, otherwise." She picks up a white remote sitting at the edge of the bed.

"Is this like a hospital bed?" I ask.

Chondra raises her finger. "No, it's a home bed with a remote that lowers it."

"Okay?" I want to ask what the difference is, but I'm not willing to poke the bear.

Chance shows me the remote raising and lowering the head of the bed. I recognise this mechanism from the nursing home I used to work at. "Yeah, I get it. About the transfers, does Irene still scream when you stand her up?"

She's about to smile and nod, but after catching a glimpse of Chondra, she suddenly shakes her head. "No. She's calmed down. She doesn't really move her legs much anymore, but she can stand and pivot as long as you use her good side. She *should* stay in bed."

Chondra chuckles. "We also got her to take a laxative earlier by sneaking it into her ice cream. That's the only thing she'll eat these days. Freakin' child. Anyway, that's our present to you."

My brain says, "Really?" But I respond with, "I'm glad." I'm sure if that's better, but Chondra doesn't seem to mind.

She bats her hand. "She's a little combative, you know! You're probably gonna have to deal with that at some point." She smiles at her sleeping mother. "Ma is so feisty!"

Chance is edging toward the door, "Okay... anymore–"

I absolutely have more questions. My brain tells me not to ask this, but it's nagging at me. I ask in a gentle, casual voice, "Oh, and just a quick question, what's your guys' policy on sleep? I wasn't sure if the caregivers sleep if Irene's doing okay, because my boss couldn't give me a clear answer."

The mood shifts. Chondra and Chance look at me like I'm insane.

I pivot my head away from them. "I mean, this is a fourteen-hour night shift. Not that I can't do it. I've done worse." Still no response. I sweat. The door is closed, and I can feel every trapped vapor of heat building.

Chondra just glares at me, eye twitching and mouth open.

I am desperate for even an expulsion of breath. "Just... uh, how do most people get through it? A fifteen-minute nap every few hours or what?"

Chance tenses up. She answers like there's a gun behind her back. "Uh, I mean, if that's what you have to do. I don't know. The other girls doze off every once in a while, but, by and large, I think they need to stay awake."

Usually, I'd kick myself for not listening to my gut, but I'm too confused. I'm asking a pretty simple question. "I-I-I don't plan on sleeping. I just want a good idea of what the other caregivers do all night. This is my first time in this house, ya know?"

Chance nods. She seems more natural now. "Yeah, I get it. Home health is weird."

Chance and I have reached an understanding, but Chondra is still looking at me as if I'm dripping in her mother's blood. I point to my bag. "I brought plenty of stuff to do, Chondra. I'm *not* gonna sleep. I was just asking a question."

She's hesitant and evasive. "Yeah... okay. Just don't scare me."

CLINK! It sounds like something fell in the kitchen. Chondra's head snaps in the direction of the sound like a curious dog. She takes one step back. "I'll go get you that water, Billy." She slinks out of the room.

"Be careful, by the way." Chance says, quickly. "I dozed off for a second and when I woke up, I had this weird splinter in my arm."

She lifts up her sleeve and shows me. It doesn't look infected.

I don't know what to do with that. "Uh, how did that happen?"

"I don't know. I just woke up and there it was. My sleeve rolled up and everything." She hears something in the kitchen. Then, she whispers, each word purposeful, "There's a nanny cam behind me. It's hiding behind the TV. They can see everything you're doing."

I pivot past her and stare into it. It's hidden between the pill bottles. My shoulders hunch. I feel Chondra watching me. I wonder if she can hear me, too, but I can't ask, because she's already back. She didn't bring any water, either.

In her presence, Chance talks with fervor and personality as if she didn't miss a beat. "Yeah, that's just there so if you have to leave the room, which you shouldn't, you can see what's going on in the living room."

Before I can ask anything else, Chance is already halfway out the door, "Anything else? No? Okay. Ask Chondra or Pat if you have any other questions."

Chondra's extending neck follows her. "Bye, Chance!" She turns to me and goofily whispers, "I'll go see her out." She leaves the door ajar. I shut it.

I sit in the recliner. Irene is sleeping. I lean my head back and sigh. "Maybe this'll be an easier night."

The hair on the back of my neck springs up. I look, and the nanny cam blinks at me. I shudder.

I understand why my discomfort at this would seem stupid. This is not my home, so why should I expect any privacy? I don't. I just want to be able to do my job in peace, and when it seems like there's always an eye on me, it interferes with my work. I'm also aware that referring to a caregiving job as "my work" sounds disingenuous. I call it work because it *is*. That is a fact I cannot stress enough.

As I'm about to get my phone out, Chondra opens the door and walks right past me. She leans over the side rails and caresses her mother's hair. "Awww. I love you, honey." She turns to me and talks way too loudly. "Isn't she the cutest when she sleeps?"

I wipe the sweat from the back of my neck, and can't shake away the earlier tightness in the air. "Hey, you don't have to worry about me dozing off. Seriously."

She slightly purses her lip and raises Irene's bed. "Oh. I get it."

Something still feels wrong, so I decide to keep talking. "Uh, so you've had Jennifer? That's cool. She trained me. One of the finest aids I've ever met."

"Mm, we tried her." She chortles to herself and half-smirks. "Didn't quite... *fit*." She nudges the side of my stomach again. "Young men are so... eager to please. The hospital workers raved about you."

My heart sinks. I step back from Chondra. "Oh," I nervously chuckle, "Did they?"

"Yeah. How's that for pretty privilege? Oh, to be young. Anyway, I'll leave you to it. I got some work to do." She walks out. I close the door behind her.

I put my head in my hands. Oh, to be young? How about: Oh, to be crippled and have dementia? I feel bad for her mother.

Before I can even pull my phone out, Chondra's opening the door. Her eyes are wide, and she's speaking a mile a minute. "You know, it is such a long shift you guys got. I never sleep at night anyway, ya know. I could come in and give you a break."

I smile and extend my palm. "I appreciate that, but please don't worry. I'm here so *you* can sleep."

She laughs. "Oh-ho no. We're all about this, right here." She casts her palm across her mother's body as if channeling energy. "Don't worry about her waking me up or anything. I'd be here all night if it were up to me and my body. I can give you a break. You could go sit on the porch or something."

"At one in the morning?" I ask.

"Sure. I can wake up then."

Not what I meant, but I nod. "Okay, okay. So, I got it from here. You can go ahead and do your thing."

She sounds withdrawn. "Oh... okay. That's fine."

I chuckle affably. "I get it. Don't worry. I've done a lot of dementia care."

"Me too. I'm a psychologist."

"Oh, cool!" My eyes widen. "We sent a *lot* of patients to psych."

"Neat." She sits on the bed. "Where'd you work?"

"PCRC, in my hometown. I..." I hang my head for a moment and hesitate. I'm embarrassed to admit this. "I don't work there anymore. I experienced the worst burnout of my life there. It was fine until I started school and saw other jobs. Then, I understood how awful it was."

She laughs. "You're burnt out? At 21?"

"22." I exhale and look out the window. "Yeah. It felt impossible to me. But it happened. That's why I'm here."

"To help your burn out?"

I shrug. "To not make it worse. I still have to pay my rent until I can get my nursing license."

Chondra scoffs. "You think being a nurse will make you *less* burnt out? Fat chance, Billy."

I tilt my head. What is she getting at? Is she trying to help me? I feel anything but uplifted, and my tone reflects this. "I'm sorry. What do you want me to say?"

"Well," she folds her arms, "I don't understand. What do you want, Billy?"

"To not do this."

She squints and moves her head toward me. "Nurses still help, ya know."

I roll my eyes in my head and flash an indifferent grin. "I'm aware. I just don't want to worry about whether I'll be able to make the rent every month. That's all." I step away from her and cross my arms. "Isn't that what all of us want?"

She scrunches her face and rolls her eyes. "You need to be passionate about–"

I hold up my hand. I've heard this a hundred times. "Passion won't put me through school. Even if it would, I'm not willing to struggle for ten years just to be able to judge people clinically." Caution floods my manner. "I appreciate the sentiment, though! I respect you for being a psychologist. Honestly, that job sounds excruciating."

She pauses. Surprise fills her expression, but after thinking for a moment, she laughs. "Right! RIGHT!! Those crazy people, man. Give 'em an inch and they'll find a way."

"Crazy people?" My eyes dart from side to side. "Shouldn't we use more empathetic word choice?"

Chondra's entire face contorts in irritation. "Pfff, yeah, okay. Maybe in your little nursing school utopia. Don't talk to your superiors like that."

"Oh." She's one of *those* people. Good to know. Careless pep enters my voice. "Yep, those dementia and psych patients are just like children."

"Right! Right!! So, do you get it? Can I trust you to watch my mother?"

I shake my head, still not comprehending whatever Chondra is trying to get at. "Do I... yeah, you can. Go ahead. You don't have to stay here."

She smiles, pats my knee, and stands up. She tosses me the remote. "She's not watching it. Go ahead and put something on while she sleeps. I need to get some work done."

"Okay, thank you!"

She nods at me and walks out. I notice that the door does not have a lock on either side.

I put on *Forensic Files*. Nothing says graveyard shift more than a show that makes me afraid to go outside. I sit in the chair and look at Irene. Much like a sleeping dog, a blanket of peace envelops her.

Chondra opens the door. "Hey, just to let you know, I could keep this door open for you, if you want."

I drop my phone. I glance back at her. I registered what she said, but still don't understand. "I'm good with keeping it closed."

She quickly talks as if trying to dig herself out of a lie. "F-for the draft. It gets so hot in that room. Anyway, we're gonna grab some dinner, do you mind?"

I shake my head.

Chondra keeps talking and talking. "Oh, you know, because it's your first time here, and I don't know what you're comfortable with. It's–"

"Not my first time doing home health," I answer.

"Ah!" She points at me and makes a clicking sound with her lip. She walks away, leaving the door ajar.

I shut it. Putting my phone on silent, I reach for my laptop and turn it on. A network connectivity warning pops up. I need a Wifi password, but not urgently. The book in my bag is calling my name, anyway. Before even putting away my laptop, Chondra returns.

Every time she opens the door, it gets hotter. "Hey, Billy, I want you to meet someone. So that you don't get confused if you see someone else wandering around the house. This is Pat."

Pat is a tall, skinny woman with short gray hair. She looks vaguely similar to Irene, just bigger and less frail. Her voice sounds about thirty years younger than her appearance. She steps right up to me and shakes my hand. "Great to meet you, Billy?" She holds out the last syllable of my name.

"Uh, Whitney? Billy *John* Whitney, if we wanna get specific."

"Don't recognize that family. Whatever." She leans right into my face and gazes into my pupils. "*Oh!* Chondra! His eyes! They're... perfect!"

Chondra smirks. "Oh yeah. I know."

Ugh. I squint. "Nice to meet you, too." Hold on. I recognize that name. "Oh! Pat! Yeah," I point back at Irene, "She was calling for you last time I was with her."

"Makes sense," responds Pat, "I sat with her a few nights ago."

"No, it doesn't," Chondra speaks sternly, as if scolding a dog. "*She* doesn't remember anything! If she was doing that, then there's no reason why she shouldn't be able to walk."

"Besides her formerly broken hip," Pat remarks.

"Broken hip?" I ask. "I didn't–"

"It was a while ago. She had the surgery. She's still weak on her right side." Pat peers at me. "You in school, Billy?"

"I am! I graduate in a month." I wait for congratulations, but instead I get stared at.

"You like movies?" Pat asks.

"Um," that came out of nowhere. It takes me a few seconds to think. "I like a good flick every once in a while, yeah. What about you?"

Chondra stomps on Pat's foot and interjects. She chuckles away the aggression in her voice. "The only director I, er, *we* care for is Hitchcock."

Pat hops a few feet away from us, clenching her lips and holding her foot.

I nod and remain casual, trying to ignore whatever Chondra just did to Pat. "Okay. He's a good one. What's your favorite?"

"*Psycho.*" Chondra answers in maybe three milliseconds.

Pat laughs, as if she didn't get her foot crushed a minute ago.

I can't even fake a laugh at this point. The stiffness of this conversation is making me feel like I'm drowning. "O...kay. I'm more of a *Rear Window* guy, myself."

"You would be, Bluey blue-eyes. Hm." Pat walks away.

Chondra follows.

I close the door. Before I can even get a thought out, Chondra jumps back into the room. She approaches her mother and quietly caresses her outer thigh. "We'll be right back, sweetie, take care." She kisses her on the forehead and points at me. "You got this under control? I need to get that work done."

My vocal cords choke out, "I sure do."

She gives me a thumbs-up, "Great," and glances around the room. "Oh! Can we turn off that TV and let her sleep?"

Didn't she just tell me to keep it on? I furrow my eyebrows. "That's fine. Should we turn off the lights, too?"

"Don't. She sleeps with those all the time." She picks up the remote, turns off the TV, and walks out. Again, I close the door behind her.

After keeping an ear out for a few minutes, I finally hear the front door close. I collapse into the chair. With Irene sleeping and Chondra gone, I breathe a sigh of relief and begin sorting my thoughts. One thing's for sure: this makes me miss the nursing home.